THE LOEB CLASSICAL LIBRARY

FOUNDED BY JAMES LOEB

EDITED BY

G. P. GOOLD

MINOR LATIN POETS
II

LCL 434

MINOR LATIN POETS

VOLUME II

WITH AN ENGLISH TRANSLATION BY

J. WIGHT DUFF

AND

ARNOLD M. DUFF

HARVARD UNIVERSITY PRESS

CAMBRIDGE, MASSACHUSETTS

LONDON, ENGLAND

First published 1934
Revised edition 1935
Reprinted 1954, 1961, 1968, 1978
Edition bound in two volumes 1982
Reprinted 1998

LOEB CLASSICAL LIBRARY® is a registered trademark
of the President and Fellows of Harvard College

ISBN 0-674-99478-7

Printed in Great Britain by St Edmundsbury Press Ltd,
Bury St Edmunds, Suffolk, on acid-free paper.
Bound by Hunter & Foulis Ltd, Edinburgh, Scotland.

CONTENTS

CONTENTS

FLORUS

INTRODUCTION

TO FLORUS

THERE is considerable plausibility in the argu-
ments which have been advanced in favour of
regarding three apparently different Flori, namely
the historian, the rhetor and the poet as one and
the same person. The acceptance of these argu-
ments commits us to taking the correct name to
have been P. Annius Florus, as the rhetor was
called, and to explaining as confusions the " Julius
Florus " or " Annaeus Florus " found in the MSS.
of the historian.[a] We no longer possess the rhetor's
dialogue discussing the problem whether Virgil was
more an orator than a poet (*Vergilius orator an
poeta*), but from a Brussels manuscript containing
an introduction to the lost theme important facts
about the author's life are recoverable.[b] He was
born in Africa about 74 A.D. While at Rome in his
younger days under Domitian he entered for the
Capitoline competition in poetry, but owing to
jealousy was denied the wreath of victory. This
injustice so rankled in his heart that he left Rome
for distant wanderings which ended with his settle-
ment at Tarraco in Spain. One day in Trajan's

[a] One MS. has " L. Annei Flori."
[b] F. Ritschl, *Rhein. Mus.* I. 302; O. Jahn, *Flori epitome*,
Leipzig, 1852, p. xli; edn. by K. Halm, Leipzig, 1854,
p. 106; edn. by O. Rossbach, Leipzig, 1896, p. 183. See
J. Wight Duff, *A Lit. Hist. of Rome in Silver Age*, p. 644.

reign a friend twitted him with his long absence from the capital, telling him that his poems had won appreciation there. By Hadrian's time he was once more in Rome, enjoying the Emperor's regard in virtue of his literary abilities and possibly because of some common links with Spain also. The intimacy was so close that it emboldened Florus to address Hadrian in a few extant trochaic lines of persiflage upon his craze for travel—*Ego nolo Caesar esse*—to which we have the imperial repartee *Ego nolo Florus esse.*[a] Happily there is more poetry in his hexameters upon spring-roses and in some at least of his trochaic tetrameters. This is the quality which has lent support to the conjecture hazarded by certain scholars, that Florus was the author of one of the most romantic poems in Latin, the *Pervigilium Veneris*. Certainly that poem would have been signally appropriate during the principate of Hadrian, who resuscitated the cult of Venus on a scale of great magnificence.[b] We cannot, however, be sure that the *Pervigilium Veneris* belongs to the second century: and a rival hypothesis claims it for the fourth century, laying stress upon its resemblance to the manner of Tiberianus.[c]

In the codex Salmasianus of the Latin *Anthologia* (Parisinus, 10318) twenty-six trochaic tetrameters appear under the superscription *Flori de qualitate vitae*. The codex Thuaneus (Parisinus 8071) has, instead of *Flori*, *Floridi*, a corruption due to a mistake in the succeeding word. Five hexameters in the codex Salmasianus also bear the heading *Flori*.

[a] Spartianus, *Hadrian*, xvi.
[b] See Introduction, p. 344, to Loeb edition of Catullus, Tibullus and *Pervigilium Veneris*.
[c] See Introduction to Tiberianus, *infra*, p. 555.

FLORUS

TEXTS OF FLORUS' VERSE

P. Burman. *Anthol. Lat.* Lib. II. No. 97; III. Nos. 288–291. Amsterdam, 1759.

[Burman ascribes 97, *Ego nolo . . .*, to "Julius Florus"; 288, *O quales . . .*, 289, *Aut hoc risit . . .*, and 290, *Hortus erat . . .*, to an unknown author; and 291, *Venerunt aliquando rosae . . .*, to "Florus." Baehrens and Buecheler follow these ascriptions.]

J. C. Wernsdorf. *Poetae Latini Minores*, III. pp. 483–488. Altenburg, 1782.

L. Mueller. *Rutilius Namatianus*, etc., p. 26 *sqq.* Leipzig, 1870.

E. Baehrens. *Poet. Lat. Min.*, IV. pp. 279, 346 *sqq.* Leipzig, 1882.

F. Buecheler and A. Riese. *Anthologia Latina*, I. i. pp. 119–121, and pp. 200–202. Leipzig, 1894.

RELEVANT WORKS

O. Mueller. *De P. Annio Poeta et de Pervig. Ven.* diss. Berlin, 1855.

F. Eyssenhardt. *Hadrian und Florus.* Berlin, 1882.

G. Costa. *Floro e Adriano, Bollettino di filol.* 13 (1907), p. 252.

FLORUS

I

Ego nolo Caesar esse,
ambulare per Britannos

. . . .

Scythicas pati pruinas.

II–IX. De Qualitate Vitae

II

Bacche, vitium repertor, plenus adsis vitibus,
effluas dulcem liquorem, comparandum nectari,
conditumque fac vetustum, ne malignis venulis
asperum ducat saporem, versus usum in alterum.

III

Mulier intra pectus omnis celat virus pestilens;
dulce de labris loquuntur, corde vivunt noxio.

II. De Qualitate Vitae *codd.*: Vitium *L. Mueller.*
II. [1] vitium *codd.*: vini tu *L. Mueller.*

---

[a] The numbering I–XIII follows L. Mueller's edition:
No. XIV is taken from Baehrens.

[b] The Latin is given by Spartianus, *Hadrian* xvi: also
Hadrian's retort (see p. 444). As the latter is in four lines, it
may be assumed that Florus' third line is lost.

FLORUS

I[a]

I've no mind to be a Caesar,
Strolling round among the Britons,

. . . .

Victim of the Scythian hoar-frosts.[b]

II–IX. THE QUALITY OF LIFE[c]

II

Bacchus, of the vine revealer, let thy fullness aid
    the vine:
Send the dulcet juice aflowing which no nectar can
    outshine.
Grant it ever-mellowing storage lest in veins inimical
It produce a smack of roughness turned to vinegar
    withal.

III

Every woman in her bosom hides a poisonous pesti-
    lence:
Though the lips speak ne'er so sweetly, yet the heart
    contrives offence.

---

  c The MS. heading for the 26 verses in II–IX is so
inappropriate that Lucian Mueller by emending *vitae* into
vitium suggested that it meant " On the Nature of Vines "
and was applicable only to poem II.

IV

Sic Apollo, deinde Liber sic videtur ignifer:
ambo sunt flammis creati prosatique ex ignibus;
ambo de donis calorem, vite et radio, conferunt;
noctis hic rumpit tenebras, hic tenebras pectoris.

V

Quando ponebam novellas arbores mali et piri,
cortici summae notavi nomen ardoris mei.
nulla fit exinde finis vel quies cupidinis:
crescit arbor, gliscit ardor: animus implet litteras.

VI

Qui mali sunt non fuere matris ex alvo mali,
sed malos faciunt malorum falsa contubernia.

VII

Sperne mores transmarinos, mille habent offucia.
cive Romano per orbem nemo vivit rectius:
quippe malim unum Catonem quam trecentos
    Socratas.

V. ³ fit *codd.*: fit iam *L. Mueller*: facta *Baehrens*.

ᵃ *Cf.* Juvenal II. 83, *nemo repente fuit turpissimus,* " no one
became an absolute villain in a moment," and St. Paul's
quotation from Menander, I. *Cor.* xv. 33 φθείρουσιν ἤθη χρήσθ'
ὁμιλίαι κακαί, " evil communications corrupt good manners."

IV

So Apollo and then Bacchus are fire-bringers, I
    opine:
Both the gods are flame-created; in their birth the
    fires take part.
Both confer their heat for guerdon, by the sunbeam
    or the vine;
One dispels the long night's darkness, one the dark-
    ness of the heart.

V

When my young pear-trees I planted, when I planted
    apple-trees,
On the bark the name I gravéd of the sweetheart
    who is mine.
Never henceforth will my passion find an end or find
    its ease.
As the tree grows, so my zeal glows: love-dreams
    through each letter shine.

VI

Rascals have not been so always—rascals from their
    mother's womb;
But false comradeship with rascals brings one to a
    rascal's doom.[a]

VII

Shun the morals brought across seas; they've a
    thousand trickeries.
None in all the world lives straighter than a citizen
    of Rome.
Why, I prize one Cato more than fifteen score like
    Socrates.

VIII

Tam malum est habere nummos, non habere quam
    malum est;
tam malum est audere semper quam malum est
    semper pudor;
tam malum est tacere multum quam malum est
    multum loqui;
tam malum est foris amica quam malum est uxor
    domi;
nemo non haec vera dicit, nemo non contra facit.

IX

Consules fiunt quotannis et novi proconsules;
solus aut rex aut poeta non quotannis nascitur.

X

DE ROSIS

Venerunt aliquando rosae. per veris amoeni
ingenium una dies ostendit spicula florum,
altera pyramidas nodo maiore tumentes,
tertia iam calathos, totum lux quarta peregit
floris opus. pereunt hodie nisi mane leguntur.

XI

DE ROSIS

A, quales ego mane rosas procedere vidi!
nascebantur adhuc neque erat par omnibus aetas.
prima papillatos ducebat tecta corymbos,
altera puniceos apices umbone levabat,
tertia iam totum calathi patefecerat orbem,   5

FLORUS

VIII

'Tis as bad possessing money as to live in penury;
Just as bad perpetual daring as perpetual modesty;
Just as bad is too much silence as too much loquacity;
Just as bad the girl you visit as the wife at home
    can be.
None can say that this is falsehood: none but does
    the contrary.

IX

Every year we get fresh consuls, every year pro-
    consuls too:
Only patrons, only poets, are not born each year
    anew.

X

ROSES IN SPRINGTIME

Roses are here at last: thanks to the mood
Of lovely Spring, one day shows barbs of bloom;
A second, pyramids more largely swoln;
A third reveals the cup: four days fulfil
Their task of flowering.   This day seals their doom
Unless the morning brings a gatherer.

XI

ROSES

What roses have I seen come with the morn!
Scarce born they were, yet not alike in age:
One showed the breast-like buds that hid the flower,
One shot its purple crest from swelling heart,
A third had opened full its rounded cup,

431

quarta simul nituit nudati germine floris.
dum levat una caput dumque explicat altera nodum,
sic, dum virgineus pudor exsinuatur amictu,
ne pereant lege mane rosas : cito virgo senescit.

XII

De Rosa

Aut hoc risit Amor aut hoc de pectine traxit
purpureis Aurora comis aut sentibus haesit
Cypris et hic spinis insedit sanguis acutis.

XIII

De Rosis

Hortus erat Veneris, roseis circumdatus herbis,
gratus ager dominae, quem qui vidisset amaret.
dum puer hic passim properat decerpere flores
et velare comas, spina libavit acuta
marmoreos digitos : mox ut dolor attigit artus   5
sanguineamque manum, tinxit sua lumina gutta.
pervenit ad matrem frendens defertque querellas :
" unde rosae, mater, coeperunt esse nocentes ?
unde tui flores pugnare latentibus armis ?
bella gerunt mecum. floris color et cruor unum
    est ! "   10

FLORUS

A fourth was bright with well-grown naked bloom,
One rears its head, while one untwines its coil:
So, while their maiden virtue's chastely garbed,
At dawn pull roses fresh: maids soon grow old.

XII

The Rose

The rose was Cupid's smile, or from her comb
Dawn drew it forth—Dawn of the lustrous hair,
Or haply Venus was by briars caught
And on the sharp thorns this her blood remained.

XIII

Venus' Rose-Garden

Venus a garden had, rose-bushes round—
Its lady's darling plot; once seen, beloved.
Her boy, in random haste to cull the blooms
And crown his tresses, pricked with pointed thorn
His marble fingers.   Soon, as pain stabbed limbs
And blood-stained hand, the tear-drop bathed his
    eye.
In rage he seeks his mother with his plaints:
" Whence comes it, mother, that the roses hurt?
Whence fight thy flowers with hidden arms?   They
    war
On me: the flower's hue is the same as blood! "

433

MINOR LATIN POETS

XIV

DE MUSIS

Clio saecla retro memorat sermone soluto.
Euterpae geminis loquitur cava tibia ventis.
voce Thalia cluens soccis dea comica gaudet.
Melpomene reboans tragicis fervescit iambis.
aurea Terpsichorae totam lyra personat aethram.   5
fila premens digitis Erato modulamina fingit.
flectitur in faciles variosque Polymnia motus.
Uranie numeris scrutatur sidera mundi.
Calliope doctis dat laurea serta poetis.

---

a Ascribed to Florus, Baehrens, *P.L.M.* IV. p. 279. *Cf.* the
verses which have come down under the name of Cato, *P.L.M.*
III. p. 243 : see *infra*, p. 634.

The Muses in Hesiod (*Theog.* 36–103, 915–918) are the nine
daughters of Zeus and Mnemosyne, born in Pieria. Some-
times represented as linked together in a dance, they formed
an allegory of the connexion among the liberal arts. For

XIV

THE NINE MUSES [a]

Clio records past ages in her prose.
Euterpe's hollow reed makes double sound.
Voice-famed Thalia revelling loves the sock.
Melpomene's notes in tragic iambs seethe.
Terpsichore's golden lyre thrills all the sky.
Strings touched by Erato sweet love-songs make.
Polymnia's odes suit swift and varying moods.[b]
Urania scans the stars of heaven in verse.
Calliope crowns epic bards with bays.

their functions and varying symbols in literature and art see
"Musen" in Roscher's *Ausführliches Lexikon der gr. und
röm. Mythologie* and "Musai" in P. W. Realencyclopädie.

  [b] *Motus* is here taken of the mind. But it is possible to
take it of bodily movement ("P. sways her body in easy and
in varied movements"); for a province assigned at a late
period to Polymnia was that of pantomime : see p. 635, note *b*.

HADRIAN

INTRODUCTION

TO HADRIAN

P. AELIUS HADRIANUS, who was born in A.D. 76, reigned as Trajan's successor from 117 till his death in A.D. 138. His contradictory traits of character, summarised by Spartianus [a] in his *Vita*, indicated a restlessness of temperament which was reflected in the physical restlessness of the perpetually travelling Emperor. He took genuine interest in army organisation, in agricultural prospects, in building schemes, and (as shown during his visit to Britain, where *Pons Aelii* [b] commemorated his name) in the establishment of frontier-lines. Prose and verse attracted his dilettante tastes: in Latin he felt a preference for archaic writers—for Ennius rather than Virgil, for Cato rather than Cicero, and for Coelius Antipater rather than Sallust: towards Hellenic thought and literature he was so much drawn that his courtiers secretly nicknamed him " Graeculus." Inscriptions have preserved fragments of his military addresses, and at one time collections of his speeches were in existence. His autobiographic books, which whether from modesty or another motive he caused to be published under the names of his literary freedmen, became the direct or indirect [c] source of much in

---

[a] *Hadr.* xiv.   [b] at Newcastle-upon-Tyne.
[c] J. Dürr, *Die Reisen d. Kaisers Hadrian*, 1881; and J. Plew, *Quellenuntersuchungen zur Gesch. d. Kaisers H.*, 890.

the life by Spartianus. A lost miscellany of his appeared under the forbidding title of *Catachannae*,[a] and he dabbled in both Greek and Latin poetry: most things by starts and nothing long, he was an epitome of contemporary culture. Possessed of an excellent memory, readiness in speech, and considerable humour, he loved to engage in discussions with the professors of the day. Sometimes he deferred to them, sometimes browbeat them; yet though he was a tormenting catechiser, he conferred generous benefactions upon teachers. Moreover, he established a library at his spacious villa whose ruins still impress the tourist under the slopes of Tivoli: he had another library at Antium, and a third at his famous academy in Rome, the Athenaeum.

The mediocrity of most of the surviving verse ascribed to him reconciles us to the rejection of the uncertain pieces. When the poet Florus took the risk of chaffing his imperial majesty on his mania for travelling (*ego nolo Caesar esse*),[b] he incurred nothing worse than the retort in the quatrain beginning *Ego nolo Florus esse*. Spartianus[c] is our authority for the simple lines of death-bed farewell

---

[a] Spartianus, *Hadrian* xvi, mentions this lost work as being in the manner of Antimachus, *Catac(h)annas* (in different MSS. *catacannos, catacrianos, catacaymos*), *libros obscurissimos Antimachum imitando scripsit*: perhaps Hadrian aped the learning of the Greek epic poet until he became obscure. *Catachanna*, in Fronto (ed. Naber, p. 35 and p. 155) was applied to a fruit-tree inoculated with alien buds (resembling the extraordinarily engrafted tree of Pliny *N.H.* XVII. 120) and to a style blended of elements from Cato and Seneca. Unger, *Jahrb. Phil.* 119 (1879), p. 493, connected it with καταχήνη, "derision", and it is therefore defined in *Thesaurus Ling. Lat.* III col. 586, as "res risu digna."

[b] Spartianus, *Hadr.* xvi.   [c] *Ibid.* xxv.

HADRIAN

to his soul, where genuine feeling, echoed in tender diminutives, has bequeathed an immortal challenge to translators in many languages.[a] The lines purporting to have been inscribed on the grave of the Emperor's favourite hunting-steed Borysthenes have been suspected. That an inscription was written is clear from Dio Cassius.[b] It is true that he does not say whether it was in Latin or Greek; but, on the whole, it seems fair to accept the testimony of Pithoeus that he found the Latin lines in an ancient manuscript.

EDITIONS

P. Burman. *Anthologia Veterum Lat. Epigram. et Poem.* Vol. I. Lib. II, Nos. 96, 98; Vol. II. Lib. IV, No. 399. Amsterdam, 1759–73.

L. Mueller. In a section *De Poetis Saeculi Urbis Conditae X* which is appended to his edition of Namatianus. Leipzig, 1870. [L. Mueller accepts as genuine only " ego nolo Florus esse . . .," " animula vagula . . ." and the verse " lascivus versu, mente pudicus eras," ten lines in all.]

E. Baehrens. *P.L.M.* Vol. IV. pp. 111 *sqq.* Leipzig, 1882. [Baehrens prints five poems ascribed to Hadrian, of which only that on Borysthenes has been included in the present edition.]

F. Buecheler and A. Riese. *Anthologia Latina*, I. i. pp. 306–7, Leipzig, 1894. I. ii. p. 132, Leipzig, 1906. [The " Hadrianic " poems in the above

---

[a] *Translations . . . of Dying Hadrian's Address to his Soul*, collected by D. Johnston, Bath, 1876.
[b] lxix. 10.

collection are identical with three in Baehrens:
as their authenticity is questionable, they are
not included in the present edition.]

RELEVANT WORKS

F. Gregorovius. *Der Kaiser Hadrian*, ed. 2. Stutt-
gart, 1884 (Eng. tr., London, 1898).

J. Dürr. *Die Reisen des Kaisers Hadrian.* Vienna,
1881.

S. Dehner. *Hadriani Reliquiae*, particula I. Diss.
Bonn, 1883. (For *adlocutiones* to the army.)

J. Plew. *Quellenuntersuchungen zur Geschichte des
Kaisers Hadrian* (pp. 11–53 on the *Vita* by
Spartianus). Strassburg, 1890.

W. Weber. *Untersuchungen zur Gesch. d. K. Hadrian.*
Leipzig, 1907.

B. Henderson. *Life and Principate of Hadrian.*
London, 1923 (" Literary Activities," pp. 240
sqq.).

J. Wight Duff. *A Literary Hist. of Rome in the
Silver Age.* London, 1927. (Sketch of Litera-
ture in the reign of Hadrian, pp. 628–649.)

HADRIAN

I

Ego nolo Florus esse,
ambulare per tabernas,
latitare per popinas,
culices pati rotundos.

II

Lascivus versu, mente pudicus eras.

III

Animula vagula blandula,
hospes comesque corporis,
quae nunc abibis in loca,
pallidula, rigida, nudula,
nec ut soles dabis iocos?

---

* Spartianus, *Hadr.* xvi : see Florus' lines, p. 426.

HADRIAN

I

Retort to Florus [a]

I've no mind to be a Florus
  Strolling round among the drink-shops,
  Skulking round among the cook-shops.
Victim of fat-gorged mosquitoes.

II

On a Poet-friend

Your lines were wanton but your heart was clean.[b]

III

Hadrian's Dying Farewell to his Soul

Dear fleeting sweeting, little soul,
My body's comrade and its guest,
What region now must be thy goal,
Poor little wan, numb, naked soul,
Unable, as of old, to jest?

[b] Apuleius, *Apolog.* xi, cites the Latin as from Hadrian's own pen to honour the tomb of his friend Voconius.

IV

Borysthenes Alanus,
Caesareus veredus,
per aequor et paludes
et tumulos Etruscos
volare qui solebat,   5
Pannonicos nec ullus
apros eum insequentem
dente aper albicanti
ausus fuit nocere:
sparsit ab ore caudam   11
vel extimam saliva,   10
ut solet evenire.
sed integer iuventa
inviolatus artus
die sua peremptus   15
hic situs est in agro.

IV. ⁴ et ruscos *Masdeus*: et ocres *Baehrens*.

⁶⁻¹¹ Pannonicos in apros (nec ullus insequentem dente aper albicanti ausus fuit notare) sparsit ab ore caldam vel extimam salivam *Baehrens*: Pannonicos nec ullus † apros insequentem *cod.*: apros eum insequentem *Scriverius*.

¹⁰⁻¹¹ caudam *cod.*: caldam *Casaubon*. extimam salivam *cod.*: extima saliva *Scriverius*. *Hos versus transposuit Riese.*

HADRIAN

IV

On his Favourite Hunting-horse

Borysthenes the Alan [a]
Was mighty Caesar's steed:
O'er marshland and o'er level,
O'er Tuscan hills, with speed
He used to fly, and never
Could any rushing boar
Amid Pannonian boar-hunt
Make bold his flank to gore [b]
With sharp tusk whitely gleaming:
The foam from off his lips,
As oft may chance, would sprinkle
His tail e'en to the tips.
But he in youthful vigour,
His limbs unsapped by toil,
On his own day extinguished,
Here lies beneath the soil.

[a] Alanus, belonging to the Ἀλανοί, warlike Scythians on the Tanais and Palus Maeotis.

[b] *nocere* governing the accusative is one of the suspicious points in these lines. Baehrens emends to *notare*.

NEMESIANUS

INTRODUCTION

TO NEMESIANUS

Towards the end of the third century A.D., M. Aurelius Olympius Nemesianus wrote bucolic and didactic poetry. He has already been mentioned in the introductions to Calpurnius Siculus and Grattius. His four eclogues for long passed under Calpurnius' name, and of his hexameter poem on the chase 325 verses have survived. He belonged to Carthage, as his designation *Carthaginiensis* in MSS. implies; and, when he says of the Spanish people *gens ampla iacet trans ardua Calpes culmina* (*Cyn.* 251–252), his attitude is that of an African author. It is recorded [a] that he won fame in poetic contests and in several kinds of literature. A love for the open air fitted him to attempt pastoral poetry, and it is in keeping with this that at the outset of his didactic poem he should echo the almost conventional renunciation of mythology to be found in Virgil, Martial and Juvenal, and should disdain it as something hackneyed, preferring to "roam the glades, the green tracts and open plains." [b] But he contemplates a more epic task when, in addressing Numerianus and Carinus, the brother emperors who were the sons of Carus, he announces his intention [c] to compose a narrative of their triumphant exploits. Of the two, Numerianus

---

[a] Vopiscus, *Carus, Numerianus et Carinus*, xi.
[b] *Cyn.* 48–49.   [c] *Cyn.* 63–78.

was at least a good speaker and had himself entered the field of poetry. The *Cynegetica* may be assigned to the period which elapsed between the death of Carus in 283 A.D. and that of Numerianus in 284; and, if we decide that in *Cynegetica* 58–62 Nemesianus is referring to his eclogues as lighter performances than his ambitious literary voyage into didactic poetry, then we may date his pastorals as earlier.

The four pastoral poems, traditionally coupled with the seven by Calpurnius, are now by general consent separated from them. In the first, Tityrus declines on the ground of age Timetas' invitation to show his poetic skill, but instead prevails on him to repeat a song inscribed by Timetas on the bark of a tree. This takes the form of a eulogy on the dead Meliboeus, who is introduced as a sort of analogue to the Meliboeus honoured by Calpurnius as his patron. But the real cue is taken from the praises of Daphnis in Virgil's fifth eclogue. Nemesianus' second eclogue, in which two shepherd lads complain that their sweetheart Donace is shut up at home by her parents, has drawn elements from Calpurnius' second and third poems. Nemesianus' third eclogue introduces Pan surprised by three rustics, who, after trying his pipe in vain, are entertained by Pan's own minstrelsy in praise of Bacchus. This eclogue is modelled on Virgil's sixth, where Silenus, caught asleep, had to pay the forfeit of a song. In the last eclogue, attractive for its glimpses of country scenes, Lycidas and Mopsus deplore the pains of unreturned affection. This is the one pastoral in which Nemesianus employs the prettily recurrent burden or refrain of the Theocritean tradition which Virgil followed in his *Pharmaceutria* or eighth eclogue. Here, then, the Virgilian influence acts directly on him; for the refrain is not one of Calpurnius' devices.

In the incomplete *Cynegetica* of 325 hexameters the first 102 lines are introductory: the remainder handles needful preliminaries to the chase rather than the chase itself—first hunting-dogs, their rearing, feeding, training, diseases and breeds; then horses, their qualities, breeds and maintenance; finally implements such as nets and snares. It will be noted that the order here is not the same as in Grattius.[a] Though Grattius was more expert in hunting than the Carthaginian poet was, it may be felt to be an advantage for Nemesianus that he enters less into details, and, if not so concentrated on imparting instruction as Grattius was, for this very reason has more chance of giving pleasure to a reader.

The diction and the metre of Nemesianus benefit undoubtedly in standard from the conscious imitation of Virgil as a model. Among the more noticeable metrical points, some of them due to his late period, are the shortened *-o* in *devotiŏ* (*Cyn.* 83) and *exercetŏ* (*Cyn.* 187),[b] the single occurrence of hiatus *catuli huc* (*Cyn.* 143) and the close of a hexameter in *fervida zonae* (*Cyn.* 147). Elision is not overdone: some 52 elisions (very many of them in *-que* or *atque*) occur in the 325 lines of the *Cynegetica.*[c]

---

[a] It has been pointed out in the Introduction to Grattius that according to some he did, according to others he did not, influence Nemesianus.

[b] *Cf.* such shortenings in Nemesianus' eclogues as *exspectŏ* (ii. 26), *coniungŏ* (iii. 14), *mulcendŏ* (i. 53), *laudandŏ* (ii. 80).

[c] Keene counts 39 elisions in the four eclogues, *i.e.* in 319 lines. Elision is much less frequent in Calpurnius.

There are in it a few rare words such as *inocciduus* (105) and *cibatus* (160); but in the main the diction is classical. And, in respect of both language and metre, broadly similar features characterise the pastoral and the didactic poetry of Nemesianus.

EDITIONS

ECLOGUES

For the chief editions and relative literature see the works given under Calpurnius Siculus, pp. 214–215.

E. Baehrens' text: *P.L.M.* III. pp. 176–190.

H. Schenkl's text is given in Postgate's *Corp. Poet. Lat.*, 1905, II. pp. 565–568.

CYNEGETICA

For editions, which usually combine Nemesianus with Grattius, see the list given under Grattius, pp. 146–147.

E. Baehrens' text: *P.L.M.* III. pp. 190–202.

J. P. Postgate's text is given in *Corp. Poet. Lat.*, II. 1905, pp. 569–571.

D. Martin. *Cynegetica of Nemesianus* (with comment.). Cornell Univ., U.S.A., 1917.

RELEVANT WORKS

M. Fiegl. *Des Grattius Faliskus Cynegetica: seine Vorgänger u. seine Nachfolger.* [Holds that Nemesianus borrowed from Grattius: P. J. Enk in his ed. of Grattius and in *Mnemos.* 45 (1917)

supports this: so does F. Muller in *Mnemos.*
46 (1918). G. Curcio in his ed. of Grattius
opposes the view.]

P. Monceaux. *Les Africains : Étude sur la littérature
latine d'Afrique.* Paris, 1894.

SIGLA

For the *Eclogues* see the Sigla for Calpurnius
Siculus, pp. 216–217.

For the *Cynegetica* :

A = Parisinus 7561, saec. x.

[B = Parisinus 4839, saec. x.]

> This codex, disfigured by many worthless
> readings, was collated by Baehrens out of re-
> spect for its age : it is ignored by Postgate in
> *C.P.L.* and its readings are not recorded in this
> edition.

C (Baehrens) = σ (Postgate) Vindobonensis 3261,
saec. xvi.

> This codex contains Nemesianus after Ovid's
> *Halieutica* and before Grattius' *Cynegetica.* σ
> denotes that it was written by Sannazarius, as
> shown by H. Schenkl, *Supplementband der Jahr-
> bücher für klass. Philol.* xxiv, 1898, pp. 387–480.

Bibliographical addendum (1982)

Nemesianus: *Oeuvres*, ed. P. Volpilhac (Budé series),
Paris 1976.

NEMESIANI CARMINA

ECLOGAE I

TIMETAS: TITYRUS

Tim. Dum fiscella tibi fluviali, Tityre, iunco
    texitur et raucis immunia rura cicadis,
    incipe, si quod habes gracili sub harundine carmen
    compositum. nam te calamos inflare labello
    Pan docuit versuque bonus tibi favit Apollo.   5
    incipe, dum salices haedi, dum gramina vaccae
    detondent, viridique greges permittere campo
    dum ros et primi suadet clementia solis.

Tit. hos annos canamque comam, vicine Timeta,
    tu iuvenis carusque deis in carmina cogis?   10
    diximus et calamis versus cantavimus olim,
    dum secura hilares aetas ludebat amores.
    nunc album caput et veneres tepuere sub annis,
    iam mea ruricolae dependet fistula Fauno.
    te nunc rura sonant; nuper nam carmine victor   15
    risisti calamos et dissona flamina Mopsi

---

[11] et calamis versus V *nonnulli* : et calamis et versu NGA :
et calamis et versum aptavimus *Baehrens.*

---

[a] The hybrid alternative title " Epiphunus " (ἐπί and
funus) refers to the obituary lament on Meliboeus.

NEMESIANUS

ECLOGUE I

Timetas : Tityrus [a]

Tim. While, Tityrus, you are weaving a basket with
river rushes, and while the country-side is free
from the harsh-toned grasshoppers,[b] strike up,
if you've got any song set to the slender
reed-pipe. Pan has taught your lips to blow
the reeds and a kind Apollo has given you the
grace of verse. Strike up, while the kids crop
the willows and the cows the grass, while the
dew and the mildness of the morning sun urge
you to let your flocks into the green meadow-
land.

Tit. Neighbour Timetas, do you constrain these years
of mine and hoary hair to sing, you a young
man beloved of the gods? Time was when I
found words; time was when I sang verses to
the reeds, so long as my care-free youth uttered
the merry lays of love. Now my head is white
and passion has cooled beneath the years.
Already hangs my pipe devoted to the country-
haunting Faunus. With your fame the country
now resounds. Victor in song of late, when I
was judge, you mocked the pipes of Mopsus

---

[b] It is morning and the cicalas are not yet noisy.

457

       iudice me. mecum senior Meliboeus utrumque
       audierat laudesque tuas sublime ferebat;
       quem nunc emeritae permensum tempora vitae
       secreti pars orbis habet mundusque piorum.   20
       quare age, si qua tibi Meliboei gratia vivit,
       dicat honoratos praedulcis tibia manes.
Tim. et parere decet iussis et grata iubentur.
       namque fuit dignus senior, quem carmine Phoe-
           bus,   24
       Pan calamis, fidibus Linus aut Oeagrius Orpheus
       concinerent totque acta viri laudesque sonarent.
       sed quia tu nostrae laudem deposcis avenae,
       accipe quae super haec cerasus, quam cernis
           ad amnem,
       continet, inciso servans mea carmina libro.
Tit. dic age; sed nobis ne vento garrula pinus   30
       obstrepat, has ulmos potius fagosque petamus.
Tim. hic cantare libet; virides nam subicit herbas
       mollis ager lateque tacet nemus omne: quieti
       adspice ut ecce procul decerpant gramina tauri.
        omniparens aether et rerum causa, liquores, 35
       corporis et genetrix tellus, vitalis et aer,
       accipite hos cantus atque haec nostro Meliboeo
       mittite, si sentire datur post fata quietis.
       nam si sublimes animae caelestia templa
       sidereasque colunt sedes mundoque fruuntur, 40
       tu nostros adverte modos, quos ipse benigno

       [37] hos cantus N : hos calamos V, *Baehrens.*

and his discordant blasts. With me the aged
Meliboeus had heard you both, and he extolled
your merits on high. He has fulfilled the
span of life's campaign, and dwells now in a
part of that secluded sphere, the heaven of
the blest. Wherefore, come, if you have a
living gratitude to Meliboeus, let the dulcet
strains of your flute tell of his glorified spirit.

Tim. 'Tis right to obey your commands, and your
commands are pleasing. The old man de-
served that the poetry of Phoebus, the reeds
of Pan, and the lyre of Linus or of Orpheus,
son of Oeagrus, should join in his praises and
should extol all the glorious deeds of the hero.
But since you ask but the praise my pipe can
give, hear now what the cherry-tree you see
beside the river keeps upon this theme; it
preserves my lay in the carving on its bark.

Tit. Come, speak: but lest the pine, made garrul-
ous by the wind, trouble us with its noise,
let us seek rather these elms and beeches.

Tim. Here 'tis my pleasure to sing: for underneath
us the soft fields spread their carpeting of
green sward, and far and wide all the grove is
still. Look! see in the distance how the bulls
are quietly browsing in the grass.

Ether, parent of all; water, primal cause of
things; and earth, mother of body; and life-
giving air! accept ye these strains; waft these
words to our loved Meliboeus, if those at rest
are permitted to have feeling after death.
For if souls sublime dwell in the celestial
precincts and the starry abodes, if the heavens
are their lot, do thou, Meliboeus, give ear to

459

pectore fovisti, quos tu, Meliboee, probasti.
longa tibi cunctisque diu spectata senectus
felicesque anni nostrique novissimus aevi
circulus innocuae clauserunt tempora vitae.　　45
nec minus hinc nobis gemitus lacrimaeque
　　fuere
quam si florentes mors invida carperet annos ;
nec tenuit tales communis causa querellas.
" heu, Meliboee, iaces mortali frigore segnis
lege hominum, caelo dignus canente senecta　　50
concilioque deum.　plenum tibi ponderis aequi
pectus erat.　tu ruricolum discernere lites
adsueras, varias patiens mulcendo querellas.
sub te iuris amor, sub te reverentia iusti
floruit, ambiguos signavit terminus agros.　　55
blanda tibi vultu gravitas et mite serena
fronte supercilium, sed pectus mitius ore.
tu calamos aptare labris et iungere cera
hortatus duras docuisti fallere curas ;
nec segnem passus nobis marcere iuventam　　60
saepe dabas meritae non vilia praemia Musae.

---

[47] pelleret V : carperet NGA : velleret *Glaeser* : tolleret
Heinsius : perderet *Burman*.
[49] mortali NG : letali V, *Baehrens*.
[50] canente *codd.* : callente *Baehrens*.
[53] patiens *codd.*: pacans *Maehly, Baehrens, H. Schenkl,
Giarratano* : sapiens *Burman*.
[54] ruris N²GV : iuris N¹, *Martellius*. iusti V, N (*in mar-
gine*) : iuris G (*corr. ex* ruris), N (*corr. ex* viris).

my lays, which your own kind heart cherished
and your judgement approved. An advanced
old age, long esteemed by all, and happy years
and the final cycle in our human span closed
the period of your life which injured none.
Neither did this make our tears and lamenta-
tions less sore than if churlish death had
plucked the years of your prime: nor did
the common cause [a] check dirges such as
these: " Ah, Meliboeus, in that chill which
awaits all men you lie strengthless, obeying
the law of all flesh, worthy though you are of
heaven in your hoary age and worthy of the
council of the gods. Your heart was full of
firmness fairly balanced. With patient ear
and soothing word for diverse plaints, you
were wont to judge the disputes of the peasants.
Under your guidance flourished a love of law
and a respect for justice; disputed land was
marked with a boundary line. You had a
courteous dignity in your countenance and
kindly brow with an unruffled forehead; but
still kindlier than your face was your heart.
You urged me to adapt the reed-pipe to my
lips and to fashion it with wax, and so taught
me to beguile oppressive cares. You would
not suffer my youth to languish in idleness;
guerdons of no mean price you often gave to
my Muse if she quitted herself well. Often

---

[a] *i.e.* that all men are mortal : *cf. Hamlet* I. ii :

"Thou know'st 'tis common; all that lives must die,
Passing through nature to eternity ";

Tennyson, *In Memoriam*, vi :

"Loss is common to the race—
And common is the commonplace."

saepe etiam senior, ne nos cantare pigeret,
laetus Phoebea dixisti carmen avena.
felix o Meliboee, vale! tibi frondis odorae
munera dat lauros carpens ruralis Apollo;　　　65
dant Fauni, quod quisque valet, de vite racemos,
de messi culmos omnique ex arbore fruges;
dat grandaeva Pales spumantia cymbia lacte,
mella ferunt Nymphae, pictas dat Flora coronas:
manibus hic supremus honos. dant carmina
　　　Musae,　　　70
carmina dant Musae, nos et modulamur avena:
silvestris te nunc platanus, Meliboee, susurrat,
te pinus; reboat te quicquid carminis Echo
respondet silvae; te nostra armenta loquuntur.
namque prius siccis phocae pascentur in arvis　　75
hirsutusque freto vivet leo, dulcia mella
sudabunt taxi, confusis legibus anni
messem tristis hiemps, aestas tractabit olivam,
ante dabit flores autumnus, ver dabit uvas,
quam taceat, Meliboee, tuas mea fistula
　　　laudes.''　　　80

Tit. perge, puer, coeptumque tibi ne desere
　　　carmen.
nam sic dulce sonas, ut te placatus Apollo
provehat et felix dominam perducat in urbem.
iamque hic in silvis praesens tibi fama benignum
stravit iter, rumpens livoris nubila pennis.　　85

---

⁶⁷ messi *Maehly* : messe NGA : campo V : messo *Burman.*
⁷³⁻⁷⁴ reboant . . . silvae (*nom. plur.*) *Baehrens.*
⁷⁴ armenta *codd.* : arbusta *Haupt, Baehrens.*
⁷⁶ hirsutusque V *nonnulli* : vestitusque NG V *plerique* : insue-
tusque *Heinsius* : villosusque *C. Schenkl.*
⁷⁸ tractabit GV : tractavit N : iactabit *Burman* : prae-
stabit *Haupt, Baehrens.*

too, lest singing might irk us, you sang joy-
fully despite your years to a flute inspired by
Phoebus. Farewell, blessed Meliboeus; Apollo
of the country-side plucks the laurel and offers
you gifts of fragrant foliage. The Fauns offer,
each according to his power, grape-clusters
from the vine, harvest-stalks from the field,
and fruits from every tree. Time-honoured
Pales offers bowls foaming with milk; the
Nymphs bring honey; Flora offers chaplets
of varied hue. Such is the last tribute to the
departed. Songs the Muses offer: the Muses
offer song: and we play your praises on the
flute. Your name, Meliboeus, is in the whisper
of the forest plane-tree and the pine: every
tuneful answer that echo makes to the wood-
land resounds your name. 'Tis you our herds
have upon their lips. For first will seals browse
in the dry meadow, the shaggy lion live in the
sea, and yew-trees drip sweet honey; first will
the year confound its laws and winter's gloom
control the harvest and summer the olive-
crop; autumn will yield blossoms, spring will
yield grapes, ere your praises, Meliboeus, are
hushed upon my flute."

Tit. Forward, my boy, leave not off the music you
have begun. Your melody is so sweet that a
favourable Apollo bears you onward and is
your auspicious guide into the queen of cities.[a]
For propitious fame has here in the woods
made smooth a kindly path for you, her
pinions piercing the clouds of malice.

---

[a] *i.e.* the imperial capital, Rome: *cf.* II. 84.

    sed iam sol demittit equos de culmine mundi,
    flumineos suadens gregibus praebere liquores.

II

Idas : Alcon

    Formosam Donacen puer Idas et puer Alcon
    ardebant rudibusque annis incensus uterque
    in Donaces venerem furiosa mente ruebant.
    hanc, cum vicini flores in vallibus horti
    carperet et molli gremium compleret acantho,   5
    invasere simul venerisque imbutus uterque
    tum primum dulci carpebant gaudia furto.
    hinc amor et pueris iam non puerilia vota :
    quis anni ter quinque† hiemes et cura iuventae.
    sed postquam Donacen duri clausere parentes,   10
    quod non tam tenui filo de voce sonaret
    sollicitumque foret pinguis sonus, improba cervix
    suffususque rubor crebro venaeque tumentes,
    tum vero ardentes flammati pectoris aestus
    carminibus dulcique parant relevare querella ;   15
    ambo aevo cantuque pares nec dispare forma,
    ambo genas leves, intonsi crinibus ambo.
    atque haec sub platano maesti solatia casus
    alternant, Idas calamis et versibus Alcon.

    ⁴ callibus *G. Hermann.*
    ⁶ venerisque H V *nonnulli* : venerique V *nonnulli* : veneris
NG. imbutus *codd.* : immitis *ed. Ald.* 1534.
    ⁹ anni *codd.* : actae *Heinsius* : aevi *Hartel.* hiemes et cura
iuventae *codd. plerique* : hiemes et cruda iuventa *Haupt* :
et mens et cura iuventae *Summers* : increscit cura iuvencae
Baehrens : *alii alia.*
    ¹⁸ haec sub *Glaeser* : hic sub NG : hi sub AH, *Baehrens* :
sub hac V : hinc sub *H. Schenkl.*

NEMESIANUS

But now the sun is driving his steeds down from the arch of heaven and prompting us to give our flocks the river waters.

ECLOGUE II

IDAS: ALCON

Young Idas and young Alcon had a burning passion for the fair Donace; both, ablaze in their inexperienced years, rushed with frenzied spirit into their love for Donace. Her they assailed together, when she was gathering flowers in the neighbouring garden vales and filling her lap with soft acanthus. Then first initiated, they both snatched the joys of Venus by a sweet robbery. Hence came love,[a] and the boys felt longings beyond their boyish age. Their years were only fifteen winters, yet they had the pangs of early manhood. But after her stern parents had imprisoned Donace, because her voice had lost its fine music, and its thickened sound caused anxious thought, because her neck grew coarse, and spreading blushes came and went and her veins showed larger,[b] then truly the youths made ready to relieve the burning heat of a love-enflamed heart with the sweet plaint of their minstrelsy—both of them equal in age and song, of well-matched comeliness, both smooth in cheek, both of unshorn locks. And beneath a plane-tree—Idas on the flute followed by Alcon in his verse—they poured out this solace for their sad plight.

---

[a] Cf. Grattius, Cyneget. 283–284.
[b] The reasons given are traditional signs of lost maidenhood.

465

I. " quae colitis silvas, Dryades, quaeque antra,
    Napaeae, 20
et quae marmoreo pede, Naiades, uda secatis
litora purpureosque alitis per gramina flores :
dicite, quo Donacen prato, qua forte sub umbra
inveniam, roseis stringentem lilia palmis ?
nam mihi iam trini perierunt ordine soles, 25
ex quo consueto Donacen exspecto sub antro.
interea, tamquam nostri solamen amoris
hoc foret aut nostros posset medicare furores,
nulla meae trinis tetigerunt gramina vaccae
luciferis, nullo libarunt amne liquores ; 30
siccaque fetarum lambentes ubera matrum
stant vituli et teneris mugitibus aera complent.
ipse ego nec iunco molli nec vimine lento
perfeci calathos cogendi lactis in usus. 34
quid tibi, quae nosti, referam ? scis mille iuvencas
esse mihi, nosti numquam mea mulctra vacare.
ille ego sum, Donace, cui dulcia saepe dedisti
oscula nec medios dubitasti rumpere cantus
atque inter calamos errantia labra petisti.
heu, heu ! nulla meae tangit te cura salutis ? 40
pallidior buxo violaeque simillimus erro.
omnes ecce cibos et nostri pocula Bacchi
horreo nec placido memini concedere somno.
te sine, vae misero, mihi lilia fusca videntur

---

[32] aera NH V *plerique* : ethera G : aethera *Ulitius,
Baehrens.*
[44] fusca NGA : nigra V, *Baehrens.*

---

[a] Line 35 closely follows Calpurnius, *Ecl.* III. 65.
[b] Lines 37–39 are copied from Calpurnius, *Ecl.* III. 55 *sqq.*

NEMESIANUS

Idas. " Ye Dryads who haunt the woodland, Napaean
nymphs who haunt the caves, and Naiads
whose marble-white feet cleave the watery
strands, who nourish the gleaming flowers
athwart the sward, say, in what meadow or
haply 'neath what shade shall I find Donace
pulling lilies with her rosy hands? Three suc-
ceeding days are now lost to me, while I have
been awaiting Donace in the grotto that was
our tryst. Meanwhile, as if this were con-
solation for my love or could heal my passion,
my cows for three morns have touched no
grass, nor sipped the waters from any stream.
Calves stand licking the dry udders of their
new-delivered mothers and fill the air with
their tender lowing. And for myself, neither
of soft sedge nor of pliant osier have I made
baskets for the purposes of curdling milk. Why
should I relate to you what you know? *a* You
are aware I have a thousand heifers; you
know my milk-pails are never empty. I am
he to whom, Donace, you gave many a tender
kiss, whose strains half-sung you did not hesi-
tate to interrupt by seeking my lips, as they
strayed o'er the reed-pipe.*b* Alack, alack, are
you touched by no thought for my health?
Paler than the box-tree and most like unto
the (white) violet I stray. See, I shrink from
all food and from the goblets of our loved
Bacchus, nor do I mind me to yield myself
to gentle sleep. Ah, without you,*c* to my
unhappy sight lilies are grey and roses pale

c Cf. 44–48 with the passage which it imitates, Calp. *Ecl.*
III. 51–54.

pallentesque rosae nec dulce rubens hyacinthus,   45
nullos nec myrtus nec laurus spirat odores.
at si tu venias, et candida lilia fient
purpureaeque rosae, et dulce rubens hyacinthus;
tunc mihi cum myrto laurus spirabit odores.
nam dum Pallas amat turgentes unguine bacas,   50
dum Bacchus vites, Deo sata, poma Priapus,
pascua laeta Pales, Idas te diligit unam."
    haec Idas calamis.   tu, quae responderit Alcon
versu, Phoebe, refer: sunt curae carmina Phoebo.
A. " o montana Pales, o pastoralis Apollo,   55
et nemorum Silvane potens, et nostra Dione,
quae iuga celsa tenes Erycis, cui cura iugales
concubitus hominum totis conectere saeclis:
quid merui? cur me Donace formosa reliquit?
munera namque dedi, noster quae non dedit Idas,
vocalem longos quae ducit aedona cantus;   61
quae licet interdum, contexto vimine clausae
cum parvae patuere fores, ceu libera ferri
norit et agrestes inter volitare volucres,
scit rursus remeare domum tectumque subire,   65
viminis et caveam totis praeponere silvis.
praeterea tenerum leporem geminasque palumbes
nuper, quae potui, silvarum praemia misi.

---

[48] et dulce rubens V *nonnulli* : *sed sine hiatu* tunc dulce
rubens *V alii* : dulce atque rubens *Baehrens.*
[50] unguine N¹GA : sanguine N²V.
[51] vites V : uvas NG.   Deo *Glaeser* : deus *codd.*
[54] curae *Haupt* : aurea *codd.*
[62] clausae *Haupt* : clausa *codd.* : caveae *Maehly.*
[64] norit *Wernsdorf* : novit *codd.*

and the hyacinth has no sweet blush, nor do
myrtle or laurel breathe any fragrance; but
if you come, lilies will grow white once more,
the roses be red, and the hyacinth regain its
sweet blush; then for me will laurel with
myrtle breathe fragrance forth. For while
Pallas loves the olive-berries that swell with
fatness, while Bacchus loves the vines, Deo [a]
her crops, Priapus his fruits and Pales the
joyous pastures, Idas loves you alone."

So Idas on the pipes. O Phoebus, recount what
Alcon answered in verse. Over poetry Phoebus
presides.

A. " O Pales, lady of the hills, Apollo of the pasture-
land, Silvanus, lord of the groves, and my Dione [b]
whose citadel is the lofty ridge of Eryx, whose
province it is throughout the aeons to rivet
the love-unions of mankind; what fate have I
merited? Why has fair Donace deserted me?
I gave her gifts, such as our friend Idas never
gave—a tuneful nightingale that trills its songs
hour after hour: and, although sometimes, when
the little cage-doors—barred with woven osier—
are opened, it can fly forth as if free and wing
its way among the birds of the field, yet it
knows how to return home again and enter its
abode and prefer the cage of osier to all the
woods that are. Besides, of late I sent her what
spoils of the forest I could, a young hare and a

[a] Deo is Δηώ, Demeter, the corn-goddess.
[b] Dione, strictly mother of Venus, is here identified with
Venus, whose temple on Mount Eryx in N.W. Sicily gave her
the epithet of " Erycina."

et post haec, Donace, nostros contemnis amores?
forsitan indignum ducis, quod rusticus Alcon   70
te peream, qui mane boves in pascua duco.
di pecorum pavere greges, formosus Apollo,
Pan doctus, Fauni vates et pulcher Adonis.
quin etiam fontis speculo me mane notavi,
nondum purpureos Phoebus cum tolleret ortus   75
nec tremulum liquidis lumen splenderet in undis:
quod vidi, nulla tegimur lanugine malas;
pascimus et crinem; nostro formosior Ida
dicor, et hoc ipsum mihi tu iurare solebas,
purpureas laudando genas et lactea colla   80
atque hilares oculos et formam puberis aevi.
nec sumus indocti calamis: cantamus avena,
qua divi cecinere prius, qua dulce locutus
Tityrus e silvis dominam pervenit in urbem.
nos quoque te propter, Donace, cantabimur
     urbi,   85
si modo coniferas inter viburna cupressos
atque inter pinus corylum frondescere fas est."

     sic pueri Donacen toto sub sole canebant,
frigidus e silvis donec descendere suasit
Hesperus et stabulis pastos inducere tauros.   90

---

89 descendere N: discedere G: descendere *vel* discedere V: decedere *Baehrens.*

pair of wood-pigeons. And after this, Donace, do you despise my passion? Perhaps you think it shame that the clownish Alcon should pine with love for you, I who lead oxen to their morning pasturage. Gods have fed herds of cattle, beauteous Apollo, skilled Pan, prophetic Fauns, and fair Adonis. Nay, I have remarked myself in a fountain's mirror of a morning, before Phoebus raised aloft the splendour of his uprising, and when no quivering light shone in the clear waters. As far as I saw, no down covers my cheeks; I let my hair grow; men call me more handsome than our Idas, and this indeed you were wont to say to me on oath,[a] while praising [b] the radiance of my cheeks, the milky whiteness of my neck, the laughter in my eyes and the comeliness of my manhood. Nor am I without skill on the reed-pipe. I sing on a flute whereon gods have sung ere now, whereon Tityrus made sweet music and so advanced from the woodland to the imperial city.[c] Me too on your account, Donace, the city will celebrate, if only the cypress with its cones be allowed to burst into leaf among the osiers or the hazel among the pines."

So the boys sang of Donace throughout the day until chilly evening bade them come down from the woods and lead the full-fed bulls to their stalls.

[a] Line 79 is repeated from Calp. III. 62.

[b] With *laudandŏ* (80) *cf.* Nemes. *Ecl.* I. 53, *mulcendŏ*.

[c] "Tityrus" means Virgil. Among frequent reminiscences of the *Eclogues* one is appropriately near; line 86 is based on *inter viburna cupressi* of Virg. *Ecl.* I. 25.

III

BACCHUS

Nyctilus atque Micon nec non et pulcher Amyntas
torrentem patula vitabant ilice solem,
cum Pan venatu fessus recubare sub ulmo
coeperat et somno laxatus sumere vires;
quem super ex tereti pendebat fistula ramo.   5
hanc pueri, tamquam praedem pro carmine possent
sumere fasque esset calamos tractare deorum,
invadunt furto; sed nec resonare canorem
fistula quem suerat nec vult contexere carmen,
sed pro carminibus male dissona sibila reddit,   10
cum Pan excussus sonitu stridentis avenae
iamque videns " pueri, si carmina poscitis " inquit,
" ipse canam: nulli fas est inflare cicutas,
quas ego Maenaliis cera coniungo sub antris.
iamque ortus, Lenaee, tuos et semina vitis   15
ordine detexam: debemus carmina Baccho."
    haec fatus coepit calamis sic montivagus Pan:
" te cano, qui gravidis hederata fronte corymbis
vitea serta plicas quique udo palmite tigres
ducis odoratis perfusus colla capillis,   20
vera Iovis proles; nam cum post sidera caeli
sola Iovem Semele vidit Iovis ora professum,
hunc pater omnipotens, venturi providus aevi,

---

    4 laxatas G : lassatas N V *plerique* : lassatus V *nonnulli* :
laxatus *Hoeufft.*
    6 praedem *Titius* : praedam *codd.*
    11 cum NG : tum V.
    21 iam tunc *codd.* : nam tunc *Burman* : nam cum *Baehrens.*

---

    a Bacchus is the subject of Pan's song: some editors prefer
" Pan " as the title.

NEMESIANUS

ECLOGUE III

Bacchus [a]

Nyctilus and Mycon and likewise fair Amyntas
were shunning the scorching heat of the sun beneath
a spreading ilex, when Pan, fatigued in the chase,
set himself to recline under an elm and gain strength
by sleep's recreation. From a rounded bough above
him hung his pipe. This the boys seized by stealth,
as though they could take it to be a surety for a
song, as though 'twere right to handle the reed-
pipes of gods. But neither would the pipe sound
its wonted music, nor would it weave its song, but
instead of songs it rendered vilely discordant
screeches, till Pan was awakened by the din of the
strident pipe, and, now seeing them, said, "Boys,
if songs ye call for, I myself will sing. No man
may blow upon the hemlock stalks which I fashion
with wax within Maenalian caves.[b] And now, O
God of the winepress, I will unfold in order due the
story of thy birth and the seeds of the vine. Song
is our debt to Bacchus."

With these words, Pan the mountain-ranger began
thus upon the reeds: "Thee I sing, who plaitest
vine-wreaths with berried clusters hanging heavy
on thine ivy-circled brow, who leadest tigers with
juice-soaked vine-branch, thy perfumed hair flowing
o'er thy neck, true offspring of Jove. For when
Semele alone, save the stars of heaven, saw Jove
wearing Jove's own countenance, this child did the
Almighty Father, careful for future ages, carry till

[b] The Arcadian mountain-range of Maenalus was sacred to
Pan.

473

pertulit et iusto produxit tempore partus.
hunc Nymphae Faunique senes Satyrique procaces,   25
nosque etiam Nysae viridi nutrimus in antro.
quin et Silenus parvum veteranus alumnum
aut gremio fovet aut resupinis sustinet ulnis,
evocat aut risum digito motuve quietem
allicit aut tremulis quassat crepitacula palmis.   30
cui deus arridens horrentes pectore setas
vellicat aut digitis aures adstringit acutas
applauditve manu mutilum caput aut breve mentum
et simas tenero collidit pollice nares.
interea pueri florescit pube iuventus   35
flavaque maturo tumuerunt tempora cornu.
tum primum laetas extendit pampinus uvas:
mirantur Satyri frondes et poma Lyaei.
tum deus ' o Satyri, maturos carpite fetus '
dixit ' et ignotos primi calcate racemos.'   40
    vix haec ediderat, decerpunt vitibus uvas
et portant calathis celerique elidere planta
concava saxa super properant: vindemia fervet
collibus in summis, crebro pede rumpitur uva
nudaque purpureo sparguntur pectora musto.   45
tum Satyri, lasciva cohors, sibi pocula quisque
obvia corripiunt: quae fors dedit, arripit usus.
cantharon hic retinet, cornu bibit alter adunco,

---

[27] veteranus *O. Schubert*: veneratus *codd.*
[37] extendit G: ostendit NVH.
[40] primi NG: pueri V: proni *Baehrens.*
[45] rubraque NG: udaque V *nonnulli*: nudaque V *reliqui.*
[47] arripit NG: hoc capit V: occupat *Ulitius, Baehrens.*

---

[a] The story of Semele's perishing amid the lightnings of
Jupiter's tremendous epiphany and of the preservation of her
child, Bacchus, in Jupiter's thigh till he reached the due hour
of birth is alluded to in Nemes. *Cyneg.* 16 *sqq.*

its full time and bring forth at the due hour of birth.[a] This child the Nymphs, the aged Fauns and wanton Satyrs, and I as well, did nurture in the green cave of Nysa.[b] Nay, the veteran Silenus, too, fondles his little nursling in his bosom, or holds him in his cradling arms, or wakes a smile with his finger, or woos repose by rocking him, or shakes rattles in tremulous hands. Smiling on him, the god plucks out the hairs which bristle on his breast, or with the fingers pulls his peaked ears, or pats with the hand his crop-horned[c] head or his short chin, and with tender thumb pinches his snub nose. Meanwhile the boy's youth blooms with the coming of manhood, and his yellow temples have swollen with full-grown horns. Then first the tendril outspreads the gladsome grapes. Satyrs are amazed at the leaves and fruitage of Lyaeus. Then said the god, ' Pluck the ripe produce, ye Satyrs, be first to tread the bunches whose full power ye know not.'

Scarce had he uttered these words, when they snatched the grapes from the vines, carried them in baskets and hastened to crush them on hollowed stones with nimble foot. On the hill-tops the vintage goes on apace, grapes are burst by frequent tread, and naked breasts are besprinkled with purple must. Then the wanton troop of Satyrs snatched the goblets, each that which comes his way. What chance offers, their need seizes. One keeps hold of a tankard; another drinks from a curved horn; one

[b] Nysa, the fabled birthplace of Bacchus, was by some accounts placed in Arabia Felix, by others in India.

[c] " crop-horned " (cf. " crop-eared ") is meant to suggest the stumpy or cropped horns with which Silenus was represented. Wernsdorf, following Heinsius, took *mutilum* as " bald " : cf. *turpe pecus mutilum*, Ovid, *A.A.* III. 249.

concavat ille manus palmasque in pocula vertit,
pronus at ille lacu bibit et crepitantibus haurit   50
musta labris; alius vocalia cymbala mergit
atque alius latices pressis resupinus ab uvis
excipit; at potus (saliens liquor ore resultat)
evomit, inque umeros et pectora defluit umor.
omnia ludus habet cantusque chorique licentes;   55
et venerem iam vina movent: raptantur amantes
concubitu Satyri fugientes iungere Nymphas
iamiamque elapsas hic crine, hic veste retentat.
tum primum roseo Silenus cymbia musto
plena senex avide non aequis viribus hausit.   60
ex illo venas inflatus nectare dulci
hesternoque gravis semper ridetur Iaccho.
quin etiam deus ille, deus Iove prosatus ipso,
et plantis uvas premit et de vitibus hastas
integit et lynci praebet cratera bibenti."   65

  haec Pan Maenalia pueros in valle docebat,
sparsas donec oves campo conducere in unum
nox iubet, uberibus suadens siccare fluorem
lactis et in niveas adstrictum cogere glebas.

---

[52] *hunc versum post* 53 *collocant codices plerique.*
[53] at potus *codd. plerique*: aes potum *Baehrens*: at potis
ed. Ald. 1534. saliensque liquore G, *Baehrens*: rediens liquor
ore *Maehly.*
[54] evomit NGH: spumeus V: ebibit *Baehrens, qui hunc
versum cum* 52 *coniungit.*
[63] prosatus ipso V *multi*: natus ab ipso V *pauci, Baehrens.*
[65] integit NG: ingerit V.

hollows his hands and makes a cup of his palms;
another, stooping forward, drinks of the wine-vat
and with smacking lips drains the new wine; another
dips therein his sonorous cymbals, and yet another,
lying on his back, catches the juice from the squeezed
grapes, but when drunk (as the welling liquid leaps
back from his mouth) he vomits it out, and the
liquor flows over shoulders and breasts. Every-
where sport reigns, and song and wanton dances.
And now love is stirred by the wine; amorous satyrs
are seized with desire to unite in intercourse with
the fleeing nymphs, whom, all but escaped, one
captor holds back by the hair, another by the dress.
Then first did old Silenus greedily quaff bowls full
of rosy must, his strength not equal to the carousal.
And ever since that time he rouses mirth, his veins
swollen with the sweet nectar and himself heavy
with yesterday's Iacchus.[a] And indeed that god
renowned, the god sprung from very Jove, presses
the grape-clusters with his feet, enwreaths the spear-
like thyrsi from the vine-wands, and proffers a mixing
bowl to a lynx that drinks thereof."

So Pan taught the boys in the Maenalian vale,
until night bade them drive together the sheep
scattered o'er the plain, urging them to drain the
udders of their milk-flow and curdle and thicken it
into snow-white clots of cheese.

[a] *i.e.* his debauch on the gifts of the Wine-god.

IV

Lycidas : Mopsus

Populea Lycidas nec non et Mopsus in umbra,
pastores, calamis ac versu doctus uterque
nec triviale sonans, proprios cantabat amores.
nam Mopso Meroe, Lycidae crinitus Iollas
ignis erat; parilisque furor de dispare sexu   5
cogebat trepidos totis discurrere silvis.
hos puer ac Meroe multum lusere furentes,
dum modo condictas vitant in vallibus ulmos,
nunc fagos placitas fugiunt promissaque fallunt
antra nec est animus solitos alludere fontes.   10
cum tandem fessi, quos dirus adederat ignis,
sic sua desertis nudarunt vulnera silvis
inque vicem dulces cantu luxere querellas.

M. immitis Meroe rapidisque fugacior Euris,
cur nostros calamos, cur pastoralia vitas   15
carmina? quemve fugis? quae me tibi gloria
        victo?
quid vultu mentem premis ac spem fronte
        serenas?
tandem, dura, nega: possum non velle negantem.
    cantet, amat quod quisque: levant et carmina
    curas.

¹⁰ ad ludere *Maehly, Baehrens.*
¹¹ durus NGA : lusus *vel* luxus V : dirus *H. Schenkl* :
torridus *Baehrens.* ederat NG V *plerique, Baehrens* : adederat
V *nonnulli.*
¹³ dixere *vulgo* : duxere V *plerique* : luxere *Glaeser* :
mulsere *Maehly.*
¹⁸ non *codd.* : iam *Baehrens* : nam *C. Schenkl.*

    ᵃ An alternative title is " Eros."
    ᵇ From Virg. *Aen.* IV. 477, *spem fronte serenat.*

478

NEMESIANUS

ECLOGUE IV

LYCIDAS: MOPSUS [a]

The shepherds, Lycidas and Mopsus too, both of them skilled on the reed-pipes and in verse, were singing each of his own love in the poplar shade, uttering no common strain. For Mopsus the flame was Meroe, for Lycidas 'twas Iollas of the flowing locks; and a like frenzy for a darling of different sex drove them wandering restlessly through all the groves. The youth and Meroe sorely mocked these shepherds in their desperate passion; now they would shun the valley-elms which had been made a trysting-place; anon they would avoid the beeches where they fixed to meet, fail to be at the promised cave, or have no mind to sport by the wonted springs; until at length in weariness, consumed by the dread fire of love, Mopsus and Lycidas thus laid bare their wounds to the solitary groves, and by turns wailed forth in song their sweet complaints.

M. Pitiless Meroe, more elusive than the rushing East wind, why do you avoid my pipes, why my shepherd songs? Or whom do you shun? What glory does my conquest bring to you? Why conceal your mind under your looks, why show fair hope on your brow? [b] At last, O heartless maid, refuse me; I may cease to want her who refuses me.

Let each sing of what he loves: song too relieves love's pangs. [c]

[c] The device of a refrain follows the examples in Theocritus, *Idyll.* I. and II. and Virgil, *Eclog.* VIII. It is effectively used in the trochaics of the *Pervigilium Veneris*: '*cras amet qui numquam amavit quique amavit cras amet.*'

L.　respice me tandem, puer o crudelis Iolla.　　　　20
　　　non hoc semper eris: perdunt et gramina flores,
　　　perdit spina rosas nec semper lilia candent
　　　nec longum tenet uva comas nec populus umbras:
　　　donum forma breve est nec se quod commodet
　　　　annis.
　　　　　cantet, amat quod quisque: levant et carmina
　　　　　curas.　　　　　　　　　　　　　　　　　25

M.　cerva marem sequitur, taurum formosa iuvenca,
　　　et Venerem sensere lupae, sensere leaenae
　　　et genus aerium volucres et squamea turba
　　　et montes silvaeque, suos habet arbor amores:
　　　tu tamen una fugis, miserum tu prodis amantem.
　　　　　cantet, amat quod quisque: levant et carmina
　　　　　curas.　　　　　　　　　　　　　　　　　31

L.　omnia tempus alit, tempus rapit: usus in arto est.
　　　ver erat, et vitulos vidi sub matribus istos,
　　　qui nunc pro nivea coiere in cornua vacca.
　　　et tibi iam tumidae nares et fortia colla,　　　35
　　　iam tibi bis denis numerantur messibus anni.
　　　　　cantet, amat quod quisque: levant et carmina
　　　　　curas.

M.　huc, Meroe formosa, veni: vocat aestus in
　　　　umbram.
　　　iam pecudes subiere nemus, iam nulla canoro
　　　gutture cantat avis, torto non squamea tractu　40
　　　signat humum serpens: solus cano. me sonat
　　　　omnis
　　　silva, nec aestivis cantu concedo cicadis.

　　　　　　　　[30] prodis NG : perdis V.

NEMESIANUS

L. Turn your gaze on me at last, Iollas, cruel boy.
You will not be ever thus. Herbs lose their
bloom, thorns lose their roses, nor are lilies
always white; the vine keeps not its leaf for
long nor the poplar its shady foliage. Beauty is
a short-lived gift nor one that lends itself to age.

Let each sing of what he loves: song too
relieves love's pangs.

M. The doe follows the buck, the comely heifer the
bull, wolves have felt the stirring of love, lionesses
have felt it, and the tribes of the air, the birds,
and the throng of scaled creatures, and moun-
tains and woods—and trees have their own
loves. You alone flee from love; you betray
your hapless lover.

Let each sing of what he loves: song too
relieves love's pangs.

L. Time nurtures all things, time snatches them
away; enjoyment lies within narrow bounds.
'Twas spring, and I saw beneath their mothers
yonder calves, which now have met in horned
battle for the snow-white cow. For you, already
your nostrils swell, already your neck grows
strong, already you count your years by twenty
harvests.

Let each sing of what he loves: song too
relieves love's pangs.

M. Come hither, fair Meroe; the heat calls us to
the shade. Now the herds have found cover in
the wood; now there is no bird that sings from
tuneful throat; the scaly serpent marks not
the ground with its sinuous trail. Alone I sing,
all the wood resounds with my strain, nor do I
yield in song to the summer cicalas.

481

cantet, amat quod quisque : levant et carmina
curas.

L. tu quoque, saeve puer, niveum ne perde colorem
sole sub hoc : solet hic lucentes urere malas.   4[

hic age pampinea mecum requiesce sub umbra ;
hic tibi lene fluens fons murmurat, hic et ab ulmis
purpureae fetis dependent vitibus uvae.

cantet, amat quod quisque : levant et carmina
curas.

M. qui tulerit Meroes fastidia lenta superbae,   5(

Sithonias feret ille nives Libyaeque calorem,
Nerinas potabit aquas taxique nocentis
non metuet sucos, Sardorum gramina vincet
et iuga Marmaricos coget sua ferre leones.

cantet, amat quod quisque : levant et carmina
curas.   5[

L. quisquis amat pueros, ferro praecordia duret,
nil properet discatque diu patienter amare
prudentesque animos teneris non spernat in annis,
perferat et fastus. sic olim gaudia sumet,
si modo sollicitos aliquis deus audit amantes.   6(

cantet, amat quod quisque : levant et carmina
curas.

M. quid prodest, quod me pagani mater Amyntac

---

[46] hic V *plerique, Leo, Giarratano* : hac G, *Baehrens.*
[47] virens NG, *H. Schenkl* : fluens V *plerique.*

ᵃ Sithonias means "Thracian"; *Sardoa gramina*, bitter
herbs from Sardinia; *Marmaricos*, belonging to the north of
Africa between Egypt and the Syrtes.

Let each sing of what he loves: song too relieves love's pangs.

L. You too, cruel youth, destroy not your snow-white colour under this sun; it is wont to scorch fair cheeks. Come, rest here with me beneath the shadow of the vine. Here you have the murmur of a gently running spring, here too on the supporting elms hang purple clusters from the fruitful vines.

Let each sing of what he loves: song too relieves love's pangs.

M. The man who can endure proud Meroe's un-responsive disdain will endure Sithonian snows and Libyan heat, will drink sea-water, and be unafraid of the hurtful yew-tree's sap; he will defy Sardinian herbs and will constrain Marmaric lions to bear his yoke.[a]

Let each sing of what he loves: song too relieves love's pangs.

L. Whoe'er loves boys, let him harden his heart with steel. Let him be in no haste, but learn for long to love with patience. Let him not scorn prudence in tender years. Let him even endure disdain. So one day he will find joy, if so be that some god hearkens to troubled lovers.

Let each sing of what he loves: song too relieves love's pangs.

M. What boots it[b] that the mother of Amyntas

[b] Lines 62–72 draw upon the magical ideas in the *Pharmaceutriae* of Theocritus, *Idyll.* II, and its adaptation by Virgil, *Ecl.* VIII. 64–109. From Virgil come the odd numbers, fillets of wool, frankincense, burning of laurel, ashes thrown in a stream, the many-coloured threads, herbs of virtue, and charms to affect the moon or a snake or corn-crops.

ter vittis, ter fronde sacra, ter ture vaporo,
incendens vivo crepitantes sulphure lauros,   65
lustravit cineresque aversa effudit in amnem,   64
cum sic in Meroen totis miser ignibus urar?
    cantet, amat quod quisque: levant et carmina
    curas.

L. haec eadem nobis quoque versicoloria fila
et mille ignotas Mycale circumtulit herbas;
cantavit, quo luna tumet, quo rumpitur anguis,   70
quo currunt scopuli, migrant sata, vellitur arbos.
plus tamen ecce meus, plus est formosus Iollas.
    cantet, amat quod quisque: levant et carmina
    curas.

CYNEGETICA

Venandi cano mille vias; hilaresque labores
discursusque citos, securi proelia ruris,
pandimus.   Aonio iam nunc mihi pectus ab oestro
aestuat: ingentes Helicon iubet ire per agros,
Castaliusque mihi nova pocula fontis alumno   5
ingerit et late campos metatus apertos
imponitque iugum vati retinetque corymbis
implicitum ducitque per avia, qua sola numquam

---

[64] *versus qui sunt in codicibus* 64 *et* 65 *transposuit Hauptius.*
[68] quoque NGA: quae V.
Cyn.   [5] alumnus *Ulitius, Baehrens.*

---

[a] The notion, imitating Virgil, *Ecl.* VIII. 82 (*fragiles
incende bitumine lauros*), is that the laurels are kindled with
divine fire, bitumen being reckoned a product of lightning.

from our village purified me thrice with chaplets,
thrice with sacred leaves, thrice with reeking
incense, while she burnt crackling laurel *a* with
live sulphur, and, turning her face away, cast
the ashes into the river? what boots it when
my unhappy heart burns thus for Meroe in all
the fires of love?

    Let each sing of what he loves: song too
relieves love's pangs.

L. Round me also this self-same dame, Mycale,
carried threads of varied colour and a thousand
strange herbs. She uttered the spell which
makes the moon grow large, the snake to burst,
rocks to run, crops to change their field, and
trees to be uprooted: yet more, lo! still more
beautiful is my Iollas.*b*

    Let each sing of what he loves: song too
relieves love's pangs.

THE CHASE

The thousand phases of the chase I sing; its merry
tasks do we reveal, its quick dashes to and fro—the
battles of the quiet country-side. Already my heart
is tide-swept by the frenzy the Muses *c* send: Helicon
bids me fare through widespread lands, and the
God of Castaly presses on me, his foster-child, fresh
draughts from the fount of inspiration: and, after
far roaming in the open plains, sets his yoke upon
the bard, holding him entangled with ivy-cluster,
and guides him o'er wilds remote, where never

---

  b *i.e.* despite all incantations, Iollas retains a beauty which
exerts an irresistible power over Lycidas.

  c Aonia = Boeotia, associated with the Muses through
Mount Helicon.

trita rotis. iuvat aurato procedere curru
et parere deo: virides en ire per herbas   1•
imperat: intacto premimus vestigia musco;
et, quamvis cursus ostendat tramite noto
obvia Calliope faciles, insistere prato
complacitum, rudibus qua luceat orbita sulcis.

    nam quis non Nioben numeroso funere maestam   15•
iam cecinit? quis non Semelen ignemque iugalem
letalemque simul novit de paelicis astu?
quis magno recreata tacet cunabula Baccho,
ut pater omnipotens maternos reddere menses
dignatus iusti complerit tempora partus?   20•
sunt qui sacrilego rorantes sanguine thyrsos
(nota nimis) dixisse velint, qui vincula Dirces
Pisaei⟨que⟩ tori legem Danaique cruentum
imperium sponsasque truces sub foedere primo
dulcia funereis mutantes gaudia taedis.   25•
Biblidos indictum nulli scelus; impia Myrrhae

---

[13] facilest *Pithoeus, Baehrens.*
[14] non placito *Baehrens*: complacito AC: complacitum *H. Schenkl.*
[20] complerit *vulgo*: compellere AC.
[21] sacrilegos orantes A: sacrilego rorantes C.

---

[a] Lines 8–14: for this almost conventional claim to be original, *cf.* Lucret. I. 926, *avia Pieridum peragro loca nullius ante trita solo*; Virg. *G.* III. 291–293; Hor. *Od.* III. i. 2–4; Milton, *P.L.* I. 16.

[b] Juno (here strikingly called *paelex*, " concubine ") tempted Semele into the fatal request that Jupiter should appear to her in all his glory.

[c] After Semele perished amidst the flames of her lover Jupiter's visitation, the god kept her unborn child, Bacchus, in his thigh until his birth was due: *cf.* Nem. *Ecl.* III. 21–24.

wheel marked ground.[a] 'Tis joy to advance in
gilded car and obey the God: lo, 'tis his behest to
fare across the green sward: we print our steps on
virgin moss; and, though Calliope meet us pointing
to easy runs along some well-known path, it is our
dear resolve to set foot upon a mead where the track
lies clear mid furrows hitherto untried.

For ere now who has not sung of Niobe saddened
by death upon death of her children? Who does
not know of Semele and of the fire that was at once
bridal and doom for her—as the outcome of her
rival's[b] craft? Who fails to record the cradling
renewed for mighty Bacchus—how the Almighty
Sire deigned to restore his mother's months and
fulfilled the time of regular pregnancy.[c] Poets
there are whose taste is to tell the hackneyed tales
of Bacchic wands dripping with unholy blood,[d] or
Dirce's bonds,[e] and the terms imposed for the wooing
at Pisa,[f] and Danaus' bloody behest, and the merci-
less brides who, fresh from plighted troth, changed
sweet joys to funeral torches.[g] No poet fails to tell
of Biblis' criminal passion;[h] we know of Myrrha's

[d] *i.e.* of Pentheus, King of Thebes, torn to pieces by his
mother and other Bacchanalian devotees.
[e] Dirce was tied to a savage bull by Amphion and Zethus
out of revenge for her part in the maltreatment of their mother,
Antiope: *cf. Aetna*, 577.
[f] To escape prophesied death at the hands of a son-in-law,
Oenomaus, King of Elis and Pisa, proclaimed that he would
give his daughter, Hippodamia, in marriage only to the suitor
who should win a chariot-race against his supernatural
steeds.
[g] The fifty Danaides, with the exception of Hypermestra,
carried out the command of their father, Danaus, to kill their
bridegrooms on their marriage-night.
[h] *i.e.* for her brother Caunus.

conubia et saevo violatum crimine patrem
novimus, utque Arabum fugiens cum carperet arva
ivit in arboreas frondes animamque virentem.
sunt qui squamosi referant fera sibila Cadmi   30
stellatumque oculis custodem virginis Ius
Herculeosque velint semper numerare labores
miratumque rudes se tollere Terea pinnas
post epulas, Philomela, tuas; sunt ardua mundi
qui male temptantem curru Phaethonta loquantur   35
exstinctasque canant emisso fulmine flammas
fumantemque Padum, Cycnum plumamque senilem
et flentes semper germani funere silvas.
Tantalidum casus et sparsas sanguine mensas
condentemque caput visis Titana Mycenis   40
horrendasque vices generis dixere priores.
Colchidos iratae sacris imbuta venenis
munera non canimus pulchraeque incendia Glauces,
non crinem Nisi, non saevae pocula Circes,

---

[27] foedo *vel* scaevo *Ulitius.*
[30] quis quā osi A.
[32] *fort.* memorare *Postgate.*
[33] se tollere ad aera (*sive* aethera) *Baehrens* : s&oller&acerea A : sustollere *Burman* : rudi s. t. T. pinna *Heinsius.*
[43] incendia *Pithoeus* : ingentia AC.

---

[a] Myrrha (or Zmyrna), daughter of King Cinyras, was metamorphosed into a fragrant tree.

[b] Juno, jealous of Jupiter's love for Io, consigned her to the guardianship of Argus of the hundred eyes, afterwards transformed into a peacock.

[c] Procne and Philomela punished Tereus for his unfaithfulness by serving to him as food Itys, his son by Procne. When Procne was changed into a swallow and Philomela into a nightingale, Tereus became a hoopoe to pursue them: *cf. Aetna,* 589.

[d] The fiery ruin which overtook Phaëthon in the Sun-God's chariot was lamented by Cycnus, who was changed into a

impious amour, of her father defiled with cruel crime, and how, traversing in her flight the fields of Araby, she passed into the greenwood life of the leafy trees.[a] There are some who relate the fierce hissing of Cadmus turned to a scaly serpent, and Maiden Io's gaoler starred with eyes,[b] or who are fain for ever to recount the labours of Hercules, or Tereus' wonderment that after your banquet, Philomela,[c] he could raise wings as yet untried ; there are others whose theme is Phaethon's ill-starred attempt upon the heights of the universe in the Sun's chariot, and whose song is of flames quenched in the thunderbolt launched forth, and of the river Padus reeking, of Cycnus and the plumage of his old age, of the (poplar-)trees for ever weeping by reason of a brother's death.[d] Bards ere now have told of the misfortunes of the Tantalids, the blood-besprinkled tables, the Titan Sun hiding his face at the sight of Mycenae and the dread vicissitudes of a race.[e] We do not sing of gifts imbued with the accursed poison of the angry Colchian dame [f] and of the burning of fair Glauce ; not of Nisus' lock ; [g] not of cruel Circe's

swan, and by his sisters, the Heliades, who were changed into poplars.

[e] Blood-guilt was transmitted through Pelops, son of Tantalus, and through his sons Atreus and Thyestes to Agamemnon and his son Orestes. Atreus, King of Mycenae, avenged himself for the seduction of his wife on his brother by slaying his two sons and setting their flesh before their father. From this " banquet of Thyestes " the Sun hid his face in horror : cf. Aetna, 20.

[f] The sorceress Medea from Colchis, infuriated by Jason's desertion of her for Glauce, sent to her bridal gifts which consumed her with fire.

[g] On the purple lock of Nisus, King of Megara, the safety of his kingdom depended. His betrayal by his daughter is told in Ciris (Appendix Vergiliana).

nec nocturna pie curantem busta sororem: 45
haec iam magnorum praecepit copia vatum,
omnis et antiqui vulgata est fabula saecli.

  nos saltus viridesque plagas camposque patentes
scrutamur totisque citi discurrimus arvis
et varias cupimus facili cane sumere praedas;   50
nos timidos lepores, imbelles figere dammas
audacesque lupos, vulpem captare dolosam
gaudemus; nos flumineas errare per umbras
malumus et placidis ichneumona quaerere ripis
inter harundineas segetes faelemque minacem   55
arboris in trunco longis praefigere telis
implicitumque sinu spinosi corporis erem
ferre domum; talique placet dare lintea curae,
dum non magna ratis, vicinis sueta moveri
litoribus tutosque sinus percurrere remis,   60
nunc primum dat vela notis portusque fideles
linquit et Adriacas audet temptare procellas.

  mox vestros meliore lyra memorare triumphos
accingar, divi fortissima pignora Cari,
atque canam nostrum geminis sub finibus orbis   65
litus et edomitas fraterno numine gentes,
quae Rhenum Tigrimque bibunt Ararisque remotum

---

[58] cursu (= *cursui*) *Baehrens*: curae AC: cymbae
Heinsius.
[65] gemini *Heinsius.*

---

[a] Circe's potions and spells transformed men into beasts.
[b] Antigone buried her brother Polynices in defiance of the
edict of Creon.
[c] *eres* (= *ericius, ericinus* or *erinaceus*) corresponds to the
Greek ἐχῖνος.
[d] This passage dates the *Cynegetica.* For the Emperor
Carus and his sons, Carinus and Numerianus, see Gibbon,

cups;[a] nor yet of the sister[b] whose conscience con-
trived a (brother's) burial by night: in all this ere
now a band of mighty bards has forestalled us, and
all the fabling of an ancient age is commonplace.

We search the glades, the green tracts, the open
plains, swiftly coursing here and there o'er all the
fields, eager to catch varied quarries with docile
hound. We enjoy transfixing the nervous hare, the
unresisting doe, the daring wolf or capturing the
crafty fox; our heart's desire is to rove along the
river-side shades, hunting the ichneumon on the quiet
banks among the crops of bulrushes, with the long
weapon to pierce in front the threatening polecat on
a tree-trunk and bring home the hedgehog[c] en-
twined in the convolution of its prickly body: for
such a task it is our resolve to set sail, while our
little barque, wont to coast by the neighbouring
shore and run across safe bays with the oar, now first
spreads its canvas to southern winds, and, leaving
the trusty havens, dares to try the Adriatic storms.

Hereafter I will gird myself with fitter lyre to
record your triumphs, you gallant sons of deified
Carus,[d] and will sing of our sea-board beneath the
twin boundaries of our world,[e] and of the subjuga-
tion, by the brothers' divine power, of nations that
drink from Rhine or Tigris or from the distant
source of the Arar or look upon the wells of

Decline and Fall, ch. xii. They succeeded their father on his
death in A.D. 283. In 284 Carinus celebrated elaborate games
at Rome in the name of himself and Numerian; but the
brothers never saw each other after their father died. Nume-
rian's death in 284 during his return journey with his army from
Persia prevented him from enjoying the triumph decreed to
the young emperors at Rome.

[e] *Fines* are the limits set by Ocean on East and West.

principium Nilique vident in origine fontem;
nec taceam, primum quae nuper bella sub Arcto
felici, Carine, manu confeceris, ipso   70
paene prior genitore deo, utque intima frater
Persidos et veteres Babylonos ceperit arces,
ultus Romulei violata cacumina regni;
imbellemque fugam referam clausasque pharetras
Parthorum laxosque arcus et spicula nulla.   75
   haec vobis nostrae libabunt carmina Musae,
cum primum vultus sacros, bona numina terrae,
contigerit vidisse mihi: iam gaudia vota
temporis impatiens sensus spretorque morarum
praesumit videorque mihi iam cernere fratrum   80
augustos habitus, Romam clarumque senatum
et fidos ad bella duces et milite multo
agmina, quis fortes animat devotio mentes:
aurea purpureo longe radiantia velo
signa micant sinuatque truces levis aura dracones.   85
   tu modo, quae saltus placidos silvasque pererras,
Latonae, Phoebe, magnum decus, heia age suetos
sume habitus arcumque manu pictamque pharetram
suspende ex umeris; sint aurea tela, sagittae;
candida puniceis aptentur crura cothurnis;   90

[68] vident *Johnson* : bibunt AC.
[69] primum AC : prima *Baehrens*.

---

   [a] The war maintained against the Sarmatians by Carus after
Probus' death was left to Carinus to finish, when Carus had to
face the Persian menace in the East. In his Gallic campaign
also, Carinus showed some degree of soldierly ability.
   [b] Numerian is here flatteringly associated with the exploits
of Carus, who after subduing Mesopotamia carried his vic-

the Nile at their birth; nor let me fail to tell what
campaigns you first ended, Carinus, beneath the
Northern Bear [a] with victorious hand, well-nigh out-
stripping even your divine father, and how your
brother [b] seized on Persia's very heart and the
time-honoured citadels of Babylon, in vengeance
for outrages done to the high dignity of the realms
of Romulus' race.[c] I shall record also the Parthians'
feeble flight, their unopened quivers, unbent bows
and unavailing arrows.

Such strains shall my Muses consecrate to you
both, as soon as it is my fortune to see your blest
faces, kindly divinities of this earth. Already my
feelings, intolerant of slow time and disdainful of
delay, anticipate the joys of my aspiration, and I
fancy I already discern the majestic mien of the
brothers, and therewith Rome, the illustrious senate,
the generals trusted for warfare, and the marching
lines of many soldiers, their brave souls stirred with
devotion. The golden standards gleam radiant afar
with their purple drapery, and a light breeze waves
the folds of the ferocious dragons.[d]

Only do thou, Diana, Latona's great glory, who
dost roam the peaceful glade and woodland, come
quickly, assume thy wonted guise, bow in hand, and
hang the coloured quiver from thy shoulder; golden
be the weapons, thine arrows; and let thy gleaming
feet be fitted with purple buskins; let thy cloak

torious arms to Ctesiphon. Numerian's subsequent retreat
surprised the Persians.

[c] The reference is to violations of the Eastern frontiers of the
Empire. *Cacumina regni* is taken, with Wernsdorf, to mean
fastigium et maiestatem imperii Romani.

[d] They were military emblems from Trajan's time.

sit chlamys aurato multum subtegmine lusa
corrugesque sinus gemmatis balteus artet
nexibus; implicitos cohibe diademate crines.
tecum Naiades faciles viridique iuventa
pubentes Dryades Nymphaeque, unde amnibus umor,
adsint, et docilis decantet Oreadas Echo.   96
duc age, diva, tuum frondosa per avia vatem:
te sequimur, tu pande domos et lustra ferarum.
huc igitur mecum, quisquis percussus amore
venandi damnas lites pavidosque tumultus   100
civilesque fugis strepitus bellique fragores
nec praedas avido sectaris gurgite ponti.

   principio tibi cura canum non segnis ab anno
incipiat primo, cum Ianus, temporis auctor,
pandit inocciduum bis senis mensibus aevum.   105
elige tunc cursu facilem facilemque recursu,
seu Lacedaemonio natam seu rure Molosso,
non humili de gente canem. sit cruribus altis,
sit rigidis, multamque trahat sub pectore lato
costarum sub fine decenter prona carinam,   110
quae sensim rursus sicca se colligat alvo,
renibus ampla satis validis diductaque coxas,
cuique nimis molles fluitent in cursibus aures.
huic parilem submitte marem, sic omnia magnum,
dum superant vires, dum laeto flore iuventas   115

   96 decantet Oreadas *vulgo* : dicant oreades A : decantet
oreades C.
   98 domos C : dolos A.
   99 huc *Ulitius* : hinc AC.
   100 avidos AC : pavidos *vel* rabidos *Ulitius* : rabidos
Baehrens : rapidos *Postgate.*

---

   a Lines 91–93 are discussed in a special excursus by Werns-
dorf. With *lusa cf.* Virg. *G.* II. 464, *illusasque auro vestes,*
"garments fancifully embroidered with gold."

be richly tricked with golden thread,[a] and a belt
with jewelled fastenings tighten the wrinkled tunic-
folds: restrain thine entwined tresses with a band.
In thy train let genial Naiads come and Dryads
ripening in fresh youth and Nymphs who give the
streams their water, and let the apt pupil Echo
repeat the accents of thine Oreads.[b] Goddess, arise,
lead thy poet through the untrodden boscage: thee
we follow; do thou disclose the wild beasts' homes
and lairs. Come hither then with me, whosoever,
smitten with the love of the chase, dost condemn
lawsuits and panic-stricken turmoil, or dost shun the
din in cities and the clash of war, or pursuest no spoils
on the greedy surge of the deep.

At the outset your diligent care of your dogs [c]
must start from the beginning of the year, when
Janus, author of the march of time, opens for each
twelve months the never-ceasing round. At that
season you must choose a bitch obedient to speed
forward, obedient to come to heel, native to either
the Spartan or the Molossian [d] country-side, and of
good pedigree.[e] She must stand high on straight
legs; with a comely slope let her carry, under a
broad breast, where the ribs end, a width of keel
that gradually again contracts in a lean belly: she
must be big enough with strong loins, spread at the
hips, and with the silkiest of ears floating in air as
she runs. Give her a male to match, everywhere
similarly well-sized, while strength holds sway, while

---

[b] *i.e.* the surroundings should reverberate to the voices of
the attendant mountain-nymphs.
[c] On dogs generally see note on Grattius, *Cyneg.* 151.
[d] *Cf.* Grattius, *Cyneg.* 181, 197, 211-212.
[e] On the mating of dogs *cf.* Grattius, *Cyneg.*, esp. 263-284.

corporis et venis primaevis sanguis abundat.
namque graves morbi subeunt segnisque senectus,
invalidamque dabunt non firmo robore prolem.
sed diversa magis feturae convenit aetas:
tu bis vicenis plenum iam mensibus acrem   120
in venerem permitte marem; sit femina, binos
quae tulerit soles. haec optima cura iugandis.
mox cum se bina formarit lampade Phoebe
ex quo passa marem genitalia viscera turgent,
fecundos aperit partus matura gravedo,   125
continuo largaque vides strepere omnia prole.
sed, quamvis avidus, primos contemnere partus
malueris; mox non omnes nutrire minores.
nam tibi si placitum populosos pascere fetus,
iam macie tenues sucique videbis inanes   130
pugnantesque diu, quisnam prior ubera lambat,
distrahere invalidam lassato viscere matrem.
sin vero haec cura est, melior ne forte necetur
abdaturve domo, catulosque probare voluntas,
quis nondum gressus stabiles neque lumina passa   135
luciferum videre iubar, quae prodidit usus
percipe et intrepidus spectatis annue dictis.
pondere nam catuli poteris perpendere vires
corporibus⟨que⟩ leves gravibus praenoscere cursu.
quin et flammato ducatur linea longe   140

<hr/>

122 *hic in codicibus sequuntur 224–230, quos traiecit Hauptius,
Schradero viam praemonstrante.*

<hr/>

a *Soles* stands here for *annos*, *i.e.* annual revolutions of the
sun according to the ancient cosmology.
b Wernsdorf, following Barth, explains *passa* as meaning
aperta (from *pandere*, not from *pati*).

bodily youth is in its joyous flower and blood
abounds in the veins of early life. For burden-
some diseases creep on and sluggish age, and they
will produce unhealthy offspring without steadfast
strength. But for breeding a difference of age in
the parents is more suitable: you should release
the male, keen for mating, when he has already
completed forty months: and let the female be
two full years old.[a] Such is the best arrangement
in their coupling. Presently when Phoebe has
completed the round of two full moons since the
birth-giving womb fertilised by the male began to
swell, the pregnancy in its due time reveals the
fruitful offspring, and straightway you see all round
an abundant noisy litter. Yet, however desirous of
dogs, you must make up your mind to put no value
on the first set born; and of the next set you must
not rear all the young ones. For if you decide to
feed a crowd of whelps, you will find them thin with
leanness and beggared of strength, and, by their
long tussle to be first to suck, harassing a mother
weakened with teat outworn. But if this is your
anxiety, to keep the better sort from being killed
or thrown out of the house, if it is your intention to
test the puppies before even their steps are steady
or their eyes have felt [b] and seen the light-bearing
sunbeam, then grasp what experience has handed
on, and assent fearlessly to well-tried words. You
will be able to examine the strength of a puppy by
its weight and by the heaviness of each body know
in advance which will be light in running.[c] Further-
more, you should get a series of flames made in a

[c] 138–139: the parallel in Grattius, *Cyn.* 298–299, is one of
the points suggesting that Nemesianus had read Grattius.

circuitu signet⟨que⟩ habilem vapor igneus orbem,
impune ut medio possis consistere circo:
huc omnes catuli, huc indiscreta feratur
turba: dabit mater partus examen, honestos
iudicio natos servans trepidoque periclo.   145
nam postquam conclusa videt sua germina flammis,
continuo saltu transcendens fervida zonae
vincla, rapit rictu primum portatque cubili,
mox alium, mox deinde alium. sic conscia mater
segregat egregiam subolem virtutis amore.   150
hos igitur genetrice simul iam vere sereno
molli pasce sero (passim nam lactis abundans
tempus adest, albent plenis et ovilia mulctris),
interdumque cibo cererem cum lacte ministra,
fortibus ut sucis teneras complere medullas   155
possint et validas iam tunc promittere vires.

    sed postquam Phoebus candentem fervidus axem
contigerit tardasque vias Cancrique morantis
sidus init, tunc consuetam minuisse saginam
profuerit tenuesque magis retinere cibatus,   160
ne gravis articulos depravet pondere moles.
nam tum membrorum nexus nodosque relaxant
infirmosque pedes et crura natantia ponunt,
tunc etiam niveis armantur dentibus ora.

---

[142] ut *Johnson* : in AC.
[144] examen AC : examine *vulgo.*
[145] exitio *Scaliger.* trepidosque *Baehrens* : *fort.* trepidansque *Postgate.*

---

[a] *Cf.* Grattius, *Cyn.* 307, *lacte novam pubem facilique tuebere maza.* For the use of the goddess' name by metonymy for bread *cf.* Gratt. *Cyn.* 398: also *Aetna*, 10.
[b] In the long days of midsummer the sun might be fancied to cross the sky more slowly. *Morantis* refers to the almost

wide circuit with the smoke of the fire to mark a con-
venient round space, so that you may stand unharmed
in the middle of the circle: to this all the puppies,
to this the whole crowd as yet unseparated must be
brought: the mother will provide the test of her
progeny, saving the valuable young ones by her
selection and from their alarming peril. For when
she sees her offspring shut in by flames, at once with
a leap she clears the blazing boundaries of the fire-
zone, snatches the first in her jaws and carries it to
the kennel; next another, next another in turn:
so does the intelligent mother distinguish her nobler
progeny by her love of merit. These then along
with their mother, now that it is clear spring, you
are to feed on soft whey (for everywhere the season
that abounds in milk has come, and sheepfolds are
white with brimming milk-pails): at times, too, add
to their food bread with milk,[a] so that they may be
able to fill their young marrows with powerful juices
and even at that time give promise of vigorous
strength.

But after the burning Sun-God has reached the
glowing height of heaven, entering on his slow paths
and on the sign of the lingering Crab,[b] then it will
be useful to lessen their regular fattening food and
retain the more delicate nourishment,[c] so that the
weight of heavy bulk may not overstrain their limbs;
for that is when they have the connecting joints of
the body slack, and plant on the ground unstable
feet and swimming legs: then too their mouths are
furnished with snowy teeth. But you should not

imperceptible lengthening and shortening of the days before
and after the solstice.

[c] *i.e.* the *molle serum* of l. 152.

sed neque conclusos teneas neque vincula collo   165
impatiens circumdederis noceasque futuris
cursibus imprudens.   catulis nam saepe remotis
aut vexare trabes, laceras aut mandere valvas
mens erit, et teneros torquent conatibus artus
obtunduntve novos arroso robore dentes   170
aut teneros duris impingunt postibus ungues;
mox cum iam validis insistere cruribus aetas
passa, quater binos volvens ab origine menses,
illaesis catulos spectaverit undique membris,
tunc rursus miscere sero Cerealia dona   175
conveniet fortemque dari de frugibus escam.
libera tunc primum consuescant colla ligari
concordes et ferre gradus clausique teneri.
iam cum bis denos Phoebe reparaverit ortus,
incipe non longo catulos producere cursu,   180
sed parvae vallis spatio septove novali.
his leporem praemitte manu, non viribus aequis
nec cursus virtute parem, sed tarda trahentem
membra, queant iam nunc faciles ut sumere praedas.
nec semel indulge catulis moderamina cursus,   185
sed donec validos etiam praevertere suescant
exerceto diu venandi munere, cogens
discere et emeritae laudem virtutis amare.
nec non consuetae norint hortamina vocis,
seu cursus revocent, iubeant seu tendere cursus.   190
quin etiam docti victam contingere praedam
exanimare velint tantum, non carpere sumptam.
sic tibi veloces catulos reparare memento

168 mandere *Heinsius* : pandere AC.
187 munera *Ulitius* : munere AC. *sic interpunxit Postgate.*

keep them shut up, nor impatiently put chains on their neck, and from want of foresight hurt their future running powers. For often young dogs, when kept separate, will take to worrying the timber-fittings, or to gnawing the doors till they are torn, and in the attempt they twist their tender limbs or blunt their young teeth by chewing at the wood or drive their tender nails into the tough door-posts. Later, when time, revolving eight months from their birth, now lets them stand on steady legs and sees the whelps everywhere with limbs unharmed, then it will be suitable again to mix the gifts of Ceres with their whey and have them given strengthening food from the produce of the fields. Only then must they be trained to have their free necks in leash, to run in harmony or be kept on chain. When Phoebe has now renewed twenty monthly risings, start to bring out the young dogs on a course not over-long but within the space of a small valley or enclosed fallow. Out of your hand let slip for them a hare, not of equal strength nor their match in speed of running, but slow in moving its limbs, so that they may at once capture an easy prey. Not once only must you grant the whelps these limited runs, but until they are trained to outstrip strong hares, exercise them long in the task of the chase, forcing them to learn and love the praise due to deserving merit. Likewise they must recognise the urgent words of a well-known voice, whether calling them in or telling them to run full-speed. Besides, when they have been taught to seize the vanquished prey, they must be content to kill, not mangle, what they have caught. By such methods see that you recruit your swift dogs every season,

semper et in parvos iterum protendere curas.
nam tristes morbi, scabies et sordida venis   19
saepe venit multamque canes discrimine nullo
dant stragem : tu sollicitos impende labores
et sortire gregem suffecta prole quotannis.
quin acidos Bacchi latices Tritonide oliva
admiscere decet catulosque canesque maritas   20
unguere profuerit tepidoque ostendere soli,
auribus et tineas candenti pellere cultro.
    est etiam canibus rabies, letale periclum.
quod seu caelesti corrupto sidere manat,
cum segnes radios tristi iaculatur ab aethra   20
Phoebus et attonito pallens caput exserit orbe ;
seu magis, ignicomi candentia terga Leonis
cum quatit, hoc canibus blandis inviscerat aestus,
exhalat seu terra sinu, seu noxius aer
causa mali, seu cum gelidus non sufficit umor   21
torrida per venas concrescunt semina flammae :
quicquid id est, imas agitat sub corde medullas
inque feros rictus nigro spumante veneno
prosilit, insanos cogens infigere morsus.
disce igitur potus medicos curamque salubrem.   21
tunc virosa tibi sumes multumque domabis
castorea, attritu silicis lentescere cogens ;
ex ebore huc trito pulvis sectove feratur,
admiscensque diu facies concrescere utrumque :
mox lactis liquidos sensim superadde fluores,   22

---

[199] olivo AC: oliva *vulgo*. Tritonide . . . *Postgate qui cum
Housmano* olivo *ut interpretamentum eiecit.*
[207] sed *Baehrens* : seu AC.

---

[a] The reference is to the heat of the sun on entering the sign
of Leo.

and again direct your anxious thoughts towards the young ones. For they have melancholy ailments, and the filthy mange often comes on their veins, and the dogs cause widespread mortality without distinction: you must yourself expend anxious efforts on them and every year fill up your pack by supplying progeny. Besides, the right thing is to blend tart draughts of wine with Minerva's olive-fruit, and it will do good to anoint the whelps and the mother dogs, expose them to the warm sun, and expel worms from their ears with the glittering knife.

Dogs also get rabies, a deadly peril. Whether it emanates from taint in a heavenly body when the Sun-God shoots but languid rays from a saddened sky, raising a pallid face in a world dismayed; or whether, rather, in striking the glowing back of the fire-tressed Lion,[a] he drives deep into our friendly dogs his feverish heats, whether earth breathes forth contagion from its bosom, or harmful air is the cause of the evil, or whether, when cool water runs short, the torrid germs of fire grow strong throughout the veins—whatever it is, it stirs the inmost marrow beneath the heart, and with black venomous foam darts forth into ferocious snarls, compelling the dog to imprint its bites in madness. Learn, therefore, the curative potions and the treatment that brings health. In such cases you will take the fetid drug got from the beaver and work it well, forcing it to grow viscous with the friction of a flint: to this should be added powder from pounded or chopped ivory, and by a long process of blending you will get both to harden together: next put in gradually the liquid flow of milk besides, to enable you to pour

ut non cunctantes haustus infundere cornu
inserto possis Furiasque repellere tristes
atque iterum blandas canibus componere mentes.
    sed non Spartanos tantum tantumve Molossos
pascendum catulos: divisa Britannia mittit   225
veloces nostrique orbis venatibus aptos.
nec tibi Pannonicae stirpis temnatur origo,
nec quorum proles de sanguine manat Hibero.
quin etiam siccae Libyes in finibus acres
gignuntur catuli, quorum non spreveris usum.   230
quin et Tuscorum non est externa voluptas
saepe canum. sit forma illis licet obsita villo
dissimilesque habeant catulis velocibus artus,
haud tamen iniucunda dabunt tibi munera praedae,
namque et odorato noscunt vestigia prato   235
atque etiam leporum secreta cubilia monstrant.
horum animos moresque simul naresque sagaces
mox referam; nunc omnis adhuc narranda supellex
venandi cultusque mihi dicendus equorum.
    cornipedes igitur lectos det Graecia nobis   240
Cappadocumque notas referat generosa propago
† armata et palmas superet grex omnis avorum.

²²⁴⁻²³⁰ *post* 122 *in codicibus.*
²³¹ extrema AC: externa *Wight Duff.*
²⁴² armata et palmas nuper grex AC: *fortasse* superet
Postgate: "*locus vexatissimus totius poematii*" *Wernsdorf,
qui proponit* harmataque (= ἅρματα) et palmas numeret:
armenti et palmas numeret *Gronov*: Martius et palmas
superans *Burman.*

ᵃ For British dogs see Grattius, 174 *sqq.* and note there:
divisa Britannia is an allusion to Virg. *Ecl.* I. 66, *penitus toto
divisos orbe Britannos.*

in through an inserted horn doses which do not stick in the throat, and so banish the melancholy Furies, and settle the dogs' minds once more to friendliness.

But it is not only Spartan whelps or only Molossian which you must rear: sundered Britain sends us a swift sort, adapted to hunting-tasks in our world.[a] You should not disdain the pedigree of the Pannonian breed, nor those whose progeny springs from Spanish blood. Moreover, keen whelps are produced within the confines of dry Libya, and their service you must not despise. Besides, Tuscan dogs often give a satisfaction not foreign to us.[b] Even allowing that their shape is covered with shaggy hair and that they have limbs unlike quick-footed whelps, still they will give you an agreeable return in game; for they recognise the tracks on the meadow, though full of scents, and actually point to where a hare lies hid. Their mettle and their habits as well, and their discerning sense of smell I shall record presently;[c] for the moment the whole equipment of the chase[d] has to be explained, and I must deal with the attention due to horses.

So then let Greece send us choice horny-hoofed coursers, and let a high-mettled breed recall the traits of the Cappadocians, and let the whole stud be soundly equipped and surpass the victorious racing-palms of their ancestors. Theirs is surface

[b] Burman gives the choice between *summa* and *minima* as equivalents to *extrema*. *Non . . . externa* seems to fit better the only Italian dogs in the passage.

[c] This shows the incomplete state in which Nemesianus has been transmitted; for these subjects are not treated in his extant work.

[d] The *supellex venandi* corresponds to Grattius' *arma*, *i.e.* nets, traps, hunting-spears, caps and so forth.

illis ampla satis levi sunt aequora dorso
immodicumque latus parvaeque ingentibus alvi,
ardua frons auresque agiles capitisque decori   245
altus honos oculique vago splendore micantes ;
plurima se validos cervix resupinat in armos ;
fumant umentes calida de nare vapores,
nec pes officium standi tenet, ungula terram
crebra ferit virtusque artus animosa fatigat.   250
quin etiam gens ampla iacet trans ardua Calpes
culmina, cornipedum late fecunda proborum.
namque valent longos pratis intendere cursus,
nec minor est illis Graio quam in corpore forma ;
nec non terribiles spirabile flumen anheli   255
provolvunt flatus et lumina vivida torquent
hinnitusque cient tremuli frenisque repugnant,
nec segnes mulcent aures, nec crure quiescunt.
sit tibi praeterea sonipes, Maurusia tellus
quem mittit (modo sit gentili sanguine firmus)   260
quemque coloratus Mazax deserta per arva
pavit et adsiduos docuit tolerare labores.
nec pigeat, quod turpe caput, deformis et alvus
est ollis quodque infrenes, quod liber uterque,
quodque iubis pronos cervix deverberet armos.   265
nam flecti facilis lascivaque colla secutus
paret in obsequium lentae moderamine virgae :
verbera sunt praecepta fugae, sunt verbera freni.

[245] decori *Baehrens* : decoris A : capitique decoro C.

---

[a] One of the fabled Pillars of Hercules, in Hispania Baetica,
now the Rock of Gibraltar. Nemesianus, writing from the
standpoint of an African, thinks of all Spain (*gens ampla*) as
beyond Calpe.

wide enough on their smooth back, an enormous
extent of side, and neat belly for their huge size, a
forehead uplifted, quick ears, high pride of comely
head, and eyes sparkling with restless gleam; an
ample neck falls back on powerful shoulders; moist
breath steams from hot nostrils, and, while the foot
does not maintain its duty to stand still, the hoof
repeatedly strikes the earth and the horse's spirited
mettle tires its limbs. Moreover, beyond the soaring
peaks of Calpe *a* lies a vast country, productive far
and wide of fine coursers. For they have the
strength to make long runs across the prairies,*b* and
their beauty is no less than that in a Grecian body;
panting they roll forth terrifying snorts, a flood of
breath; they shoot out spirited glances; all a-quiver
they raise whinnyings and fight against the bridle,
never giving their ears smooth rest nor their legs
repose. Besides, you may select the courser sent
by Mauretania (if he be a stout descendant of good
stock), or the horse which the dusky Mazax tribes-
man *c* has reared in desert fields and taught to under-
go ceaseless toil. No need to repine at their ugly
head and ill-shapen belly, or at their lack of bridles,
or because both breeds have the temper of freedom,
or because the neck lashes the sloping shoulders
with its mane. For he is an easy horse to guide,
and, following the turn of an unconfined neck, com-
plies obediently under the control of a limber switch:
its strokes are the orders for speed, its strokes are

b The commendation of Spanish horses is supported by
Martial I. xlix. 21-25 : *cf.* XIV. cxcix. But, according to
Oppian, *Cyneg.* I. 284-286, the Iberian horses, although fleet
(θοοί), were found wanting in staying power (δρόμον ἐν παύροισιν
ἐλεγχόμενοι σταδίοισιν).

c Belonging to the Numidian tribe of Mazaces in Africa.

quin et promissi spatiosa per aequora campi
cursibus acquirunt commoto sanguine vires   270
paulatimque avidos comites post terga relinquunt.
haud secus, effusis Nerei per caerula ventis,
cum se Threicius Boreas superextulit antro
stridentique sono vastas exterruit undas,
omnia turbato cesserunt flamina ponto: 275
ipse super fluctus spumanti murmure fervens
conspicuum pelago caput eminet: omnis euntem
Nereidum mirata suo stupet aequore turba.
   horum tarda venit longi fiducia cursus,
his etiam emerito vigor est iuvenalis in aevo.   280
nam quaecumque suis virtus bene floruit annis,
non prius est animo quam corpore passa ruinam.
pasce igitur sub vere novo farragine molli
cornipedes venamque feri veteresque labores
effluere adspecta nigri cum labe cruoris.   285
mox laetae redeunt in pectora fortia vires
et nitidos artus distento robore formant;
mox sanguis venis melior calet, ire viarum
longa volunt latumque fuga consumere campum.
inde ubi pubentes calamos duraverit aestas   290
lactentesque urens herbas siccaverit omnem
messibus umorem culmisque aptarit aristas,
hordea tum paleasque leves praebere memento:
pulvere quin etiam puras secernere fruges

[269] permissi *Heinsius.*
[276] pater fluctus (*id est Neptunus*) *Baehrens* : super fluctus
AC.   marmore *Heinsius.*
[282] passa *vulgo* : posse AC.
[292] culmisque armarit *Burman* : culmusque *Baehrens, Post-
gate* : aptarit *Wight Duff.*
508

as bridles too. Nay, once launched across the spacious levels of the plain, with blood stirred, the steeds win fresh strength in the race, leaving by degrees their eager comrades behind. Even so, on the outburst of the winds across the blue waters of Nereus, when Thracian Boreas has uprisen o'er his cavern and with shrill howling dismayed the dreary waves, all the blasts on the troubled deep give way to him: himself[a] aglow mid foaming din, above the billows he o'ertops them in mastery manifest upon the sea: the whole band of the Nereids is mazed in wonderment as he passes over their watery domain.

These horses are slow to attain confidence in prolonged running; also, theirs is youthful vigour even in age that has served its time. For no quality which has bloomed full at its due period suffers collapse in spirit ere physical powers fail. In the fresh spring-time, then, feed the coursers on soft mash, and, lancing a vein, watch old-standing ailments flow out with the ooze of the tainted blood. Soon strength returns joyously to their gallant hearts, moulding the sleek limbs with strength diffused: soon a better blood runs warm in their veins, and they wish for long stretches of road, and to make the broad plain vanish in their career. Next, when summer has hardened the ripening stalks and, scorching the juicy blades, has dried all the moisture for harvest and joined corn-ears to stems, then be sure to furnish barley and light chaff: moreover, there must be care to winnow the produce free from dust, and to run the hands

---

[a] Boreas.

cura sit atque toros manibus percurrere equorum, 295
gaudeat ut plausu sonipes laetumque relaxet
corpus et altores rapiat per viscera sucos.
id curent famuli comitumque animosa iuventus.
  nec non et casses idem venatibus aptos
atque plagas longoque meantia retia tractu 300
addiscant raris semper contexere nodis
et servare modum maculis linoque tenaci.
linea quin etiam, magnos circumdare saltus
quae possit volucresque metu concludere praedas,
digerat innexas non una ex alite pinnas. 305
namque ursos magnosque sues cervosque fugaces
et vulpes acresque lupos ceu fulgura caeli
terrificant linique vetant transcendere septum.
has igitur vario semper fucare veneno
curabis niveisque alios miscere colores 310
alternosque metus subtegmine tendere longo.
dat tibi pinnarum terrentia milia vultur,
dat Libye, magnarum avium fecunda creatrix,
dantque grues cycnique senes et candidus anser,
dant quae fluminibus crassisque paludibus errant 315
pellitosque pedes stagnanti gurgite tingunt.
hinc mage puniceas nativo munere sumes:
namque illic sine fine greges florentibus alis
invenies avium suavique rubescere luto
et sparsos passim tergo vernare colores. 320
his ita dispositis hiemis sub tempus aquosae
incipe veloces catulos immittere pratis,
incipe cornipedes latos agitare per agros.

---

  [a] *Cf.* Grattius, *Cynegeticon*, 75–88 (the "formido").
  [b] *e.g.* the ostrich.
  [c] *i.e.* aquatic fowl.

over the horses' muscles, so that the courser may enjoy being patted and relax his body in pleasure and quickly pass the nourishing juices throughout his frame. This must be the task of the servants and brave young attendants.

Besides they too must learn always to weave with knots far enough apart the hollow nets fit for the chase, and the toils set on tracks, and the nets which run in a long stretch; they must learn to preserve the right size for the openings between the knots and for the binding cord. Moreover, the line which can enclose great glades and by reason of terror shut in winged game as prey must carry here and there, entwined on it, feathers of different birds.[a] For the colours, like lightning-flashes, frighten bears, big boars, timid stags, foxes and fierce wolves, and bar them from surmounting the boundary of the cord. These then you will always be careful to diversify with various hues, mixing other colours with the whites, and thus stretching all along the line one terror after another. In feathers you draw a thousand means of fright from the vulture, from Africa, fertile mother of great-sized birds,[b] from cranes and aged swans and the white goose, from fowl that haunt rivers and thick marshes and dip webbed feet in standing pools. Of these [c] you will rather take birds with red plumage by nature's gift; for among the former you will find endless flocks of birds with bright-hued wings, their colours reddening with pleasant orange tint and gleaming everywhere in flecks upon the back. With such arrangements made towards the season of rainy winter, begin to send your swift dogs across the meadows; begin to urge your horses over the broad

venemur dum mane novum, dum mollia prata
nocturnis calcata feris vestigia servant.   325

TWO FRAGMENTS ON BIRD-CATCHING
ASCRIBED TO NEMESIANUS

Introduction

Gybertus Longolius (de Longueil, 1507–1543), in
a *Dialogus de avibus* printed at Cologne in 1544, is
the authority for ascribing the two following frag-
ments to Nemesianus. He records that they were
surreptitiously copied by a young friend of his,
Hieronymus Boragineus of Lübeck, from a poem
De Aucupio by Nemesianus " in bibliotheca porcorum
(*sic*) Salvatoris Bononiensis." This account is not

VERSUS DE AUCUPIO

I

. . . et tetracem, Romae quem nunc vocitare taracem
coeperunt. avium est multo stultissima ; namque
cum pedicas necti sibi contemplaverit adstans,
immemor ipse sui tamen in dispendia currit.
tu vero adductos laquei cum senseris orbes   5
appropera et praedam pennis crepitantibus aufer.
nam celer oppressi fallacia vincula colli
excutit et rauca subsannat voce magistri

ª a black grouse. The bird is identified with the *urogallus*
by Longolius. Pliny's form is *tetras*.

fields. Let us go hunting while the morning is young, while the soft meads retain the tracks imprinted by the wild beasts of the night.

---

free from suspicion, any more than certain points in the Latinity and prosody of the lines. *Contemplaverit* in l. 3 may be an archaistic return to the active form of the verb as used in early Latin; but the metrical quantity of *notae* which Longolius read in l. 13 and of *gulae* in the last line of all is unclassical, and the frequent elision of a long vowel (ll. 5, 6, 14 and 27) is noticeable. Teuffel considers the lines a late production, though they are usually printed along with the *Cynegetica*.

E. Baehrens' text, *P.L.M.* III. pp. 203–204.
J. P. Postgate's text, *C.P.L.* II. p. 572.

FRAGMENTS ON BIRD-CATCHING

I

. . . and the *tetrax*,[a] which they have now begun to call *tarax* at Rome. It is far the silliest of birds; for although it has perched and has watched the snare laid for it, yet reckless of self it darts upon its own hurt. You, however, on finding the circles of the noose drawn tight, must hasten up and carry off your prey with its whirring wings. For it is quick to shake off the treacherous bonds of the neck when caught, deriding [b] with hoarse cry the hunter's

[b] *Subsannare*, a late Latin verb, used by Tertullian, and in the Vulgate.

consilium et laeta fruitur iam pace solutus.
hic prope † Peltinum ⟨ad⟩ radices Apennini   1
nidificat, patulis qua se sol obicit agris,
persimilis cineri collum, maculosaque terga
inficiunt pullae cacabantis imagine guttae.
Tarpeiae est custos arcis non corpore maior
nec qui te volucres docuit, Palamede, figuras.   1.
saepe ego nutantem sub iniquo pondere vidi
mazonomi puerum, portat cum prandia, circo
quae consul praetorve novus construxit ovanti.

II

cum nemus omne suo viridi spoliatur honore,
fultus equi niveis silvas pete protinus altas   2.
exuviis: praeda est facilis et amoena scolopax.
corpore non Paphiis avibus maiore videbis.
illa sub aggeribus primis, qua proluit umor,
pascitur, exiguos sectans obsonia vermes.
at non illa oculis, quibus est obtusior, etsi   2.
sint nimium grandes, sed acutis naribus instat:
impresso in terram rostri mucrone sequaces
vermiculos trahit et vili dat praemia gulae.

    ¹⁰ Pelt(u)inum *Buecheler*: Pentinum *Longolius*: Pontinum
Ulitius. in radicibus *Burman*: et radices *Haupt*: ad radices
Baehrens.
    ¹² dorsum *Longolius* : collum *Gesner.*
    ¹³ notae *Longolius* : guttae *Ulitius.*
    ¹⁷ mazonomi *Gesner*: mazonoim *Longolius.* circo *Bur-
man* : cirro *Longolius.*
    ²¹ facilis praeda est et amoena *Riese.*
    ²⁸ atque gulae d. pr. vili *Wernsdorf.*

    ᵃ The geese of the Capitol saved it from surprise by the
Gauls, in 390 B.C., Livy, V. xlvii.

design and now in freedom delighting in the joy of
peace. Near Peltinum by the foot of the Apennine
range it builds its nest where the sun presents him-
self to the outspread lands: at the neck it is very
like ashes in colour, and its spotted back is marked
with dark flecks in the fashion of a partridge. The
guardian of the Tarpeian citadel[a] is no larger in
size, nor the bird that taught you, Palamedes, wing-
like letters.[b] Often have I seen a slave swaying
beneath the unfair weight of a huge dish of such
dainties,[c] as he carries the collation which a consul
or a new praetor has furnished for the circus at a
fête.

II

When the woodland everywhere is despoiled of
its green honours, make straight for the deep forest,
mounted on the snow-white housing of your steed.
The snipe is an easy and an agreeable prey. You
will find it no larger in body than Venus' doves. It
feeds close to the edge of embankments, by the
wash of the water, hunting tiny worms, its favourite
fare. But its pursuit thereof is rather with keen-
scented nose than with the eyes, in which its sense
is rather dull, too big for the body though they be.
With the point of the beak driven into the ground it
drags out the little worms which needs must follow,
therewith rewarding an appetite cheap to satisfy.[d]

[b] Palamedes was said to have invented some of the Greek
letters (Υ, Θ, Ξ, Φ, X) by observing the flight of cranes: cf.
Martial, IX. xiii. 7, XIII. lxxv.; Ausonius, *Idyll.* xii. (*Techno-
paegnion de literis monosyllabis*) 25; Pliny *N.H.* VII. 192.

[c] For the *mazonomus* (μαζονόμος) see Hor. *Sat.* II. viii. 86.

[d] For the unclassical lengthening of *gŭla*, Wernsdorf cites as
a parallel from Nemesianus' fellow-African Luxorius, *quid
festinus abis gula impellente, sacerdos?*

REPOSIANUS
AND SOME CONTEMPORARIES

INTRODUCTION

TO REPOSIANUS, MODESTINUS, " CUPIDO AMANS " AND PENTADIUS

THE codex Salmasianus [a]—a title which records the previous ownership of Claude de Saumaise—is the chief authority for the surviving poems by three authors of the third century here selected from it —Reposianus, Modestinus and Pentadius, with the additional piece *Cupido Amans* by an unknown hand. The codex represents, though imperfectly, the extensive and varied *Anthologia Latina* compiled from poets of different periods, originally in twenty-four books, at Carthage in the time of the Vandal kings about A.D. 532. Owing to the disappearance of the first eleven quaternions, half-a-dozen books at the beginning are lost except in so far as the missing contents are represented by codex Leid. Voss. Q. 86 [" V "], by codex Paris. 8071 (or Thuaneus, " T "), both of the ninth century, and by other MSS.[b] The 182 hexameters by Reposianus on the *liaison* between Mars and Venus depend solely on the codex Salmasianus; for Modestinus we have the additional authority of T; and for Pentadius we have V as well as S and T.

Reposianus' theme is the discovery of the intrigue

---

[a] It is also the manuscript for Florus' poems, see p. 424.

[b] See Baehrens' prolegomena *P.L.M.* IV. pp. 3–54; Buecheler and Riese, *Anth. Lat.* I. i. praefatio, pp. xii. *sqq.*

between the Goddess of Love and the God of War by the injured husband, as first related in European literature by Homer, *Odyssey* VIII. 266–366. The Roman poet exhibits a turn for description, especially in depicting the flowery grove where the lovers meet; but there is in him a certain poverty of style—a certain want of variety in language, in thought and in structure. Manifestly he overdoes the use of *forte* (*e.g.* 68, 83, 87, 95, 114, 121, 126, 156, 166). The archaism *mage* of line 9 is an artificiality which he shares with Nemesianus (*Cyneg.* 317), with Sulpicius Lupercus Servasius and other late poets. The most noticeable metrical points are his use of *tuo* (93) as a monosyllable and *gratiosa* (126) as a trisyllable. A few turns of phrase suggest the Lucretian picture of Mars in Venus' lap (Lucret. I. 31–40); but Reposianus shows signs of independence in treating his sensuous theme. Thus, he alters the scene of the amour from the traditional house of the Fire-God, Vulcan, to a forest, which gives the cue for his introduction of some beauties in external nature (33–50). Further, the chains fastened upon the offending lovers are not, according to earlier forms of the fable, prepared as a trap in anticipation of their continued guilt, but fashioned at Vulcan's forge after Phoebus has informed him of Venus' infidelity.

The three longer pieces by Pentadius, *On Fortune*, *On the Coming of Spring* and *On Narcissus*, have " echoic " lines: the rest are short epigrams. Among these the quatrain *On Woman's Love*, beginning *Crede ratem ventis*, may be a tetrastichon combining a pair of independent elegiac distichs. It has been ascribed to a variety of authors besides Pentadius—to Marcus Cicero, to his brother, to Petronius, to Ausonius, and to Porphyrius, the panegyrist of Constantine. The epigram has been claimed for Quintus Cicero [a] as a vigorous expression of a thought which might have been in his mind after his divorce (*Ad Att.* XIV. 13. 3). But it cannot be argued that either the situation or the reflection was by any means peculiar to him.

EDITIONS

Reposianus : P. Burman. *Anthol. Lat.* Lib. I. No. 72. Amsterdam, 1759.

J. C. Wernsdorf. *Poet. Lat. Min.* IV. pp. 319 *sqq.* Altenburg, 1785.

E. Baehrens. *Poet. Lat. Min.* IV. pp. 348 *sqq.* Leipzig, 1882.

F. Buecheler and A. Riese. *Anth. Lat.* I. i. No. 253. Leipzig, 1894.

Modestinus : P. Burman. *Anthol. Lat.* Lib. I. No. 31.

E. Baehrens. *Poet. Lat. Min.* IV. p. 360.

F. Buecheler and A. Riese. *Anth. Lat.* I. i. No. 273, p. 217.

Pentadius : P. Burman. *Anthol. Lat.* Lib. I. Nos. 139, 141, 165; III. No. 105; V. No. 69.

J. C. Wernsdorf. *Poet. Lat. Min.* III. pp. 262–80, pp. 405–407.

E. Baehrens. *Poet. Lat. Min.* IV. pp. 343–5, 358–9.

F. Buecheler and A. Riese. *Anth. Lat.* I. i. Nos. 234–5, 265–8.

[a] Jas. Stinchcomb, "The Literary Interests of a Roman Magnate," *Class. Weekly*, Oct. 3, 1932.

INTRODUCTION TO REPOSIANUS

SIGLA

S = codex Salmasianus sive Parisinus 10318: saec. vii.

T = codex Thuaneus sive Parisinus 8071: saec. ix. exeunte.

V = codex Vossianus L.Q. 86: medio saec. ix.

Bibliographical addendum (1982)

Reposianus: *Concubitus Martis et Veneris* (introduction, text, commentary, Italian translation) ed. U. Zuccarelli, Naples 1972.

REPOSIANUS

DE CONCUBITU MARTIS ET VENERIS

DISCITE securos non umquam credere amores.
ipsa Venus, cui flamma potens, cui militat ardor,
quae tuto posset custode Cupidine amare,
quae docet et fraudes et amorum furta tuetur,
nec sibi securas valuit praebere latebras.   5
improbe dure puer, crudelis crimine matris,
pompam ducis, Amor, nullo satiate triumpho!
quid conversaª Iovis laetaris fulmina semper?
ut mageᵇ flammantes possis laudare sagittas,
iunge, puer, teretes Veneris Martisque catenas: 10
gestet amans Mavors titulos et vincula portet
captivus, quem bella timent! utque ipse veharis,
iam roseis fera colla iugis submittit amator:
post vulnus, post bella potens Gradivusᶜ anhelat
in castris modo tiro tuis, semperque timendus   15
te timet et sequitur qua ducunt vincla marita.
ite, precor, Musae: dum Mars, dum blanda Cythereᵈ
imis ducta trahunt suspiria crebra medullis

ª *conversa*, either thrown back by the power of love or
exchanged for the disguises which Jove used in his amours.

ᵇ *mage*, an artificial archaism, as in Sulpicius Lupercus
Servasius, II. (*De Cupiditate*) 16, and in the *Dicta Catonis*,
Praef. II. 2, *Distich.* II. 6; IV. 42.

ᶜ An ancient form of *Mars*: his surname *Gradivus* (14) marks
him as god of the march (*gradus*).

ᵈ *Cythere* (cf. 172), a late Latin collateral form of *Cytherea*
(153), refers to the birth of Venus from the sea at the island

REPOSIANUS

THE INTRIGUE OF MARS WITH VENUS

LEARN ye the creed that amours are never free
from care. Venus herself of the potent flame, Venus
of the blazing campaign, who might indulge love
with Cupid as her safe warden, instructress in deceits,
protectress of the stealth of love, did not avail to
furnish herself with a secure lurking-place. Harsh
tyrant Boy, cruel in a mother's fault, O Love, you
lead your victorious procession, never sated with any
triumph! Why do you always rejoice that Jove's
thunderbolts have been reversed? [a] That you may
the better [b] praise your flaming arrows, draw tight,
Boy, the well-woven chains of Venus and of Mars:
let Mavors [c] in love wear the label of a slave, let him
whom wars do dread be a prisoner bearing bonds!
To let you ride triumphant, the lover yields his savage
neck to a rosy yoke. After wounds dealt and battles
fought, powerful Gradivus pants as a new-enlisted
recruit in your camp; he that should ever be feared
fears you, following where wedlock's bonds do lead.
Pray, come, ye Muses: while Mars, while alluring
Cythere [d] draw fast-following sighs from the depth

of Cythera. *Cypris* (35, 79, 141, 146) recalls her cult in Cyprus,
and *Paphie*, Reposianus' favourite epithet for Venus (23, 50,
61, 64, 80, 105, 109, 136, 139, 178), alludes to her temple at
Paphos in Cyprus. Reposianus shares the epithets *Cythere*,
Cypris and *Paphie* with Ausonius (4th cent. A.D.), though
Paphie is used by Martial.

525

dumque intermixti captatur spiritus oris,
carmine doctiloquo Vulcani vincla parate,   20
quae Martem nectant Veneris nec bracchia laedant
inter delicias roseo prope livida serto.
    namque ferunt Paphien, Vulcani et Martis amorem,
inter adulterium nec iusti iura mariti
indice sub Phoebo captam gessisse catenas.   25
illa manu duros nexus tulit, illa mariti
ferrea vincla sui.   quae vis fuit ista doloris?
an fortem faciebat amor? quid, saeve, laboras?
cur nodos Veneri Cyclopia flamma paravit?
de roseis conecte manus, Vulcane, catenis!   30
nec tu deinde liges, sed blandus vincla Cupido,
ne palmas duro nodus cum vulnere laedat.
    lucus erat Marti gratus, post vulnera Adonis
pictus amore deae; si Phoebi lumina desint,
tutus adulterio, dignus quem Cypris amaret,   35
quem Byblos coleret, dignus quem Gratia servet.

    22 divitias S : delicias *Burman.* prope S : modo *Baehrens.*
    26 manus S : manu *Schrader* : Venus *Baehrens.*
    32 comodus S : nodus cum *Baehrens, alii alia.*
    34 pictus S : dictus *vel* lectus *vel* dignus *Wernsdorf* : huius *Baehrens* : laetus *Riese (in not.).*

    [a] *i.e.* arms so delicate that rose-leaves might almost make them black and blue.
    [b] Addressed to Vulcan as the injured husband of Venus.
    [c] *i.e.* to fashion iron chains.
    [d] After the death of her beloved Adonis from a wound inflicted by a boar in the forest, Venus might be imagined to dislike all woods. The passage implies that she made an exception in the case of the grove where she met her lover Mars, and so it is "decorated," "lit up" by the beautiful presence of the enamoured goddess. *pictus* may be right, though *amore* is less directly instrumental than the concrete ablatives in Lucr. V. 1395–1396, *anni tempora pingebant viridantes floribus herbas*; Sen. *Med.* 310, *stellisque quibus pingitur*

of their being, and while they woo the breath of
intermingled kisses, do ye with dulcet strain make
ready Vulcan's bonds to twine round Mars and yet
do no hurt to Venus' arms that mid their dalliance
are half-discoloured with the pressure of even a
garland of roses.[a]

The tale is told that the Paphian goddess, darling
of Vulcan and of Mars, amid her adulterous inter-
course and rights usurped by one not her lawful
husband, was 'neath the revealing Sun-god caught,
and wore the chains. She bore on her hand the
cruel coils, she bore the iron bonds of her own hus-
band. What was that violence in your resentment?[b]
Did love make strength?[c] Why toil, O ruthless one?
Why did the flame of the Giants' forge prepare
entanglements for Venus? Rather, Vulcan, make
the linking for the hands from chains of roses!
And then *you* must not tie the bonds, but coaxing
Cupid must, lest the knotting hurt the palms and
inflict harsh pain.

There was a grove dear to Mars, adorned [d] by the
goddess' love after Adonis' death-wound; if only
sunlight were lacking, safe for unlawful passion, meet
for the Cyprian's affection, meet for worship from
Byblos,[e] meet for the regard of one of the Graces.[f]

---

aether; Pentadius, *De Adventu Veris*, line 11, *floribus innu-
meris pingit sola flatus Eoi*: cf. Lucr. II. 374–5, *concharum
genus . . . videmus pingere telluris gremium*. The meta-
phorical use seems a not unnatural extension from the idea
of *pingunt* in 38, or in *sic mea flaventem pingunt vineta
Garumnam* (of vineyards throwing their green reflection on
the yellow Garonne), Auson. *Mosella* 160, or in *quis te naturae
pinxit color? ib.* 110.

[e] This Phoenician coast-town was the chief seat of the wor-
ship of Adonis : *cf.* 66 and *Bybliades*, 90.

[f] *Cf.* line <u>51</u>. The singular is used in Ovid. *Met.* VI. 429.

527

vilia non illo surgebant gramina luco :
pingunt purpureos candentia lilia flores ;
ornat terra nemus : nunc lotos mitis inumbrat,
nunc laurus, nunc myrtus. habent sua munera
    rami ;   40
namque hic per frondes redolentia mala relucent.
hic rosa cum violis, hic omnis gratia odorum,
hic inter violas coma mollis laeta hyacinthi :
dignus amore locus, cui tot sint munera rerum.
non tamen in lucis aurum, non purpura fulget : 45
flos lectus, flos vincla tori, substramina flores ;
deliciis Veneris dives Natura laborat.
texerat hic liquidos fontes non vilis harundo,
sed qua saeva puer componat tela Cupido.
hunc solum Paphie puto lucum fecit amori : 50
hic Martem exspectare solet.   quid Gratia cessat,
quid Charites ?   cur, saeve puer, non lilia nectis ?
tu lectum consterne rosis, tu serta parato
et roseis crinem nodis subnecte decenter.
haec modo purpureum decerpens pollice florem, 55
cum delibato suspiria ducat odore.
ast tibi blanda manus ⟨flores⟩ sub pectore condat !
tunc ne purpurei laedat te spina roseti,
destrictis teneras foliis constringe papillas !
sic decet in Veneris luco gaudere puellas : 60
ut tamen illaesos Paphiae servetis amores,

    [39] locos vitis S : lotos mitis *Burman.*
    [40] rami *Baehrens, Riese* : lauri *vulgo.*
    [41] lilia pendent S : mala relucent *Baehrens.*
    [52] licia *vulgo.*
    [56] diligatum . . . odorem S : delibat eum . . . odorem
Baehrens : delibato . . . odore *Klappius.*

---

    [a] There are no purple coverlets.

REPOSIANUS

No common herbage grew within that grove: white
lilies set off its bright-hued flowers. The earth gives
adornment to the woodland: now the mild lotus
casts its shade, now the laurel, now the myrtle.
The boughs have their own gifts; for here mid
leafage fragrant apples shine out. Here the rose is
neighbour to violets, here is every charm of scent,
here among the violets are the joyous bells of the
delicate hyacinth. Meet for love is a place which
hath such wealth of boons. Still, gold there is none
in all the grove, no gleam of purple [a]: flowers are
the bed, flowers the frame of the couch, flowers
the support beneath. Rich Nature toils for Venus'
luxury. Here had no common reeds shaded the
crystal wells, but such as those whence young Cupid
fashions his cruel weapons. I trow our Lady of
Paphos made this grove for naught but love. Here
'tis her way to wait for Mars. Why be the Graces
slow to come—the sisterhood of the Charites? [b]
Why, cruel Boy, do you not twine lilies? Nay, *you*
must strew the couch with roses, *you* must make
garlands ready and with rosy knots bind up Venus'
hair in seemly wise. [c] Even as her finger culls the
bright-hued bloom, let her draw long sighs as she
drinks in its fragrance. But for thyself let a caress-
ing hand store the flowers beneath thy bosom!
Then, lest a thorn of the bright-hued rose-bush
hurt thee, strip off the leaves ere thou bind together
the tender buds! [d] Even thus 'tis seemly that
maids rejoice within the grove of Venus: yet that
ye may preserve amours uninjured for the Paphian,

[b] The Greek Χάριτες corresponded to the Latin *Gratiae*.
[c] Wernsdorf thinks *tu* is addressed to one of the Graces.
[d] For *papillae* as rosebuds *cf. Pervig. Ven.* 14 and 21.

vincula sic mixtis caute constringite ramis,
ne diffusa ferat per frondes lumina Titan.
his igitur lucis Paphie, dum proelia Mavors
horrida, dum populos diro terrore fatigat,   65
ludebat teneris Bybli permixta puellis.
nunc varios cantu divom referebat amores
inque modum vocis nunc motus forte decentes
corpore laeta dabat, nunc miscens † denique plantas,
nunc alterna movens suspenso pollice crura,   70
molliter inflexo subnitens poplite sidit.
saepe comam pulchro collectam flore ligabat
ornans ambrosios divino pectine crines.

    dum ludos sic blanda Venus, dum gaudia miscet   75
et dum flet, quod sera venit sibi grata voluptas,
et dum suspenso solatia quaerit amori:
ecce furens post bella deus, post proelia victor
victus amore venit.   cur gestas ferrea tela?
ne metuat Cypris, comptum decet ire rosetis.
a, quotiens Paphie vultum mentita furentis   80
lumine converso serum incusavit amantem!
verbera saepe dolens minitata est dulcia serto
aut, ut forte magis succenso Marte placeret,
amovit teneris suspendens oscula labris
nec totum effundens medio blanditur amore.   85

    decidit aut posita est devictis lancea palmis
et, dum forte cadit, myrto retinente pependit.
ensem tolle, puer, galeam tu, Gratia, solve;   89

---

⁸² mentita S : minitata *Higtius.*
⁸⁴ atmovet S : admovit *vulgo* : amovit *Wakkerus.*

ᵃ An imitation of Virg. *Georg.* IV. 347.

carefully knit together bonds of branches inter-
twined to keep the Sun-god from shedding a flood
of light through the foliage. In these woodlands,
then, the Paphian used to sport amid a bevy of
tender damsels from Byblos, while Mavors plied
savage warfare, while he wearied the nations with
dread alarm. Now she would rehearse in song the
chequered amours of the gods *a* and to the vocal
measure now joyously, as it befell, made seemly
movements with her body; now in turn plying
intricate steps, now on light fantastic toe moving
alternate feet, she sinks down resting upon grace-
fully bended haunch. Oft she would bind her hair
close-drawn with pretty blooms, ordering ambrosial
tresses with comb divine.

While thus sweet Venus engages in various sports
and joys, and turns to tears for that her darling
pleasure cometh late, and seeks some solace for her
love deferred, behold in frenzy after warfare comes
the god, after his battles the vanquisher vanquished
by love. Why dost thou wear weapons of steel?
Lest Cypris feel alarm, 'tis seemly to come with
roses garlanded. Ah, how often did the Paphian's
look feign anger as her averted eye reproached her
lover's tardiness! Oft, piqued, did she threaten
sweet lashes from festoons of flowers, or, mayhap
the more to please when Mars was afire with
passion, withheld those kisses which she poised on
tender lips, alluring in the midst of love by checking
love's full flood.

Down fell his lance or with love-vanquished hands
was laid aside, and, as it happened to fall, hung
on a myrtle-bough which caught it. Take, Boy, his
sword: let one of the Graces unlace his helmet: ye

solvite, Bybliades, praeduri pectora Martis: 90
haec laxet nodos, haec ferrea vincula temptet   89
loricaeque moras, vos scuta et tela tenete.   91
nunc violas tractare decet.   laetare, Cupido,
terribilem divum tuo solo numine victum:
pro telis flores, pro scuto myrtea serta,
et rosa forte loco est gladii, quem iure tremescunt!   95
    iverat ad lectum Mavors et pondere duro
floribus incumbens totum turbarat honorem.
ibat pulchra Venus vix presso pollice cauta,
florea ne teneras violarent spicula plantas,
et nunc innectens, ne rumpant oscula, crinem,   100
nunc vestes fluitare sinens, vix lassa retentat,
cum nec tota latet nec totum nudat amorem.
ille inter flores furtivo lumine tectus
spectat hians Venerem totoque ardore tremescit.
incubuit lectis Paphie.   proh sancte Cupido,   105
quam blandas voces, quae tunc ibi murmura fundunt!
oscula permixtis quae tunc fixere labellis!
quam bene consertis haeserunt artubus artus!
stringebat Paphiae Mavors tunc pectore dextram
et collo innexam ne laedant pondera laevam,   110
lilia cum roseis supponit candida sertis.
saepe levi cruris tactu commovit amantem
in flammas, quas diva fovet.   iam languida fessos
forte quies Martis tandem compresserat artus;
non tamen omnis amor, non omnis pectore cessit   115
flamma dei: trahit in medio suspiria somno

⁹⁵ iura S : iure *Riese* : bella *Baehrens.*
¹⁰¹ sinū S : sinens *Oudendorp.*   laxa S : lassa *Baehrens.*
¹⁰³ tectus S : tectam *Baehrens.*
¹⁰⁴ motoque *Baehrens.*

ᵃ *Cf.* Lucret. I. 36, of Mars in Venus' lap, *pascit amore avidos inhians in te, dea, visus.*

damsels of Byblos, unlace the breast of stalwart
Mars—let one slacken the knots, one try the iron
bands which guard his breastplate, you others keep
the shield and weapons. 'Tis the fitting moment to
handle violets. Rejoice, O Cupid, that the awe-
inspiring god is conquered by your divinity alone :
instead of weapons there be flowers, instead of shield
the myrtle wreaths ; the rose, it so befalls, takes the
place of the sword at which men have cause to
tremble !

Mavors had come to the couch and resting his hard
weight upon the flowers disordered all their graceful-
ness. Fair Venus came scarce leaving footprint in
her caution lest the prickly flowers should mar her
tender feet, and, now entwining her tresses lest kisses
might ruffle them, now letting her robes flow loose,
can scarce confine them in her languor : she is not
wholly hid nor wholly bares her charms. He in his
covering of flowers with stealthy eye gazes agape at
Venus, quivering in the full flame of passion.ᵃ The
Paphian goddess sank upon the couch. Ah ! Cupid
the august, how coaxing the words, what the mur-
murs they then did utter there ! What kisses did
they then imprint upon commingled lips ! How well
did limb clasp limb in close embrace ! Then Mavors
drew his right hand from the Paphian's breast and
lest his weight should hurt the left arm twined around
her neck, sets white lilies and rose-wreaths under-
neath. Oft the leg's light touch stirred the lover
into flames by the goddess fanned. At last, it
befell, the languor of repose had mastered the
weary limbs of Mars ; yet did not all love's rapture,
yet did not all the flame, quit the god's breast :
amidst his slumber he heaves sighs and from the

et venerem totis pulmonibus ardor anhelat.
ipsa Venus tunc tunc calidis succensa venenis
uritur ardescens, nec somnia parta quieta.
o species quam blanda! o quam bene presserat artus   120
nudos forte sopor! niveis suffulta lacertis
colla nitent: pectus gemino quasi sidere fulget.
non omnis resupina iacet, sed corpore flexo
molliter et laterum qua se confinia iungunt.
Martem respiciens deponit lumina somno,   125
sed gratiosa, decens. pro lucis forte Cupido
Martis tela gerit; quae postquam singula ⟨lustrat⟩,
loricam clipeum gladium galeaeque minacis
cristas, flore ligat; tunc hastae pondera temptat
miraturque suis tantum licuisse sagittis.   130

  iam medium Phoebus radiis possederat orbem,
iam tumidis calidus spatiis libraverat horas:
flammantes retinebat equos. proh conscia facti
invida lux! Veneris qui nunc produntur amores
lumine, Phoebe, tuo! stant capti iudice tanto   135
Mars Amor et Paphie, ramisque inserta tremescunt
lumina, nec crimen possunt te teste negare.
viderat effusis Gradivum Phoebus habenis
in gremio Paphiae spirantem incendia amoris.
o rerum male tuta fides! o gaudia et ipsis   140
vix secura deis! quis non, cum Cypris amaret,

    [120] *sic Baehrens*: o quam blanda quies S, *Riese*.
    [122] turget S: fulget *Baehrens*.
    [124] quo . . . iungant *Baehrens*.
    [127] regens S: gerit *Riese*. tela; rigens *Baehrens*. lustrat
Burman, Baehrens; *om.* S: vidit *vulgo*: sumpsit *Riese*.
    [132] *sic Burman*: iam mediis *Maehly*: dimidiis *Riese*.
calidum spatium . . . horis *Baehrens, Riese*.
    [136] ramis cum *Baehrens*.

_____

   [a] The manuscript reading *quam blanda quies* seems an over-
bold contradiction of the preceding line.

depths of his lungs hot passion still pants love.
Venus herself then, even then, enkindled with
glowing poison, is afire and burns: she wins no
restful dreams. How winning the sight![a] How
fit the slumber that has o'ercome the naked limbs!
A fair neck rests on snowy arms: the breast seems
lit up by a pair of stars. Not wholly on her back
is she reclined, but with a gentle bend of the body
where side meets side. Looking at Mars, she drops
her eyes in sleep, charming as ever, comely.[b] In
front of the grove meanwhile Cupid is handling
Mars' weapons: and after scanning them one by one,
breastplate, shield, sword, plumes of the threatening
helmet, he binds them each with flowers; then tests
the spear's weight, marvelling that his own arrows
have been allowed such power.

Already had Phoebus taken possession of the mid-
world with his rays, already in the heat of his proud
course had he balanced the hours of day and was
restraining his flaming steeds. Ah! envious day-
light privy to the deed! What love-intrigues of
Venus are now betrayed, O Phoebus, by thy sun-
shine! With a judge so mighty there stand as
prisoners Mars and Love and Paphos' queen; shed
through the branches, sunbeams quiver; they cannot
disown their guilt confronted by thy testimony.
From his chariot in full career Phoebus had espied
Gradivus breathing love's fires in the Paphian god-
dess' lap. O ill-placed confidence! O joys even
for the very gods scarce free from care! Who but
would hope, when Cypris was in love, that loving

[b] Baehrens marks a lacuna here because of the abrupt
transition.

535

praeside sub tanto tutum speraret amare?
criminis exemplum si iam de numine habemus,
quid speret mortalis amor? quae vota ferenda?
quod numen poscat, quo sit securus, adulter? 145
Cypris amat, nec tuta tamen! compressit habenas
Phoebus et ad lucos tantummodo lumina vertit
et sic pauca refert: " nunc spargis tela, Cupido;
nunc nunc, diva Venus, nati devicta sagittis
das mihi solamen; sub te securus amavi: 150
fabula, non crimen, nostri dicentur amores."
    haec ait et dictis Vulcanum instigat amaris:
" dic ubi sit Cytherea decens, secure marite!
te exspectat lacrimans, tibi castum servat amorem?
vel si forte tuae Veneris fera crimina nescis, 155
quaere simul Martem, cui tu modo tela parasti."
dixit et infuso radiabat lumine lucum
inque fidem sceleris totos demiserat ignes.
haeserat Ignipotens stupefactus crimine tanto.
iam quasi torpescens (vix sufficit ira dolori) 160
ore fremit maestoque modo gemit ultima pulsans
ilia et indignans suspiria pressa fatigat.
antra furens Aetnaea petit. vix iusserat, omnes
incubuere manus, multum dolor addidit arti.
quam cito cuncta gerunt ars numen flamma maritus 165
ira dolor! nam vix causam tunc forte iubendo

142 amorem *vulgo*.
148 sparge tela S: spargis *Riese*: sparge o *Baehrens*.
150 da S: das *Oudendorp*. securus S: si lusus *Baehrens*.

---

a Apollo mischievously argues that Venus' example has shown him that conscience need not trouble a lover: so his own amours will be handed down as entertaining stories, not moral offences.

should be safe 'neath overseer so mighty? If now we take our pattern of wrongdoing from deity, what may a mortal's love expect? What prayers must be offered? What deity should a paramour entreat for an easy mind? Cypris is in love, yet not in safety. Phoebus held tight his reins and towards the grove turned but his eyes, uttering these brief words: "Now dost thou shower thy darts, O Cupid; now, now, divine Venus, quite vanquished by thy son's arrows, thou givest me solace; 'neath thy power I have learned to love care-free. My amours will be recounted for a fable, not a crime."[a]

So speaking he stirs up Vulcan with bitter words: "Say, heedless husband, where is the comely Lady of Cythera! Does she await thee in tears, preserving her chaste love for thee? Or, if mayhap thou knowest not the wild offences of thy Venus, search at the same time for Mars, whom of late thou didst provide with weapons." As he spoke, he lit up the grove with a flood of light, sending straightway his full fires down in proof of guilt. The Lord of Fire was at a loss, stunned by so great a crime: now half-benumbed (anger scarce meets his pain) he growls aloud, and groaning in melancholy wise convulses his sides to their very depth and wrathfully heaves sigh on sigh unceasing.[b] In his frenzy he makes for the cavern-forge of Aetna. Scarce were his orders given, when all hands fell to work—much did resentment add to skill. How quickly is all accomplished by skill, deity, flame, husband, anger, pain! Scarce in the moment of his ordering had he explained the

[b] *Cf.* phrases like Virg. *Aen.* IX. 415, *longis singultibus ilia pulsat*; VIII. 94, *noctemque diemque fatigant*; Sil. Ital. XII. 496, *curasque ita corde fatigat*.

dixerat, et vindex coniunx iam vincla ferebat.
pervenit ad lucos, non ipsi visus Amori,
non Chariti: totas arti mandaverat iras.
vincula tunc manibus suspenso molliter ictu   17❁
illigat et teneris conectit bracchia palmis.
excutitur somno Mavors et pulchra Cythere.
posset Gradivus validos disrumpere nexus,
sed retinebat amor, Veneris ne bracchia laedat.
tunc tu sᴜb galea, tunc inter tela latebas,   17❁
saeve Cupido, timens.   stat Mavors lumine torvo
atque indignatur, quod sit deprensus adulter.
at Paphie conversa dolet non crimina facti;
sed quae sit vindicta sibi tum singula volvens
cogitat et poenam sentit, si Phoebus amaret.   18❁
iamque dolos properans decorabat cornua tauri,
Passiphaae crimen mixtique cupidinis iram.

MODESTINUS

Forte iacebat Amor victus puer alite somno
myrti inter frutices pallentis roris in herba.

176 stans S : stat *Burman* : flat *Baehrens.*
180 sancit *Baehrens.*   181 reparans *Baehrens.*
182 Passifę S.

ᵃ *i.e.* for the full satisfaction of his anger he depended on the
skill at the forge with which the avenging chains were made.

ᵇ Reposianus departs from the traditional story according to
which the lovers were entrapped in a snare previously contrived
by the Fire-god: see *Odyss.* viii. 276 *sqq.*; Ovid. *Met.* IV.
176 *sqq.*; *Ars. Am.* II. 577 *sqq.*; Statius, *Silv.* I. ii. 59–60.   He
also substitutes a grove for the Fire-god's house as the scene
of the amour.

MODESTINUS

reason before the avenging husband was already
bringing the chains. He reaches the grove, unseen
by Love himself, unseen by any Grace: to his art
he had entrusted all his rage.[a] Then with light
soft touch he bound the chains upon the sleepers'
hands, linking their arms with gentle movement.[b]
Mars shakes himself free of sleep: so too the fair
Cytherean. Gradivus well might burst asunder the
strong bonds, but love restrained him lest he hurt
Venus' arms. Then did *you* lurk hidden 'neath
Mars' helmet, then did you lurk among his weapons,
cruel Cupid, in cowardice. Mavors stands sullen
of look, chafing because he is an adulterer caught.
But the Paphian feels no grief that her guilty deed
has turned awry: instead, she thinks of what re-
venge is hers, revolving point by point, and feels it
were fit penalty if Phoebus fell in love: and now,
hastening forward her guile, she set to ornament
the horns of the bull which would mean Pasiphaë's
guilt and the wrath involved in blended lust.[c]

MODESTINUS

Cupid Asleep

Young Love lay once with wingéd sleep o'ercome
Mid myrtle shrubs where pale dew soaked the grass.

[c] The fable ran that Venus took revenge on Phoebus through
his offspring. Pasiphaë, daughter of the Sun-god, and wife of
Minos, king of Crete, was the victim of Venus, who caused her
to become enamoured of the bull: cf. Virg. *Aen.* VI. 25,
Pasiphaë mixtumque genus prolesque biformis (in reference to
the Minotaur).

Here, as occasionally elsewhere, *cupido* (= " desire ") is
masculine: there is no need to personify it as " Cupid," nor
to adopt the suggestion in Burman of *mixtaeque libidinis.*

hunc procul emissae tenebrosa Ditis ab aula
circueunt animae, saeva face quas cruciarat.
" ecce meus venator ! " ait " hunc " Phaedra
    " ligemus ! "   5
crudelis " crinem " clamabat Scylla " metamus ! "
Colchis et orba Procne " numerosa caede necemus ! "
Didon et Canace " saevo gladio perimamus ! "
Myrrha " meis ramis," Euhadneque " igne creme-
    mus ! "
" hunc " Arethusa inquit Byblisque " in fonte
    necemus ! "   10
ast Amor evigilans dixit " mea pinna, volemus."

AUCTOR INCERTUS

Cupido Amans

Quis me fervor agit ? nova sunt suspiria menti.
anne aliquis deus est nostro vehementior arcu ?
quem mihi germanum fato fraudante creavit
diva parens ? satis an mea spicula fusa per orbem
vexavere polum laesusque in tempore mundus   5
invenit poenam ? sed si mea vulnera novi,

Cupido Amans: ³ fato S: furto *Wakkerus*: partu *Baehrens*.

ᵃ The ten victims of unhappy love are represented as making
allusions to their own misfortunes. Thus Phaedra seems to
see a second Hippolytus, eager for the chase ; Scylla remembers
the lock she treacherously clipped from her father's head ;
Dido and Canace recall their death by a sword ; Myrrha her
transformation into a tree ; Euhadne or Evadne her suicide
on a blazing pyre ; Byblis and Arethusa their metamorphosis
into a fountain.

ANONYMOUS

Round him came ghosts, from Pluto's gloomy hall
Set free, ghosts whom his cruel brand had scorched.[a]
" Look! 'tis my hunter! " Phaedra said: " bring
    bonds! "
But ruthless Scylla cried " Let's shear his hair! "
The Colchian dame [b] and Procne sore-bereaved
Said " We must make him die full many a death! "
Dido and Canace urged death by steel:
" Nay, by my branches! " Myrrha claimed. " Let's
    burn
Him in the fire! " Euhadne thought his due.
Byblis and Arethusa wished him drowned.
But Love awoke and said " My wings, let's fly! "

ANONYMOUS

CUPID IN LOVE [c]

WHAT is the glow of passion that impels me?
Sighs be new for me to think of. Can it be that
some god has mightier force than Cupid's bow? To
whom by some trick of fate has my goddess mother
given birth to be a brother for me? Have my
darts, shot through the globe, harassed the heavens
enough, and an injured world at the fit moment dis-
covered a penalty? Nay, if I know wounds of my

---

  [b] Medea.
  [c] This poem by an unknown author was first printed by
Burman, *Anth. Lat.* I. Lib. I. No. 30 immediately before
Modestinus' poem (. . . " ex Divionensi codice primi
producimus et Salmasianis schedis "). It is here included as a
companion picture to "Cupid Asleep." See Buecheler–Riese,
Anth. Lat. I. i. No. 240, p. 197; Baehrens, *P.L.M.* IV.
pp. 345–346.

hic meus est ignis: meus est, qui parcere nescit.
in furias ignesque trahor! licet orbe superno,
Iuppiter, et salsis undis, Neptune, tegaris,
abdita poenarum te cingant Tartara, Pluton,   10
impositum rumpemus onus! volitabo per axem
mundigerum caelique plagas pontique procellas
umbriferumque Chaos; pateant adamantina regna,
torva venenatis cedat Bellona flagellis!
poenam mundus amet: stupeat vis maior! anhelat   15
in se saevus Amor fraudemque in vulnere quaerit!

PENTADIUS

I

DE FORTUNA

RES eadem adsidue momento volvitur uno
    atque redit dispar res eadem adsidue.
vindice facta manu Progne pia dicta sorori,
    impia sed nato vindice facta manu.
carmine visa suo Colchis fuit ulta maritum,
    sed scelerata fuit carmine visa suo.
coniugis Eurydice precibus remeabat ad auras,
    rursus abit vitio coniugis Eurydice.

⁹ ex altis S: et salsis *Wakkerus*: exultes *Riese*.
¹⁰ poenarum *vulgo*: terrarum *Maehly*: Taenarium *Baeh-
rens*. te cingant *Oudendorp*: est ingum (*sic*) S.
¹⁵ vix S: vis *schedae*: mox *Baehrens*: stupeat, vincatur,
anhelet *Riese*.
¹⁶ vulnera *Baehrens*.
PENTADIUS: ³, ⁴ functa *L. Mueller, Baehrens*: facta *codd.*
⁵, ⁶ visa *codd.*: fisa *Baehrens*: nisa *Riese*.

PENTADIUS

dealing, this is my own fire—that fire of mine which
knows not how to spare. Into a frenzy of fires am I
dragged! Although thou, O Jupiter, be concealed
in the sphere above, and thou, O Neptune, in the
salt-sea waves, although the hidden Hell of punish-
ment encircle thee, Pluto, we will burst the burden
laid on us! I will fly across the axis that supports the
world, through the tracts of the sky and the tempests
of ocean, and through shadowy Chaos: let adaman-
tine realms ope wide, let the War-Goddess, sullen
mid her envenomed whips, retreat! Let the world
love its punishment! Let mightier force stand
mazed!—So pants fell Cupid inly and, though him-
self wounded,[a] aims at guile.

PENTADIUS

I

On Changing Fortune

THE same thing constantly rolls on with uniform
movement, and unlike its old self returns the same
thing constantly. By her avenging hand,[b] legend
says, Progne proved loyal to her sister but proved
disloyal to her son by her avenging hand. Through
her incantation the Colchian (Medea) was seen to
have revenged herself on her husband, but she was
seen to be guilt-stained through her incantation.
Her consort's entreaties all but won Eurydice's return
to upper air: again is Eurydice lost through the fault

[a] Cupid forgets his own wound in his desire to do mischief.
[b] Progne or Procne : cf. Nemes. *Cyneg.* 33. She avenged on
her husband King Tereus his outrage on her sister Philomela by
slaying Itys her own son by Tereus : cf. Nem. *Cyn.* 33–34.

543

sanguine poma rubent Thisbae nece tincta repente :
   candida quae fuerant, sanguine poma rubent.   1

Daedalus arte sua fugit Minoia regna,
   amisit natum Daedalus arte sua.

munere Palladio laeti qua nocte fuere,
   hac periere Phryges munere Palladio.

nate quod alter ades caelo, sunt gaudia Ledae ;   1
   sed maeret mater, nate quod alter abes.

hostia et ipse fuit diri Busiridis hospes
   Busirisque aris hostia et ipse fuit.

Theseus Hippolyto vitam per vota rogavit,
   optavit mortem Theseus Hippolyto.   2

stipite fatifero iuste quae fratribus usa est,
   mater saeva fuit stipite fatifero.

sola relicta toris flevisti in litore, Cnosis ;
   laetaris caelo sola relicta toris.

aurea lana fuit, Phrixum quae per mare vexit ;   2
   Helle qua lapsa est, aurea lana fuit.

---

[9] tristi nece *codd.* : **Thysbaeo tincta** *Heinsius* : Thisbae nece *L. Mueller.*

[17], [18] saepe *codd.* : et ipse *Heinsius* : sacra *Baehrens.*

[23] litore *codd.* : in litore *vulgo* : litora (*coniungendum cum* sola) *Baehrens.*

---

[a] Heinsius saw that the reference was to the trysting-place of Pyramus and Thisbe, and altered the *tristi* of the manuscripts. L. Mueller's *Thisbae* saves *nece.*

[b] Castor and Pollux, Leda's twins, were granted an alternate immortality ; when changed into the constellation Gemini, one had to be above the horizon, the other below. This is the one instance among these Latin " echoic " verses in which the opening of a couplet is not exactly repeated at the close. Here there is the slight change of *ades* to *abes.*

[c] The Egyptian king who sacrificed strangers was in turn immolated by Hercules.

544

PENTADIUS

of her consort. Red with blood is the fruit suddenly
stained by Thisbe's death : [a] the fruit which once was
white is red with blood. By his skill (in flying)
Daedalus escaped from the realms of Crete : his son
(Icarus) was lost to Daedalus by his skill. Minerva's
gift ruined the Trojans on that same night in which
they were gladdened by Minerva's gift (of the
wooden horse). O son, because thou, the one twin,
art present in the sky, Leda feels joy ; but her
maternal heart is sore, O son, because thou, the
other twin, art not present.[b] A victim of dread
Busiris [c] was the stranger his very self, and Busiris
at the altar his very self was a victim. For Hippo-
lytus Theseus sought long life in his prayers ; yet
Theseus' (final) prayer was death for Hippolytus.[d]
A fatal brand Althaea used justly for avenging her
brothers, and a cruel mother she proved herself with
that same fatal brand.[e] Left alone on thy couch, O
Cretan lady, thou didst weep upon the strand ; thou
now rejoicest in the sky because thou wast left alone
on thy couch.[f] The Golden Fleece it was which bore
Phrixus o'er the sea : that from which (his sister)
Helle fell was the Golden Fleece.[g] The Tantalid

[d] *i.e.* after the false charge brought against Hippolytus by
Phaedra.
[e] Althaea avenged her brothers, whom her son Meleager had
slain, by burning the brand on which his life depended (*im-
pietate pia est*, Ovid, *Met.* VIII. 477): *cf.* Rutilius, II. 53.
[f] Ariadne, deserted by Theseus, was consoled by Bacchus
and eventually made a constellation.
[g] Phrixus, in danger of death by sacrifice through the
malignity of his stepmother Ino, escaped overseas with his
sister Helle on the ram of the Golden Fleece provided by Zeus.
Helle was drowned by falling from the ram into the strait which
was called the Hellespont after her ; but her brother reached
Colchis in safety.

545

Tantalis est numero natorum facta superba,
  natorum afflicta † Tantalis est numero.
Pelias hasta fuit, vulnus grave quae dedit hosti;
  hoc quae sanavit, Pelias hasta fuit.   3
per mare iacta ratis pleno subit ostia velo,
  in portu mersa est per mare iacta ratis.
lux cito summa datur natusque exstinguitur infans
  atque animae eximiae lux cito summa datur.
sunt mala laetitiae diversa lege creata,   3
  iuncta autem adsidue sunt mala laetitiae.

II

DE ADVENTU VERIS

Sentio, fugit hiemps; Zephyrisque animantibus orbem
  iam tepet Eurus aquis: sentio, fugit hiemps.
parturit omnis ager, persentit terra calores,
  germinibusque novis parturit omnis ager.
laeta virecta tument, folio sese induit arbor:
  vallibus apricis laeta virecta tument.
iam Philomela gemit modulis, Ityn impia mater
  oblatum mensis iam Philomela gemit.
monte tumultus aquae properat per levia saxa,
  et late resonat monte tumultus aquae.   1
floribus innumeris pingit sola flatus Eoi,

---

²⁷⁻²⁸ afflicta *codd.* (*contra metrum*): *fortasse* infelix *Wight
Duff. Metri causa coniecit Oudendorp* T. e numero . . . afflicta
est T. e numero.
³² versa *codd.*: mersa *Heinsius.*
³⁴ prima *codd.* (*corruptum*): primae *Oudendorp*: pretium
Heinsius: *fortasse* eximiae *A. M. Duff.*
³⁵ e lege creandi *Baehrens.*
³⁶ autem *Riese*: etiam *Baehrens.*

PENTADIUS

(Niobe) grew proud over the number of her children:
in the number of her children grief crushed the
Tantalid. Achilles' spear[a] it was which dealt the
enemy a heavy blow: what also cured the wound was
Achilles' spear. The sea-tost barque enters the
river-mouth under full sail; but in harbour sinks the
sea-tost barque. Soon is the final day assigned and
the new-born child cut off: likewise to illustrious
life soon is the final day assigned. Evils and joy
are made on a different pattern: yet are they
constantly linked—evils and joy.

II

On the Arrival of Spring

Winter, I feel, has fled; and while Zephyrs quicken
the world, Eurus is already genial on the waters:
winter, I feel, has fled. Every field is in travail:
earth feels thrills of warmth throughout: with the
new buds every field is in travail. Green copses swell
joyously: the tree robes herself with leaves: in
sunlit dales green copses swell joyously. Now doth
Philomel lament in tuneful notes; now, for that
Itys was served at the board,[b] doth the impious
mother Philomel lament. From the hill the tumul-
tuous stream speeds among the smooth-worn stones:
far and wide resounds from the hill the tumultuous
stream. With flowers beyond all count the breath
of the Orient wind decks the ground; and vales like

[a] See note on *Laus Pisonis*, 177.
[b] *i.e.* as food to Tereus. Philomela here takes the place of
Procne: *cf. De Fortuna*, 3–4.

547

Tempeaque exhalant floribus innumeris.
per cava saxa sonat pecudum mugitibus Echo,
   voxque repulsa iugis per cava saxa sonat.
vitea musta tument vicinas iuncta per ulmos;   1⁵
   fronde maritata vitea musta tument.
nota tigilla linit iam garrula luce chelidon;
   dum recolit nidos, nota tigilla linit.
sub platano viridi iucundat somnus in umbra,
   sertaque texuntur sub platano viridi.   2⁰
tunc quoque dulce mori, tunc fila recurrite fusis :
   inter et amplexus tunc quoque dulce mori.

III

NARCISSUS

Cui pater amnis erat, fontes puer ille colebat,
   laudabatque undas, cui pater amnis erat.
se puer ipse videt, patrem dum quaerit in amne,
   perspicuoque lacu se puer ipse videt.
quod Dryas igne calet, puer hunc irridet amorem ;
   nec putat esse decus, quod Dryas igne calet.
stat stupet haeret amat rogat innuit adspicit ardet
   blanditur queritur stat stupet haeret amat.
quodque amat, ipse facit vultu prece lumine fletu ;
   oscula dat fonti, quodque amat ipse facit.   1⁰

[14] visque T : usque V : bisque S : voxque *corr. Salmasius,
Baehrens.*
[19] iucunda *codd.* : iucundat *Meyer.*

---

[a] *musta,* usually of new wine, here by metonymy means the
clusters containing the promise of wine.
   [b] *i.e.* in the spring season restore the by-gone days of youth.
   [c] The River-god Cephisus was the father of Narcissus, who
fell in love with his own reflection in water. The story is
beautifully told by Ovid, *Met.* III. 346–510.

548

PENTADIUS

Tempe are fragrant with flowers beyond all count.
Mid hollow rocks resounds Echo to the lowing herd;
the note reverberated by the heights mid hollow
rocks resounds. Wine-filled clusters *a* swell, linked
among their neighbour elms: mid married leafage
wine-filled clusters swell. The familiar roof-timber
already at daybreak is being smeared with mud by
the twittering swallow; as she repairs her nest, she
smears the familiar roof-timber. Under the green
plane-tree sleep takes pleasure in the shade: and
garlands are a-twining under the green plane-tree.
Then too 'twere sweet to die: then run, ye threads
of destiny, back on the spindles: *b* amid embraces
then too 'twere sweet to die.

III

NARCISSUS

The youth who had a river for sire *c* was ever fond
of fountains: the waters won praise from him who
had a river for sire. The youth beholds himself as
he seeks his sire in the river; in the translucent pool
the youth beholds himself. When a Dryad is fired
with passion, the youth flouts such love: he deems
it ne'er an honour that a Dryad is fired with passion.
He stands astonished; halts and falls in love, ques-
tions, nods, gazes all aflame; now coaxing, now
reproaching, he stands astonished; halts and falls
in love. And what he loves, himself he makes *d* in
look, entreaty, eye and tears; prints kisses on the
fountain, and what he loves, himself he makes.

d i.e. he makes his own reflection, with which he is in love.

549

IV

NARCISSUS

Hic est ille, suis nimium qui credidit undis,
　　Narcissus vero dignus amore puer.
cernis ab irriguo repetentem gramine ripas,
　　ut per quas periit cernere possit aquas.

V

CHRYSOCOME

Chrysocome gladium fugiens stringente marito
　　texit adulterium iudice casta reo.

VI

DE FEMINA

Crede ratem ventis, animum ne crede puellis;
　　namque est feminea tutior unda fide.
femina nulla bona est, vel, si bona contigit una,
　　nescio quo fato est res mala facta bona.

IV. ¹ undis *codd.* : umbris *Baehrens.*
⁴ crescere *codd.* : cernere *Baehrens (in not.).*

ᵃ The *Anthologia Latina* contains also two elegiac couplets
on Narcissus (Baehrens, *P.L.M.* IV. p. 305 and p. 340); but
their authorship is uncertain. The *Tumulus Hectoris* given
to Pentadius in Cabaret-Dupaty's *Poetae Minores* is by
Baehrens assigned to Pompilianus (*P.L.M.* IV. p. 149), while
the *Tumulus Acidis* is of uncertain authorship (*P.L.M.* V.
p. 404).

PENTADIUS

IV

NARCISSUS [a]

This is he who trusted overmuch in the pools
which were his kin—the youth Narcissus, worthy
of no counterfeit love. You behold him making
again from the moist meadow for the river-banks in
hope of beholding the waters which wrought his
doom.[b]

V

GOLDILOCKS

Chrysocome escaping from the sword as her
husband drew it (to punish her) veiled her adultery
by being found innocent when the culprit acted as
judge.[c]

VI

ON WOMAN'S LOVE [d]

Trust to the winds thy barque, but to a girl
Never thy heart's affections; for the swirl
Of ocean wave is less to be eschewed
Than woman's faith. No woman can be good,
Or if a good one comes, then freakish fate
Good out of ill has managed to create.

[b] *crescere* would imply his perennial growth as a flower after
metamorphosis.
[c] Convinced of her infidelity, her husband had been within
an ace of killing her; but in court the judge pronounced her
not guilty—he had been her partner in the offence!
[d] Variously ascribed to the Ciceros, to Ausonius and other
poets besides Pentadius. See Introduction.

TIBERIANUS

INTRODUCTION

TO TIBERIANUS

From Jerome's Chronicle (ad ann. 2352) we learn that Tiberianus, " vir disertus," was a governor in Gaul as " praefectus praetorio " in A.D. 335. Possibly he is the same as the Tiberianus whom we find holding official positions in Africa and Spain slightly earlier in the fourth century. His poetry is represented by a few surviving poems and quotations. The feeling for the beauty of nature pervading the twenty trochaic tetrameters [a] in his *Amnis ibat* gives some countenance to Baehrens' suggestion that he composed the metrically similar *Pervigilium Veneris*; [b] and the almost entire avoidance of quadrisyllabic endings in that poem bears, it has been argued, a resemblance to the manner of Tiberianus.[c] His authorship of the twenty-eight hexameters on the pernicious influence of gold is attested by Servius' citation of its third line on *Aeneid* VI. 136. The twelve hendecasyllabics

[a] Tiberianus apparently uses greater metrical licence than is found in the *Pervigilium Veneris*. He allows an anapaest in the fifth foot, if either Baehrens' *violarum sub spiritu* or Garrod's *violarum suspiritu* is accepted in line 7, and a spondee in the fifth foot, if the MS. readings are correct in lines 6 and 14.

[b] See Introduction to Florus for the contention that the *Pervigilium* is much earlier: *cf.* also Introduction to the poem in Loeb ed. of Catullus, Tibullus and *Pervig. Ven.*

[c] See Appendix to J. A. Fort's ed. of *Pervig. Ven.*, Oxford, 1922.

on a bird may be somewhat less confidently ascribed to him. Based on different manuscript authority is the poem purporting to be translated from Greek into Latin " a quodam Tiberiano," and in its invocation of the Supreme Being blending Orphic, Pythagorean and Platonic elements. There are, besides, a few fragments referred explicitly to Tiberianus by Servius and Fulgentius.[a]

EDITIONS

M. Haupt. *Ovidii Halieutica*, etc. Leipzig, 1838. [Haupt first printed poem No. iv " Omnipotens . . . "][b]

E. Baehrens. *Unedirte lateinische Gedichte*, p. 27 *sqq.* Leipzig, 1877.

—— *Poet. Lat. Minores*, III. pp. 263–269. Leipzig, 1881.

F. Buecheler and A. Riese. *Anthologia Latina*, I. ii. Nos. 490, 719*b*, 809–810.

The text here given is in the main that of Baehrens, with the chief departures indicated.

SIGLUM for Poems I–III.

H = codex Harleianus 3685: saec. xv. (Containing also various medieval verses.)

---

[a] These scraps are given by Baehrens, *P.L.M.* III. 269, and are included in this edition.

[b] See also L. Quicherat, *Biblioth. de l'école des chartes*, IV. p. 267 *sq.*

TIBERIANUS

SIGLA for Poem IV.

R = Reginensis 215 : saec. ix. (Collated by Baehrens.)
P = Parisinus 2772 : saec. x–xi. (Collated by Quicherat and by Riese.)
S = Parisinus 17160 : saec. xii. (Collated by Baehrens.)
V = Vindobonensis 143 : saec. xiii. (Used by Haupt.)

Bibliographical addendum (*1982*)

A new edition and commentary on the *Pervigilium Veneris* is awaited from Alan Cameron, who has definitively established, at least to this writer's satisfaction, that the work is to be ascribed to Tiberianus.

TIBERIANUS

I

Amnis ibat inter arva valle fusus frigida,
luce ridens calculorum, flore pictus herbido.
caerulas superne laurus et virecta myrtea
leniter motabat aura blandiente sibilo.
subter autem molle gramen flore adulto creverat:
et croco solum rubebat et lucebat liliis,
et nemus fragrabat omne violarum ⟨sub⟩ spiritu.
inter ista dona veris gemmeasque gratias
omnium regina odorum vel colorum Lucifer
auriflora praeminebat, flamma Diones, rosa.
roscidum nemus rigebat inter uda gramina:
fonte crebro murmurabant hinc et inde rivuli,
antra muscus et virentes intus ⟨hederae⟩ vinxerant,
qua fluenta labibunda guttis ibant lucidis.

⁶ tum croco *Baehrens* : et croco H.
⁷ violarum spiritu H (*contra metrum*): sub *addidit Baehrens*:
spiritu violarii *Fort.*
¹⁰ *sic Garrod (Oxford Book of Latin Verse)*: auro flore
praeminebat forma dionis H : aureo flore eminebat cura
Cypridis *Baehrens*.
¹³ hederae *addidit Mackail* : myrtus *Baehrens* : om. H.
¹⁴ qua *Ziehen* : quae H, *Baehrens, qui hunc versum ante* 13
transposuit. guttis ibant lucidis H : gurgite i. lucido *Fort.*

TIBERIANUS

I

THROUGH the fields there went a river; down the
  airy glen it wound,
Smiling mid its radiant pebbles, decked with flowery
  plants around.
Dark-hued laurels waved above it close by myrtle
  greeneries,
Gently swaying to the whispers and caresses of the
  breeze.
Underneath grew velvet greensward with a wealth
  of bloom for dower,
And the ground, agleam with lilies, coloured 'neath
  the saffron-flower,
While the grove was full of fragrance and of breath
  from violets.
Mid such guerdons of the spring-time, mid its
  jewelled coronets,
Shone the queen of all the perfumes, Star that love-
  liest colours shows,
Golden flame of fair Dione, passing every flower—the
  rose.
Dewsprent trees rose firmly upright with the lush
  grass at their feet:
Here, as yonder, streamlets murmured tumbling from
  each well-spring fleet.
Grottoes had an inner binding made of moss and
  ivy green,
Where soft-flowing runlets glided with their drops of
  crystal sheen.

has per umbras omnis ales plus canora quam putes   15
cantibus vernis strepebat et susurris dulcibus;
hic loquentis murmur amnis concinebat frondibus,
quis melos vocalis aurae musa Zephyri moverat.
sic euntem per virecta pulchra odora et musica
ales amnis aura lucus flos et umbra iuverat.   20

II

Aurum, quod nigri manes, quod turbida versant
flumina, quod duris extorsit poena metallis!
aurum, quo pretio reserantur limina Ditis,
quo Stygii regina poli Proserpina gaudet!
aurum, quod penetrat thalamos rumpitque pudorem,   5
qua ductus saepe illecebra micat impius ensis!
in gremium Danaes non auro fluxit adulter
mentitus pretio faciem fulvoque veneno?
non Polydorum hospes saevo necat incitus auro?
altrix infelix, sub quo custode pericli   10
commendas natum? cui regia pignora credis?
fit tutor pueri, fit custos sanguinis aurum!
immitis nidos coluber custodiet ante
et catulos fetae poterunt servare leaenae.
sic etiam ut Troiam popularet Dorica pubes,   15
aurum causa fuit . . . .
. . . . pretium dignissima merces:
infami probro palmam convendit adulter.

---

    a Jupiter: *cf.* Sulpicius Lupercus Servasius, II. 7–8 (*De Cupiditate*).
    b Polydorus, son of Priam, was murdered by Polymnestor, King of Thrace, for the gold which Priam had sent with Polydorus: *cf.* Virgil, *Aeneid* III. 41–57, esp. *auri sacra fames.*
    c Paris gave his judgement in favour of Venus for the promise of Helen's love, and his award of the golden apple to her thus led to the Trojan war.

TIBERIANUS

Through those shades each bird, more tuneful than
    belief could entertain,
Warbled loud her chant of spring-tide, warbled low
    her sweet refrain.
Here the prattling river's murmur to the leaves made
    harmony,
As the Zephyr's airy music stirred them into melody.
To a wanderer through the coppice, fair and filled
    with song and scent,
Bird and river, breeze and woodland, flower and shade
    brought ravishment.

II

O Gold, whirled onward by dark hell and muddy
rivers, wrested by the convict from cruel mines :
gold, the bribe unbarring Pluto's doors, and the
delight of Proserpine, queen of the Stygian world !
gold which invades the marriage-bower and shatters
chastity, and at whose enticement the unholy sword
often flashes from scabbard drawn ! Was it not in
golden stream that to Danaë's lap there came the
adulterer [a] who masked his appearance in his bribe
of yellow poison ? Was not barbarous gold the
motive when Polydorus [b] was slain by his host ?
Unhappy nurse, under what guardian against danger
dost thou entrust a son ? To whom dost thou com-
mit children of royal line ? Gold becomes protector
of the boy, gold the guardian of the blood ! Sooner
will ruthless serpent guard nestlings, and lionesses
be ready to save the whelps of a newly delivered
dam. So too for Troy's destruction by the young
manhood of Greece the reason lay in gold . . . a
bribe the worthiest recompense. At the price of
infamous scandal the paramour sold his award. [c]

denique cernamus, quos aurum servit in usus.
auro emitur facinus, pudor almus venditur auro,
tum patria atque parens, leges pietasque fidesque :   20
omne nefas auro tegitur, fas proditur auro.
porro hoc Pactolus, porro fluat et niger Hermus?
aurum, res gladii, furor amens, ardor avarus,
te celent semper vada turbida, te luta nigra,
te tellus mersum premat infera, te sibi nasci   25
Tartareus cupiat Phlegethon Stygiaeque paludes!
inter liventes pereat tibi fulvor harenas,
nec post ad superos redeat faex aurea puros!

III

Ales, dum madida gravata nube
udos tardius explicat volatus,
decepta in medio repente nisu
capta est pondere depremente plumae :
cassato solito vigore pennae,   5
quae vitam dederant, dedere letum ;
sic, quis ardua nunc tenebat alis,
isdem protinus incidit ruinae.
quid sublimia circuisse prodest?
qui celsi steterant, iacent sub imis!   10
exemplum capiant, nimis petendo
qui ventis tumidi volant secundis.

III. ¹ madida g. pennis H : madidis g. p. *Garrod* : madida g.
nube *Baehrens*.
   ⁷ ac *Baehrens*.
   ⁹ sublima circuisse H : sublima requisiisse *Baehrens*.
   ¹⁰ sub ictu *Baehrens*.
   ¹² vanis t. tonant H : ventis t. volant *Rohde*.

TIBERIANUS

Let us then see for what uses gold doth serve. It is the buying-price of crime, it is the sale-price of kind modesty, of fatherland and parent, of laws and piety and faith: all guilt is hidden by gold, by gold all righteousness betrayed. With it must Pactolus still flow on, and likewise the dark Hermus-stream ?[a] O gold, thou murderous thing, thou frenzied madness and passionate greed, let muddy shallows and a stream's dark silt conceal thee evermore; let earth below whelm and bury thee, let Tartarean Phlegethon and the Stygian pools covet thy birth for themselves! Perish thy yellow gleam among the sombre sands! Never hereafter let the golden dregs return to clean-handed men of the world above!

III

A bird with drenching rain o'erweighted,
Hindered by wet, her flight abated,
And sudden, mid her efforts foiled,
Was caught as 'neath her load she toiled.
When her old strength of wing grew nought,
What once brought life now ruin brought:
So pinions used for soaring high
Straight dashed her on the ground to die.
What boots it round the heavens to fly?
Who stood exalted, lowest lie!
Learn this, who aim beyond the scale
And haughtily ride the favouring gale.

[a] The golden sands of the Lydian river Hermus and its tributary, the Pactolus, were renowned in antiquity.

IV

Omnipotens, annosa poli quem suspicit aetas,
quem sub millenis semper virtutibus unum
nec numero quisquam poterit pensare nec aevo,
nunc esto affatus, si quo te nomine dignum est,
quo sacer ignoto gaudes, quom maxima tellus   5
intremit et sistunt rapidos vaga sidera cursus.
tu solus, tu multus item, tu primus et idem
postremus mediusque simul mundique superstes.
nam sine fine tui labentia tempora finis.
altus ab aeterno spectas fera turbine certo   10
rerum fata rapi vitasque involvier aevo
atque iterum reduces supera in convexa referri,
scilicet ut mundo redeat quod partubus haustus
perdiderit refluumque iterum per tempora fiat.
tu (siquidem fas est in temet tendere sensum   15
et speciem temptare sacram, qua sidera cingis
immensus longamque simul complecteris aethram)
fulmineis forsan rapida sub imagine membris
flammifluum quoddam iubar es, quo cuncta coruscans
ipse vides nostrumque premis solemque diemque.   20
tu genus omne deum, tu rerum causa vigorque,
tu natura omnis, deus innumerabilis unus,
tu sexu plenus toto, tibi nascitur olim

---

⁸ mundique   superstes   RS: mundoque   superstans
Baehrens.
¹⁰ altus et *Baehrens.* spectans *codd.*, *Baehrens* : spectas
Riese.
¹³ austrum R : abstrum P : abstui S : astra V : haustum
Quicherat : haustus *Baehrens.*
¹⁸ fulgentis . . . Phoebi *Baehrens.*
¹⁹ choruscas S : coruscant R : coruscas P, *Baehrens* :
coruscans *Riese.*
²⁰ ipse vides *codd.* : ipseque das *Baehrens.*

IV

Almighty Being, to whom heaven's age, ancient of years, showeth reverence, whom for ever One amid a thousand attributes, no man shall e'er have power to appraise in number or in time, now be thou addressed if under any name it is fitting to address thee; yet even in name unknown thou hast thy hallowed joy, when mightiest earth shuddereth and wandering constellations stay their rapid courses. Thou art alone, yet in thyself many, thou art first and likewise last, and midway in time withal, outliving the world. For without end for thyself, thou bringest the gliding seasons to an end. On high from everlasting thou beholdest the cruel destinies of the world awhirl in their predestined cycle, living souls in the coils of time, and again on their return restored to the vault above,[a] doubtless so that there may come back to the world what it has lost, exhausted by births, and that this may again flow through the seasons of time. Thou (if indeed it is allowed towards thee to direct the senses and essay to grasp the hallowed beauty wherewith in thine immeasurable power thou dost invest the stars and dost embrace withal the far-stretched upper air) in some quick guise mayhap with lightning limbs art like a flame-flowing radiance wherewith thou dost cause to flash all the world beneath thine own eyes and speedest onward the sunlight of our day. Thou art the whole kindred of the gods, thou art the cause and energy of things, thou art all nature, one god beyond reckoning, thou art full of the whole of sex, for thee cometh to birth upon a day here a god, here

[a] *Cf.* Virg. *Aen.* VI. 241, *supera ad convexa ferebat.*

hic deus hic mundus, domus haec hominumque
    deumque,
lucens, augusto stellatus flore iuventae.   2
quem (precor, adspires), qua sit ratione creatus,
quo genitus factusve modo, da nosse volenti;
da, Pater, augustas ut possim noscere causas,
mundanas olim moles quo foedere rerum
sustuleris animamque levi quo maximus olim   3
texueris numero, quo congrege dissimilique,
quidque id sit vegetum, quod per cita corpora vivit.

FRAGMENTA

1. *Servius ad Verg. Aen. VI.* 532 :

     Tiberianus etiam inducit epistolam vento
allatam ab antipodibus, quae habet: " superi
inferis salutem."

2. Fulgentius, *Mythologiarum I.* 26 :

     . . . unde Tiberianus: " Pegasus hinniens
transvolat aethram."

3. Fulgentius, *Mythologiarum III.* 7 :

     nam et Tiberianus in Prometheo ait, deos
singula sua homini tribuisse.

4. Fulgentius, *Vergiliana Continentia*, p. 154 :

     . . . memores Platonis sententiae, cuius here-
ditatem Diogenes Cynicus invadens nihil ibi plus
aurea lingua invenit, ut Tiberianus in libro de
Socrate memorat.

---

[24] hic deus hic mundus *codd.* : hic cunctus m. *Baehrens*.
domus hic *codd.* : d. haec *Riese* : d. una *Baehrens*.

a world—this home of men and gods—lucent, starred
with the majestic bloom of youth. Touching this
world (vouchsafe thy favour, I pray), grant to a
willing mind the knowledge of the principles on which
it was created, the manner of its origin and making.
Grant, O Sire, that I may have power to learn causes
majestic, by what alliance of things [a] thou didst of
old upraise the world's masses of matter, and of what
light texture, intimate yet dissimilar, thou didst of
old in thy might weave the soul, and what that
vigorous element is which in quick-moving bodies
constitutes life.

FRAGMENTS

1. Tiberianus also introduces a letter brought by
the wind from the antipodes, with the words " Those
above greet those beneath."

2. Hence Tiberianus says: " Pegasus neighing
flies across the upper air."

3. For Tiberianus too says in the Prometheus that
the gods have assigned to a man his individual traits.

4. (We used " golden " of brilliant eloquence),
recalling the utterance of Plato on whose inheritance
Diogenes the Cynic encroached and found there
nothing more than a golden tongue, as Tiberianus
records in his book on Socrates.

[a] Or " law of nature."

5. Fulgentius, *Expositio sermonum antiquorum*, p. 183 :

   sudum dicitur serenum.   Tiberianus : " Aureos
subducit ignes sudus ora Lucifer."

[6. *Servius ad Verg. Aen. VIII.* 96 :

   ostendit adeo perspicuam fuisse naturam
fluminis ut in eo apparerent imagines nemorum,
quas Troianae naves secabant.   Tiberianus :

> " natura sic est fluminis,
> ut obvias imagines
> receptet in lucem suam."]

   6 [3] Tiberianus *Baehrens* : Terentianus *vulgo*.

5. The word *sudum* means serene: *e.g.* Tiberianus: " Lucifer, serene to look on, draws away his golden fires."

[6. He shows that so transparent was the nature of the river that in it appeared clear reflections of the woods across which the Trojan vessels cut their way, as Tiberianus says:

" Such is the nature of the stream
    That images which meet it seem
    Clear-mirrored in its own bright gleam."] [a]

[a] The ascription of this to Tiberianus depends on Baehrens' suggestion that Terentianus in Servius' text is a blunder for Tiberianus.

SULPICIUS LUPE
SERVASIUS JU

ERCUS
NIOR

INTRODUCTION

TO SERVASIUS

THE codex Leidensis Vossianus of Ausonius contains two poems ascribed to Sulpicius Lupercus Serbastus Junior. Schryver (Scriverius) altered " Serbastus " to " Sebastus," which Baehrens retains; Wernsdorf printed " Servastus," and Riese proposed " Servasius." From this schoolman author, whose very name is imperfectly known, there are thus preserved three Sapphic stanzas on the transitoriness of everything in nature and a longer elegiac complaint on the ruinous result which the prevalence of money-getting produces upon rhetorical studies. The archaisms *mage* and *fundier* (II. 16 and 18), artificially introduced into these laboured verses of the fourth century, contribute to the effect of unreality.

EDITIONS

P. Burman. *Anthol. Lat.* Lib. III. No. 97 (*De Vetustate*). Amsterdam, 1759.

J. C. Wernsdorf. *Poet. Lat. Min.* III. p. 235 and p. 408. Altenburg, 1782.

E. Baehrens. *Poet. Lat. Min.* IV. Nos. 118–119 (pp. 107–109). Leipzig, 1882.

F. Buecheler and A. Riese. *Anthol. Latina* I. ii. Nos. 648–649. Leipzig, 1906.

(The main departures from Baehrens' text are indicated.)

INTRODUCTION TO SERVASIUS

SIGLUM

E (Baehrens' siglum) = codex nobilissimus Ausonii,
  Leidensis Vossianus 111 : saec. viii–ix.

(In West-Gothic writing it contains, after its text
of Ausonius, other poems including the two ascribed
to Sulpicius Lupercus " Serbastus.")

SULPICIUS LUPERCUS
SERVASIUS JUNIOR

I

De Vetustate

Omne quod Natura parens creavit,
quamlibet firmum videas, labascit:
tempore ac longo fragile et caducum
 solvitur usu.

amnis insueta solet ire valle,
mutat et rectos via certa cursus,
rupta cum cedit male pertinaci
 ripa fluento.

decidens scabrum cavat unda tofum,
ferreus vomis tenuatur agris,
splendet attrito digitos honorans
 anulus auro.

II

De Cupiditate

Heu misera in nimios hominum petulantia census!
 caecus inutilium quo ruit ardor opum,
auri dira fames et non expleta libido
 ferali pretio vendat ut omne nefas!

SULPICIUS LUPERCUS
SERVASIUS JUNIOR

I

THE WORK OF TIME

ALL that Nature ever bore,
Firm to look at, time makes hoar,
Frail and fleeting more and more,
  Its strength in service losing.

Streams fresh valley-routes pursue,
Ancient courses change to new,
When their banks are broken through
  By floods' persistent oozing.

Cascades make rough tufa yield;
Ploughs wear thinner in the field;
Rings that jewelled fingers wield
  Show gold rubbed bright by using.

II

GREED

  Alas for the wretched craving after excessive incomes! What is the end on which the blind passion for useless wealth rushes, so that the cursed hunger for gold and greed unsatisfied may barter any enormity for a recompense fraught with destruction?

sic latebras Eriphyla viri patefecit, ubi aurum
  accepit, turpis materiam sceleris;
sic quondam Acrisiae in gremium per claustra puellae
  corruptore auro fluxit adulterium.
o quam mendose votum insaturabile habendi
  imbuit infami pectora nostra malo!   1(
quamlibet immenso dives vigil incubet auro,
  aestuat augendae dira cupido rei.
heu mala paupertas numquam locupletis avari!
  dum struere immodice quod tenet optat, eget.
quis metus hic legum quaeve est reverentia veri,   15
  crescenti nummo si mage cura subest?
cognatorum animas promptum est patrumque cruorem
  fundier: affectus vincit avara fames.
divitis est, semper fragiles male quaerere gazas:
  nulla huic in lucro cura pudoris erit.   2(
istud templorum damno excidioque requirit;
  hoc caelo iubeas ut petat: inde petet.

mirum ni pulchras artes Romana iuventus
  discat et egregio sudet in eloquio,
ut post iurisonae famosa stipendia linguae   2[
  barbaricae ingeniis anteferantur opes.
at qui sunt, quos propter honestum rumpere foedus
  audeat illicite pallida avaritia?

---

16 crescenti nummo *vulgo*: crescentis nummi *Baehrens*.
17 fratrumque *cod.*, *Baehrens*: patrumque *vulgo*.
21 exitioque *vulgo*.
25 iurgisonae clamosa impendia *Heinsius*.
27 atqui *vulgo*.

---

^a Amphiaraus, for whom it meant death to take part in the
Theban War, was betrayed by his wife for a golden necklace:
cf. Hor. *Od.* III. xvi. 11–13: Statius, *Theb.* IV. 187–213.

SULPICIUS LUPERCUS SERVASIUS JUNIOR

Thus it was that Eriphyla betrayed her husband's [a] hiding-place when she received the gold that was the cause of her foul crime: thus it was that long ago through prison-bars there rained in corrupting gold an adulterous stream on the lap of Acrisius' daughter.[b] How culpably the unquenchable longing for possession stains our hearts with scandalous wickedness! However boundless the gold o'er which Dives broods wakefully, within there seethes the accursed lust for adding to his wealth. Alas for the baleful poverty of the miser who is never rich! His desire for a limitless heap of what he holds makes him a beggar. What fear is here of laws, what respect for what is fair, if 'neath his growing bullion-heap there lurk still more the pains of greed? Taking the lives of kinsmen, shedding a father's blood comes readily to his mind: miserly hunger masters feeling. An evil quest after frail treasures is ever the rich man's way: in the matter of gain he will have no qualms of shame. Such gain it is he pursues, though it mean loss or destruction to temples: [c] bid him seek this in heaven and from heaven he will fetch it.[d]

It is not unlikely that the young men of Rome learn fine accomplishments and sweat at distinguished rhetoric only in order that, after the glorious campaigns [e] of an eloquent lawyer's tongue, they may prize barbaric wealth above talent. Yet who are those (glib pleaders) thanks to whom pale avarice ventures on the forbidden crime of breaking an

[b] Danaë: cf. Hor. *Od.* III. xvi. 1–8; and Tiberianus' poem on gold, II. 7–8.

[c] *i.e.* he sacrilegiously robs or fires them.

[d] An echo of Juvenal III. 78, *in caelum iusseris, ibit.*

[e] Heinsius' emendation (meaning literally "the bawling outlay of a loud litigious tongue") gets rid of *ă* before *stipendia*.

Romani sermonis egent, ridendaque verba
    frangit ad horrificos turbida lingua sonos.   30
sed tamen ex cultu appetitur spes grata nepotum?
    saltem istud nostri forsan honoris habent?
ambusti torris species, exesaque saeclo
    amblant ut priscis corpora de tumulis!
perplexi crines, frons improba, tempora pressa,   35
    exstantes malae deficiente gena,
simataeque iacent pando sinuamine nares,
    territat os nudum caesaque labra tument.
defossum in ventrem propulso pondere tergum
    frangitur et vacuo crure tument genua.   40
decolor in malis species, hoc turpius illud,
    quod cutis obscure pallet in invidiam.

    [29] egens *vulgo*.
    [31] ultu *cod.*: vultu *Scaliger*: cultu *Oudendorp*.
    [34] amblant ut *Baehrens*: abtantur *cod.*: abduntur *vulgo*:
aptantur *Vinetus*.
    [38] caesaque *cod.*: scissaque *vel* fissaque *Heinsius*: crassaque
Wernsdorf.
    [41] discolor *cod.*: *corr. Heinsius.* in manibus *cod.*: in
malis *Baehrens*.

SULPICIUS LUPERCUS SERVASIUS JUNIOR

honourable compact? They are beggared of Latin
style, and their confused jargon minces ridiculous
words to an accompaniment of shocking sounds. Yet
does their dress prompt the younger generation to
indulge pleasing hopes (of legacies)?[a] Have they
mayhap such a share at least of our Roman dignity?
No, theirs is the appearance of a burnt-out fire-
brand: they walk like skeletons gnawed by time
from ancient graves! Their hair is tangled, fore-
head impudent, temples thin, jaws protruding while
their cheeks are sunken, and their flattened nostrils
rest on a tip-tilted curve: the toothless mouth is a
terror and the chapped lips are swollen. Forced down
by the impetus of weight, back sinks to belly; and
the knees swell on a shrunken leg. Sallow is the
look of their jaws, and it is an uglier feature that the
skin wears a mysterious pallor suggestive of envy.

[a] *i.e.* Can it be said for the misers that they dress well and
in accordance with their wealth?

DICTA CATONIS

INTRODUCTION

TO DICTA CATONIS

In the educational training of the Middle Ages, when Donatus supplied the rudiments, an early and safe reading-book was the compendium of practical ethics which passed under the name of " Cato." Here was a work with much of the unimpeachable but hackneyed morality of the copy-book headline, and a useful repertory of material for adorning the letters of a young student desirous of creating a good impression when he wrote home. It is significant that Chaucer accounts for the foolish marriage of the carpenter in the *Miller's Tale* by remarking that " he knew not Catoun, for his wit was rude." This *vade mecum* of proverbial wisdom has, however, bequeathed an extraordinary number of enigmas: its title and the meaning of the title, the date of different *strata* in our collections, the proportion borne by what we now possess to the larger *corpus* of *Dicta Catonis* once in existence, the relation of the single lines to the couplets, the disentanglement of pagan elements from Christian additions or alterations, and the textual criticism of what has been handed down to us, all constitute problems of considerable difficulty.

Inscriptional evidence proves that about the end of the second century A.D. some of the proverbs were well enough known to be quoted.[a] It is likely that an unknown author gave to his collection of wise saws the title of *Cato*, as an echo of the moral instruction addressed generations earlier by Cato the Censor to his son. The name " Dionysius," sometimes added, rests upon a doubtful testimony by Scaliger to the effect that it existed in a manuscript belonging to Bosius. If " Dionysius " has to be considered at all, it may be explained, on Haupt's theory,[b] as due to a contamination of Cato's name with that of Dionysius, whose *Periegesis*, translated by Priscian, might have immediately preceded Cato in Bosius' manuscript.

By the fourth century we have evidence that the *Disticha* enjoyed an extensive vogue, and the Irish monk Columbanus at the turn of the sixth century had access to a large body of moral verses whence to draw part of the collection of separate hexameters to which he added many lines from Christian sources. But wide use did not guarantee the preservation of the text. Some *disticha* became less popular for school-work than others; extracts, excisions and transpositions were made; and couplets were, by intention or chance, reduced to single lines (*monosticha*) amidst the confusion into which the collection had fallen by the eighth century. It is, then, not an unreasonable supposition that a re-editing of the Catonian *corpus* took place in the Carolingian era; and it is possible that the brief verses prefixed to Books II, III and IV of the *Disticha* date from that period. Our present collection opens with a

[a] *Distich.* II. 3 is used in *C.I.L.* VI. 11252.
[b] M. Haupt, *Opusc.* I. 376. *Cf.* Boas, *Phil. Woch.* 1930, 649 *sqq.*

prose preface ostensibly directing its precepts to a son (*fili karissime*) in what we might call a Cato-like manner, and between this preface and the *Disticha* are 57 brief prose *sententiae*, some only two words long. About these opinion is sharply divided. It has been, on the one hand, argued that some of them may be the oldest part of the sayings, that some may even go back to Cato the Censor himself, and that some at least were expanded later into *disticha*; on the other hand, it has been argued that these *breves sententiae* may have constituted a summary introduction based, as excerpts, upon a once much fuller collection of verse sayings.[a]

Despite the excisions and alterations to which Christian re-editing subjected the inferior ethics of the original collection, there have survived evident traces not merely of antiquity (*e.g.* in the prose sentences *foro par(c)e* or *ad praetorium stato*), but of pagan principles in the religious thought or the practical advice. Thus, in the *Disticha* the polytheistic *an di sint* of II. 2 must be the original text, and is combined with monotheism (*mitte arcana dei*) in one manuscript only: II. 12, on divination, and IV. 38, on sacrifice, may be called pre-Christian, while IV. 14, on cleansing by a victim's blood, may possibly be directed against the doctrine of the atonement. Occasionally the ring is that of worldly cunning, I. 26, or selfishness in I. 11 and in the second line of III. 12. A wife's tears, III. 20, or her complaints about her husband's favourite slave, I. 8, must not, readers are enjoined, be too

---

[a] Skutsch, in *P.W. Realencycl.* V., on "Dicta Catonis," maintains the priority of the prose sentences in opposition to Bischoff.

much regarded. But, taken all in all, it is a sound if homely morality that is preached—respect for the lessons of books and of life, diligence in work, loyalty to friends, avoidance of quarrels, bravery in misfortune, temperance in prosperity, and—as Stoicism had taught—consideration for slaves.

In the maxims can be discerned the human experience of many generations, some of it going back to Greek originals and some of it touched with a literary reminiscence of Horace or Ovid. On the whole, the language is simple and clear, as befits proverbial wisdom, so that an archaism like *mage* (*Praef.* II. 2; *Distich.* II. 6; IV. 42) or a compound like *officiperdi* (IV. 42) stands out as something unusual. The closing distich emphasises the brevity aimed at in the couplets. Yet the very condensation led to a monotony of clause-structure and of expression; and this monotony is not redeemed by any great metrical variety in the hexameters. The prevailing merit, however, remains of a neat intelligibility which suited both teacher and taught; and this ensured for the collection its long career as an educational manual. "Catho" was one of the books printed during the early years of Caxton's work at Westminster. The distichs were paraphrased by Caxton's contemporary, Benedict Burgh, who expanded each couplet into the Chaucerian seven-lined stanza or rhyme-royal. Both text and paraphrase are extant in many fifteenth-century MSS., *e.g.* the Harleian 4733, and the volume, handsomely illustrated with coloured miniatures, which is now Peniarth MS. 481 in the National Library of Wales, Aberystwyth. The educational vogue of these *disticha moralia* is exemplified by their use

DICTA CATONIS

during the eighteenth century in Scotland as an adjunct to Ruddiman's *Rudiments of the Latin Tongue* : they were, for example, included among the *Prima Morum et Pietatis Praecepta*, printed as a schoolbook at Edinburgh in 1784.

EDITIONS

D. Erasmus. *Disticha moralia titulo Catonis . . . mimi Publiani . . . cum scholiis Erasmi.* (?) London, 1514.

M. Corderius. *Catonis Disticha Lat. et Gall. interpret.* Oliva, 1561.

P. Pithou. *Catonis Disticha.* Paris, 1577.

M. Corderius. *Disticha moralia nomine Catonis inscripta c. Gall. interpretatione . . . et Graeca Planudae interpretatione.* Paris, 1585.

Jos. Scaliger. *P. Syri sentent. et Dion. Catonis disticha graece redd.* Leyden, 1598.

P. Scriverius. *Dionysii Catonis Disticha.* Amsterdam, 1635 and 1636.

M. Z. Boxhorn. *Catonis Disticha.* Amsterdam, 1646.

O. Arntzen. Utrecht 1735; Amst. 1754 (with the dissertations of Boxhorn, Cannegieter, and Withof).

F. Hauthal. Berlin, 1869.

E. Baehrens. *Poet. Lat. Min.* III. pp. 205–246. Leipzig, 1881.

G. Némethy. Ed. 2. Budapest, 1895.

RELEVANT WORKS

F. Zarncke. *Der Deutsche Cato.* Leipzig, 1852.

H. J. Mueller. *Symbolae ad emendandos scriptores Latinos.* II. *Quaestiones Catonianae.* Berlin, 1876.

J. Nehabs. *Der altenglische Cato.* Berlin, 1879.

M. O. Goldberg. *Die Catonischen Distichen während des Mittelalters in englischen und französischen Literatur.* Leipzig, 1883.

E. Bischoff. *Proleg. zu Dionysius Cato.* Diss. Erlangen, 1890.

F. Skutsch. *Pauly-Wissowa, Realencycl.* V. (1905) *s.v.* " Dicta Catonis."

E. Stechert. *De Catonis quae dicuntur distichis.* Greifswald, 1912.

M. Boas. *Der Codex Bosii der Dicta Catonis* in *Rhein. Mus.* 67 (1912), pp. 67–93.

For a list of translations into other languages see M. Schanz, *Gesch. der röm. Lit.*, ed. 3, 1922, pp. 38–39 : to which may be added *The Distichs of Cato* translated into couplets, with introductory sketch by Wayland J. Chase, Madison, U.S.A., 1922.

SIGLA FOR DISTICHA

(As in Baehrens, *P.L.M.* III. 206–211.)

A = codex biblioth. capit. Veronensis 163 : saec. ix. (Imperfect and in confused order, though preserving many good readings.[a])

B = codex Matritensis 14, 22 : saec. ix. (Contains *disticha* up to I. 27, 1.)

C = codex Turicensis 78 : saec. ix.

D = codex scholae medicinalis Montepessulanae 306 : saec. ix.

[a] On this, the oldest codex, see K. Schenkl, *Zeitschr. für österr. Gymn.* 24 (1873), p. 485; C. Cipolla, *Riv. di filol.* 8 (1880).

DICTA CATONIS

E = codex Vossianus L.Q. 86 : saec. ix.[a]
F = codex Ambrosianus C 74 : saec. x. [The last
    four are from a common original, CD and EF
    showing close agreement.]
ς = codices inferiores, including Reginenses and
    Parisini.

[The codex Matritensis is regarded by M. Boas,
along with Paris. 8093 saec. ix and Vaticanus Reg.
2078 saec. x, as representing a Spanish-Gallic
tradition of the vulgate collection, in contrast to a
" Neben-vulgata " and " Vor-vulgata " represented
by Paris. 9347, Monacensis 19413 saec. xi, Vaticanus
Barber. 8, 41 saec. xiii–xiv. See references at close
of the Sigla given for the *Monosticha*.]
The main departures from Baehrens' text are
indicated in the apparatus criticus.

* See H. J. Mueller, *op. cit.*, pp. 17 *sqq.*

CATO

I. COLLECTIO DISTICHORUM VULGARIS

Prologus

Cum animadverterem quam plurimos graviter in via morum errare, succurrendum opinioni eorum et consulendum famae existimavi, maxime ut gloriose viverent et honorem contingerent. nunc te, fili karissime, docebo quo pacto morem animi tui componas. igitur praecepta mea ita legito, ut intellegas. legere enim et non intellegere neglegere est.

Deo supplica.
Parentes ama.
Cognatos cole.
Datum serva.
Foro parce.
Cum bonis ambula.
Antequam voceris, ne accesseris.
Mundus esto.
Saluta libenter.
Maiori concede.

Incep dicta marci catonis ad filium suum A: Marci Catonis ad filium salutem *litt. mai. rubr.* B: Incipiunt libri Catonis philosophi *litt. mai.* D: *tit. om.* C: *totum prologum om.* EF.

Prologus: ² graviter in via morum BC *ʒ omnes*: gravitate murum A.

Sententiolae: ⁵ parce A: pare B *ʒ nonnulli*: para CD *ʒ nonnulli*.

CATO

I. THE COMMON COLLECTION OF DISTICHS

Prologue

As I noticed the very great number of those who go seriously astray in the path of conduct, I decided that I should come to the aid of their belief and take thought for their reputation, so that they might live with the utmost glory and attain honour. Now I will teach you, dearest son, how to fashion a system for your mind. Therefore, so read my precepts as to understand; for to read and not to understand is to give them the go-by.[a]

Pray to God.
Love your parents.
Respect your kindred.
Guard what is given you.
Avoid the market-place.[b]
Walk in good company.
Don't approach, until you're invited.
Be tidy.
Salute willingly.
Yield to your senior.

[a] On the manuscript authority for the order of these *sententiolae* see Baehrens, *P.L.M.* III. pp. 206 and 214–215.
[b] This seems to anticipate Bacon's warning against *idola fori*, misconceptions due to the careless notions of the crowd.

Magistratum metue.
Verecundiam serva.
Rem tuam custodi.
Diligentiam adhibe.
Familiam cura.   15
Mutuum da.
Cui des videto.
Convivare raro.
Quod satis est dormi.
Coniugem ama.   20
Iusiurandum serva.
Vino tempera.
Pugna pro patria.
Nihil temere credideris.
Meretricem fuge.   25
Libros lege.
Quae legeris memento.
Liberos erudi.
Blandus esto
Irascere ob rem ⟨gravem⟩.   30
Neminem riseris.
In iudicio adesto.
Ad praetorium stato.
Consultus esto.
Virtute utere.   35
Trocho lude.
Aleam fuge.
Litteras disce.

²² te tempera *s pauci.*

CATO

Honour a magistrate.
Preserve your modesty.
Guard your own property.
Practise diligence.
Take trouble for your household.
Be willing to lend.
Consider to whom you should give.
Let your banquets be few.
Sleep as much as suffices.
Love your wife.
Keep an oath.
Be moderate with wine.
Fight for your country.
Believe nothing rashly.
Shun a harlot.
Read books.
Remember what you read.
Instruct your children.
Be kind.
Be angry for a serious cause.
Mock no one.
Support a friend in the law-court.
Maintain your standing at the praetor's residence.[a]
Be conversant with the law.
Practise virtue.
Play with the hoop.
Eschew dice.
Study literature.

---

[a] The *praetorium* may be the official residence of a provincial governor, or the headquarters in a camp, or sometimes a great private mansion (*e.g.*, Juvenal I. 75). The advice here apparently is " keep in with the powers that be " or " keep in with your patron." Erasmus took *praetorium* of a law-court, explaining " multa enim discuntur in agendis causis."

Bono benefacito.
Tute consule.   40
Maledicus ne esto.
Existimationem retine.
Aequum iudica.
Nihil mentire.
Iracundiam rege.   45
Parentem patientia vince.
Minorem ne contempseris.
Nihil arbitrio virium feceris.
Patere legem quam ipse tuleris.
Benefici accepti esto memor.   50
Pauca in convivio loquere.
Miserum noli irridere.
Minime iudica.
Alienum noli concupiscere.
Illud aggredere quod iustum est.   55
Libenter amorem ferto.
Liberalibus stude.

CATONIS DISTICHA

LIBER I

1. Si deus est animus, nobis ut carmina dicunt,
   hic tibi praecipue sit pura mente colendus.
2. Plus vigila semper neu somno deditus esto;
   nam diuturna quies vitiis alimenta ministrat.
3. Virtutem primam esse puto, compescere linguam:
   proximus ille deo est qui scit ratione tacere.
4. Sperne repugnando tibi tu contrarius esse:
   conveniet nulli qui secum dissidet ipse.

40 tute *corruptum videtur*: *fortasse* tuta consule *A. M. Duff.*
2, 1 neu A : nec BCDEF : ne ς.

596

CATO

Do good to a good man.
Give safe advice.
Do not be abusive.
Hold fast to your reputation.
Judge fairly.
Tell no lie.
Control your anger.
Overcome your parent with patience.
Do not despise a younger man.
Do nothing with the caprice of might.
Accept the law which you yourself made.
Bear in mind a benefit received.
Say little at a banquet.
Do not deride the wretched.
Judge not at all.
Do not covet what is another's.
Undertake what is fair.
Show affection gladly.
Put zeal into noble pursuits.

THE DISTICHS OF CATO

BOOK I

1. If God be spirit, as bards represent,
   He must be worshipped with a clean intent.
2. Watch always more: sleep must not thee entice:
   Prolonged inaction serves up food for vice.
3. To rule the tongue I reckon virtue's height:
   He's nearest God who can be dumb aright.
4. Avoid the clash of inconsistency:
   Who fights with self, with no one will agree.

597

5. Si vitam inspicias hominum, si denique mores,
   cum culpant alios: nemo sine crimine vivit.

6. Quae nocitura tenes, quamvis sint cara, relin-
   que:
   utilitas opibus praeponi tempore debet.

7. Clemens et constans, ut res expostulat, esto:
   temporibus mores sapiens sine crimine mutat.

8. Nil temere uxori de servis crede querenti:
   semper enim mulier quem coniunx diligit odit.

9. Cum moneas aliquem nec se velit ille moneri,
   si tibi sit carus, noli desistere coeptis.

10. Contra verbosos noli contendere verbis:
    sermo datur cunctis, animi sapientia paucis.

11. Dilige sic alios, ut sis tibi carus amicus;
    sic bonus esto bonis, ne te mala damna sequan-
    tur.

12. Rumores fuge neu studeas novus auctor haberi;
    nam nulli tacuisse nocet, nocet esse locutum.

13. Spem tibi polliciti certam promittere noli:
    rara fides ideo est, quia multi multa loquuntur.

14. Cum te aliquis laudat, iudex tuus esse memento;
    plus aliis de te quam tu tibi credere noli.

15. Officium alterius multis narrare memento;
    at quaecumque aliis benefeceris ipse, sileto.

16. Multorum cum facta senex et dicta reprendis,
    fac tibi succurrant iuvenis quae feceris ipse.

17. Ne cures, si quis tacito sermone loquatur:
    conscius ipse sibi de se putat omnia dici.

18. Cum fueris felix, quae sunt adversa caveto:
    non eodem cursu respondent ultima primis.

12, 1 neu studeas *Baehrens* : ne studeas A : ne (nec D)
incipias *ceteri omnes.*
13, 1 polliciti A : promissi BCDE : promissam F (*et sic*
CE *m.* 2 *corr.*).

5. Test but the life and ways of them who blame
   Their fellows; all, you'll find, have faults the
      same.
6. Gear that may harm forgo, however dear:
   Wealth yields to usefulness in time of fear.
7. Be mild or firm as circumstances claim:
   A sage may change his outlook free from blame.
8. A wife's complaints about the slaves mistrust:
   Her husband's favourite wakens her disgust.
9. In warning one who fain would not attend,
   Drop not the endeavour, should he be your
      friend.
10. To fight the wordy you must words eschew:
    Speech is bestowed on all, sound sense on few.
11. Love other men; yet be your own true friend:
    Do good to good men so no loss attend.
12. Shun tattling, and the newest thing to say
    Seek not: closed lips hurt no one—speaking
       may.
13. Think not hopes built on promises are sure:
    Much said by many seldom proves secure.
14. When someone praises you, be judge alone:
    Trust not men's judgement of you, but your
       own.
15. Let others' kindness frankly be revealed;
    Your own good turns to others keep concealed.
16. When you, grown old, blame what folk do or
       say,
    Think what you did in your own youthful day.
17. Reck not of what the whispering lip lets
       fall:
    Self-conscious men think they're the talk of all.
18. In happy hours beware the hapless lot:
    What the start promises, the end is not.

19. Cum dubia et fragilis nobis sit vita tributa,
    in morte alterius spem tu tibi ponere noli.
20. Exiguum munus cum dat tibi pauper amicus,
    accipito laetus, plene et laudare memento.
21. Infantem nudum cum te natura crearit,
    paupertatis onus patienter ferre memento.
22. Ne timeas illam quae vitae est ultima finis:
    qui mortem metuit, quod vivit, perdit id ipsum.
23. Si tibi pro meritis nemo succurrit amicus,
    incusare deos noli, sed te ipse coerce.
24. Ne tibi quid desit, quod quaesisti, utere parce;
    utque, quod est, serves, semper tibi desse
        putato.
25. Quod dare non possis, verbis promittere noli,
    ne sis ventosus, dum vir bonus esse videris.
26. Qui simulat verbis nec corde est fidus amicus,
    tu quoque fac simules: sic ars deluditur arte.
27. Noli homines blando nimium sermone probare:
    fistula dulce canit, volucrem dum decipit auceps.
28. Cum tibi sint nati nec opes, tunc artibus illos
    instrue, quo possint inopem defendere vitam.
29. Quod vile est, carum, quod carum, vile putato:
    sic tu nec cupidus nec avarus nosceris ulli.
30. Quae culpare soles ea tu ne feceris ipse:
    turpe est doctori, cum culpa redarguat ipsum.
31. Quod iustum est petito vel quod videatur hones-
        tum;
    nam stultum petere est quod possit iure negari.
32. Ignotum tibi tu noli praeponere notis:
    cognita iudicio constant, incognita casu.

²¹, 1 quod quaesisti *Baehrens*: quod quaeris A.
²⁵, 1 verbis promittere noli *Baehrens*: nec bis (*ex* vis *corr.*
m. 2) promittere noli A: noli promittere verbis *Columb.*
³⁰, ² redarguat *Baehrens*: arguat A: redarguit *ceteri codd.*

19. Our life is but a frail uncertain breath:
    Rest not thy hopes, then, on another's death.
20. When your poor friend gives of his poverty,
    Accept well pleased and thank him handsomely.
21. A naked babe since nature fashioned thee,
    With patience bear the load of poverty.
22. Fear not lest life's concluding lap be nigh:
    He makes his life no life who dreads to die.
23. If no friend helps you as your deeds demand,
    Tax not the gods but hold yourself in hand.
24. Save up your gains lest you go short some day:
    To keep possessions, fancy they're away.
25. Utter no promise that you can't redeem,
    Lest you inconstant prove, while kind you seem.
26. The glib dissembler, faithless friend at heart,
    See that you copy: so art baffles art.
27. Approve not men who wheedling nothings say:
    Fowlers pipe sweetly to delude their prey.
28. Since sons you have—not wealth—such training give
    Their minds that they, though poor, unharmed may live.
29. Hold dear the cheap, and cheaply hold the dear:
    So none can say you hunt or hoard your gear.
30. Do not yourself what you are wont to blame:
    When sin convicts the preacher's self, 'tis shame.
31. Ask what is right or fair to human eye:
    Fools ask what others rightly may deny.
32. Do not the unknown o'er the known advance:
    Known things on judgement hang, unknown on chance.

---

[32], 1 notis noli praeponere amicis *Baehrens.*

33. Cum dubia in certis versetur vita periclis,
   pro lucro tibi pone diem quicumque sequetur.

34. Vincere cum possis, interdum cede sodali,
   obsequio quoniam dulces retinentur amici.

35. Ne dubita, cum magna petes, impendere parva:
   his etenim pressos contingit gloria raro.

36. Litem inferre cave, cum quo tibi gratia iuncta
   est:
   ira odium generat, concordia nutrit amorem.

37. Servorum culpa cum te dolor urguet in iram,
   ipse tibi moderare, tuis ut parcere possis.

38. Quem superare potes interdum vince ferendo;
   maxima enim est hominum semper patientia
   virtus.

39. Conserva potius, quae sunt iam parta, labore:
   cum labor in damno est, crescit mortalis egestas.

40. Dapsilis interdum notis et largus amicis
   cum fueris, dando semper tibi proximus esto.

LIBER II

Telluris si forte velis cognoscere cultus,
Vergilium legito; quodsi mage nosse laboras
herbarum vires, Macer haec tibi carmina dicit;

35, 2 pressos contingit gloria raro *Baehrens* : rebus coniungit
gratia caros *codd. omnes, sine sensu.*
40, 1 largus *edd. vett.* : carus *codd.* ² cum ς *nonnulli* : dum
CDEF ς *nonnulli.* dando *Par.* 2772 *m.* 1, *Regin.* 2078 *in
ras.* : felix *codd. ceteri, quod ortum videtur ex* I. 18, 1.

CATO

33. Since our frail life through dangers sure must
    run,
    Count every day that comes as something won.
34. Yield to your mate some points you well might
    score:
    Compliance keeps your friends attached the
    more.
35. In mighty aims small cost you must not spare;
    For those whom trifles cramp high fame is rare.
36. Beware of strife with one close linked to thee:
    Anger breeds hate, love feeds on harmony.
37. If, stung by slaves' misdeeds, you've angry grown,
    Control yourself and so hurt not your own.
38. Sometimes put up with him you might beat
    down;
    Of human virtues patience is the crown.
39. What you have won conserve at cost of pains:
    Want must increase, when labour brings no
    gains.
40. Though sometimes on your friends you lavish
    gear,
    In giving always to yourself keep near.[a]

BOOK II

If perchance you fain would acquaint yourself
with farming, read Virgil; but if your struggle
rather is to know the virtue of herbs, this is the
poetry that Macer [b] offers you; if you long to know

[a] The self-regarding morality of this distich advises the generous man never to depart too far from his own interest.
[b] The didactic poet Aemilius Macer of Verona (d. 16 B.C.) wrote a work De Herbis (Ovid, Trist. IV. x. 43-44).

si Romana cupis et Punica noscere bella,
Lucanum quaeres, qui Martis proelia dixit;
si quid amare libet vel discere amare legendo,
Nasonem petito; sin autem cura tibi haec est,
ut sapiens vivas, audi quae discere possis,
per quae semotum vitiis deducitur aevum:
ergo ades et quae sit sapientia disce legendo.   10

1. Si potes, ignotis etiam prodesse memento:
   utilius regno est meritis acquirere amicos.

2. An di sint caelumque regant, ne quaere doceri:
   cum sis mortalis, quae sunt mortalia cura.

3. Linque metum leti; nam stultum est tempore
   in omni,
   dum mortem metuas, amittere gaudia vitae.

4. Iratus de re incerta contendere noli:
   impedit ira animum, ne possis cernere verum.

5. Fac sumptum propere, cum res desiderat ipsa;
   dandum etenim est aliquid, dum tempus postu-
   lat aut res.

6. Quod nimium est fugito, parvo gaudere memento:
   tuta mage est puppis modico quae flumine
   fertur.

7. Quod pudeat, socios prudens celare memento,
   ne plures culpent id quod tibi displicet uni.

---

⁴ romam velis et p. cognuscere (*sic*) A: civica *pro* punica
Scriverius.
². ¹ *codd. omnes habent:* mitte arc(h)ana dei caelumque
inquirere quid sit, *nisi quod* C *unus ante versum* 2 *inserit:*
an dii sint caelum qui (i *ex corr.*) regant nequere (*sic*)
doceri; *haec altera versus forma genuina iudicanda est, cum
prior illa colorem christianum prae se ferat.*

of Roman and Punic [a] warfare, you will seek Lucan, who has recounted the combats of Mars; if your fancy is to have a love-affair or by reading learn how to love, make for Ovid. But if your serious aim is a life of wisdom, hear what you may learn of things that ensure a course of life divorced from vice. Come then and, as you read, learn what wisdom is.

1. To help even strangers, if you can, take pains:
   A crown counts less than friends whom kindness gains.
2. Ask not if Gods exist or are Heaven's kings:
   As thou art mortal, think of mortal things.
3. Cease fearing death: 'tis folly day by day,
   For fear of death, to cast life's joys away.
4. Temper in fighting rival claims eschew:
   Temper bars minds from seeing what is true.
5. Make haste to spend when so the case desires;
   For something must be given, as need requires.
6. Pleased with small store, take care to avoid the extreme:
   Safer the craft that sails a moderate stream.
7. What makes you blush 'fore friends decline to own,
   Lest many blame what you dislike alone. [b]

---

[a] If *Punica* be the right reading, did an erroneous superscription on a manuscript of Lucan mislead the author of these lines? (*Cf.* H. Blass, *Rhein. Mus.* xxxi. p. 134.) Or has a verse referring to a poet other than Lucan, *e.g.* Silius Italicus, dropped out of the text? Lucan's *Pharsalia* narrated the civil war between Caesar and Pompey; Silius' *Punica* the struggle of Rome against Hannibal.

[b] One of the many prudential maxims: to confess openly a secret fault may invite ill-natured comment about what is really your own concern.

8. Nolo putes pravos homines peccata lucrari:
   temporibus peccata latent, et tempore parent.

9. Corporis exigui vires contemnere noli:
   consilio pollet cui vim natura negavit.

10. Cui scieris non esse parem, pro tempore cede:
    victorem a victo superari saepe videmus.

11. Adversum notum noli contendere verbis:
    lis verbis minimis interdum maxima crescit.

12. Quid deus intendat, noli perquirere sorte:
    quid statuat de te, sine te deliberat ille.

13. Invidiam nimio cultu vitare memento:
    quae si non laedit, tamen hanc sufferre moles-
       tum est.

14. Esto animo forti, cum sis damnatus inique:
    nemo diu gaudet qui iudice vincit iniquo.

15. Litis praeteritae noli maledicta referre:
    post inimicitias iram meminisse malorum est.

16. Nec te collaudes nec te culpaveris ipse;
    hoc faciunt stulti, quos gloria vexat inanis.

17. Utere quaesitis modice: cum sumptus abundat,
    labitur exiguo quod partum est tempore longo.

18. Insipiens esto, cum tempus postulat aut res:
    stultitiam simulare loco, prudentia summa est.

19. Luxuriam fugito, simul et vitare memento
    crimen avaritiae; nam sunt contraria famae.

20. Nolito quaedam referenti credere saepe:
    exigua est tribuenda fides, qui multa loquuntur.

8, 2 tempore si *Baehrens*: temporibus *codd. omnes.*
14, 1 ferto *Baehrens*: esto *codd.*
18, 1 ipsum A, *Baehrens*: aut res *ceteri codd.*   2 ioco *Baehrens*: loco *codd.* cum tempore laus est A: prudentia summa est *ceteri codd.*

606

CATO

8. Think not that wicked men find wrongdoing
    gain:
    At times the wrong lies hid—in time 'tis plain.
9. Strength housed in little frame do not disdain:
    In counsel men of slight physique may reign.
10. When you're outmatched, to meet the case,
    retreat:[a]
    Oft-times the vanquished will the victor beat.
11. In wordy war do not engage thy friend;
    For trivial words in mighty strife may end.
12. What God intendeth seek not to divine:
    His plans for thee require no aid of thine.
13. Proud pomp will rouse men's jealousy, be
    sure:
    Though it mayn't hurt, it's irksome to endure.
14. When judged unfairly, your own courage trust:
    None long has joy who wins through judge
    unjust.
15. The quarrel past, its bitter words ignore:
    'Tis ill to think of wrath, when strife is o'er.
16. Praise not yourself, nor to yourself take blame:
    Fools do so, plagued by love of empty fame.[b]
17. Make temperate use of gains: when all is cost,
    What took long time to get is quickly lost.
18. Play the fool's part, if time or need advise:
    To act the fool at times is truly wise.
19. Flee luxury, avoiding all the same
    The charge of avarice: both blot a name.
20. Trust not those who for ever news relate:
    Slight faith is due to tongues that glibly prate.

[a] *Cf.* the French *reculer pour mieux sauter.*
[b] The second line refers more obviously to the first part of
the preceding line, but insincere self-depreciation may be the
form of vanity known as " fishing for compliments."

21. Quae potus peccas ignoscere tu tibi noli;
nam crimen vini nullum est, sed culpa bibentis.
22. Consilium arcanum tacito committe sodali,
corporis auxilium medico committe fideli.
23. Successu indignos noli tu ferre moleste:
indulget Fortuna malis, ut vincere possit.
24. Prospice qui veniant casus hos esse ferendos:
nam levius laedit, quicquid praevidimus ante.
25. Rebus in adversis animum submittere noli:
spem retine; spes una hominem nec morte relinquit.
26. Rem tibi quam nosces aptam dimittere noli:
fronte capillata, post est Occasio calva.
27. Quod sequitur specta quodque imminet ante videto:
illum imitare deum, partem qui spectat utramque.
28. Fortius ut valeas, interdum parcior esto:
pauca voluptati debentur, plura saluti.
29. Iudicium populi numquam contempseris unus:
ne nulli placeas, dum vis contemnere multos.
30. Sit tibi praecipue, quod primum est, cura salutis;
tempora nec culpes, cum sis tibi causa doloris.
31. Somnia ne cures; nam mens humana quod optat,
dum vigilans sperat, per somnum cernit id ipsum.

23, 1 successus nolito indigni (*vel* indignos) ferre *Baehrens.* 2 vincere A: laedere *ceteri codd.*

26, 1 noris *Baehrens*: noscis CDEF ς *plerique*: nosces ς *pauci*: scieris A.

30, 2 sit *codd.*: sis ς *pauci.*

31, 2 vigilat *codd. omnes*: vigilans *edd. vet.* verum *Baehrens*: sperat *codd. omnes.*

CATO

21. Your faults in drink should not your pardon
    win :
    The wine is guiltless : 'tis the drinker's sin.
22. Trust secret plans to friend who guards his
    speech,
    And bodily treatment to a faithful leech.
23. Chafe not against men's undeserved success :
    To bring it low Luck smiles on wickedness.
24. Ills, as they come, prepare to undergo :
    What we've foreseen deals us a lighter blow.
25. Let not your courage droop in darkest hours :
    Hope on ; for hope alone at death is ours.[a]
26. Do not let slip the thing that suits your mind :
    Chance wears a forelock, but is bald behind.[b]
27. Observe the past and what impends foresee,
    Like Janus, facing both ways equally.
28. For growth in strength, at times eat food in
    measure ;
    You owe more to your health than to your
    pleasure.
29. Ne'er stand alone to flout the general view :
    If you flout many, none may care for you.
30. Your health, the chief thing, guard with might
    and main :
    Don't blame the season for your self-caused
    pain.
31. Reck not of dreams ; in things which men
    pursue,
    Sleep sees the hopes of waking hours come
    true.

[a] This is probably an instance where Christian thought has
coloured the *Disticha* : " hope alone does not desert man—not
even in death."

[b] The Latin is quoted by Wm. Herman in letter to Cornelius
Gerard, A.D. 1494: *cf.* P. S. Allen, *Erasmi Epistolae* (1906),
no. 36.

LIBER III

Hoc quicumque volet carmen cognoscere lector,
cum praecepta ferat quae sunt gratissima vitae,
commoda multa feret; sin autem spreverit illud,
non me scriptorem, sed se fastidiet ipse.

1. Instrue praeceptis animum, ne discere cessa;
   nam sine doctrina vita est quasi mortis imago.
2. Cum recte vivas, ne cures verba malorum:
   arbitrii non est nostri quid quisque loquatur.
3. Productus testis, salvo tamen ante pudore,
   quantumcumque potes, celato crimen amici.
4. Sermones blandos blaesosque cavere memento:
   simplicitas veri forma est, laus ficta loquentis.
5. Segnitiem fugito, quae vitae ignavia fertur;
   nam cum animus languet, consumit inertia
   corpus.
6. Interpone tuis interdum gaudia curis,
   ut possis animo quemvis sufferre laborem.
7. Alterius dictum aut factum ne carpseris umquam,
   exemplo simili ne te derideat alter.
8. Quod tibi sors dederit tabulis suprema notato,
   augendo serva, ne sis quem fama loquatur.
9. Cum tibi divitiae superant in fine senectae,
   munificus facito vivas, non parcus, amicis.
10. Utile consilium dominus ne despice servi:
    si prodest, sensum nullius tempseris umquam.
11. Rebus et in censu si non est quod fuit ante,
    fac vivas contentus eo quod tempora praebent.

III *prologum ita habet* A : *ceteri codices interponunt
distichon primum inter versum* 2 *et versum* 3 *prologi.*
    4, ² forma *Barth*: fama *codd. omnes*: norma *Scriverius.*
laus f. loquentis A : fraus f. loquendi CDEF *ς.*

CATO

BOOK III

Any reader who decides to study this poem will reap many advantages, as it offers maxims most acceptable for life; but if he spurn it, he will show disdain not for me, its author, but for himself.

1. Fail not to learn: equip your mind with rules;
   Count as but death the life that never schools.
2. Mind not ill tongues, if you live straight of soul:
   A neighbour's words are not in our control.
3. If called to witness, hide as best you can
   A friend's misdeeds, but be an honest man.
4. Beware of softly whispered flatteries:
   Frankness is mark of truth, flattery of lies.
5. Shun slackness, which means idling all your days:
   With lazy minds sloth on the body preys.
6. Sandwich occasional joys amidst your care
   That you with spirit any task may bear.
7. Another's word or act ne'er criticise,
   Lest others mock at you in selfsame wise.
8. A heritage bequeathed to you by will
   Keep and increase: so save your good name still.
9. If you've abundant wealth, as old age ends,
   Be generous, not close-fisted, with your friends.
10. Sound counsel from your slave do not despise:
    Spurn no man's view at all, if it is wise.
11. If goods and income are not what they were,
    Live satisfied with what the times confer.

8, 2 auge servando *vel* augendo cura ne segnem *Withof.*

12. Uxorem fuge ne ducas sub nomine dotis,
    nec retinere velis, si coeperit esse molesta.

13. Multorum disce exemplo, quae facta sequaris,
    quae fugias : vita est nobis aliena magistra.

14. Quod potes id temptato, operis ne pondere
      pressus
    succumbat labor et frustra temptata relinquas.

15. Quod factum scis non recte, nolito silere,
    ne videare malos imitari velle tacendo.

16. Iudicis auxilium sub iniqua lite rogato :
    ipsae etiam leges cupiunt ut iure regantur.

17. Quod merito pateris patienter ferre memento,
    cumque reus tibi sis, ipsum te iudice damna.

18. Multa legas facito, perlectis neglege multa ;
    nam miranda canunt, sed non credenda poetae.

19. Inter convivas fac sis sermone modestus,
    ne dicare loquax, cum vis urbanus haberi.

20. Coniugis iratae noli tu verba timere ;
    nam lacrimis struit insidias, cum femina plorat.

21. Utere quaesitis, sed ne videaris abuti :
    qui sua consumunt, cum dest, aliena sequuntur.

22. Fac tibi proponas mortem non esse timendam :
    quae bona si non est, finis tamen illa malorum
      est.

23. Uxoris linguam, si frugi est, ferre memento ;
    namque malum est non velle pati nec posse
      tacere.

24. Aequa diligito caros pietate parentes,
    nec matrem offendas, dum vis bonus esse parenti.

14, 2 inceptata *Baehrens* : temptata *s nonnulli*.
15, 2 velle inritare *Baehrens*.
16, 2 rogentur (*i.e.* adeantur) *Baehrens* : regantur E *m.*1.
18, 1 facito tum lectis *Baehrens* : factorum lectis CD.
23, 2 tacere *codd.* : carere *Withof*.

CATO

. Do not for dowry's sake espouse a wife,
Nor wish to keep her, if she causes strife.

. From men's behaviour learn what to pursue
Or shun. The life of others gives the cue.

. Try what you can, lest by hard task foredone
You fail and drop what you've in vain begun.

. Do not conceal ill deeds within your ken,
Lest silence look like aping wicked men.

. If sued unfairly, ask the judge for aid:
The very laws would fain be justly swayed.

. What you deserve to bear, with patience bear:
And, when you're judge of self, you must not
spare.

. Read much, but, having read, with much dis-
pense;
Bards' themes are wonders, but revolt the sense.

. Upon your talk, at dinners, set a bit,
Lest you're dubbed "rattle," when you'd fain
be "wit."

. Fear not the words your angry wife may say:
A weeping woman plots but to waylay.

. Use your estate, yet shun extravagance:
Want follows waste and begs for maintenance.

. Be this thy motto—" I do not dread death ":
Death, if no boon, our troubles finisheth.

. A thrifty wife may talk and talk: endure:
Lost patience and loud brawling are no cure.

. Love both your parents, one as much as other:
To please your father never wound your mother.

LIBER IV

Semotam a curis si vis producere vitam
nec vitiis haerere animi, quae moribus obsunt,
haec praecepta tibi saepe esse legenda memento:
invenies, quo te possis mutare, magistrum.

1. Despice divitias, si vis animo esse beatus;
   quas qui suspiciunt, mendicant semper avari.
2. Commoda Naturae nullo tibi tempore derunt,
   si contentus eo fueris quod postulat usus.
3. Cum sis incautus nec rem ratione gubernes,
   noli Fortunam, quae non est, dicere caecam.
4. Dilige † te ornari, sed parce dilige formam,
   quam nemo sanctus nec honestus captat habere.
5. Cum fueris locuples, corpus curare memento:
   aeger dives habet nummos, se non habet ipsum.
6. Verbera cum tuleris discens aliquando magistri,
   fer patris imperium, cum verbis exit in iram.
7. Res age quae prosunt; rursus vitare memento,
   in quis error inest nec spes est certa laboris.
8. Quod donare potes gratis concede roganti;
   nam recte fecisse bonis in parte lucrorum est.
9. Quod tibi suspectum est confestim discute quid
   sit;
   namque solent, primo quae sunt neglecta,
   nocere.
10. Cum te detineat veneris damnosa libido,
    indulgere gulae noli, quae ventris amica est.

4, 1 olens nardum *Baehrens*: denarium *codd.*: te ornari
Cannegieter. defuge odorem *Baehrens*: dilige formam *codd.*
2 quem *codd.* (*quod non congruit cum* formam): quam *vulgo.*
habere *codd.*: ab aere *Scaliger.*

CATO

BOOK IV

If you would lead a long life divorced from anxieties, and not cling to faults in the mind which harm character, then remember that you must often read these rules. You will find a teacher through whom you will be able to transform yourself.

1. Scorn wealth, if you would have a mind care-freed:
   Its votaries are but beggars in their greed.
2. Ne'er will you lack supplies from Nature's hands,
   If you're content with that which need demands.
3. Reckless, haphazard steersman of your lot,
   Do not call Fortune blind: blind she is not.
4. Love neatness: showiness love not amain,
   Which good and honest folk seek not to gain.
5. Yourself, when you grow rich, treat well; for pelf
   The invalid owns, but does not own himself.
6. At school you sometimes bear the teacher's cane:
   So 'gainst a father's angry words don't strain.[a]
7. Do what is helpful; but from things recoil
   Where hazard leaves dim hope to honest toil.
8. Give gratis what you can upon request:
   Befriending friends may be as gain assessed.
9. Test quickly what it is that you suspect:
   Men end by suffering from what they neglect.
10. When on some ruinous amour forced to spend,
    Indulge not gluttony, the belly's friend.[b]

[a] *verbera* and *verbis* make an excellent contrast in the Latin.
[b] *i.e.* love in itself is ruinous enough; but expensive feasts given in honour of a sweetheart may prove ruinous to health and purse.

11. Cum tibi praeponas animalia bruta timore,
    unum hominem scito tibi praecipue esse timen-
    dum.
12. Cum tibi praevalidae fuerint in corpore vires,
    fac sapias: sic tu poteris vir fortis haberi.
13. Auxilium a notis petito, si forte labores;
    nec quisquam melior medicus quam fidus amicus.
14. Cum sis ipse nocens, moritur cur victima pro te?
    stultitia est morte alterius sperare salutem.
15. Cum tibi vel socium vel fidum quaeris amicum,
    non tibi fortuna est hominis sed vita petenda.
16. Utere quaesitis opibus, fuge nomen avari:
    quid tibi divitiae, si semper pauper abundes?
17. Si famam servare cupis, dum vivis, honestam,
    fac fugias animo quae sunt mala gaudia vitae.
18. Cum sapias animo, noli ridere senectam;
    nam quoicumque seni puerilis sensus inhaeret.
19. Disce aliquid; nam cum subito Fortuna recessit,
    ars remanet vitamque hominis non deserit
    umquam.
20. Prospicito tecum tacitus quid quisque loquatur:
    sermo hominum mores et celat et indicat idem.
21. Exerce studio quamvis perceperis artem:
    ut cura ingenium, sic et manus adiuvat usum.
22. Multum venturi ne cures tempora fati:
    non metuit mortem qui scit contemnere vitam.
23. Disce sed a doctis, indoctos ipse doceto:
    propaganda etenim est rerum doctrina bonarum.

11.1 bruta *Arntzen*: cuncta *codd.* timore D: timere *ceteri codd.*
16.2 divitias DF, *Baehrens*: divitiae C.
18.2 cuicumque seni *edd. vet.*: quocumque sene *codd.*: quicumque senet *Scaliger.* pueri bis *Withof.* inhaeret *Baehrens*: in illo est *codd.*

11. When fear of brute beasts harasses your mind,
    Know what you most should dread is human
    kind.
12. If you have bodily strength in high degree,
    Add wisdom : so win fame for bravery.
13. In straits ask those you know their aid to lend ;
    No doctor can surpass a trusty friend.
14. Why dies a victim for you in your sin ?
    Grace through another's blood fools hope to win.
15. Seeking a mate or friend who will be true,
    A man's life, not his fortune, you must view.
16. Employ your gains : earn not a niggard's name :
    What boots your wealth, if you're in want the
    same ?
17. If throughout life you'd keep an honoured name,
    Shun in your thought the joys which end in
    shame.
18. Don't mock old age, though you've a gifted
    brain :
    Old age must ever show a childish vein.
19. Learn something ; for when Luck is sudden
    gone,
    Art stays nor ever leaves man's life alone.
20. Look quietly out on what the city says :
    Men's talk at once reveals and hides their
    ways.
21. Practise with zeal an art once learned : as pains
    Help talent, so the hand, used deftly, trains.
22. For fated hours to come show small concern :
    He fears not death who knows how life to spurn.
23. Learn from the learnéd, but the unlettered
    teach :
    Far should the spread of wholesome knowledge
    reach.

24. Hoc bibe quo possis si tu vis vivere sanus:
    morbi causa mali minima est quaecumque
    voluptas.
25. Laudaris quodcumque palam, quodcumque pro-
    baris,
    hoc vide ne rursus levitatis crimine damnes.
26. Tranquillis rebus semper diversa timeto,
    rursus in adversis melius sperare memento.
27. Discere ne cessa: cura sapientia crescit,
    rara datur longo prudentia temporis usu.
28. Parce laudato; nam quem tu saepe probaris,
    una dies, qualis fuerit, ostendit, amicus.
29. Non pudeat, quae nescieris, te velle doceri:
    scire aliquid laus est, culpa est nil discere velle.
30. Cum venere et baccho lis est et iuncta voluptas:
    quod lautum est animo complectere, sed fuge
    lites.
31. Demissos animo et tacitos vitare memento:
    quod flumen placidum est, forsan latet altius unda.
32. Dum fortuna tibi est rerum discrimine prava,
    alterius specta cui sit discrimine peior.
33. Quod potes id tempta; nam litus carpere remis
    utilius multo est quam velum tendere in altum.
34. Contra hominem iustum prave contendere noli;
    semper enim deus iniustas ulciscitur iras.
35. Ereptis opibus noli maerere dolendo,
    sed gaude potius, tibi si contingat habere.
36. Est iactura gravis quaesitum amittere damno;
    sed tibi cum valeat corpus, superesse putato.

24. [1] hoc adhibe vitae quo possis v. s. *Baehrens.* [2] mali est
nimia est *Baehrens.*
32. [1] tibist rerum *Baehrens*: rerum tibi sit A: tua rerum tibi
ceteri codd. discrimine prava *Baehrens*: discrimine peior A:
displicet ipsi *ceteri codd.*

CATO

24. If you'd live healthy, drink in temperate measure:
    Oft ill diseases spring from trivial pleasure.
25. What you've approved and lauded openly,
    Shun the reproach of damning flightily.
26. When all is calm, dread ever fortune's change:
    Then, in bad times, your hope towards good must range.
27. Fail not to learn; for wisdom grows by pains:
    Mere long-drawn waiting rarely prudence gains.
28. Praise sparingly; for him you oft commend—
    One day reveals how far he has been friend.
29. Blush not to wish, where ignorant, to be taught:
    Knowledge wins praise: drones wish to study naught.
30. With love and wine are strife and pleasure knit:
    Take to your heart the joy: the strife omit.
31. Gloomy and silent men take care to shun;
    Still waters haply all too deep may run.
32. When fortune at a crisis serves thee ill,
    Look at that other who is served worse still.
33. Try only what you can: 'tis wiser far
    To row inshore than sail beyond the bar.
34. Strive not unfairly 'gainst an upright man:
    On wrath unjustified God sets a ban.
35. When robbed of wealth, in anguish sorrow not:
    Rather rejoice in what falls to thy lot.
36. To part with what toil won the loss is sore:
    Yet think, if health be thine, thou hast full store.

33, 2 utilius multo est A : tutius est multo *s*.

36, 1 quaesitum a. damno A : quae sunt a. dam(p)nis *ceteri codd.*

37. Tempora longa tibi noli promittere vitae:
    quocumque incedis, sequitur Mors corporis
    umbra.

38. Ture deum placa, vitulum sine crescat aratro:
    ne credas gaudere deum, cum caede litatur.

39. Cede locum laesus Fortunae, cede potenti:
    laedere qui ⟨potuit⟩ poterit prodesse aliquando.

40. Cum quid peccaris, castiga te ipse subinde:
    vulnera dum sanas, dolor est medicina doloris.

41. Damnaris numquam post longum tempus ami-
    cum:
    mutavit mores, sed pignora prima memento.

42. Gratior officiis, quo sis mage carior, esto,
    ne nomen subeas quod dicunt officiperdi.

43. Suspectus cave sis, ne sis miser omnibus horis;
    nam timidis et suspectis aptissima mors est.

44. Cum servos fueris proprios mercatus in usus
    et famulos dicas, homines tamen esse memento.

45. Quam primum rapienda tibi est occasio prona,
    ne rursus quaeras iam quae neglexeris ante.

46. Morte repentina noli gaudere malorum:
    felices obeunt quorum sine crimine vita est.

47. Cum coniunx tibi sit, ne res et fama laboret,
    vitandum ducas inimicum nomen amici.

48. Cum tibi contigerit studio cognoscere multa,
    fac discas multa a vita te scire doceri.

49. Miraris versus nudis me scribere verbis?
    hoc brevitas fecit, sensu uno iungere binos.

45, 1 prona *Baehrens*: prima *codd.* 2 iam quae *Baehrens*:
quae iam *codd.*

48, 2 multa a vita *Baehrens*: multa vita *codd.* te scire
Baehrens: nescire *codd.* doceri EF: docere C.

49, 2 sensu uno iungere *Baehrens*: sensu (-sum *m.* 2 *corr.*)
coniungere A: sensus coniungere *ceteri codd.*

CATO

37. Thyself to promise years of life forbear;
    Death, like thy shadow, dogs thee everywhere.
38. Spare calves to plough: heaven's grace with
    incense gain:
    Think not God loves the blood of victims slain.
39. When stricken, yield to Fortune, yield to power:
    Who once could hurt may help in happier hour.
40. For faults committed, oft yourself arraign:
    In treating wounds, the cure for pain is pain.
41. Never condemn your friend of many a year:
    If changed his ways, think how he once was dear.
42. Show gratitude to bind affection's tie:
    Lest "ingrate" be the name you justify.
43. Earn not suspicion lest you live in grief:
    Suspected cravens find in death relief.
44. When you've bought slaves to serve your own
    sweet will,
    Though servants called, they're men, remember,
    still.
45. The lucky chance you must secure with speed,
    Lest you go seeking what you failed to heed.
46. Joy not when knaves come by a sudden end:
    Their death is blest whose life you can commend.
47. Having a wife, wouldst save thy gear and fame?
    Beware the friend who is but friend in name.
48. Great knowledge you have gained from books,
    you own:
    Yet note that life has lessons to be known.
49. You wonder that I write in these bare lines?
    Terseness the couplet in one thought combines.[a]

---

[a] An apology for the unadorned language of the distichs:
the aim at brevity has prevented expansion, the object being
to clinch one general thought in a couplet (or, if *sensus
coniungere binos* be read, "to combine two allied thoughts").

II. CODICUM TURICENSIS ET
VERONENSIS APPENDIX

1. LAETANDUM est vita, nullius morte dolendum;
   cur etenim doleas a quo dolor ipse recessit.
2. Quod scieris opus esse tibi, dimittere noli;
   oblatum auxilium stultum est dimittere cui-
   quam.
3. Perde semel, socium ingratum quom noveris
   esse;
   saepe dato, quom te scieris bene ponere dona.
4. Dissimula laesus, si non datur ultio praesens:
   qui celare potest odium pote laedere quem vult.
5. Qui prodesse potest non est fugiendus amicus,
   si laesit verbo: bonitas sine crimine nil est.
6. Contra hominem astutum noli versutus haberi:
   non captare malos stultum est, sed velle cluere.
7. Dat legem Natura tibi, non accipit ipsa.
8. Quod tacitum esse velis verbosis dicere noli.
9. Fortunae donis parvum tribuisse memento:
   non opibus bona fama datur, sed moribus ipsis.

5, 2 nihil est A : *an* nulla est ? *Baehrens in not.*
6, 2 velle cluere *Baehrens* : velle nocere A *sine sensu.*

SIGLA FOR MONOSTICHA

(As used by Baehrens in constituting his text.)

[For the contribution of single lines from each
manuscript, see *P.L.M.* III. pp. 212–213.]

A = Vaticano-Palatinus 239: saec. x.
B = Vaticano-Reginensis 711: saec. xi.
C = Vaticano-Reginensis 300: saec. xi.

CATO

II. APPENDIX OF ADDITIONAL LINES FROM ZÜRICH AND VERONA MSS. (= C and A)

1. FIND joy in life; grieve for the death of none.
   Why grieve for him from whom all grief has gone?
2. Never let slip the thing you know you need:
   They're fools who fail the proffered aid to heed.
3. Your friend, ungrateful proved, dismiss with haste:
   Give often, when you know your gifts well placed.
4. Conceal your wrong, if vengeance must be slow:
   Who hides his hate can injure any foe.
5. Your useful friend, though by his words annoyed,
   Drop not; there is no goodness unalloyed.
6. To outwit craft, court not for guile a name:
   Trap rogues you may, but not therefrom seek fame.
7. On you falls Nature's law, not on herself.
8. Don't tell a chatterbox what you'd keep quiet.
9. As slight in worth the gifts of Fortune view:
   To character, not wealth, renown is due.

D = Parisinus 8069: saec. xi.
E = Voravensis 111: saec. xii.
F = Marbodi codex S. Gatian. Turonensis 164.

[For the Cambridge MS. in Gonville and Caius College, saec. ix, see H. Schenkl, *Wien. Sitzungsber.* 143 (1901). For further views on the MSS. see M. Boas, *Mnemos.* 43 (1915), 44 (1916); *Philol.* 74 N.F. 28 (1917); *Rhein. Mus.* 72 (1917).]

III. COLLECTIO MONOSTICHORUM

UTILIBUS monitis prudens accommodet aurem.
Non laeta extollant animum, non tristia frangant.
Dispar vivendi ratio est, mors omnibus una.
Grande aliquid caveas timido committere cordi.
Numquam sanantur deformis vulnera famae.
Naufragium rerum est mulier male fida marito.
Tu si animo regeris, rex es ; si corpore, servus.
Proximus esto bonis, si non potes optimus esse.
Nullus tam parcus, quin prodigus ex alieno.
Audit quod non vult, qui pergit dicere quod vult.   1•
Non placet ille mihi, quisquis placuit sibi multum.
Nulli servitium si defers, liber haberis.
Vel bona contemni docet usus vel mala ferri.
Ex igne ut fumus, sic fama ex crimine surgit.
Paulisper laxatus amor decedere coepit.   1
Splendor opum sordes vitae non abluit umquam.
Improbus officium scit poscere, reddere nescit.
Irridens miserum dubium sciat omne futurum.
Mortis imago iuvat somnus, mors ipsa timetur.
Quanto maior eris, tanto moderatior esto.   2
Alta cadunt odiis, parva extolluntur amore.
Criminis indultu secura audacia crescit.
Quemlibet ignavum facit indignatio fortem.
Divitiae trepidant, paupertas libera res est.
Haut homo culpandus, quando est in crimine casus.   2
Fac quod te par sit, non alter quod mereatur.
Dissimilis cunctis vox vultus vita voluntas.
Ipsum se cruciat, te vindicat invidus in se.
Semper pauperies quaestum praedivitis auget.
Magno perficitur discrimine res memoranda.   3
Terra omnis patria est, qua nascimur et tumulamur.

---

a i.e. the very fact of envying a man is in itself (*in se*) a
testimony to his merit.

III. COLLECTION OF SINGLE LINES

LET prudence to sound warnings lend an ear.
Gladness must not transport, nor sorrow break.
Life's way will vary: death is one for all.
Trust not a faint heart with some high emprise.
The wounds of base repute are never cured.   5
The wife who tricks her husband wrecks the home.
King art thou, ruled by mind; by body, slave.
If short of best, then emulate the good.
No thrift but will be free with others' gear.
Say all you like; you'll hear what you mislike.   10
Who much hath pleased himself doth not please me.
To none subservient, you are reckoned free.
Life's rule is—spurn your goods and face your ills.
As fire gives smoke, a charge gives rise to talk.
Love gradually relaxed begins to go.   15
Wealth's glitter never washed a foul life clean.
Rascals can ask a service, but not give.
Mockers at woe should know the future's hid.
Death's copy, sleep, delights: death's self affrights.
The greater you are, be all the more restrained.   20
Hate ruins high things, love exalts the small.
Give rein to guilt, and daring grows secure.
Wrath forces any coward to be brave.
Where wealth brings panic, poverty is free.
Man's not to blame when fortune is arraigned.   25
Act as befits you, not as men deserve.
In voice, look, life and will all are unlike.
Self-racking Envy clears you in herself.[a]
The rich man's gain aye grows by poverty.
Great crises foster deeds enshrined in thought.   30
All the Earth's our home; there we are born and
    buried.

Aspera perpessu fiunt iucunda relatu.
Acrius appetimus nova quam iam parta tenemus.
Labitur ex animo benefactum, iniuria durat.
Tolle mali testes: levius mala nostra feremus.
Saepe labor siccat lacrimas et gaudia fundit.
Tristibus afficiar gravius, si laeta recorder.
Quid cautus caveas aliena exempla docebunt.
Condit fercla fames, plenis insuavia cuncta.
Doctrina est fructus dulcis radicis amarae.
Cum accusas alium, propriam prius inspice vitam.
Qui vinci sese patitur pro tempore, vincit.
Dum speras, servis, cum sint data praemia sensis.
Nemo ita despectus, quin possit laedere laesus.
Ille nocet gravius quem non contemnere possis.
Quod metuis cumulas, si velas crimine crimen.
Consilii regimen virtuti corporis adde.
Cum vitia alterius satis acri lumine cernas
nec tua prospicias, fis verso crimine caecus.
Suffragium laudis quod fert malus, hoc bonus odit.
Si piget admissi, committere parce pigenda.
Quod nocet interdum, si prodest, ferre memento:
dulcis enim labor est, cum fructu ferre laborem.
[Laetandum est vita, nullius morte dolendum:
cur etenim doleas, a quo dolor ipse recessit?]
Spes facit illecebras visuque libido movetur.
Non facit ipse aeger quod sanus suaserit aegro.
Ipsos absentes inimicos laedere noli.
Ulcus proserpit quod stulta silentia celant.

43 *solus habet* A. cum data sint A. sensis *Baehrens*:
saevis A: servis *Mai.*

---

^a *Cf.* Tennyson's "For a sorrow's crown of sorrow is
remembering happier things" and Dante's "nessun maggior
dolore che ricordarsi del tempo felice nella miseria."
^b *i.e.* you are a slave if you cherish extravagant hopes.
because your thoughts have no freedom from the imaginary

CATO

Things hard to bear grow pleasant to relate.
Keener our zest for the new than our grasp on the old.
A good turn slips the mind, a wrong endures.
No witness near—we'll easier bear our ills.   35
Work often dries the tear and spreads delight.
Memory of joys will aggravate my woes.*a*
Caution and care you'll learn from others' case.
Hunger is sauce: no dishes please the gorged.
Learning is pleasant fruit from bitter root.   40
Ere you accuse, your own life first inspect.
Who at fit moment yields is conqueror.
Your hopes enslave you; for your thoughts are bribed.*b*
None so despised as cannot hurt when hurt.*c*
The man you could not slight can harm you more.*d*   45
Cloak crime with crime and you increase your fear.
To bodily courage add the sway of thought.
When with sharp eye another's faults you mind,
Not seeing yours, you're blamed in turn as blind.
Praise voted to the bad disgusts the good.   50
If irked by what you've done, don't do what irks.
Harm sometimes must be borne, if found to suit;
For sweet the toil of bearing toil with fruit.
[Find joy in life; grieve for the death of none.
Why grieve for him from whom all grief has gone?]*e* 55
Hope makes allurements: lust is stirred by sight.
What you prescribe when well, you drop when sick.
Don't hurt e'en enemies behind their backs.
Sores spread in stealth by foolish silence hid.

advantages you are counting on and allotting to yourself
as if already won.

c *i.e.* the veriest craven will retaliate: " even a worm will
turn."

d The thought is not very deep: the man with no chinks
in his armour is one to be reckoned with.

e In D: also in Appendix from Zürich and Verona MSS.
supra.

Nemo reum faciet qui vult dici sibi verum.　　　60
Vincere velle tuos satis est victoria turpis.
Nonnumquam vultu tegitur mens taetra sereno.
Quisque miser casu alterius solatia sumit.
Vera libens dicas, quamquam sint aspera dictu.
Vir constans quicquid coepit complere laborat.　　65
Iniustus, qui sola putat proba quae facit ipse.
Omne manu factum consumit longa vetustas.
Haut multum tempus mentis simulata manebunt.
Quicquid inoptatum cadit, hoc homo corrigat arte.
Durum etiam facilem facit adsuetudo laborem.　　70
Robur confirmat labor, at longa otia solvunt.
Ut niteat virtus, absit rubigo quietis.
Sat dulcis labor est, cum fructu ferre laborem.
Magni magna parant, modici breviora laborant.
Ne crede amissum, quicquid reparare licebit.　　75
Non pecces tunc cum peccare impune licebit.
Tristis adest messis, si cessat laeta voluptas.
Absentum causas contra maledicta tuere.

68 haut multum E : haud ullum CF.　mentis E : vanitas
CF : bonitas *Riese* : gravitas *vel* virtus *Buecheler*.

IV. LINES FROM COLUMBANUS

WHICH MAY BE REGARDED AS CATONIAN

Under the name of the Irish monk Columbanus
(A.D. 543–615) there has come down a *carmen mono-
stichon* in 207 verses constituting a set of rules for
life (*praecepta vivendi*). While many are of Chris-
tian origin, Baehrens selects about a quarter of
these as being Catonian in source; and Manitius
thinks considerably more might be claimed under
this head.[a] Baehrens bases his text on Canisius in

CATO

None him arraigns who wants truth said to him. 60
'Tis a poor win to seek to beat your own.
Calm looks do sometimes cloak a loathsome mind.
Another's woe consoles all wretched folk.
Speak the truth freely, though the truth be hard.
The steadfast strive to end a task begun. 65
Unfair the man who approves his own acts only.
Long lapse of time consumes all handiwork.
The mind's pretences will not long endure.
Let man by skill make good unwelcome chance.
Hard work grows easy to the practised hand. 70
Long leisure saps the strength which work upbuilds.
That worth may shine, let rest be free from rust.
Sweet task it is to face a task and win.[a]
The great aim high ; plain folk ply humbler tasks.
Whate'er may be recovered think not lost. 75
Sin not in the hour when you may safely sin.
Sad reaping comes, if joyful pleasure wanes.
Champion the absent 'gainst backbiting tongues.

[a] *Cf.* line 53 *supra*.

---

his *Thesaurus* (Amsterdam, 1725),[b] who used a *codex Frisingensis*. It gives the ascription to Columbanus —*incipit libellus cuiusdam sapientis et ut fertur beati Columbani*. In the word *sapientis* may be detected an echo of " Cato the Philosopher." [c] Other manuscripts are the *codices Sangallenses, Lugdunensis* 190, and *Parisinus* 8092.

[a] *Gesch. der latein. Lit. des Mittelalters*, I. (1911), pp. 181 *sqq.*: *cf.* E. Dümmler, *Poet. lat. aevi Karolini*, I. 275–281.
[b] First ed. Ingolstad, 1601.
[c] The Disticha are entitled in the Parisinus 2659, saec. ix. *liber (quartus) Catonis philosophi.* The Montepessulanus has *libri Catonis philosophi.*

IV. EX COLUMBANO QUAE VIDENTUR
CATONIS ESSE

CORPORIS exsuperat vires prudentia mentis.
Ne tua paeniteat caveas victoria temet.
Vir bonus esse nequit nisi qui siet omnibus aequus.
Non tu quaeso iocis laedas nec carmine quemquam.
Sit servus mentis venter, sit serva libido.
Eripe, si valeas, non suggere tela furenti.
Saepe nocet puero miratio blanda magistri.
Cum sapiente loquens perpaucis utere verbis.
Egregios faciet mentis constantia mores.
Felix, qui causam loquitur prudentis in aurem.   10
Tantum verba valent, quantum mens sentiat illa.
Non erit antiquo novus anteferendus amicus.
Moribus egregiis facias tibi nomen honestum.
Cui prodest socius qui non prodesse probatur?
Res se vera quidem semper declarat honeste.   15
Actibus aut verbis noli tu adsuescere pravis.
Praemeditata animo levius sufferre valebis.
Quae subito adveniunt multo graviora videntur.
Felix, alterius cui sunt documenta flagella.
Praemia non capiet, ingrato qui bona praestat.   20
Omnis paulatim leto nos applicat hora.
Ante diem mortis nullus laudabilis exstat.
Doctor erit magnus, factis qui quod docet implet.
Quod tibi vis fieri, hoc alii praestare memento.
Quod tibi non optes, alii ne feceris ulli.   25
Corripe prudentem: reddetur gratia verbis.
Plus tua quam alterius damnabis crimina iudex.

---

^a *Cf.* Publilius Syrus, line 2.

CATO

IV. LINES FROM COLUMBANUS

Presumably of Catonian origin

Foresight of mind surpasses bodily strength.
Take care your victory bring you no regrets.
He can't be good who is not fair to all.
Wound no one, pray, with either jest or verse.
Let appetite and lust be slaves of mind. 5
Seize, if you can, a madman's arms : lend none.
A teacher's flattering wonder harms a boy.
Talking with sages, use but scanty words.
Firmness of mind will make fine character.
Blest he who states his case to wisdom's ear. 10
As the heart feels, so much the worth of words.
New friends must not be set before the old.
By noble traits make yours an honoured name.
Who gains by friend who stands no test of use?
Truth ever honourably declares herself. 15
Do not grow used to evil acts or words.
You'll bear more lightly what the mind fore-knew.
Far heavier seem the strokes which sudden fall.
Blest he who from another's scourging learns.
Goods given to ingrates will bring no reward. 20
Each hour slow moving steers us nearer death.
Praiseworthy none stands out till day of death.
Great teacher he who as he teaches acts.
As you'd be treated, see you treat another.[a]
What you'd not like yourself, don't do to any. 25
Reprove the wise: your words will bring you thanks.
Thy faults, when judge, condemn more than another's.

Sis bonus idque bonis, laesus nec laede nocentem.
Vir prudens animo est melior quam fortis in armis.
Divitias animo iniustas attendere noli.   30
Semper avarus amat mendacia furta rapinas.
Invidiae maculat famam mala pestis honestam.
Nil sine consilio facias : sic facta probantur.
Instanter facias, sors quae tibi tradat agenda.
Improperes numquam, dederis munuscula si qua.   35
Omnia pertractet primum mens verba loquelae.
Sic novus atque novum vinum veterascat amicus.
Alma dies noctem sequitur somnosque labores.
Tempora dum variant, animus sit semper honestus.
Corripe peccantem, noli at dimittere, amicum.   40
Observat sapiens sibi tempus in ore loquendi ;
insipiens loquitur spretum sine tempore verbum.
Iam magnum reddis modico tu munus amico,
si ipsum ut amicus amas : amor est pretiosior auro.
Dives erit semper, dure qui operatur in agro.   45
Otia qui sequitur, veniet huic semper egestas.
Omnibus est opibus melior vir mente fidelis.
Qui bona sectatur prima bene surgit in hora.
Multorum profert sapientis lingua salutem.
Hostili in bello dominatur dextera fortis.   50
Lingua ligata tibi multos acquirit amicos.
Diligit hic natum, virga qui corripit illum.

41 forte *Baehrens* : in ore *cod. Fris.*
50 hostili *Baehrens* : hostibus *cod. Fris.*
51 ligata tibi *Baehrens* : placata sibi *cod. Fris.*

Treat well the good: though harmed, harm not the
    bad.
Men sage in mind excel the brave in arms.
To unfair money-getting give no heed.   30
Greed ever loves lies, theft and robbery.
Fair fame is soiled by envy's cursed plague.
Do naught uncounselled: so are deeds approved.
What chance hands you to do, do earnestly.
Never upbraid for any gifts you give.   35
Thought, words and language first must handle all.[a]
Let time mature new friends just like new wine
Kind day comes after night, toil after sleep.
Times change: let honour always rule the mind.
Reprove, but don't let go, your erring friend.   40
Wise men respect the hour for utterance ;
Fools out of season utter worthless trash.
To a humble friend you give a handsome gift
In friendly love: love counts for more than gold.
Rich he'll be ever who toils hard afield.   45
The quest of ease will in its trail bring want.
The man of trusty mind excels all wealth.
Who aims at gear is smart to rise at dawn.
The sage's tongue reveals the health of many.[b]
In fighting foes, the strong right hand is lord.   50
A tongue fast bound procures you many a friend.[c]
He loves his son who chides him with the rod.[d]

---

  [a] *i.e.* reflection and discussion should precede action.
  [b] *i.e.* gives advice which, if acted on, will secure the general
welfare.
  [c] *i.e.* silence may be golden in avoiding offence to others.
  [d] This may be influenced by the Scriptures : *e.g. Prov.* xiii.
24 " He that spareth his rod hateth his son; but he that
loveth him chasteneth him betimes."

MINOR LATIN POETS

LINES ON THE MUSES

The lines on the Muses were well known in the Middle Ages, and, according to Baehrens, may well be the work of the composer of the *Disticha*. They are found in the following, among other, MSS.:—

A = Turicensis 78: saec. ix.
B = Caroliruhensis 36 f.: saec. ix–x.

CATONIS DE MUSIS VERSUS

Cᴌɪᴏ gesta canens transactis tempora reddit.
dulciloquis calamos Euterpe flatibus urguet.
comica lascivo gaudet sermone Thalia.
Melpomene tragico proclamat maesta boatu.
Terpsichore affectus citharis movet impetrat auget.
plectra gerens Erato saltat pede carmine vultu.
signat cuncta manu loquiturque Polymnia gestu.
Urania ⟨arce⟩ poli motus scrutatur et astra.
carmina Calliope libris heroica mandat.
mentis Apollineae vis has movet undique Musas,   1
in medioque sedens complectitur omnia Phoebus.

³ comicolas civo A : lascivio E.
⁵ impetrat *Baehrens* : imperat *codd. omnes.*
⁷⁻⁹ *ita ponunt* DE : 8, 9, 7 *collocant* ABC *et ceteri omnes.*
⁸ Urania arce poli *Baehrens* : Urania poli *codd. omnes* (poliq. B) : Uranie caeli *vulgo.*
¹¹ medioque sedens *Baehrens* : medio residens *codd. omnes* (*aut* 10 *aut* 11 *spurium putat Riese*).

ᵃ *Cf.* p. 434, *supra*, lines *De Musis* ascribed to Florus. The ascription of the above verses to "Cato" is doubtful. Burman, *Anthol. Lat.*, *Lib. I.* No. 74, gives the heading "Musarum

CATO

C = Vossianus L.Q. 33 : saec. x.
D = Cantabrigiensis, Collegii S. Trinit. O. 4. 11 :
    saec. x–xi.
E = Parisinus 7930 : saec. xi.

The title in A is simply *Nomina Musarum* ; but
two MSS. ascribe the lines to Cato, viz. B *Versus
Catonis de musis vel nominibus philorum* (*sic*) and
C *Incipiunt versus Catonis philosophi de novem musis.*

LINES ON THE MUSES [a]

To recreate the past is Clio's theme :
Euterpe plies the pipes with tuneful breath
Thalia's joy is playful comedy :
Melpomene utters woe with tragic cry :
Terpsichore's lute moves, wins and swells the heart :
Lyric the song, dance, smile of Erato :
Polymnia's hand marks all—she speaks in act : [b]
Urania scans the sky and moving stars :
Calliope records heroic lays.
Apollo's varied thought each Muse inspires : [c]
So Phoebus, mid them throned, combines their
    charms.

Inventa " and cites the parallel lines from the *Anthologia
Graeca.*

[b] Polymnia or Polyhymnia was traditionally the Muse
of sacred song, but varied provinces were at different periods
assigned to her—rhetoric and even agriculture and geometry.
A wall-painting from Herculaneum associated her with μύθους
(*fabulas*). It was a late development to assign *pantomimus*
to her patronage, and the line refers to the expression of
everything by gesture.

[c] Apollo, as their patron, was known as *Musagetes.*

EPITAPH ON VITALIS THE MIME-ACTOR

This poem is subjoined to the *Disticha Catonis* in the following manuscripts:
A = Turicensis 78 : saec. ix.
B = Reginensis 2078 : saec. ix–x.
C = Parisinus 2772 : saec. x–xi.
D = Reginensis 1414 : saec. xi.
E = Parisinus 8319 : saec. xi.

A gives no title : D gives *Epitaphium Vitalis Mimi Filii Catonis*, which Baehrens accepts : BC give

---

EPITAPHIUM VITALIS MIMI [FILII CATONIS]

QUID tibi, Mors, faciam, quae nulli parcere nosti ?
  nescis laetitiam, nescis amare iocos.
his ego praevalui toto notissimus orbi,
  hinc mihi larga domus, hinc mihi census erat.
gaudebam semper.   quid enim, si gaudia desint,   5
  hic vagus ac fallax utile mundus habet ?
me viso rabidi subito cecidere furores ;
  ridebat summus me veniente dolor.
non licuit quemquam curis mordacibus uri
  nec rerum incerta mobilitate trahi.   10
vincebat cunctos praesentia nostra timores
  et mecum felix quaelibet hora fuit.
motibus ac dictis, tragica quoque veste placebam
  exhilarans variis tristia corda modis.
fingebam vultus, habitus ac verba loquentum,   15
  ut plures uno crederēs ore loqui.

² amara *coni. Burman.*
⁹ curis mordacibus uri *Baehrens* : mordacibus urere curis *codd.* (ordac. B.   curris B, C *m.* 1).
636

CATO

Epitafium filii Cat(h)onis ; and E *Epitaphiū Vitalis mimi.* Burman, *Anth. Lat., Lib.* IV. No. 20, and Meyer, *Anth. vet. Lat.*, 1173, have the poem under the heading *Vitalis mimi.* Its late period is shown in the shortening of the final syllable in *nescis* l. 2 and *crederes* l. 16. The German monk Ermenrich of the ninth century, writing to Grimald, cites *nescis* as a trochee " in epitaphio Catonis Censorini dicentis " (where *dicentis*, it may be guessed, is an attempt to include the lines as among *Dicta Catonis*).

EPITAPH ON VITALIS THE MIME-ACTOR

How shall I treat thee, Death, who sparest none?
Thou knowst not mirth, knowst not the love of fun :
Yet all the world in these my merit knew—
Hence came my mansion, hence my revenue.
I always wore a smile : if smiles be lost,
What boots a world in wayward trickery tossed?
At sight of me wild frenzy met relief :
My entrance changed to laughter poignant grief.
None felt the canker of anxiety
Nor worried mid this world's uncertainty.
O'er every fear my presence won success :
An hour with me was ever happiness.
In tragic rôle my word and act could please,
Cheering in myriad ways hearts ill at ease :
Through change in look, mien, voice I so could run
That many seemed to use the lips of one.

---

¹³ veste *Buecheler* : verba *codd.* : voce *Pithoeus.*
¹⁵ angebam CD.   loquentū E *corr.* : loquentur *codd.*
¹⁶ crederis *codd., nisi quod in* A e *supra* i m. 1 *est positum.*

ipse etiam, quem nostra oculis geminabat imago,
 horruit in vultus se magis isse meos.
o quotiens imitata meos per femina gestus
 vidit et erubuit totaque muta fuit! 2●
ergo quot in nostro vivebant corpore formae,
 tot mecum raptas abstulit atra dies.
quo vos iam tristi turbatus deprecor ore,
 qui titulum legitis cum pietate meum:
" o quam laetus eras, Vitalis " dicite maesti, 2●
 " sint tibi di tali, sint tibi fata modo ! "

---

[19] meos per femina *Baehrens* : meo ≡ se ≡ femine A : meos es semina BCD : meo se femina E. gestus *Baehrens* : gestu *codd.*
[20] muta *Baehrens* : mata CD : mota E : nata B : compta A *interpolate.*
[21] vivebant *Goetz* : videbantur *codd.* (videantur E) : ridebant *Hauthal.*

CATO

The man whose double on the stage I seemed
Shrank, as my looks his very own he deemed.
How oft a woman whom my gestures played
Saw herself, blushed, and held her peace dismayed!
So parts which I made live by mimicry
Dark death hath hurried to the grave with me.[a]
To you who with compassion read this stone
I utter my request in saddened tone:
Say sadly: " Glad, Vitalis, did you live:
Such gladness may the Gods and fates thee give! "

[a] *abstulit atra dies* (22) is from Virg. *Aen.* VI. 429.

---

[22] raptas *Pithoeus* : raptor *codd.* (rapitor E).
[24] titulum *Burman, Schrader* : tumulum *codd.*
[26] di tali *Baehrens* : vitalis *codd., nisi quod* vitalis *m.* l *in* dii tales *corr.* A.   fata *Heinsius* : laeta *codd. e glossa.*

PHOENIX

INTRODUCTION

TO PHOENIX

It is not surprising that poets and historians, Latin as well as Greek, should have felt the magnetism of legends concerning the phoenix, a strange Eastern bird of brilliantly varied plumage, reappearing in loneliness at long cyclic intervals after an aromatic and musical death, which was at once a mysterious loss and a mysterious renewal of life. Even in its pagan forms—for it varied considerably in detail—the story had undeniable attraction.[a] The earliest reference traceable is one in Hesiod[b] to the bird's longevity. Herodotus' contact with Egypt impelled him to mention the story of its re-emergence at Heliopolis every 500 years—a cyclic period doubled and even further increased by other

---

[a] See W. H. Roscher *Ausführliches Lexicon der griech. u. röm. Mythologie*, 1902–1909, III. 2. col. 3450–3472 for an account of the Phoenix (Φοῖνιξ) in literature and in both pagan and Christian art, *e.g.* on coins as a symbol of eternity and rejuvenation. Here it must suffice to select some representative references : Herod. II. 73 ; Ovid *Am.* II. vi. 54, *Met.* XV. 392–407 ; Stat. *Silv.* II. iv. 36 ; Sen. *Epist.* xlii. 1 ; Pliny, *N.H.* X. 3–5 ; Tac. *Ann.* VI. 28 ; Aur. Vict. *De Caesaribus* 4 ; Claudian, *De Cons. Stil.* II. 414–420, *Carm. min.* xxvii (xliv).

[b] Fragm. 163 (222), 3–4, ed. Goettling, 1878 = Loeb ed. of Hesiod, etc., p. 74. αὐτὰρ ὁ φοῖνιξ ἐννέα μὲν κόρακας (sc. γηράσκεται), "the phoenix lives nine times longer than the raven." The idea is echoed in the "reparabilis ales" of Ausonius, Bk. VII. *Eclog.* v. 5–6 (Loeb ed.).

authorities. Ovid fitted the description of the nest into the last book of his *Metamorphoses*; and at a subsequent date Statius conceived the fancy of a still happier phoenix untouched by the lethargy of age. The rarity of the fabulous bird struck Seneca as a good analogy to the infrequent occurrence of a perfect Stoic sage. Pliny in his *Natural History* touches with considerable minuteness upon the bird's nest of spices, its habits, and the growth of its offspring; while the news that it had been seen in Egypt in the year A.D. 34 draws from Tacitus an account of its periodic death and the transport of the father's body by the new phoenix to the altar of the Sun. Towards the end of the classical period we note the continued attraction of the theme for Claudian, not only in an elaborate simile of half a dozen lines in his *De Consulatu Stilichonis*, but also in the 110 hexameters which he almost certainly modelled upon our extant elegiac *Phoenix*. This is most commonly ascribed to Lactantius, the pupil of Arnobius in oratory, who was professor of rhetoric at Nicomedia early in the fourth century and who later in the West became the instructor of Prince Crispus by the invitation of Constantine. As his conversion from paganism did not divorce him from ancient culture, Lactantius attained distinction among early Christian authors for the beauty and eloquence of his Latin style.

But no more surprising than the semi-romantic pagan appeal of the phoenix fable is the fact that Christian writers should have found an added symbolic fascination in such features as its Oriental paradise and its resurrection to life through death. *Prima facie*, then, there seems little to startle one

in the ascription to Lactantius; but, in fact, the
authorship of the *Phoenix* has long been under dis-
cussion. It is easy to discover in the poem both
pagan and Christian constituents. Baehrens indeed
argues that the pagan element is enough to invali-
date the traditional ascription (supported by certain
MSS.[a] of the poem) to so unquestionably Christian
an author. To meet this objection Brandt has
argued that the *Phoenix* was composed by Lactantius
before his conversion; and Pichon, who minimises
the Christian colour, is so sure that the pagan
touches would have been unacceptable to a Christian,
that he holds the only possible alternatives to be
the composition of the poem either by Lactantius
at a pre-Christian stage or by a different author who
was pagan. Yet such "contamination" of con-
flicting strains does not seem to be an insuperable
barrier to the prevailing belief: indeed it is rather
to be expected in the age and circumstances of
Lactantius. Baehrens, who, like Ribbeck, rejects
the Lactantian authorship, is not convinced by
Dechent's study of similarities in phraseology be-
tween our poem and the unquestioned works of
Lactantius. As regards the testimony by Gregory
of Tours [b] in the sixth century to a poem on the
phoenix which he summarises and ascribes to Lac-
tantius, Baehrens eventually concluded [c] that Gregory

---

[a] See the Sigla.

[b] *De cursu stellarum* 12, p. 861. Our poem is quoted eight
times under the name of Lactantius in a short anonymous
treatise *de dubiis nominibus* (between Isidore of Seville and the
ninth century); and it is significant that Alcuin cites Lactantius
as a Christian poet in his list of books in the library at York
(F. Dümmler, *Poet. lat. aev. Carol.* I. p. 204).

[c] *P.L.M.* III. pp. 250–252.

had not before him the same poem as we have, but a lost one by Lactantius. On Jerome's authority we know that Lactantius wrote a ὁδοιπορικόν from Africa to Nicomedia, presumably when he went on Diocletian's invitation to teach rhetoric in that city; and it is Baehrens' suggestion that into this narrative of his own journey eastwards he might have appropriately worked an account of the fabled Oriental bird, using our extant poem (according to Baehrens, by a pagan) but adding Christian colour. The hypothesis next assumes that after the supposed disappearance of Lactantius' poem monkish copyists made an incorrect ascription of the surviving poem to the " Christian Cicero," being misled by the outward resemblances in it to Christian ideas and by the knowledge that a *Phoenix* had actually been composed by Lactantius. It will be noted that the monks, if this guess be true, did not find the paganism of the poem so much of a stumbling-block as Baehrens and Pichon have done. But the majority of critics, including Ebert, Manitius, Riese, Birt and Dechent, have been satisfied with a less elaborate theory and have accepted our poem as Lactantius' authentic work.

For English readers the *Phoenix* possesses special historical and literary interest as the basis of an early Anglo-Saxon *Phoenix* in alliterative accentual verse. Its author, whether the Northumbrian Cynewulf or not—for here too there is a dispute—undoubtedly modelled the earlier portion of his poem upon the extant Latin poem. Here again, as in the original, we meet the earthly paradise, partly a plain, partly " a fair forest where fruits fall not " (*wuduholt wynlic, waestmas ne dreosaδ*).

PHOENIX

Here too, familiar as in the ancient source, are the bird's unrivalled notes of song, its flight to the Syrian palm-tree in the fullness of a thousand years, the building of its nest, its own admirable beauty, its strange death and birth to fresh life. But the adaptation is free. The English borrower omits as he wishes. Phaethon and Deucalion vanish. Phoebus' car becomes " God's candle." Even the texture of the Anglo-Saxon proem on the far Eastern land where the marvellous bird dwells is interwoven with Biblical thought. Such expansion is still more noticeable in the later part, where a transition is made from the mystery of the phoenix's sex and birth to analogies with the life of the elect; and, when the ways of the phoenix are treated as symbolic of the Christian life, the English poem departs entirely from the Latin original.

EDITIONS

Apart from editions of Lactantius (*e.g. ed. princeps*, Rome, 1468; M. Thomasius, Antwerp, 1570; Gallaeus, Leyden, 1660):

Gryphiander. Jena, 1618.
Burman. In his *Claudian*. Amsterdam, 1760.
Wernsdorf. In *P.L.M.* III. Altenburg, 1782.
A. Martini. Lüneburg, 1825.
H. Leyser. Quedlinburg, 1839.
A. Riese. In *Anthol. Lat.* 1863; ed. 2. Leipzig, 1906.
L. Jeep. In his *Claudian*, vol. ii. Leipzig, 1879.
E. Baehrens. In *P.L.M.* III. Leipzig, 1881.

INTRODUCTION TO

RELEVANT WORKS

A. **Ebert.** In *Allgemeine Geschichte der Lit. des Mittelalters im Abendlande.* Leipzig, 1874, ed. 2, 1889.

G. **Goetz.** In *Acta Societ. philol. Lips.* V. p. 319 *sqq.*

H. **Klapp.** In *Progr. gymn. Wandsbeckiani.* 1875.

A. **Riese.** *Ueber den Phoenix des Lactantius, Rh. Mus.* xxxi. 1876.

H. **Dechent.** *Ueber die Echtheit des Phoenix von Lactantius, Rh. Mus.* xxxv. 1880, pp. 39–55.

M. **Manitius.** In *Geschichte der christl.-latein. Poesie.* Stuttgart, 1891.

O. **Ribbeck.** In *Geschichte der röm. Dichtung,* III. p. 364. Stuttgart, 1892.

S. **Brandt.** *Zum Phoenix des Lactantius, Rh. Mus.* xlvii. 1892.

A. **Knappitsch.** *De Lactantii Ave Phoenice.* Graz, 1896.

R. **Pichon.** *Lactance : Étude sur le mouvement philosophique et religieux sous le règne de Constantin.* Paris, 1901.

C. **Pascal.** *Sul carme de ave Phoenice.* Naples, 1904.

————. *I carmi De Phoenice* in *Letteratura latina medievale*: Nuovi Saggi. Catania, 1909.

C. **Landi.** *De Ave Phoenice : il carme e il suo autore* in *Atti e memorie di Padova,* 31, 1914–1915.

SIGLA

(As in Baehrens' *P.L.M.* III. pp. 247–249.)

A = Parisinus 13048 : saec. viii, scriptura langobardica exaratus inter Venantii Fortunati poemata, fol. 47ᵃ–48ᵇ versus 1–110, sine titulo exhibens.

PHOENIX

B = codex bibliothecae capitularis Veronensis 163:
saec. ix, continens Claudianum maxime cuius
post " Phoenicem " legitur nostrum carmen,
fol. 14ᵃ–19ᵇ, cum hac inscriptione *item Lacta(n)tii
de eadem ave.*

C = Vossianus L.Q. 33: saec. x: fol. 73ᵃ–75ᵇ,
versus Lactantii de ave Phoenice habet.

O = consensus codicum melioris notae vel communis
archetypus.

CODICES INTERPOLATI

D = codex Cantabrigiensis [Bibl. Univers. Gg. 5.35]:
saec. xi, qui inter multa poemata christiana
fol. 168ᵃ–170ᵇ, habet " Phoenicem " praemisso
titulo: *Incipit libellus de fenice, paradisi ut
fertur habitatrice. Quidam ferunt Lactantium
hunc scripsisse libellum.*

E = Bodleianus F. 2. 14: saec. xii, fol. 126ᵇ–128ᵇ,
sine inscriptione libellum continens.

ς = pauca quae correctiora leguntur in codicibus
saeculo xiv maximeque xv scriptis.

[For the large number of late and inferior manu-
scripts see A. Martini's edition, 1825.]

DE AVE PHOENICE

Est locus in primo felix oriente remotus,
   qua patet aeterni maxima porta poli,
nec tamen aestivos hiemisve propinquus ad ortus,
   sed qua Sol verno fundit ab axe diem.
illic planities tractus diffundit apertos,   5
   nec tumulus crescit nec cava vallis hiat,
sed nostros montes, quorum iuga celsa putantur,
   per bis sex ulnas imminet ille locus.
hic Solis nemus est et consitus arbore multa
   lucus perpetuae frondis honore virens.   10
cum Phaethonteis flagrasset ab ignibus axis,
   ille locus flammis inviolatus erat;
et cum diluvium mersisset fluctibus orbem
   Deucalioneas exsuperavit aquas.
non huc exsangues Morbi, non aegra Senectus   15
   nec Mors crudelis nec Metus asper adest
nec Scelus infandum nec opum vesana Cupido
   aut Ira aut ardens caedis amore Furor;
Luctus acerbus abest et Egestas obsita pannis
   et Curae insomnes et violenta Fames.   20
non ibi tempestas nec vis furit horrida venti
   nec gelido terram rore pruina tegit;

[16] adest AB : adit CDE.
[18] aut metus O (*cf. v. 16*) : aut Mars *edd. vet.* : Venus *Oudendorp* : Pavor *Goetz* : Letum *Riese* : huc meat *Birt* : aut Ira *Baehrens*.

PHOENIX

There is a far-off land, blest amid the first streaks of dawn, where standeth open the mightiest portal of the everlasting sky, yet not beside the risings of the summer or the winter Sun, but where he sheds daylight from the heavens in spring. There a plain spreads out its open levels; no knoll swells there, no hollow valley gapes, yet that region o'ertops by twice six ells our mountains whose ridges are reckoned high. Here is the grove of the Sun, a woodland planted with many a tree and green with the honours of eternal foliage. When the sky went ablaze from the fires of Phaethon's car, that region was inviolate from the flames;[a] it rose above the waters on which Deucalion sailed, when the flood had whelmed the world in its waves.[b] Hither no bloodless Diseases come, no sickly Eld, nor cruel Death nor desperate Fear nor nameless Crime nor maddened Lust for wealth or Wrath or Frenzy afire with the love of murder; bitter Grief is absent and Beggary beset with rags and sleepless Cares and violent Hunger.[c] No tempest raveth there nor savage force of wind: nor does the hoar-frost shroud the ground in chilly

[a] For Phaethon's disastrous driving of the car of his father Apollo see Ovid, *Met.* II. 1–332.
[b] Deucalion's ark saved him and Pyrrha during the primeval deluge.
[c] The personifications are largely based on Virg. *Aen.* VI. 274 *sqq.*

nulla super campos tendit sua vellera nubes
   nec cadit ex alto turbidus umor aquae.
sed fons in medio, quem vivum nomine dicunt,   25
   perspicuus, lenis, dulcibus uber aquis;
qui semel erumpens per singula tempora mensum
   duodeciens undis irrigat omne nemus.
hic genus arboreum procero stipite surgens
   non lapsura solo mitia poma gerit.   30

hoc nemus, hos lucos avis incolit unica Phoenix,
   unica, si vivit morte refecta sua.
paret et obsequitur Phoebo memoranda satelles:
   hoc Natura parens munus habere dedit.
lutea cum primum surgens Aurora rubescit,   35
   cum primum rosea sidera luce fugat,
ter quater illa pias immergit corpus in undas,
   ter quater e vivo gurgite libat aquam.
tollitur ac summo considit in arboris altae
   vertice, quae totum despicit una nemus,   40
et conversa novos Phoebi nascentis ad ortus
   exspectat radios et iubar exoriens.
atque ubi Sol pepulit fulgentis limina portae
   et primi emicuit luminis aura levis,
incipit illa sacri modulamina fundere cantus   45
   et mira lucem voce ciere novam,
quam nec aedoniae voces nec tibia possit
   musica Cirrheis adsimulare modis;

[25] sed O : est *Baehrens*.
[32] sed O : si (= siquidem) *Baehrens*.
[33] memoranda O : veneranda *Baehrens*.
[47] voces O : fauces *Baehrens*.

damp. Above the plains no cloud stretches its fleece, nor falleth from on high the stormy moisture of rain. But there is a well in the midst, the well of life they call it, crystal-clear, gently-flowing, rich in its sweet waters: bursting forth once for each several month in its season, it drenches all the grove twelve times with its flood. Here is a kind of tree that rising with stately stem bears mellow fruits which will not fall to the ground.

In this grove, in these woods, dwells the peerless bird,[a] the Phoenix, peerless, since she lives renewed by her own death. An acolyte worthy of record,[b] she yields obedience and homage to Phoebus: such the duty that parent Nature assigned to her for observance. Soon as saffron Aurora reddens at her rising, soon as she routs the stars with rosy light, thrice and again that bird plunges her body into the kindly waves, thrice and again sips water from the living flood. Soaring she settles on the topmost height of a lofty tree which alone commands the whole of the grove, and, turning towards the fresh rising of Phoebus at his birth, awaits the emergence of his radiant beam. And when the Sun has struck the threshold of the gleaming portal and the light shaft of his first radiance has flashed out, she begins to pour forth notes of hallowed minstrelsy and to summon the new day in a marvellous key which neither tune of nightingale nor musical pipe could rival in

[a] " alone of its kind," " unparalleled " : *cf.* Ovid *Am.* II. vi. 54, *et vivax phoenix, unica semper avis.*

[b] In most accounts the phoenix appears as a male bird (*pater*, etc.). Contrast, however, Ovid's *unica avis* (*l.c.*) with Claudian's *Titanius ales* (*Carm. Min.* xxvii.7) and his *idem* (masc.) in *De Cons. Stil.* II. 415. Aurelius Victor, *De Caesaribus* 4, has *quam volucrem* in reference to the phoenix.

sed neque olor moriens imitari posse putetur
    nec Cylleneae fila canora lyrae.   50

postquam Phoebus equos in aperta effudit Olympi
    atque orbem totum protulit usque means,
illa ter alarum repetito verbere plaudit
    igniferumque caput ter venerata silet.
atque eadem celeres etiam discriminat horas   55
    innarrabilibus nocte dieque sonis,
antistes luci nemorumque verenda sacerdos
    et sola arcanis conscia, Phoebe, tuis.
quae postquam vitae iam mille peregerit annos
    ac sibi reddiderint tempora longa gravem,   60
ut reparet lapsum spatiis vergentibus aevum,
    adsuetum nemoris dulce cubile fugit;
cumque renascendi studio loca sancta reliquit,
    tunc petit hunc orbem, Mors ubi regna tenet.
derigit in Syriam celeres longaeva volatus,   65
    Phoenicen nomen cui dedit ipsa vetus,
securosque petit deserta per avia lucos,
    hic ubi per saltus silva remota latet.
tum legit aerio sublimem vertice palmam,
    quae Graium Phoenix ex ave nomen habet,   70
in quam nulla nocens animans prorepere possit,
    lubricus aut serpens aut avis ulla rapax.

    [49] sed O : et *Baehrens.*
    [60] ac si A : ac se BCDE : et sic *Barth* : ac sibi *Hoeufft.*
    [65] dirigit O : derigit *Baehrens.*
    [66] vetus DE : vaetus A : vetustas BC : Venus *Heinsius.*
    [68] sic ubi post DE : hic ubi per *edd. vet.*
    [70] Graium A : gratum *ceteri.*
    [71] prorepere A : proripere B : prorumpere *ceteri.*

---

    [a] From Cirrha near Parnassus.
    [b] An allusion to Mercury's early association with Mount
Cyllene in Arcadia.

PHOENIX

Cirrhean [a] modes; nay, let not the dying swan be thought capable of imitating it, nor yet the tuneful strings of Cyllenean [b] lyre.

After Phoebus has given his steeds the rein into the open heavens and in ever onward course brought forth his full round orb,[c] then that bird with thrice repeated beat of the wing yields her applause, and after three obeisances to the fire-bearing prince holds her peace. She it is also who marks off the swift hours by day and night in sounds which may not be described, priestess of the grove and awe-inspiring ministrant of the woods, the only confidant of thy mysteries, Phoebus. When she has already fulfilled a thousand years of life [d] and long lapse of time has made it burdensome to her, she flees from her sweet and wonted nest in the grove, so that in the closing span she may restore her bygone existence, and when in passion for re-birth she has left her sacred haunts, then she seeks this world where Death holds sovereignty. Despite her length of years she directs her swift flight into Syria, to which she herself of old gave the name of " Phoenice," and seeks through desert wilds the care-free groves, here where the sequestered woodland lurks among the glades. Then she chooses a palm-tree towering with airy crest which bears its Greek name " Phoenix " from the bird: against it no hurtful living creature could steal forth, or slippery serpent, or any bird of

[c] Possibly " revealed the whole wide world " (*cf.* Virg. *Aen.* IV. 118).

[d] Tac. *Ann.* VI. 28 gives 500 years as the usually accepted length of the Phoenix-cycle, but he mentions also 1461 years (*i.e.* the "magnus annus" = $365\frac{1}{4} \times 4$). Martial V. vii. 2 gives *decem saecula*, and Pliny 1000 years, a round figure adopted by Claudian and Ausonius.

tum ventos claudit pendentibus Aeolus antris,
    ne violent flabris aera purpureum,
neu concreta Noto nubes per inania caeli   7
    submoveat radios solis et obsit avi.
construit inde sibi seu nidum sive sepulcrum:
    nam perit ut vivat, se tamen ipsa creat.
colligit huic sucos et odores divite silva,
    quos legit Assyrius, quos opulentus Arabs,   8
quos aut Pygmeae gentes aut India carpit
    aut molli generat terra Sabaea sinu.
cinnamon hic auramque procul spirantis amomi
    congerit et mixto balsama cum folio.
non casiae mitis nec olentis vimen acanthi   8
    nec turis lacrimae guttaque pinguis abest.
his addit teneras nardi pubentis aristas
    et sociat murrae vim, Panachaea, tuae.
protinus instructo corpus mutabile nido
    vitalique toro membra vieta locat.   9
ore dehinc sucos membris circumque supraque
    inicit exsequiis immoritura suis.
tunc inter varios animam commendat odores,
    depositi tanti nec timet illa fidem.

       [79] hinc O : huc *Riese* : huic *Baehrens.*
       [88] panacea *ς Wernsdorf.*
       [90] quieta CDE : quiete AB : vieta *Heinsius.*

    [a] Cf. Claudian, *Carm. Min.* xxvii. 44, *bustumque sibi partumque futurum.*
    [b] The Pygmies were considered legendary dwarfs of Egypt or Ethiopia : the allusions are to both African and Asiatic spices.
    [c] *terra Sabaea* = Arabia Felix, whose chief town Saba was famed for its myrrh and frankincense.
    [d] Cf. Ovid, *Met.* XV. 398, *nardi lenis aristas.*

prey. Then Aeolus imprisons the winds in over-arching grottoes, lest their blasts harass the bright-gleaming air, or the cloud-wrack from the South banish the sunrays throughout the empty tracts of heaven and do harm to the bird. Thereafter she builds herself a cradle or sepulchre [a]—which you will—for she dies to live and yet begets herself. She gathers for it from the rich forest juicy scented herbs such as the Assyrian gathers or the wealthy Arabian, such as either the Pygmaean races or India [b] culls or the Sabaean [c] land produces in its soft bosom. Here she heaps together cinnamon and effluence of the aromatic shrub that sends its breath afar and balsam with its blended leaf. Nor is there lacking a slip of mild casia or fragrant acanthus or the rich dropping tears of frankincense. Thereto she adds the tender ears [d] of downy spikenard, joining as its ally the potency of thy myrrh, Pana-chaea.[e] Forthwith in the nest she has furnished she sets her body that awaits its change—withered limbs on a life-giving couch: thereafter with her beak she casts the scents on her limbs, around them and above, being appointed to die in her own funeral.[f] Then she commends her soul [g] amid the varied fragrances without a fear for the trustworthiness of

[e] The usual form is *Panchaïa*, a fabled island east of Arabia, famous for precious stones and myrrh. *Cf.* Virg. *Georg.* II. 139 : Plin. *N.H.* X. 4.

[f] This paradoxical idea is introduced by the preceding lines which picture the bird as laying out her own body, and, by throwing perfumes on herself, performing a ritual usually assigned to mourners: *immoritura* is echoed in 95, *corpus genitali morte peremptum.*

[g] One of the Christian notes in the poem : *cf.* 64, *hunc orbem mors ubi regna tenet.* With 94 *cf.* 2 Timothy I. 12.

interea corpus genitali morte peremptum   9]

  aestuat et flammam parturit ipse calor,

aetherioque procul de lumine concipit ignem :

  flagrat et ambustum solvitur in cineres.

quos velut in massam cineres umore coactos

  conflat ; et effectum seminis instar habet.   10(

hinc animal primum sine membris fertur oriri,

  sed fertur vermi lacteus esse color :

creverit immensum subito cum tempore certo

  seque ovi teretis colligit in speciem,

inde reformatur quali fuit ante figura   105

  et Phoenix ruptis pullulat exuviis :

ac velut agrestes, cum filo ad saxa tenentur,

  mutari tineae papilione solent.

non illi cibus est nostro consuetus in orbe

  nec cuiquam implumem pascere cura subest ;   11(

ambrosios libat caelesti nectare rores,

  stellifero tenues qui cecidere polo.

hos legit, his alitur mediis in odoribus ales,

  donec maturam proferat effigiem.

ast ubi primaeva coepit florere iuventa,   115

  evolat ad patrias iam reditura domus.

ante tamen, proprio quicquid de corpore restat,

  ossaque vel cineres exuviasque suas,

    [99] in more ABC : in morte D, *Wernsdorf* : in monte E : umore *Ritschl, Baehrens* : *alii alia.*
    [103] it tener in densum duratus *Baehrens* : *alii alia.*
    [107-108] *post* 102 *ponit Baehrens.*
    [108] pinnae AB : pennae *ceteri* : tineae *Didacus Couarruvias episcopus Segobiensis, teste Thomasio* : *cf. Ovid, Met.* XV. 372-4.
    [109] concessus O : consuetus *Baehrens.*
    [110] *in verbis* cura subest *desinit codex* A.

658

PHOENIX

a deposit so great. Meanwhile her body, by birth-giving death destroyed, is aglow, the very heat producing flame and catching fire from the ethereal light afar: it blazes and when burned dissolves into ashes. These ashes she welds together, as if they were concentrated by moisture in a mass, possessing in the result what takes the place of seed.[a] Therefrom, 'tis said, rises a living creature first of all without limbs, but this worm is said to have a milky colour: when suddenly at the appointed hour it has grown enormously, gathering into what looks like a rounded egg, from it she is remoulded in such shape as she had before, bursting her shell and springing to life a Phoenix: 'tis even so that larvae in the country fastened by their threads[b] to stones are wont to change into a butterfly. Hers is no food familiar in this world of ours: 'tis no one's charge to feed the bird as yet unfledged: she sips ambrosial dews of heavenly nectar fallen in a fine shower from the star-bearing sky. Such is her culling, such her sustenance, encompassed by fragrant spices until she bring her appearance to maturity. But when she begins to bloom in the spring-time of her youth, she flits forth already bent on a return to her ancestral abodes. Yet ere she goes, she takes all that remains of what was her own body—bones or ashes and the shell that was hers—and stores it

[a] The simile from metallurgy seems violent as applied to a substance endowed with the seeds of life. With *umore coactos* cf. Virg. *G.* IV. 172–173 *stridentia tingunt aera lacu*, of dipping metal in the blacksmith's watertank.

[b] The passage, like Ovid, *Met.* XV. 372–4, has silkworms in view. Thomasius thought *saxa* should be *taxa*, presumably in the sense of yew branches, an invention of which Wernsdorf does not approve.

unguine balsameo murraque et ture soluto
  condit et in formam conglobat ore pio.   12

quam pedibus gestans contendit Solis ad urbem
  inque ara residens ponit in aede sacra.

mirandam sese praestat praebetque videnti:
  tantus avi decor est, tantus abundat honor.

principio color est qualis sub sidere caeli   12
  mitia quem corio punica grana tegunt;

qualis inest foliis, quae fert agreste papaver,
  cum pandit vestes Flora rubente polo.

hoc umeri pectusque decens velamine fulget,
  hoc caput, hoc cervix summaque terga nitent;   13

caudaque porrigitur fulvo distincta metallo,
  in cuius maculis purpura mixta rubet;

alarum pennas lux pingit discolor, Iris
  pingere ceu nubes desuper acta solet;

albicat insignis mixto viridante smaragdo   1
  et puro cornu gemmea cuspis hiat;

---

121 ortus O (*e versu* 41): urbem *ed. Gryphiandri* 1618.
123 vehentes B: vehentis E: videnti *vulgo*: verendam
Baehrens.
124 ubi B: ibi CDE: avi *Heinsius*.
125-6 principio O: puniceus *Heinsius*: purpureus *Burman*:
praecipuus *Baehrens*: qualis sub sidere caeli O: qualis sub
cortice laevi *Heinsius*. qu(a)e croceo BE: qui croceo CD:
quem croceum *Heinsius*: quae corio *Goetz*. legunt O: tegunt
Heinsius: quali sunt, sidere Cancri mitia quae corio, Punica,
grana tegunt *Baehrens*.
128 flore O: Flora *vulgo*. caelo BC: polo B *m.* 2: flore
rubente novo *Baehrens*.
131 fulvo BC: flavo DE. distenta BC: distincta DE: *cf.
vers.* 141.

in balsam oil, myrrh, and frankincense set free,[a]
rounding it into ball-shape with loving beak. Bear-
ing this in her talons she speeds to the City of the
Sun,[b] and perching on the altar sets it in the hallowed
temple. Marvellous is her appearance and the show
she makes to the onlooker: such comeliness has the
bird, so ample a glory. To begin with, her colour
is like the colour which beneath the sunshine of the
sky ripe pomegranates cover under their rind[c];
like the colour in the petals of the wild poppy when
Flora displays her garb at the blush of dawn. In
such a dress gleam her shoulders and comely breast:
even so glitter head and neck and surface of the
back, while the tail spreads out variegated with a
metallic yellow, amid whose spots reddens a purple
blend. The wing-feathers are picked out by a con-
trasted sheen, as 'tis the heaven-sent rainbow's way
to illuminate the clouds. The beak is of a fine
white with a dash of emerald green, glittering jewel-
like in its clear horn as it opens. You would take

[a] *i.e.* dissolved from the form of roundish tears of gum resin.
[b] The usual form of the legend, as in Ovid, Mela and Tacitus,
gives Heliopolis as the destination, *i.e.* a westward instead of
the eastward flight suggested by *solis ad ortus* of the MSS.
Pliny, *N.H.* X. 4, has *in Solis urbem.*
[c] The text of 125–126 is difficult. Wernsdorf reads *principio
color est, qualis sub cortice laevi* (= *levi*), *mitia quem croceum
punica grana legunt.* Baehrens' text is given in the apparatus
criticus. The editors do not consider either reading satisfact-
ory. For *qualis* followed by the relative *cf.* Liv. VIII. 39,
acies qualis quae esse instructissima potest: Calp. Sic. iv. 160,
talis erit qualis qui . . .

---

[133] harum inter pennas insigneque desuper iris DE:
clarum *Wernsdorf*: alarum *Ritschl.* lux pingit discolor, Iris
Baehrens.
[134] aura O: alta *ς*: acta *Heinsius, Baehrens.*

MINOR LATIN POETS

ingentes oculos credas geminos hyacinthos,
   quorum de medio lucida flamma micat;
aptata est toto capiti radiata corona
   Phoebei referens verticis alta decus;   140
crura tegunt squamae fulvo distincta metallo,
   ast ungues roseo tingit honore color.
effigies inter pavonis mixta figuram
   cernitur et pictam Phasidis inter avem.
magnitiem terris Arabum quae gignitur ales   145
   vix aequare potest, seu fera seu sit avis.
non tamen est tarda, ut volucres quae corpore
     magno
   incessus pigros per grave pondus habent,
sed levis ac velox, regali plena decore:
   talis in adspectu se tenet usque hominum.   150
huc venit Aegyptus tanti ad miracula visus
   et raram volucrem turba salutat ovans.
protinus exsculpunt sacrato in marmore formam
   et titulo signant remque diemque novo.
contrahit in coetum sese genus omne volantum,   155
   nec praedae memor est ulla nec ulla metus.
alituum stipata choro volat illa per altum
   turbaque prosequitur munere laeta pio.
sed postquam puri pervenit ad aetheris auras,
   mox redit; illa suis conditur inde locis.   160
a fortunatae sortis finisque volucrem,
   cui de se nasci praestitit ipse deus!

---

[139] aequataq; O: aptatur *Oudendorp*: aptata est *Ritschl*:
arquata est *Baehrens.* noto BD: notho C: nota E:
toto *Wernsdorf*: croceo *Klapp*: summo *vel* nitido *Ritschl*:
rutilo *Baehrens.*
[161] ad B: at C: a *Is. Vossius*: sat *Baehrens.* filisque
volucrum BC: fatique volucrem *edd. vet.*: finisque volu-
crem *Is. Vossius.*

for twin sapphires those great eyes from between
which shoots a bright flame. All over the head is
fitted a crown of rays, in lofty likeness to the glory
of the Sun-god's head. Scales cover the legs, which
are variegated with a metallic yellow, but the tint
which colours the claws is a wonderful rose. To
the eye it has a blended semblance between the
peacock's appearance and the rich-hued bird from
Phasis.[a] Its size [b] the winged thing that springs
from the Arabs' lands is scarce able to match,
whether wild animal it be or bird.[c] Yet 'tis not
slow like large-sized birds which are of sluggish
movement by reason of their heavy weight, but 'tis
light and swift, filled with a royal grace: such is its
bearing ever to the eyes of men. Egypt draws
nigh to greet the marvel of so great a sight and the
crowd joyfully hails the peerless bird. Straightway
they grave its form on hallowed marble and with a
fresh title mark both the event and the day.[d] Every
breed of fowl unites in the assemblage: no bird
has thoughts of prey nor yet of fear. Attended by
a chorus of winged creatures, she flits through the
high air, and the band escorts her, gladdened by
their pious task. But when the company has reached
the breezes of ether unalloyed, it presently returns:
she ensconces herself in her true haunts. Ah,
bird of happy lot and happy end to whom God's
own will has granted birth from herself! Female or

---

[a] The pheasant.
[b] *magnitiem* is unparalleled.
[c] *ales* is a reference to the ostrich or *strouthiocamelos*,
which was so called from its camel-like neck, and which might
be considered either land animal or bird.
[d] *i.e.* in their joy over the periodic return of the Phoenix.

femina vel mas haec, seu neutrum, seu sit utrumque,
    felix quae veneris foedera nulla colit:
mors illi venus est, sola est in morte voluptas: 16
    ut possit nasci, appetit ante mori.
ipsa sibi proles, suus est pater et suus heres,
    nutrix ipsa sui, semper alumna sibi—
ipsa quidem, sed non eadem quia et ipsa nec ipsa est,
    aeternam vitam mortis adepta bono.   17

[163] *sic Heinsius et Wernsdorf: discrepant codices*: femina
seu mas est seu neutrum: belua felix *Baehrens*.

[164] colit O: coit *Baehrens*.

[169] *sic* ς *et Wernsdorf: omiserunt* et CD: non ⟨eadem est⟩
eademque nec ipsa est *Baehrens*.

male she is, which you will—whether neither or both, a happy bird, she regards not any unions of love: to her, death is love; and her sole pleasure lies in death: to win her birth, it is her appetite first to die. Herself she is her own offspring, her own sire and her own heir, herself her own nurse, her own nurseling evermore—herself indeed, yet not the same; because she is both herself and not herself, gaining eternal life by the boon of death.

AVIANUS

INTRODUCTION

TO THE FABLES OF AVIANUS

In most of the extant MSS. the name of the author of these forty-two fables is given (in the genitive) *Aviani*. Two of our principal MSS. (A and *Rawl.*), however, have *Avieni*. If one may judge from inscriptions, Avianius was a commoner name than Avianus. Between Avienus and Avienius there is not enough material on which to form a judgement. Since, however, there is no trace of the ending *-ii* in any of our MSS., we may venture to limit ourselves to the question of Avianus as against Avienus.

The suggestion has been made that the writer of the fables was identical with Rufius Festus Avienus, author of works entitled *Aratea* and *Descriptio Orbis Terrae*. Chronology agrees, it is true; but there are two grave objections: the fables and the *Aratea* are poles asunder in style; and the author of the *Aratea* is designated in full in the MSS. *Rufi Festi Avieni*, while the prevailing description of the fabulist is simply *Aviani*. A more possible suggestion is that our fabulist was the Avienus who took part in the symposium described in the *Saturnalia* which was written early in the fifth century by Macrobius Theodosius. The theory appears more likely, if we agree that *ad Theodosium* in the title of the dedicatory letter means Macrobius Theodosius [a] and neither of the emperors named Theodosius, although two MSS. (*Ranl.* and *Reg.*) have *imperatorem* in apposition to *Theodosium*. Other arguments are given by Ellis (*Proleg.* p. xiv) in favour of this particular Avienus; but nothing in the way of proof is forthcoming, and the prevalence of " Aviani " in the MSS. militates against it. It seems, then, best to conclude that the fables are the work of an unknown Avianus, who wrote about A.D. 400 in the lifetime of Macrobius and dedicated his work to him.

Cannegieter and Lachmann, denying that the Theodosius of the preface was either of the emperors or Macrobius, argued that Avianus lived in the middle of the second century A.D. Cannegieter based his theory partly on the fact that the preface omits Julius Titianus (a fabulist of about A.D. 200 mentioned by Ausonius) from the list of Avianus' predecessors. Therefore, he held, Avianus must have preceded Titianus. This argument from silence is demolished by Wernsdorf's reply that Avianus' list of fabulists does not profess to be exhaustive. But Cannegieter (like Lachmann in the following century) argued from Avianus' style also. The first impression is that of general metrical correctness marred by some glaring licences and of a Latinity, partly Augustan, partly Silver, combined with a number of violent departures from classical usage. Therefore, according to Cannegieter and Lachmann, the original

---

[a] This hypothesis, originally propounded by Pithou, *Poemat. Vet.* p. 474, has been accepted by many scholars, including Voss, *De Histor. Latinis* ii. 9; Wernsdorf, *P.L.M.* V. 669; L. Müller, *De Phaedri et Av. Libellis*, 32; Baehrens, *P.L.M.* V. 31; Unrein, *De Aviani Aetate*, 60.

THE FABLES OF AVIANUS

Avianus lived in the second century and wrote in classical Latin and in correct metre, while school-masters, rhetoricians, interpolators and copyists are responsible for the depravations.

Since Lachmann's day, however, the date of Babrius [a] the fabulist, whom Avianus mentions and upon whom (as we shall see) he models a great part of his work, has been established by Otto Crusius.[b] Babrius, we now know, wrote under Severus Alexander (222–235 A.D.); and so Avianus must belong to a subsequent age. Moreover, arguments from style really support the view that Avianus flourished about 400 A.D. Many couplets, it may be conceded, particularly in the " promythia " and " epimythia," employed to introduce or conclude some fables, as we now have them, are quite late additions; others can be plausibly emended into classical Latin. Still, there remain some violations of prosody,[c] both defying emendation and occurring in couplets which cannot be dismissed as interpolations without destroying the sense of the fable; while much of the late Latin (see Ellis, *Proleg.* xxx *sqq.*) is embedded in the core of a fable, and must therefore come from the original Avianus. These violations of prosody and this late Latin prevent us from putting the period of Avianus earlier than the later part of the fourth century.

[a] Valerius Babrius composed two books of fables in Greek scazons. The dedication of one of his books is to the son of Severus Alexander. We have in all 137 fables along with fragments. There is in the Bodleian a Greek prose paraphrase of many of his fables, including some no longer extant in Babrius : see W. G. Rutherford, *Babrius*, London 1883.

[b] *De Babrii Aetate, Leipz. Stud.* II. 238.

[c] *Cf.* remarks on metre later in Introduction.

Avianus in his preface or dedicatory letter makes
no claim to be original. He claims that he has
put into elegiac verse 42 fables from the Aesopic
collection—a collection from which Socrates and
Horace [a] had drawn to illustrate moral maxims and
which Phaedrus [b] and Babrius had abridged in their
Latin and Greek iambics respectively. It is strange
that Avianus should mention Phaedrus and Babrius
together in such a way as to suggest he was no more
indebted to one than to the other. The truth is that
he owes practically nothing to Phaedrus and nearly
everything to Babrius. Avianus 2, 5, 9, 34, 37 are
respectively more or less similar in subject-matter
to Phaedrus II. vi, I. xi, V. ii, IV. xxiv, III. vii. In
fable 37 Avianus is as near to Phaedrus as he is to
Babrius and (though a lion has taken the place of a
wolf) Phaedrian influence may be admitted; the
other four Avianus could have composed without
reading Phaedrus. Fables 2, 9, 34 are much closer
to Babrius than to Phaedrus, and 5, which is not in
our Babrius, is closer to the Aesopic prose version.
As for single lines, apart from Av. xi. 10 and xxxi. 12
(which perhaps are echoes of Phaedrus I. v. 1 and
IV. vi. 13) there is scarcely a trace of indebtedness
to the first-century fabulist. The case is very
different in regard to Babrius.[c] With a few excep-
tions the 42 fables can be traced to a Babrian source—
either to the scazons of Babrius or to the Greek prose

[a] Cf. notes on the dedicatory letter.
[b] Phaedrus, of Thracian origin, composed his five books in
Latin iambic senarii. His first two books were written under
Tiberius (14–37 A.D.); see J. Wight Duff, *Lit. Hist. of Rome in
Silver Age*, pp. 133–154.
[c] The Greek text of the extant Babrian versions is given
in Ellis' commentary.

paraphrase now in the Bodleian. Probably, if our
Babrius were complete, we should be able to account
for all Avianus' *fabulae*. In most cases Avianus'
version is longer than that of Babrius. Avianus
expands his Babrian material, sometimes to make an
alteration in the story (*e.g.* 32, 35, 36), but more often
to elaborate the descriptive element with poetical
diction which contains frequent echoes of Virgil or
Ovid. Thus a strained, even grotesque, artificiality
displaces the simple directness of Babrius. For a
forcible instance, one may examine fable 7, which is
based on Babrius 104. Here Avianus takes four lines
(3–6) to paraphrase λάθρη κύων ἔδακνε, virtually
repeats in lines 9 and 10 the preceding couplet, and
introduces the Virgilian *crepitantia aera*, perhaps as a
tardy recognition of χαλκεύσας in Babrius' opening
line. Then the couplet 15–16

" Infelix, quae tanta rapit dementia sensum,
        munera pro meritis si cupis ista dari ? "

represents ὦ τάλαν, τί σεμνύνῃ; and combines a
mock-heroic imitation of Virgil with a colloquial
post-classical use of *si cupis* for " if you want to make
out that . . ." Other expansions, largely descrip-
tive, are observable in most fables where the Babrian
original has survived (*e.g.* in 14, 18, 34). To such
expansions throughout the fables a very noticeable
contribution is made by Avianus' habit of drawing
poetical phrases freely from Virgil and, to a less
extent, from Ovid. They may be pleasantly pictur-
esque reminiscences like *glaucas salices* (xxvi. 6) and
querulo ruperat arva sono of the grasshopper (xxxiv.
12) ; [a] or they may lend a quaint epic turn to the story

[a] *Cf.* Virg. *Georg.* IV. 182; III. 328.

as in *pependit onus* (ix. 8), *rumpere vocem* (xiv. 11, xxv. 13), *surgentes demoror austros* (xvi. 15), *generis fiducia vestri* (xxiv. 11);[a] or they may be still more positively mock-heroic as in *circumstetit horror* of the ass in the lion's skin (v. 9) and *lacrimis obortis* of a weeping fish (xx. 5).[b]

Mingled with this poetical language of a pre-Avianian age we have frequent instances of a degenerate Latin. These have been collected and tabulated by Ellis (*Proleg.* xxxvi *sqq.*). The use of *nimius* for *magnus*, of *tanti* for *tot*, and of *datur* for *dicitur*, are among the most noticeable as far as single words are concerned. Indirect statement is sometimes introduced by *quod* or expressed by the subjunctive without a conjunction. *Que* and *atque* according to the manuscripts (though emendation is generally possible) may be used illogically to connect participles with finite verbs; and the gerundive once or twice does the work of a future participle passive.

To the prosody of Avianus a reference has already been made. In general, he gives us correct Ovidian elegiacs. Occasionally, according to the traditional text, at the end of the first half of a pentameter, hiatus is admitted or a short syllable takes the place of a long one (Ellis xxiv–xxv). In most of these cases the text can be easily emended and Avianus himself absolved from a metrical fault. Some other violations of classical prosody (*velĭs* iii. 6; *nŏlam* vii. 8; *dispăr* xi. 5; *herĕs* xxxv. 14) cannot be explained away; they come from Avianus' own hand and attest

---

[a] *Cf.* Ovid, *Her.* ix. 98, *Rem. Am.* 18, *Fasti* II. 760; Virg. *Aen.* II. 129, etc.; III. 481; I. 132.
[b] *Cf.* Virg. *Aen.* II. 559; XI. 41.

the decline of metrical strictness at the end of the fourth century.

There is no trace of Christian influence in the Fables. Pagan gods and sacrifices are introduced after a pre-Christian fashion in 4, 8, 14, 22, 23, 32, 36 and 42.

The popularity of Avianus in the schools of the Middle Ages is attested by accretions, paraphrases, scholia and quotations. As rhetorical exercises, promythia or epimythia were composed at the beginning or end of many fables to point the moral. A few of these came to be included in the text. Some epimythia (those contained in the earliest MSS.), it is likely, come from Avianus himself; but the four promythia (to fables 5, 7, 8, 34) are probably the work of a rhetorician, although, being contained in the tenth century MSS., they are of an early date. A number of undoubtedly spurious epimythia (found only in later MSS.) are omitted in most editions. Froehner prints them separately in his edition of 1862. Paraphrases were often made of Avianus. One collection entitled *Apologi Aviani* [a] is attached to two of the later Paris MSS. Here the paraphrast usually turns the first half or more of each fable into prose and ends by copying the last few lines of Avianus' own version, so that occasionally his work is useful for determining the text. Alexander Neckam (1157–1217) composed verse paraphrases, perhaps of the whole of Avianus, entitling his work *Novus Avianus*. His versions of the first six fables are contained in a St. Germain MS. of the thirteenth century. [b] Scholia of varying

[a] Published by Froehner in his ed. of Avianus 1862.
[b] Published by Edelestand du Meril (*Poésies Inédites*, 260–267) and afterwards by Froehner, *op. cit.*

extent and value are included in nearly all MSS. of Avianus, indicating the assiduity with which he was studied. He is extensively quoted or alluded to by medieval grammarians and anthologists,[a] and the fables were to be found in many libraries of the Middle Ages.[b]

EDITIONS

H. Cannegieter. Amsterdam, 1731.
J. A. Nodell. Amsterdam, 1787.
K. Lachmann. Berlin, 1845.
W. Froehner. Leipzig, 1862.
E. Baehrens. In *Poetae Latini Minores*, Vol. V. Leipzig, 1883.
R. Ellis. Oxford, 1887.
L. Hervieux. In *Fabulistes latins*, iii. Paris, 1894.

RELEVANT WORKS

T. Wopkens. *Observationes Criticae*. Amsterdam, 1736, VII. ii, pp. 197–253.
J. H. Withof. *Encaenia Critica*. 1741.
J. C. Wernsdorf. In *P. L. M.*, V. 2, pp. 663 *sqq.*
K. Lachmann. *De aetate Fl. Aviani.* Berlin, 1845 = *Kl. Schriften*, II. 51.
E. Baehrens, *Miscell. Critica.* Groningen, 1878.
K. Schenkl. *Ztschr. f. österr. Gymn.* xvi. 397.
O. Unrein. *De Aviani aetate.* Jena, 1885.
Draheim. *De Aviani elegis, J. f. Philologie*, cxliii. 509.
J. E. B. Mayor. *Class. Rev.* I. (1887), 188 *sqq.*

---

[a] Manitius, *Gesch. der lat. Lit. des Mittelalters*, Index, *s.v.* Avianus; *Philologus* LI (1892), 533 *sqq.*
[b] G. Becker, *Catalogi Bibliothecarum Antiqui*, 306.

THE FABLES OF AVIANUS

F. Heidenhain. *Zu den Apologi Aviani. Progr.*
    Strassburg, 1894.
Jenkinson. *Fables of Avianus, The Academy,* XLV.
    (1894), 129.
O. Crusius. *De Babrii Aetate, Leipz. Stud.,* II. 238.
——— *Avian und die sogenannten Apologi Aviani,*
    Philologus LIV. (1895), 474–488.
——— s.v. *Avianus* in Pauly-Wissowa, *Realencyclop.*

SIGLA

(following Ellis in the main)

A = Paris. 8093 : saec. ix.
P = Paris. 13206 : saec. ix.
C = Paris. 5570 : saec. ix (Froehner), x (Ellis),
    xi (Baehr.).
O = Oxon. Auct. F. 2. 14 : saec. xi.
Rawl. = Oxon. B. N. Rawl. 111 : saec. xi–xii.
X = Oxon. Auct. F. 5. 6 : *circ.* 1300.
G = Cantab. Trinity, Gale 0. 3. 5 : saec. xii.
Pet^1. = Cantab. Peterhouse, 4 (fabulis i–xxii derep-
    tis) : saec. xiii–xiv.
Pet^2. = Cantab. Peterhouse, 25 (continens Avianum
    et Maximianum) : saec. xiii–xiv.
B = Londin. Brit. Mus. Harl. 4967 : saec. xiii.
b = Londin. Brit. Mus. 21, 213 (saepe inter-
    polatus) : saec. xiii.
b^2 = Londin. Brit. Mus. A. xxxi (xvii–xxi omissis) :
    circ. 1300.
b^3 = Londin. Brit. Mus. 10090 (interpolatus).
T = Trevirensis. 1464 (continens Avianum et
    Prudentium) : saec. x.
V = Lugdun. Batav. Vossianus L.Q. 86 : saec. ix.

W = Lugdun. Batav. Vossianus L.O. 15: saec. xi.
Ashb. [= B in Baehrens' ed.] = Ashburnhamensis
  (Libri 1813): saec. xi–xii.
Reg. = Reginensis. 1424: saec. xi.
L = Laurentianus, lxviii 24: saec. xi.
S = Fragmentum Sangallense. 1396: saec. xi.
K = Fragmentum Karoliruhense (ab Froehnero
  adhibitum): saec. ix.
Cab. = readings reported by Cabeljau from a
  " codex vetustissimus " and reprinted by Canne-
  gieter in D'Orville's *Miscellanea Nova*, 1734.
Paraphr. = readings of the paraphrast, author of
  the *apologi Aviani*.

Of the MSS. Baehrens collated the Leyden manu-
scripts V and W, the Trèves one, T, the Florence one,
L, and the Ashburnhamensis (his B). G was collated
for Baehrens by H. A. J. Munro. Baehrens cites
the readings of the Paris MSS. P, A, C and of the
Carlsruhe fragment, K, from Froehner's edition.
Ellis based his text largely on a personal examination
of the three Paris codices, those at Oxford, and those
in the British Museum, besides T and S. The most
important MSS. are C, Rawl., G, B (in Ellis' sigla,
i.e. Harl. 4967), T and V.

Bibliographical addendum (1982)

On the author's name see Alan Cameron, *CQ* 17
  (1967) 392ff.

Avianus, ed. (with French translation) L. Herrmann
  (Coll. Latomus), Bruxelles 1968.

J. Kueppers: *Die Fabeln Avians, Studien zu Dar-
  stellung und Erzählweise spätantiken Fabeldichtung*,
  Bonn 1977.

FABULAE AVIANI

EPISTULA EIUSDEM AD THEODOSIUM

Dubitanti mihi, Theodosi optime, quoinam litte-
rarum titulo nostri nominis memoriam mandaremus,
fabularum textus occurrit, quod in his urbane con-
cepta falsitas deceat et non incumbat necessitas ve-
ritatis. nam quis tecum de oratione, quis de poemate
loqueretur, cum in utroque litterarum genere et
Atticos Graeca eruditione superes et Latinitate
Romanos? huius ergo materiae ducem nobis Aesopum
noveris, qui responso Delphici Apollinis monitus
ridicula orsus est, ut legenda firmaret. verum has pro 1(
exemplo fabulas et Socrates divinis operibus indidit
et poemati suo Flaccus aptavit, quod in se sub iocorum
communium specie vitae argumenta contineant.

Titulus : Incipiunt fabulae Aviani poetae : epistola
eiusdem ad Theodosium C : ad imperatorem Theodosium
Reg. : ad Teodosium imperatorem *Rawl.*
⁴ falsitas *codd.* : salsitas *Baehrens.* veritatis *codd.* :
severitatis *Lachmann.*
¹⁰ legenda *codd.* : sequenda *Lachmann.*

---

a *i.e.* probably Macrobius Theodosius, author of the
Saturnalia : see Introduction. The tone of the dedication
suits a literary addressee.
b The historical " Aisopos " was a slave in Samos, 6th cent.
B.C., who used beast-stories to convey moral lessons. Later
generations freely ascribed to him a mass of fables, and the
supposed Aesopic fables were collected about 300 B.C. by

THE FABLES OF AVIANUS

DEDICATORY LETTER TO THEODOSIUS [a]

I was in doubt, most excellent Theodosius, to
what class of literature I should entrust the memory
of my name, when the narration of fables occurred to
my mind; because in these, fiction, if gracefully
conceived, is not out of place, and one is not
oppressed by the necessity of adhering to the truth.
Who could speak in your company on oratory or
on poetry? In both these divisions of literature
you outstrip the Athenians in Greek learning as
well as the Romans in mastery of Latin. My
pioneer in this subject, you must know, is Aesop,[b]
who on the advice of the Delphic Apollo started
droll stories in order to establish moral maxims.
Such fables by way of example have been intro-
duced by Socrates [c] into his inspired works and fitted
by Horace [d] into his poetry, because under the guise
of jests of general application they contain illustrations

Demetrius of Phaleron. The authority for Avianus' statement
that Aesop was advised by the Delphic oracle is unknown.

[c] The reference is to Plato's dialogues (*Socraticis sermonibus*,
Hor. *Od*. III. xxi. 9–10) which represent much of Socrates'
teaching. In Plato's *Phaedo*, 60–61, Socrates says a dream
led him to turn Aesopic fables into verse. Avianus here
refers to apologues in fable style : *e.g.* of Grasshoppers,
Phaedr. 259; of Plenty and Poverty, *Symp*. 203; of Prome-
theus and Epimetheus, *Protag*. 320–321.

[d] *e.g.* the Town Mouse and the Country Mouse in *Sat*. II. vi.

quas Graecis iambis Babrius repetens in duo volumina
coartavit. Phaedrus etiam partem aliquam quinque 15
in libellos resolvit. de his ego ad quadraginta et duas
in unum redactas fabulas dedi, quas rudi Latinitate
compositas elegis sum explicare conatus. habes ergo
opus, quo animum oblectes, ingenium exerceas,
sollicitudinem leves totumque vivendi ordinem cautus 20
agnoscas. loqui vero arbores, feras cum hominibus
gemere, verbis certare volucres, animalia ridere
fecimus, ut pro singulorum necessitatibus vel ab
ipsis ⟨in⟩animis sententia proferatur. ⟨vale.⟩

I

De Nutrice et Infante

Rustica deflentem parvum iuraverat olim,
    ni taceat, rabido quod foret esca lupo.
credulus hanc vocem lupus audiit et manet ipsas
    pervigil ante fores, irrita vota gerens.
nam lassata puer nimiae dat membra quieti ;   5
    spem quoque raptoris sustulit inde fami.

[16] ergo *plerique* : ego OP.
I. [1] iuraverat *Pet.*[2] : iuraverat *cett. codd.* : iurgaverat
Froehner secutus Cabellavium.
[6] *sic Wopkens* : fami (*ex* -mes *corr.*) T : famis PV*m*[1]W :
fames V*m*[2] *cum cett.*

---

[a] See Introduction and note.
[b] *Ibid.*
[c] *Cf.* Phaedrus, I. *prol.* 6–7 *quod arbores loquantur non
tantum ferae, fictis iocari nos meminerit fabulis,* and Babrius,

of life.   They were taken up by Babrius [a] in Greek
choliambics and abridged into two volumes.   A
considerable portion also was expanded by Phaedrus [b]
to a length of five books.   I have compressed forty-
two of these into one book for publication—writing
in unembellished Latin and attempting to set them
forth in elegiacs.   You have, therefore, a work to
delight the mind, to exercise the brain, to relieve
anxiety—one that will give you a wary knowledge
of the whole course of life.   I have made trees talk,[c]
beasts growl in conversation with men, birds engage
in wordy disputes, and animals laugh, so that to meet
the needs of each individual a maxim may be proffered
even by inanimate things.   Farewell.

I

The Nurse and her Child

Once upon a time when her little boy was crying, a
peasant-woman had sworn that if he were not quiet
he would be given as a tit-bit [d] for a ravenous wolf.
A credulous wolf overheard these words and waited
on guard close in front of the cottage doors, cherishing
hopes in vain.   For the child let a deep sleep come
over his weary limbs, and besides deprived the
hungry robber thereby of his expectation.   The wolf

---

praef. 9 ἐλάλει δὲ πέτρη καὶ τὰ φύλλα τῆς πεύκης.   In Avianus,
pine and bramble argue xix, and a reed speaks xvi.   His
other remarks in this sentence are illustrated by the follow-
ing: tigress challenges hunter xvii; lion and hunter dispute
xxiv; crane and peacock quarrel xv; fox laughs vi; ant
laughs xxxiv; and among "inanimate things" a jar speaks
xi; a statue xxiii and a trumpet xxxix.

[d] *quod foret esca* replaces the classical accus. and infin.
Cf. xxv. 16.

hunc ubi silvarum repetentem lustra suarum
　ieiunum coniunx sensit adesse lupa,
" cur " inquit " nullam referens de more rapinam
　languida consumptis sic trahis ora genis ? "　　　1[

" ne mireris " ait " deceptum fraude maligna
　vix miserum vacua delituisse fuga :
nam quae praeda, rogas, quae spes contingere posset,
　iurgia nutricis cum mihi verba darent ? "[a]

haec sibi dicta putet seque hac sciat arte notari,　　　1[
　femineam quisquis credidit esse fidem.

II

DE TESTUDINE ET AQUILA

Pennatis avibus quondam testudo locuta est,
　si quis eam volucrum constituisset humi,
protinus e Rubris conchas proferret harenis,
　quis pretium nitido cortice baca daret :
indignum, sibimet tardo quod sedula gressu　　　　　[
　nil ageret toto proficeretque die.
ast ubi promissis aquilam fallacibus implet,
　experta est similem perfida lingua fidem ;
et male mercatis dum quaerit sidera pennis,
　occidit infelix alitis ungue fero.　　　　　　　　1[

II. ² volucrem P A m² : volucrum A m¹ cum ceteris codd.
⁶ perficeretque ACOTW Ash. : proficeretque Pet.² G Rawl.
B b b² Cab.
¹⁰ occidit plerique codd. : excidit Baehrens.

---

[a] verba darent in the classical sense of tricking. Contrast
ix. 20; xxiv. 10; xxxvii. 2; xxxviii. 6, where the sense is
simply that of speaking.

repaired to the lair in his native woods, and his mate, seeing him arrive famished, said, "Why don't you bring back the usual prey? Why are your cheeks wasted and your jaws so drawn and emaciated?" "A mean trick took me in," he said; "so don't be surprised that I have been hard put to it to skulk pitifully away—with no spoil. What kill, do you ask, could come my way? what prospect could there be, when a scolding nurse befooled me?" [a]

Let anyone who believes in a woman's sincerity reflect that to him these words are spoken and that it is he whom this lesson censures.

II

THE TORTOISE AND THE EAGLE

Once a tortoise said to the feathered birds that if one of the swift fliers could carry her away and set her safe on the ground [b] she would at once from the sands of the Erythraean Sea produce shells [c] on which their bright-crusted pearl conferred a value. She felt it an outrage that, despite her diligence, her slow pace prevented her doing anything or making any progress the whole day. She loaded an eagle with false promises, but her untruthful tongue found a broken troth to match her own. While soaring aloft on the wings whose aid she had bought so ill, the wretched tortoise met her death by the bird's

[b] Line 2 presents difficulties. It has *eam* for *se*; *quis* implying the rare masc. gender for *volucrum*; and *constituisset* involving a latent idea. The alternative *volucrem* means that the tortoise asked to be made a bird : this is accepted by Baehrens, who reads *ibi* for *humi*.

[c] Late Latin for *se prolaturam esse conchas*.

tum quoque sublimis, cum iam moreretur, in auras
    ingemuit votis haec licuisse suis;
nam dedit exosae post haec documenta quieti
    non sine supremo magna labore peti.

sic quicumque nova sublatus laude tumescit,   1
    dat merito poenas, dum meliora cupit.

III

De Cancro et Matre Eius

Curva retro cedens dum fert vestigia cancer,
    hispida saxosis terga relisit aquis.
hunc genetrix facili cupiens procedere gressu
    talibus alloquiis emonuisse datur:
" ne tibi transverso placeant haec devia, nate,
    rursus in obliquos neu velis ire pedes,
sed nisu contenta ferens vestigia recto
    innocuos proso tramite siste gradus."
cui natus " faciam, si me praecesseris " inquit,
    " rectaque monstrantem certior ipse sequar.   1
nam stultum nimis est, cum tu pravissima temptes,
    alterius censor si vitiosa notes."

          [12] licuisse *plerique codd.* : libuisse *Cannegieter.*
          III. [3] procedere CT : praecedere *plerique codd.*
          [4] praemonuisse *codd.* : emonuisse *Ellis.*
          [12] ut *codd.* : si *Ellis* (*servans metrum*).

cruel talons. Then it was that, raised on high,[a] in the hour of death, she filled the breezes with her moaning plaint that such had been the answer to her prayers. For she gave surly sloth a warning for the future that great achievement is only reached by the utmost toil.

So anyone elated and puffed up with new-found glory pays a just penalty in hankering after what is too high for him.

III

The Crab and its Mother

While a crab was walking backwards and tracing its crooked way, it banged its scaly back in the rocky pools. Its mother, eager to go forward with step unhindered, is said to have delivered a warning to it in such words as these: " Don't go zigzag and choose these crooked ways, my child, and don't seek to move backwards and slantwise on your feet. Step out vigorously with straightforward effort and plant your footsteps safely in the onward path." " I will do so," the young crab replied, " if you go ahead of me ; and, if you show me the correct road, I will follow the more surely. For it is exceedingly foolish of you, when you are attempting the most crooked of courses yourself, to set up as censor and criticise the faults of another."

[a] *sublimis* is emphatic : *cf.* the application in 15–16. *sublimes*, the variant in several MSS., goes with *auras*, " breezes of heaven."

IV

De Vento et Sole

Immitis Boreas placidusque ad sidera Phoebus
  iurgia cum magno conseruere Iove,
quis prior inceptum peragat: mediumque per aequor
  carpebat solitum forte viator iter.
convenit hanc potius liti praefigere causam,   5
  pallia nudato decutienda viro.
protinus impulsus ventis circum tonat aether
  et gelidus nimias depluit imber aquas:
ille magis lateri duplicem circumdat amictum,
  turbida submotos quod trahit aura sinus.   10
sed tenues radios paulatim increscere Phoebus
  iusserat, ut nimio surgeret igne iubar,
donec lassa volens requiescere membra viator
  deposita fessus veste sederet humi.
tunc victor docuit praesentia numina Titan,   15
  nullum praemissis vincere posse minis.

V

De Asino Pelle Leonis Induto

[Metiri se quemque decet propriisque iuvari
  laudibus, alterius nec bona ferre sibi,
ne detracta gravem faciant miracula risum,
  coeperit in solitis cum remanere malis.]

IV. ¹ sidera *codd.*: cetera *Lachmann*: ludicra *Baehrens.*
³ aequor *Cm¹*: orbem *cett. codd.*
V. ⁴ solitis *Pet.²* b: solis *plerique codd.*

THE FABLES OF AVIANUS

IV

THE WIND AND THE SUN

Savage Boreas and gentle Phoebus joined strife in the presence of the stars with great Jupiter, to decide which should first achieve his task; and over the midst of the plain it happened a traveller was plying his wonted way. They agree to preface their dispute with this case for trial—to get the man stripped by tearing off his cloak.[a] Straightway with the onset of the wind the sky thunders around, and the chill rain-storm pours down torrents of water. The traveller folds his cloak double and draws it round his sides all the more, because the tempestuous blast pushes the folds aside and tugs at them. But Phoebus had bidden his penetrating rays grow stronger little by little, so that his splendour might emerge in excessive heat,—until the traveller, anxious to rest his weary limbs, threw down his cloak and sat on the ground exhausted. Then in his triumph the Titan taught the assembled gods[b] that no one can win victory by an advance guard of threats.

V

THE DONKEY IN THE LION'S SKIN

[Everyone should take his true measure and be content with his own merits, and not claim for himself his neighbour's goods, lest the stripping of the finery lead to painful ridicule as soon as he is left in possession of his usual defects.]

---

[a] *nudato* is proleptic.   [b] *i.e.* the stars and Jupiter.

Exuvías asinus Gaetuli forte leonis
  repperit et spoliis induit ora novis.
aptavitque suis incongrua tegmina membris
  et miserum tanto pressit honore caput.
ast ubi terribilis mimo circumstetit horror
  pigraque praesumptus venit in ossa vigor,   10
mitibus ille feris communia pabula calcans
  turbabat pavidas per sua rura boves.
rusticus hunc magna postquam deprendit ab aure,
  correptum vinclis verberibusque domat;
et simul abstracto denudans corpora tergo   15
  increpat his miserum vocibus ille pecus:
" forsitan ignotos imitato murmure fallas;
  at mihi, qui quondam, semper asellus eris."

VI

De Rana et Vulpe

Edita gurgitibus limoque immersa profundo
  et luteis tantum semper amica vadis,
ad superos colles herbosaque prata recurrens
  mulcebat miseras turgida rana feras,
callida quod posset gravibus succurrere morbis
  et vitam ingenio continuare suo;
nec se Paeonio iactat cessisse magistro,
  quamvis perpetuos curet in orbe deos.

---

    5 getuli *plerique codd.* : defuncti PV.
    9 mimo *Cannegieter* : animo *plerique codd.* : animū *Ashb.*
    VI. 1 limoque W *Nevelet* : olimque *cett. codd.*
    7 P(a)eonio *plerique codd.* : Paeoni *Lachmann.*

THE FABLES OF AVIANUS

It happened that a donkey discovered a Gaetulian lion's skin and clothed his face with the new-found spoil. To his own limbs he fitted the ill-assorted covering and burdened his wretched head with trappings so majestic. But when the grim appearance, awe-inspiring in its mimicry,[a] enveloped him, and the courage he had assumed in advance entered his sluggish bones, then, trampling the pasture which he shared with the tame animals, he drove the scared cattle in confusion over their fields. The farmer, after catching him by his long ear, hustled him off and subdued him by tying him up and thrashing him; and as he stripped the stolen skin off his body he scolded the poor beast with these words: "Perhaps your mimic roar may cheat strangers. To me you will always be a donkey as before."

VI

THE FROG AND THE FOX

Sprung from pools, immersed in depths of mud, the constant friend of naught but miry shallows, a distended frog, revisiting the hills above and the grassy meadows, sought to comfort the afflicted beasts with the assurance that her leech-craft could relieve their sore diseases and her genius could prolong their lives. Her boast was that she had never been surpassed by the Paeonian master,[b] though he attended the ever-

[a] *mimo* goes with *terribilis* as an ablative. The reading *animū* tempts one to suggest *mimum*: "when the awful appearance enveloped this farcical actor" (*i.e.* the ass). For the diction *cf.* Virg. *Aen.* II. 559, *me . . . circumstetit horror.*
[b] Paeon was the Master Healer: *cf.* Rut. Namat. I. 75 *Paeoniam artem.*

tunc vulpes pecudum ridens astuta quietem,
   verborum vacuam prodidit esse fidem: 1
" haec dabit aegrotis " inquit " medicamina membris,
   pallida caeruleus cui notat ora color? "

VII

DE CANE QUI NOLUIT LATRARE

[Haud facile est pravis innatum mentibus ut se
   verberibus dignas suppliciove putent.]

Forte canis quondam nullis latratibus horrens
   nec patulis primum rictibus ora trahens,
mollia sed pavidae submittens verbera caudae,
   concitus audaci vulnera dente dabat.
hunc dominus, ne quem probitas simulata lateret,
   iusserat in rabido gutture ferre nolam.
faucibus innexis crepitantia subligat aera,
   quae facili motu signa cavenda darent.   1
haec tamen ille sibi credebat praemia ferri,
   et similem turbam despiciebat ovans.
tunc insultantem senior de plebe superbum
   aggreditur tali singula voce monens:
" infelix, quae tanta rapit dementia sensum,
   munera pro meritis si cupis ista dari?   1

---

[10] vacuam *codd.*: vanam *Cannegieter.*
   VII. [2] muneribus *codd.*: verberibus *Withof*: vulneribus
Froehner in not.
   [8] nolam *plerique codd.*: molam Vm^1W: notam *Cab.*
   [14] singula voce *codd.*: monens *plerique codd.*: sibila voce
movens *Lachmann*: voce severa monens *Baehrens*: cingula
voce moves? *Ellis.*

lasting gods in turn. Then a cunning vixen, laughing at the acquiescence of the cattle, disclosed the futility of giving credence to words: " Is physic," she asked, " going to be prescribed for diseased limbs by this frog, whose pale face is sicklied o'er with a livid hue? "

VII

THE DOG THAT WOULD NOT BARK

[Not readily is it the nature of evil dispositions to believe themselves deserving of stripes and punishment.]

It happened once there was a dog with no gruff bark, that did not open its mouth in a wide gape as a first sign of mischief, but put its soft-wagging tail in fear beneath it, and then would fly into a fury and snap recklessly with its teeth. To prevent anyone being taken unawares by its pretended good character, its master had made it wear a bell *a* round its savage throat. He fastened its neck and tied the tinkling brass underneath to give signals of warning by its ready motion. The dog, however, believed this was worn by it as a reward, and triumphantly began to look down on the crowd of dogs like itself. Then an older dog of humble rank accosted the swaggerer in its exaltation, giving each word of advice *b* after the following strain: " Wretch, what is this monstrous madness that steals away your senses, if indeed you will have it that those rewards are given you for your

---

a *nolam* elsewhere has a long *o*.
b Ellis' reading is attractive, " tali cingula voce moves? " " what, so loud in shaking your collar? "

non hoc virtutis decus ostentatur in aere,
 nequitiae testem sed geris inde sonum.''

VIII

De Camelo et Iove

[Contentum propriis sapientem vivere rebus
 nec cupere alterius fabula nostra monet,
indignata cito ne stet Fortuna recursu
 atque eadem minuat quae dedit ante rota.]

Corporis immensi fertur pecus isse per auras
 et magnum precibus sollicitasse Iovem:
turpe nimis cunctis irridendumque videri,
 insignes geminis cornibus ire boves,
et solum nulla munitum parte camelum
 obiectum cunctis expositumque feris.
Iuppiter irridens postquam sperata negavit,
 insuper et magnae sustulit auris onus.
" vive minor merito, cui sors non sufficit " inquit,
 " et tua perpetuum, livide, damna geme."

IX

De Duobus Sociis et Ursa

Montibus ignotis curvisque in vallibus artum
 cum socio quidam suscipiebat iter,

VIII. ³ det . . . recursum *Baehrens* (*ex* recursū *in* W).
⁵ auras *plerique codd.* : aras b : arva *Pet.*² : Afros *Withof.*

THE FABLES OF AVIANUS

deserts? This is not an ornament of merit displayed in a brass setting: no, by wearing it you carry a sound as witness of your bad character."

VIII

JUPITER AND THE CAMEL

[Our fable counsels a man if he be wise to live contented with his own property and not to covet what belongs to another, lest Fortune be angry and run quickly back to a standstill, and the same wheel that once bestowed favours end in lessening them.]

The story goes that an animal of vast bulk went through the air and besought high Jove with entreaties, saying that everyone thought it a monstrous scandal and theme for ridicule that oxen should strut about in the glory of a pair of horns, while the camel alone should be undefended in every quarter, at the mercy of all the animal world and open to their attacks. Jupiter, mocking the camel, after refusing the expected boon, went further and relieved it of the weight of its large ears, saying, " Live beneath your deserts, as you are not satisfied with your lot; bewail your loss for ever, you jealous creature."

IX

THE TWO COMPANIONS AND THE BEAR

A man was once journeying along a narrow road with a companion among unknown hills and in

---

[11] adridens *vel* arridens *plerique codd.* : irridens B *Rawl. Pet.*[2] : at ridens *Cannegieter.*

securus, cum quodque malum Fortuna tulisset,
    robore collato posset uterque pati.
dumque per inceptum vario sermone feruntur,
    in mediam praeceps convenit ursa viam.
horum alter facili comprendens robora cursu
    in viridi trepidum fronde pependit onus;
ille trahens nullo iacuit vestigia gressu,
    exanimem fingens, sponte relisus humi.   10
continuo praedam cupiens fera saeva cucurrit
    et miserum curvis unguibus ante levat;
verum ubi concreto riguerunt membra timore
    (nam solitus mentis liquerat ossa calor),
tunc olidum credens, quamvis ieiuna, cadaver   15
    deserit et lustris conditur ursa suis.
sed cum securi paulatim in verba redissent,
    liberior iusto, qui fuit ante fugax:
" dic, sodes, quidnam trepido tibi rettulit ursa?
    nam secreta diu multaque verba dedit."   20
" magna quidem monuit, tamen haec quoque maxima
      iussit,
    quae misero semper sunt facienda mihi:
'ne facile alterius repetas consortia,' dixit,
    ' rursus ab insana ne capiare fera.' "

X

DE CALVO EQUITE

Calvus eques capiti solitus religasse capillos
    atque alias nudo vertice ferre comas,

IX. ³ quodcumque *plerique codd.* : cum quodque *Baehrens.*
  ⁵ inceptum *plerique co*ld. : incertum T : inseptum *Ellis.*
  ⁶ convenit *codd.* : en venit *Canneg.* : convolat *Baehrens.*
X. ¹ religasse PVW *Ashb. Rawl.* : religare *plerique codd.*

winding valleys. He felt safe because, whatever adversity Fortune might bring, both would be able to unite their strength and face it. While with varied conversation they were pursuing the journey they had started, a she-bear came headlong to meet them in the middle of the way. One of the travellers with an easy run grasped an oak branch and suspended his panic-stricken weight among the green foliage. The other, without advancing his course a single step, feigned death, and lay down, throwing himself intentionally on the ground. At once, eager for the spoil, the savage beast ran up and, to start with, lifted the poor man in her crooked claws. But when icy fear stiffened his limbs (for the usual vital warmth had left his bones), then the bear, thinking him a rank corpse, abandoned him in spite of her hunger and vanished into her own haunts. But after they recovered their nerve and gradually resumed their talk, the man who before had run away grew now over-merry and said, " Tell me, please, what was it the bear told you when you were trembling there? She spoke much with you in a long private talk." "Yes, she gave me important advice, but laid also this command especially on me, and I, poor wretch, must always carry it out. ' Be chary of returning to partnership with another,' she said, ' lest a rabid beast get hold of you a second time.' "

X

THE BALD HORSEMAN

A bald horseman, accustomed to fasten hair to his head and wear strange locks on his bare crown,

ad Campum nitidis venit conspectus in armis
    et facilem frenis flectere coepit equum.
huius ab adverso Boreae spiramina praeflant
    ridiculum populo conspiciente caput;
nam mox deiecto nituit frons nuda galero,
    discolor apposita quae fuit ante coma.
ille sagax, tantis quod risus milibus esset,
    distulit admota calliditate iocum,
" quid mirum " referens " positos fugisse capillos,
    quem prius aequaevae deseruere comae? "

XI

De Duabus Ollis

Eripiens geminas ripis cedentibus ollas
    insanis pariter flumen agebat aquis.
sed diversa duas ars et natura creavit:
    aere prior fusa est, altera ficta luto.
dispar erat fragili et solidae concordia motus,
    incertumque vagus amnis habebat iter.
ne tamen allisam confringeret, aerea testa
    iurabat solidam longius ire viam.

---

[5] praeflant *Ellis*: perfl = ant *Ashb.*: praestant *cett. codd.*
[8] apposita *codd.*: ab posita *Baehrens.*
XI. [4] facta CX b² *Pet.*² *Reg.*: ficta *plerique codd.*
[6] vagans B, *Ellis*: vagus *cett. codd.*
[7] elisam *codd.*: allisam *Barth, Baehrens*: illisam *Schenkl.*
[8] solitam *codd.*: solidam *Ellis*: sociam *Nevelet.* longius
codd.: comminus *Canneg.*: urgebat coctam, comminus
Baehrens.

came to the Campus[a] conspicuous in shining armour
and began manœuvring his nimble horse with the
bridle. The blasts of the North wind driving against
him blew upon the front of his head and made it a
figure of fun in the sight of the people. For soon his
wig flew off and his uncovered forehead shone
brightly, which just before had another hue while
the false hair was fixed on. As the horseman
saw that he was the laughing-stock of so many
thousands, he shrewdly brought cunning to his aid
and turned away the jest from himself. "Why be
surprised," he remarked, "that my assumed locks
have gone, when my natural hair deserted me first?"

XI

THE TWO JARS

Two jars were once swept away by a river owing to
a collapse of its banks and were being carried down
together in the wild current. Different craftsmanship
and material had created the two; the first was of
fused bronze, the other of moulded clay. The
brittle and the solid jar kept up an uneven harmony
of progress,[b] while the meandering river took its way-
ward course. The bronze jar, however, swore to pursue
its metallic route at a distance from the other lest it
should strike against it and smash it to pieces. The

---

[a] *i.e.* the *Campus Martius*, the ancient open exercise-
ground of Rome: *cf.* Hor. *Sat.* I. vi. 126 *fugio Campum
lusumque trigonem.*

[b] *dispăr*: *cf.* xxiii. 8, and *impăr*, xviii. 10. The oxymoron
dispar concordia means that in general the pots kept together,
but irregularly so. Each in turn might drop behind and
afterwards catch up.

illa timens ne quid levibus graviora nocerent,
    et quia nulla brevi est cum meliore fides,
" quamvis securam verbis me feceris " inquit,
    " non timor ex animo decutiendus erit;
nam me sive tibi seu te mihi conferat unda,
    semper ero ambobus subdita sola malis."

XII

DE RUSTICO ET THESAURO

Rusticus impresso molitus vomere terram
    thesaurum sulcis prosiluisse videt.
mox indigna animo properante reliquit aratra,
    gramina compellens ad meliora boves.
continuo supplex Telluri construit aras,
    quae sibi depositas sponte dedisset opes.
hunc Fortuna novis gaudentem provida rebus
    admonet, indignam se quoque ture dolens:
" nunc inventa meis non prodis munera templis
    atque alios mavis participare deos;
sed cum surrepto fueris tristissimus auro,
    me primam lacrimis sollicitabis inops."

XIII

DE HIRCO ET TAURO

Immensum taurus fugeret cum forte leonem
    tutaque desertis quaereret antra viis,

¹⁴ subruta sola modis *Lachmann.*
XII. ⁴ semina *plerique codd.*: gramina *Canneg.*: *fortasse*
vimina *vel* stramina *Ellis.*

clay jar, through fear that it might be an instance of the light damaged by the heavy, and because weakness has no confidence in dealings with the stronger, said, " Though you relieve me of anxiety as far as your promises go, still I cannot shake my mind clear of fear. For whether the water brings me up against you or you against me, I shall always be the sole victim of either disaster."

XII

The Peasant and the Treasure

On breaking up the earth by the impact of his plough a peasant noticed a treasure-hoard leap into view from the furrows. Presently with quickened heart he abandoned the plough, now disesteemed, and drove his oxen to better pastures. At once with vows he raised altars in honour of Earth, since she unasked had given him the wealth entrusted to her. As he rejoiced in his new estate, Fortune with an eye to the future gave him a warning; for she was piqued that he did not think her also deserving of incense. " For the moment you neglect to hand over your treasure-trove to any temple of mine, and prefer to share it with other gods; but when the gold is stolen and you are in the depths of grief, I shall be the first whom you will tearfully entreat in your beggary."

XIII

The Goat and the Bull

It happened once that a bull was running away from a mighty lion, seeking by lonely paths for some

speluncam reperit, quam tunc hirsutus habebat
    Cinyphii ductor qui gregis esse solet.
ast ubi submissa meditantem irrumpere fronte
    obvius obliquo terruit ore caper,
tristis abit longaque fugax de valle locutus
    (nam timor expulsum iurgia ferre vetat):
" non te demissis saetosum, putide, barbis,
    illum, qui super est consequiturque, tremo;   1
nam si discedat, nosces, stultissime, quantum
    discrepet a tauri viribus hircus olens."

XIV

De Simia

Iuppiter in toto quondam quaesiverat orbe,
    munera natorum quis meliora daret.
certatim ad regem currit genus omne ferarum,
    permixtumque homini cogitur ire pecus;
sed nec squamigeri desunt ad iurgia pisces
    vel quicquid volucrum purior aura vehit.
inter quos trepidae ducebant pignora matres,
    iudicio tanti discutienda dei.
tunc brevis informem traheret cum simia natum,
    ipsum etiam in risum compulit ire Iovem.   1

XIII. ³ repetit C *Rawl.* m¹.
  ⁵ post *plerique codd.*: ast BX *Pet.*² b².
  ⁷ longaque *plerique codd.*: longeque *Canneg.*: longumque
Ellis. valle (vale P) *codd.*: calle *Lachmann.*
XIV. ⁴ homini *codd.*: cicur *Baehrens.*
  ⁷ inter quos *codd.*: in tergo *Baehrens.*

safe cavern, when he discovered a cave which was then occupied by a shaggy goat accustomed to lead the Cinyphian herd.[a] Thereupon, when the goat met him and with sidelong look frightened him out of his intention to lower his head and burst in, he went off mournfully and in his flight sent a reply from the far reaches of the valley (fear forbade him to quarrel over his rebuff). " It's not you I tremble at, you stinking creature, with your bristly hair and trailing beard; it's that lion—which is still to come and which follows in my track. If he abandons the chase, you'll learn, you arrant fool, the difference between a bull in his strength and a smelly goat."

XIV

The Monkey

Jupiter had once inquired through the whole world which animal it was that could present the gift of the finest offspring. In eager rivalry there hastened to the king every sort of creature of the wild, and every beast that has dealings with man was constrained to come. Nor did the scale-covered fish fail to contest their claim, or any bird borne on the clearer air. Among this gathering nervous mothers led up their progeny to be inspected at the judgement-seat of the powerful god. Just then, as a dwarfish monkey pulled forward her ugly offspring, she forced even Jove himself to laugh. But for all her

---

[a] The epithet refers to the long-haired goats bred in the Mauritanian territory washed by the Cinyps.

hanc tamen ante alios rupit turpissima vocem,
    dum generis crimen sic abolere cupit:
" Iuppiter hoc norit, maneat victoria si quem;
    iudicio superest omnibus iste meo."

XV

De Grue et Pavone

Threiciam volucrem fertur Iunonius ales
    communi sociam conteruisse cibo—
namque inter varias fuerat discordia formas,
    magnaque de facili iurgia lite trahunt—
quod sibi multimodo fulgerent membra decore,   5
    caeruleam facerent livida terga gruem;
et simul erectae circumdans tegmina caudae
    sparserat arcatum sursus in astra iubar.
illa licet nullo pennarum certet honore,
    his tamen insultans vocibus usa datur: 10
" quamvis innumerus plumas variaverit ordo,
    mersus humi semper florida terga geris:
ast ego deformi sublimis in aera penna
    proxima sideribus numinibusque feror."

    [11] haec BX *Rawl.*: hec *Ashb.*: hanc *cett. codd.*
    XV. [2] contenuisse P: continuisse *vel* continuasse *cett. codd.*:
corripuisse *Froehner*: commonuisse *vel* detinuisse *vel* con-
teruisse *Ellis.*
    [7] agmina *Ellis.*
    [8] arcanum *codd.*: arcatum *Barth.* rursus *codd.*: sursus
Lachmann.

ugliness the monkey flung out these words before others could speak, anxious by so doing to remove the reproach upon her race: "Let Jupiter determine whether victory is in store for anyone; to *my* mind the little monkey before you beats the lot."

XV

THE CRANE AND THE PEACOCK

The story goes that Juno's bird disparaged the Thracian fowl,[a] when she shared their joint feeding-ground. For a quarrel had arisen involving their different kinds of beauty and they were protracting a long argument on a case easy to settle. The peacock contended that the parts of his body gleamed in manifold loveliness, but that a dingy back gave the crane a dun colour, and at the word he arrayed about him the canopy of his uplifted tail and shot an arc of light upwards to the sky. The crane, though unable to rival the other in any glory of plumage, is nevertheless said to have used these words in mockery: "Countless may be the array of colours variegating your plumage, yet you, the wearer of that gaudy tail, are for ever kept close to earth. But I soar aloft into the air on my wing for all its ugliness, and am wafted nigh to the stars and heavenly powers."

[a] *i.e.* the crane : *cf.* Ovid, *A. A.* iii. 182, *Threiciamve gruem*; Virg. *Aen.* X. 265, *Strymoniae grues.*

XVI

De Quercu et Harundine

Montibus e summis radicitus eruta quercus
  decidit insani turbine victa Noti,
quam tumidis subter decurrens alveus undis
  suscipit et fluvio praecipitante rapit.
verum ubi diversis impellitur ardua ripis,
  in fragiles calamos grande residit onus.
tunc sic exiguo conectens caespite ramos
  miratur liquidis quod stet harundo vadis:
se quoque tam vasto necdum consistere trunco,
  ast illam tenui cortice ferre minas.   10
stridula mox blando respondens canna susurro
  seque magis tutam debilitate docet.
" tu rabidos " inquit " ventos saevasque procellas
  despicis et totis viribus acta ruis.
ast ego surgentes paulatim demoror Austros   15
  et quamvis levibus provida cedo Notis;
in tua praeruptus se effundit robora nimbus,
  motibus aura meis ludificata perit."

haec nos dicta monent magnis obsistere frustra,
  paulatimque truces exsuperare minas.   20

XVI. ⁹ necdum *plerique codd.*: rectum C *Reg.*: rectam
Ellis.   consistere *plerique codd.*: non sistere *Ellis.*
  ¹⁷ offendit *codd. praeter* X: se effundit *Lachmann.*
  ¹⁹ frusta b: lustra B: rebus b³: frustra *cett. codd.*: fluxa
Ellis.

THE FABLES OF AVIANUS

XVI

THE OAK AND THE REED

An oak was torn up by its roots, a victim of the mad South Wind's whirling force, and fell down from the mountain heights. A river-channel, flowing below in high spate, took it and bore it off in the headlong current. But after the tall trunk had been thrust from bank to bank, its mighty bulk came to rest among slender reeds. Then it marvelled that a reed, fastening its stalks in but a tiny tuft, should stand firm in the flowing water; it marvelled that, for all its massive trunk, even it could not yet[a] stand unmoved, while the reed with its slender rind endured the menaces of nature.[b] Presently the creaking reed, answering with meek whisper, declared that its weakness increased its safety. "You," it said, " scorn the ravening winds and cruel tempests, and fall beneath the onset of their full strength. I keep in dalliance the gradually rising Auster and, with an eye to the future, let myself be swayed by Notus, however light his breath. Against your strength the rain-storm hurls itself sheer; but, baffled by my motion, the breeze sinks into nothing."

This teaches us that it is in vain we resist the mighty and that it is by slow degrees that we surmount the fury of their menaces.

---

[a] *necdum.* The years in which the *truncus* had grown *tam vastus* had not yet made it strong enough to resist the storm. *Cf.* J. E. B. Mayor, *C. R.* I. (1887) p. 191.

[b] *miratur* (8) is first followed by *quod stet* to express indirect statement, then by two accus. and infin. clauses (9–10).

XVII

De Venatore et Tigride

Venator iaculis haud irrita vulnera torquens
  turbabat trepidas per sua lustra feras.
tum pavidis audax cupiens succurrere tigris
  verbere commoto iussit adesse minax.
ille tamen solito contorquens tela lacerto   5
  " nunc tibi, qualis eam, nuntius iste refert."
et simul emissum transegit vulnere ferrum,
  praestrinxitque citos hasta cruenta pedes.
molliter at fixum traheret cum saucia telum,
  a trepida fertur vulpe retenta diu,   10
nempe quis ille foret, qui talia vulnera ferret,
  aut ubinam iaculum delituisset agens.
illa gemens fractoque loqui vix murmure coepit
  (nam solitas voces ira dolorque rapit):
" nulla quidem medio convenit in aggere forma   15
  quaeque oculis olim sit repetenda meis,
sed cruor et validis in nos directa lacertis
  ostendunt aliquem tela fuisse virum."

XVIII

De Quattuor Iuvencis et Leone

Quattuor immensis quondam per prata iuvencis
  fertur amicitiae tanta fuisse fides,

XVII. ² pavidas BGOX *Rawl. Ashb. Pet.*² : rapidas L :
rabidas *cett. codd.* : trepidas *Lachmann*.
  ⁴ commoto O : commotas *plerique codd.*   minas *codd.* :
minax *Froehner*.
  ⁶ eram *plerique codd.* : eam T*m*², *Froehner*.
  ¹¹ dum quis *plerique codd.* : quis deus *Baehrens* : nempe
quis *Ellis*.

THE FABLES OF AVIANUS

XVII

The Hunter and the Tigress

A huntsman who dealt effective wounds with the javelins he discharged used to drive the wild animals in terrified confusion through their coverts. Then a bold tigress, eager to succour the panic-stricken beasts, lashing with her tail in threatening wise, bade him come up against her. But he hurled as usual his missile from his shoulder, saying, " That is the messenger which in this hour tells you my prowess as I go my way "; and at that moment the weapon which he discharged pierced and wounded her, and the blood-stained shaft grazed her swift feet. When the wounded tigress was gently drawing forth the tight-fixed weapon, she is said to have been kept in converse a long time by a fox asking in dismay, who was the man that could deal such wounds or where had he hid himself to shoot his javelin. The tigress with moans and broken growls found speech with difficulty; for rage and pain robbed her of her usual utterance; " No shape that my sight could afterwards recall confronted me in the middle of the road,[a] but the blood and the weapon aimed at me by a powerful arm show that it was some man of might."

XVIII

The Four Oxen and the Lion

Once among four huge oxen in the meadows there existed, as the story goes, so trusty a bond of affection,

---

[a] Servius on Virg. *Aen.* V. 273, *viae deprensus in aggere*, explains *agger est media viae eminentia coaggeratis lapidibus strata*: *cf.* Rut. Namat. I. 39 *Aurelius agger = Via Aurelia*.

ut simul emissos nullus divelleret error,
    rursus et e pastu turba rediret amans.
hos quoque collatis inter se cornibus ingens
    dicitur in silvis pertimuisse leo,
dum metus oblatam prohibet temptare rapinam
    et coniuratos horret adire boves;
et quamvis audax factisque immanior esset,
    tantorum solus viribus impar erat.   1
protinus aggreditur pravis insistere verbis,
    collisum cupiens dissociare pecus.
sic postquam dictis animos disiunxit acerbis,
    invasit miserum diripuitque gregem.
tunc quidam ex illis " vitam servare quietam   1
    qui cupit, e nostra discere morte potest;
neve cito admotas verbis fallacibus aures
    impleat aut veterem deserat ante fidem."

XIX

DE ABIETE AC DUMIS

Horrentes dumos abies pulcherrima risit,
    cum facerent formae iurgia magna suae,
indignum referens cum istis certamen haberi,
    quos meritis nullus consociaret honor:
" nam mihi deductum surgens in nubila corpus
    verticis erectas tollit in astra comas,
puppibus et patulis media cum sede locamur,
    in me suspensos explicat aura sinus;
at tibi deformem quod dant spineta figuram,
    despectum cuncti praeteriere viri."   1

XVIII. ⁴ ovans WBX b *Pet.*² : amans *cett. codd.*
 ⁹ sed *co l d.* : et *vulgo.*
¹⁴ invasit BX *Pet.*² : invadit *cett. codd.*
XIX. ³ cunctis *codd.* : cum istis *Baehrens* : dumis *Ellis.*
 ⁴ quos GTOX *Reg. Rawl.* : quod *cett. codd.*

that on being sent from their stalls together no straying would sunder them, and then again the group would return from pasture still friends. Now, before these oxen, with their horns united in line, a mighty lion in the forest is said to have quailed, so long as fear forbade him to make trial of the quarry facing him, and he shrank from approaching the allied cattle; and, though courageous and more savage in his deeds, he was no match by himself for the strength of such powerful beasts. Thereupon he began to urge evil counsels, anxious to divide the herd by making them quarrel. So after he had sown disunion with embittering words, he rushed upon the poor herd and tore them limb from limb. Then one of them said, "Anyone who wants to preserve an untroubled life may learn from our death. Let him not be in a hurry to suffer a ready ear to be filled with guile, or to desert over soon an ancient loyalty."

XIX

The Pine and the Bramble Bush

A very lovely pine made mockery of a prickly bramble bush in a serious dispute touching their claims to beauty. The pine said it was unfair it should have to contend with such as no title brought by merit into its own class. " For my tapering trunk rises towards the clouds, and rears starward the lofty foliage of my tree-top; and when I am placed on the ship's open deck in the centre, the sails unfurled by the wind hang upon me. But you—everyone passes you by with scorn, because your growth of thorns gives you an ugly appearance." The bramble

ille refert: " nunc laeta quidem bona sola fateris
    et nostris frueris imperiosa malis;
sed cum pulchra minax succidet membra securis,
    quam velles spinas tunc habuisse meas! "

XX

De Piscatore et Pisce

Piscator solitus praedam suspendere saeta
    exigui piscis vile trahebat onus.
sed postquam superas captum perduxit ad auras
    atque avido fixum vulnus ab ore tulit,
" parce, precor " supplex lacrimis ita dixit obortis;   5
    " nam quanta ex nostro corpore dona feres?
nunc me saxosis genetrix fecunda sub antris
    fudit et in propriis ludere iussit aquis.
tolle minas, tenerumque tuis sine crescere mensis:
    haec tibi me rursum litoris ora dabit: 10
protinus immensi depastus caerula ponti
    pinguior ad calamum sponte recurro tuum."
ille nefas captum referens absolvere piscem,
    difficiles queritur casibus esse vices:
" nam miserum est " inquit " praesentem amittere
    praedam,   15
stultius et rursum vota futura sequi."

XX. ⁶ damna *codd.*: dona *Lachmann.*
¹⁴ casibus *codd.*: cassibus *Froehner, Baehrens, Ellis.*

rejoins : " True, now you rejoice and all you profess is fair, and in your domineering way you take pleasure in my defects. But in that day when the threatening axe shall hew your fine limbs, how you would then wish that you had possessed my thorns ! "

XX

The Angler and the Fish

A fisherman who used to catch his prey hanging on a horsehair line was drawing in a tiny fish of trumpery weight. But after he had brought his catch up into the air and the fish had been pierced with a wound *a* through its hungry mouth, in entreaty amid starting tears it said, " Have mercy, I pray you ; for how much gain will you derive from my flesh ? Just now has a fertile mother spawned me 'neath the rocky caves, and bidden me disport myself in our own waters. Banish your fell designs ; I am young ; let me grow up for your table. This bank of the shore will give me to you again. In a little time, when I have fed on the blue waters of the boundless deep, I shall willingly return the fatter to your rod." The fisherman, declaring it a crime to let go a fish once caught, complained that hazards are beset with turns incalculable : " It is a pity," he said, " to lose the spoil in hand, and a worse folly to start afresh in pursuit of future hopes."

---

a *vulnus ferre* here means to endure a wound : contrast XVII. 11, where it means to deal a wound.

XXI

De Alite et Messione

Parvula progeniem terrae mandaverat ales,
    qua stabat viridi caespite flava seges.
rusticus hanc fragili cupiens decerpere culmo
    vicinam supplex forte petebat opem.
sed vox implumes turbavit credita nidos,   5
    suasit et e laribus continuare fugam.
cautior hos remeans prohibet discedere mater:
    " nam quid ab externis proficietur? " ait.
ille iterum caris operam mandavit amicis;
    at genetrix rursum tutior inde manet.   10
sed postquam curvas dominum comprendere falces,
    frugibus et veram sensit adesse manum,
" nunc " ait, " o miseri, dilecta relinquite rura,
    cum spem de propriis viribus ille petit."

XXII

De Cupido et Invido

Iuppiter ambiguas hominum praediscere mentes
    ad terras Phoebum misit ab arce poli.
tunc duo diversis poscebant numina votis;
    namque alter cupidus, invidus alter erat.

XXI. [5] credula *plerique codd.*: sedula b: credita *Withof*:
acredula (*in casu vocativo*) *Ellis*.
   [6] suaserat e X: suaserat et *cett. codd.*: suasit et *Ellis*.
   XXII. [4] invidus *codd.* (*contra metrum*): lividus *Withof*.

---

[a] Babrius makes the bird a lark. Gellius, *N. A.* ii. 29,
who paraphrases the fable from Ennius' trochaic septenarii,

THE FABLES OF AVIANUS

XXI

The Bird and the Reaping of the Corn

A tiny little bird [a] had entrusted her young to the
ground where with its root-stem green stood the
yellow corn-crop. It so happened that a farmer
wanting to cut the corn from its fragile stalk begged
and prayed for a neighbour's help. Now these words,
which the unfledged nestlings believed, struck panic
into them and counselled instant flight from their
home. Their mother was more wary; on her return
she told them not to go away, saying, "What good will
come from outsiders?" The farmer once more en-
trusted the task to his dear friends; but the mother
again stayed where she was, all the safer for that
reason. But when she perceived that the owner was
gripping the curved sickle and that his true hand was
near the crops, she said, "Now, my poor dears,
abandon the fields you love so well, now that he seeks
the fulfilment of his hopes from his own powers."

XXII

The Greedy Man and the Jealous Man

Jupiter sent Phoebus to the earth from the citadel
of the sky to discover in advance the doubtful hearts
of mankind. Just then two men were beseeching
the gods to satisfy different desires, for one had a
covetous and the other a jealous nature. The Sun-

describes it as *cassita*, "helmeted" or "crested." Ellis'
acredula strictly means a nightingale. While the Ennian
moral is explicitly "Do not expect friends to do what you
can do yourself," it is noticeable that Avianus gives no
epimythion.

his sese medium Titan scrutatus utrumque   5
   obtulit et precibus cum peteretur, ait:
" praestant di facilis; quae namque rogaverit unus,
   protinus haec alter congeminata feret."
sed cui longa iecur nequeat satiare cupido,
   distulit admotas in nova damna preces,   10
spem sibi confidens alieno crescere voto
   seque ratus solum munera ferre duo.
ille ubi captantem socium sua praemia vidit,
   supplicium proprii corporis optat ovans;
nam petit exstinctus sic lumine degeret uno.   15
   alter ut hoc duplicans vivat utroque carens.
tum sortem sapiens humanam risit Apollo,
   invidiaeque malum rettulit ipse Iovi,
quae, dum proventis aliorum gaudet iniquis,
   laetior infelix et sua damna cupit.   20

XXIII

DE VENDITORE ET BACCHO

Venditor insignem referens de marmore Bacchum
   expositum pretio fecerat esse deum.
nobilis hunc quidam funesta in sede sepulcri
   mercari cupiens compositurus erat;

[6] confiteretur X : ut peteretur *cett.* : cum peteretur *Ellis* :
Iuppiter aecus *Lachmann.*
[7] praestabit C *Reg.* : praestandi *cett. codd.* : praestandist
Baehrens : praestant di *Ellis.* facilis *codd.* nam quae spera-
verit VW : nam quaeque rogaverit *plerique codd.* : quae
namque rogaverit *Ellis.*
[15] ut *plerique codd.* : sic *Ellis.*

---

[a] Ellis' conjecture and interpretation have been followed,
though *facilis* is a rare form for the nom. plur. (See Neue,
Formenlehre d. lat. Sprache, II. 1875, pp. 34 *sqq.*)

God, scrutinising both, presented himself as a mediator between them, and when entreated with prayers said, "The gods being kind grant fulfilment;[a] for what one of you asks, that shall the other forthwith receive, doubled." But the one, whose far-reaching desires could not satisfy his heart, put off addressing his prayer—with a surprising loss as the sequel.[b] He was sure the desires of the other would increase his own prospects, calculating that in his single person he was thus winning two boons. The other, when he saw his companion grasping at his own prizes, gleefully prayed for a punishment to be inflicted on his own body. For he asked that he might lose one eye for the rest of his life in order that the other, doubling this misfortune, might live deprived of both. Then Apollo, learning the truth, smiled at human lot, and with his own lips reported to Jupiter the curse of jealousy, which, as it rejoices in other people's untoward fortunes, is unlucky enough the more gladly to desire its own harm also.

XXIII

The Salesman and his Statue of Bacchus [c]

A trading craftsman who had fashioned a fine Bacchus in marble had put up the god for sale. A nobleman who wanted to buy it intended to place it in the funereal resting-place containing his tomb.

---

[b] *i.e.* the loss of both his eyes, described later.
[c] The fable is so full of difficulties that Ellis questions its authenticity. The use of the participles in lines 1 and 4 marks the deterioration of syntax; *expositum fecerat esse* cannot be called good Latin; and the obscurity of lines 7–9 led Baehrens to rewrite them with more than usual infelicity.

alter adoratis ut ferret numina templis,   5
  redderet et sacro debita vota loco.
" nunc " ait " ambiguum facies de mercibus omen,
  cum spes in pretium munera dispar agit,
et me defunctis seu malis tradere divis,
  sive decus busti seu velis esse deum;   10
subdita namque tibi est magni reverentia sacri
  atque eadem retines funera nostra manu."

convenit hoc illis, quibus est permissa potestas,
  an prodesse magis seu nocuisse velint.

XXIV

De Venatore et Leone

Certamen longa protractum lite gerebant
  venator quondam nobilis atque leo.
hi cum perpetuum cuperent in iurgia finem,
  edita continuo forte sepulcra vident.
illic docta manus flectentem colla leonem   5
  fecerat in gremio procubuisse viri.
" scilicet affirmas pictura teste superbum
  te fieri? exstinctam nam docet esse feram."
ille graves oculos ad inania signa retorquens
  infremit et rabido pectore verba dedit: 10

XXIII. ⁹ et me licet addere vivis *Baehrens.*
  ¹¹ fati *plerique codd.*: facti AGO *m. pr.* b *Pet.*²: sati P: sacri
Ellis: fani *Baehrens.*
  ¹⁴ prodesse X: praestare *plerique codd.*
  XXIV. ⁴ contigue *Baehrens* (*in not.*): continuo *codd.*
fronte *Ellis*: forte *codd.*
  ⁷ affirmans *plerique codd.*: affirmas *Ellis.*
  ⁸ se *codd.*: te *Ellis.*

Another wished to present [a] the god in the temple
where he worshipped and in the hallowed precincts
to fulfil a vow that was owing. "Now," said the
statue, "you will make a puzzling forecast about
your wares, when two far different prospects set a
price upon your work,[b] and you will be in doubt
whether you prefer to consign me to the dead or to
the gods, whether you wish me to adorn a tomb or
to be a deity. To your arbitrament is submitted the
reverence of a great religious act; in your hand also
you hold my death-warrant." [c]

This is applicable to those who have it in their
power to do a good or a bad turn according as they
wish.[d]

XXIV

THE HUNTER AND THE LION

A huntsman of renown and a lion were once
engaged in a contest protracted by long dispute.
As they desired to put an end once for all to their
quarrel, they saw on the instant, it so happened, a
lofty tombstone. Thereon a cunning hand had
represented a lion bowing its neck in submission and
prostrate in a man's embrace. "Can you really
assert that the evidence of that work of art makes
you proud? Why, it shows the death of the beast."
The lion, turning downcast eyes to the unreal figures,
growled and in fierceness of heart broke into speech :

[a] *ut ferret* depends on *mercari cupiit* supplied from *mercari
cupiens.*
[b] *munera* seems more suitably translated as " result of your
employment " than as " gift."
[c] *i.e.* to make of me a sepulchral ornament.
[d] *i.e.* the salesman had the option of benefiting or injuring
the statue.

" irrita te generis subiit fiducia vestri,
    artificis testem si cupis esse manum.
quod si nostra novum caperet sollertia sensum,
    sculperet ut docili pollice saxa leo,
tunc hominem adspiceres oppressum murmure
        magno,   15
    conderet ut rabidis ultima fata genis."

XXV

DE PUERO ET FURE

Flens puer extremam putei consedit ad undam,
    vana supervacuis rictibus ora trahens.
callidus hunc lacrimis postquam fur vidit obortis,
    quaenam tristitiae sit modo causa rogat.
ille sibi abrupti fingens discrimina funis   5
    hac auri queritur desiluisse cadum.
nec mora, sollicitam traxit manus improba vestem :
    exutus putei protinus ima petit.
parvulus exiguo circumdans pallia collo
    sentibus immersus delituisse datur.   10
sed post fallaci suscepta pericula voto
    tristis ut amissa veste resedit humi,
dicitur his sollers vocem rupisse querellis
    et gemitu summos sollicitasse deos :
" perdita, quisquis erit, post haec bene pallia credat,   15
    qui putat in liquidis quod latet urna vadis."

15 expressum marmore *Lachmann.*
XXV. 6 atque *plerique codd.* : ac C *Reg.* : hac *Froehner.*
16 natat *vel* natet *codd.* : latet *Wight Duff.*

---

a *latet* implies that the thief ought not to have been fool
enough to be cheated by the boy's story about letting a golden
pitcher drop into the well : he had not paused (*nec mora,* 7)

" Vain is the confidence in your human birth that
has entered into you, if you desire to have for a wit-
ness an artist's hand.   If *our* ingenuity admitted of
an extra sense, allowing a lion to engrave stones with
skilful touch, then you would behold how the man,
overwhelmed by a loud roar, closed his final destiny
in ravening jaws."

XXV

The Boy and the Thief

A boy sat down in tears at the edge of the water
of a well, deceitfully opening wide his mouth in
groundless blubbering.   A smart thief, on seeing him
with tears starting from his eyes, asked what was the
cause of his distress now.   The boy pretended his
rope had parted in two; thereby, he sobbed, his
golden pitcher had fallen down the well.   At once
the rascal's hand dragged off his hampering garment,
and, when stripped, he made straight for the bottom
of the well.   The youngster, so the story has it, put
the cloak round his own little neck, plunged into the
brambles and was lost to sight.   But when, after
encountering danger on a deceptive hope, he had
seated himself again on the ground, miserable over
the loss of his cloak, the shrewd knave (so the story
goes) gave utterance to these laments and made
moaning supplication to the high gods: " Hence-
forth let anyone, whoever he be, who thinks a jar
lies hid in clear water,[a] reckon that he has richly
deserved to lose his cloak."

to see if the gold was visible in the water. *Natet* or *natat*
implies that anyone who expected a jar to be floating at the
bottom of a well would be served right by losing his cloak.

XXVI

De Capella et Leone

Viderat excelsa pascentem rupe capellam,
  comminus esuriens cum leo ferret iter,
et prior " heus " inquit " praeruptis ardua saxis
  linque nec hirsutis pascua quaere iugis ;
sed cytisi croceum per prata virentia florem
  et glaucas salices et thyma grata pete."
illa gemens " desiste, precor, fallaciter " inquit
  " securam placidis instimulare dolis.
vera licet moneas, maiora pericula tollas,
  tu tamen his dictis non facis esse fidem :
nam quamvis rectis constet sententia verbis,
  suspectam hanc rabidus consiliator habet."

XXVII

De Cornice et Urna

Ingentem sitiens cornix adspexerat urnam,
  quae minimam fundo continuisset aquam.
hanc enisa diu planis effundere campis,
  scilicet ut nimiam pelleret inde sitim,
postquam nulla viam virtus dedit, admovet omnes
  indignata nova calliditate dolos ;
nam brevis immersis accrescens sponte lapillis
  potandi facilem praebuit unda viam.

XXVI. ⁸ instimulare b ² *et paraphr.* : insimulare *plerique*
codd. : insinuare *Cab.*
  ¹² rabidus *Ashb.* : gravidus *cett. codd.* : pravus *Baehrens.*
habes b³, *Lachmann, Ellis* : habet *cett. codd.*

722

XXVI

The Lion and the Goat

A hungry lion while passing near by had spied a she-goat grazing on a rocky height. He opened conversation with "Ho, there! leave these steeps with their precipitous crags and don't look for pasture on prickly ridges. No, you should go through the green meadows in quest of the yellow lucerne-flower and pale green willow and sweet thyme." "Please stop," said the goat with a groan, "your lying attempts to rouse me from my security with your gentle wiles. Though your advice has truth in it, though you suppress the greater dangers, yet you do not make me trust what you say. For however correct your words be and however sound their meaning, yet a famished counsellor has his meaning under suspicion."

XXVII

The Crow and the Jar

A thirsty crow had spied a huge jar containing a very little water at the bottom. Long did the crow strive to spill this water on the level plain, to banish, of course, thereby her excessive thirst; but, when no valiant effort could provide a way, she lost her temper and with fresh cunning applied all her crafty devices. She threw pebbles in, and the low level of water rose naturally and so supplied an easy way of drinking.

viribus haec docuit quam sit prudentia maior,
qua coeptum cornix explicuisset opus.   10

XXVIII

De Rustico et Iuvenco

Vincla recusanti dedignantique iuvenco
  aspera mordaci subdere colla iugo
rusticus obliqua succidens cornua falce
  credidit insanum defremuisse pecus,
cautus et immenso cervicem innectit aratro   5
  (namque erat hic cornu promptior atque pede),
scilicet ut longus prohiberet verbera temo
  neve ictus faciles ungula saeva daret.
sed postquam irato detractans vincula collo
  immeritam vacua calce fatigat humum,   10
continuo eversam pedibus dispergit harenam,
  quam † in domini Boreas ora sequentis agat.
tunc hic informi squalentes pulvere crines
  discutiens imo pectore victus ait:
"nimirum exemplum naturae derat iniquae,   15
  qua fieri posset quis ratione nocens."

XXVII. [10] volucris *plerique codd.*: cornix *Ellis (servans
metrum).*
XXVIII. [9] bos quom *Baehrens*: postquam *codd.*
[10] vacuo (*masc.*) *nonnulli codd., Ellis.*
[12] quam ferus in domini ora *plerique codd.*: q. in d. aura
ferens ora *Lachmann*: q. feriens Boreas ora *Withof*: q. in d.
Boreas ora *Baehrens in not.* agat ACPT b: agit *cett. codd.*
[13] sic *codd.*: hic *Lachmann.*
[16] cum *codd.*: quis *Baehrens.*

This fable has proved the superiority of foresight over stout efforts, as by it the crow accomplished the task she had undertaken.

XXVIII

THE FARMER AND HIS OX

There once was an ox that chafed at ropes and shirked submitting its rebellious neck to the grip of the yoke. The farmer cut its horns with a knife used slantwise and thought the frenzied animal had abated its rage. Carefully he fastened its neck to the weighty plough (for it was over-ready with horn and hoof), doubtless so that the long pole might obstruct any butting and that its cruel hoof might find it difficult to kick. But when the animal, its neck angrily struggling against the straps, worried the inoffensive earth with impotent hoof, its feet at once churned up the sand broadcast for the North wind to blow into its master's face as he followed. Then the farmer, while he shook his locks begrimed with unsightly dust, said, in deep discomfiture of heart, " Truly, I needed an instance of a vicious temper to show how anyone could contrive to do mischief." [a]

---

[a] This new instance proved how a low nature, in spite of all precautions, could work harm.

XXIX

De Viatore et Satyro

Horrida congestis cum staret bruma pruinis
  cunctaque durato stringeret arva gelu,
haesit in adversa nimborum mole viator;
  perdita nam prohibet semita ferre gradum.
hunc nemorum custos fertur miseratus in antro   5
  exceptum Satyrus continuisse suo.
quem simul adspiciens ruris miratur alumnus
  vimque homini tantam protinus esse pavet;
nam gelidos artus vitae ut revocaret in usum,
  afflatas calido solverat ore manus.   10
sed cum depulso coepisset frigore laetus
  hospitis eximia sedulitate frui,
namque illi agrestem cupiens ostendere vitam
  silvarum referens optima quaeque dabat,
obtulit et calido plenum cratera Lyaeo,   15
  laxet ut infusus frigida membra tepor.
ille ubi ferventem labris contingere testam
  horruit, algenti rursus ab ore reflat.
obstipuit duplici monstro perterritus hospes
  et pulsum silvis longius ire iubet: 20
" nolo " ait " ut nostris umquam successerit antris,
  tam diversa duo qui simul ora ferat."

XXIX. ⁸ protinus *codd.*: pectoris *Lachmann*: providus
Froehner.
¹⁰ foverat *Lachmann*: solverat *plerique codd.*
¹¹ sed cum *codd.*: donec *Baehrens.*
¹⁸ sufflat *vel* suflat *codd.*: reflat *Schenkl.*

THE FABLES OF AVIANUS

XXIX

The Traveller and the Satyr

When mid-winter stood bristling with thick frost and bound every field in hardened ice, a traveller came to a halt in a heavy barrier of mist; for the losing of his path prevented his advance. They say one of the guardians of the woodland, a Satyr, felt pity and gave him welcome and shelter in his cave. This nurseling of the country [a] looked upon him wondering the while, and straightway was afeared to see a mortal possess power so great. For, to bring back his chilled limbs to the tasks of life, the traveller had blown into his hands and thawed them with his warm breath. But it was different when he had banished the cold and had delightedly begun to enjoy his host's generous attentions; since, anxious to show him how they lived in the country, the Satyr kept bringing out and serving all the best that the woodland yielded; he set before him also a bowl full of warm wine so that its pervasive heat might loosen the chilliness of his limbs. The traveller, fearing to touch the glowing cup with his lips, blew this time with a cooling breath. His host was alarmed and astounded at the double miracle, and driving him from the woods bade him begone still further off. " I desire no one," he said, " ever to approach my cave who owns at the same moment two such different sorts of mouth."

[a] The Satyr is called *ruris alumnus* as one of the ape-like and goat-footed demigods of the forest: *cf.* Ovid *Met.* I. 192–3 *sunt mihi semidei, sunt rustica numina Nymphae, Faunique Satyrique et monticolae Silvani*; ib. VI. 392–3 *ruricolae, silvarum numina, Fauni et Satyri fratres.*

XXX

De Sue et Illius Domino

Vastantem segetes et pinguia culta ruentem
  liquerat abscisa rusticus aure suem,
ut memor accepti referens monumenta doloris
  ulterius teneris parceret ille satis.
rursus in exsculpti deprensus crimine campi   5
  perdidit indultae perfidus auris onus.
nec mora, praedictae segeti caput intulit horrens;
  poena sed insignem congeminata facit.
tunc domini captum mensis dedit ille superbis,
  in varias epulas plurima frusta secans.   10
sed cum consumpti dominus cor quaereret apri,
  impatiens fertur quod rapuisse cocus,
rusticus hoc iustam verbo compescuit iram,
  affirmans stultum non habuisse suem—
nam cur membrorum demens in damna redisset,   15
  atque uno totiens posset ab hoste capi?

haec illos descripta monent, qui saepius ausi
  numquam peccatis abstinuere manus.

XXX. ⁵ exculpti G : excepti *cett. codd.* : excerpti *Guiet.*
  ⁷ praedictae *plerique codd.* : praedator *Lachmann* : praeve-
titae *Baehrens.*
  ⁸ quod O *Rawl., Pet.*² : sed *cett. codd.* indignum *codd.* :
indictum *Cab.* : insignem *Lachmann.*

THE FABLES OF AVIANUS

XXX

THE PIG AND ITS OWNER

A pig was ruining a farmer's corn and trampling his fertile fields; so he cut its ear off and let it go, hoping that, carrying home a reminder of the pain suffered, it would remember in future and keep off the tender crops. It was caught again in the crime of grubbing up the soil, and for its thieving lost the ear it had—the one previously spared. Immediately afterwards it thrust its mutilated [a] head into the aforementioned corn; but the twice-repeated punishment made it a marked trespasser.[b] This time the farmer, having captured it, gave it for its owner's sumptuous banquet, cutting a great number of slices for the various dishes. But when they had been eating the boar and the owner asked for its heart, which the ravenous cook is said to have purloined, then the farmer soothed his reasonable anger with these words, remarking that the pig was stupid and never had a heart [c]—for why had it been mad enough to return just to lose parts of its body? why let itself be caught so many times by the same enemy?

This sketch is a warning to those who have ventured too often and never kept their hands off iniquity.

[a] *Horrens* is glossed in the Trèves MS. as *truncatum*.
[b] If *indignum* of the MSS. is kept, the sense is that the two previous punishments made this new trespass by the pig an outrage. Nothing, therefore, but death could meet the case.
[c] The *cor* was considered the seat of understanding.

MINOR LATIN POETS

XXXI

De Mure et Bove

Ingentem fertur mus quondam parvus oberrans
  ausus ab exiguo laedere dente bovem.
verum ubi mordaci confecit vulnera rostro,
  tutus in anfractus conditur inde suos.
ille licet vasta torvum cervice minetur,   5
  non tamen iratus quem petat esse videt.
tunc indignantem mus hoc sermone fatigans
  distulit hostiles calliditate minas:
" non quia magna tibi tribuerunt membra parentes,
  viribus effectum constituere tuis.   10
disce tamen brevibus quae sit fiducia rostris,
  ut faciat quicquid parvula turba cupit."

XXXII

De Aratore et Bobus

Haerentem luteo sub gurgite rusticus axem
  liquerat et nexos ad iuga tarda boves,
frustra depositis confidens numina votis
  ferre suis rebus, cum resideret, opem.
cui rector summis Tirynthius infit ab astris   5
  (nam vocat hunc supplex in sua vota deum):

XXXI. ⁷ iusto *codd.*: mus hoc *Withof*: lusor *Ellis.*
¹¹ monstris *plerique codd.*: membris B: rostris *Froehner.*
¹² ut W *Reg., Pet.*¹: et *plerique codd.* faciat *plerique codd.*:
facias *Pet.*¹, B *m. sec., paraphr.*
XXXII. ³ depositis *plerique codd.*: dispositis PX *Rawl.* b².

ᵃ For *ab cf.* Ovid. *Met.* viii. 513, *invitis correptus ab ignibus arsit.*

730

THE FABLES OF AVIANUS

XXXI

The Mouse and the Ox

They tell how once upon a time a little mouse on its wanderings ventured with [a] its tiny teeth to attack a mighty ox. When its nibbling mouth finished biting, it thereupon hid safely in its winding hole. Though the ox made sullen threats with his huge neck, yet for all his anger he could not see that there lived an enemy for him to attack. Then the mouse dispersed [b] the foe's threats with its cleverness, bantering the enraged ox with these words: "Because your parents transmitted strong limbs to you, it does not follow that they added efficiency to your strength. Learn, however, the self-reliance that our tiny mouths possess, and learn how our pigmy band does whatever it wants."

XXXII

The Ploughman and his Oxen [c]

A peasant had left his cart sticking in a muddy pool and his oxen fastened to a yoke that would not move. He trusted in vain that thanks to the vows he lodged the gods would assist his fortunes though he sat idle himself. From the starry heights he was addressed by the Lord of Tiryns [d] (for he was one of the gods whom his entreaties invoked to further his prayers).

[b] Cf. x. 10.
[c] This represents De aratore et bobus, Rawl. Other titles are De rustico et axe, O, and De pigro Tyrint(h)ium frustra orante, C.
[d] Hercules.

" perge laborantes stimulis agitare iuvencos,
    et manibus pigras disce iuvare rotas.
tunc quoque congressum maioraque viribus ausum
    fas superos animis conciliare tuis.   10
disce tamen pigris non flecti numina votis
    praesentesque adhibe, cum facis ipse, deos."

XXXIII

De Ansere Ova Aurea Pariente

Anser erat cuidam pretioso germine feta,
    ovaque quae nidis aurea saepe daret.
fixerat hanc volucri legem Natura superbae,
    ne liceat pariter munera ferre duo.
sed dominus, cupidum sperans vanescere votum,   5
    non tulit exosas in sua lucra moras,
grande ratus pretium volucris de morte referre,
    quae tam continuo munere dives erat.
postquam nuda minax egit per viscera ferrum
    et vacuam solitis fetibus esse videt,   10
ingemuit tantae deceptus crimine fraudis;
    nam poenam meritis rettulit inde suis.

sic qui cuncta deos uno male tempore poscunt,
    iustius his etiam vota diurna negant.

    [10] animis *codd.* : athlis *Baehrens.*
    XXXIII. [5] cupidus . . . augescere *Wopkens.*

" Go on and drive your bullocks with the goad through their difficulties, and learn to aid with your hands the sluggish wheels. After you have come to grips and used your strength for greater efforts, then it is allowable also to win the gods over to your wishes. Learn, however, that the deities are not swayed by indolent vows: bring the gods to your help by acting yourself."

XXXIII

THE GOOSE THAT LAID THE GOLDEN EGGS

A man owned a goose teeming with precious offspring, one that often laid golden eggs in its nest. Nature had ordained this rule for the noble bird, that it should not lay more than one egg at the same time. But the owner, anticipating the disappearance of his greedy expectations,[a] could not brook delays, hateful when his profits were considered; [b] he thought to win a handsome prize by killing the bird, rich as it was in such unfailing bounty. When he plunged his dread knife into its open [c] breast, and found the bird empty of the usual eggs, he groaned aloud, tricked by the iniquity of so gross a fraud; for thereupon he ascribed the punishment to his own deserts.

So to those wicked enough to ask the gods for everything at once, they refuse the more justly even the prayers of a single day.

[a] The golden harvest, he feared, was too good to last.
[b] He wished more than one golden egg at a time.
[c] *nuda = nudata.* Ellis explains as " stript of feathers " to make the opening with more dexterity.

XXXIV

De Formica et Cicada

[Quisquis torpentem passus transisse iuventam
  nec timuit vitae providus ante mala,
confectus senio, postquam gravis adfuit aetas,
  heu frustra alterius saepe rogabit opem.]

Solibus ereptos hiemi formica labores
  distulit et brevibus condidit ante cavis.
verum ubi candentes suscepit terra pruinas
  arvaque sub rigido delituere gelu,
pigra nimis tantos non aequans corpore nimbos
  in laribus propriis umida grana legit.   1

discolor hanc precibus supplex alimenta rogabat,
  quae quondam querulo ruperat arva sono:
se quoque, maturas cum tunderet area messes,
  cantibus aestivos explicuisse dies.
parvula tunc ridens sic est affata cicadam   1
  (nam vitam pariter continuare solent):
" mi quoniam summo substantia parta labore est,
  frigoribus mediis otia longa traho;
at tibi saltandi nunc ultima tempora restant,
  cantibus est quoniam vita peracta prior."   2

XXXIV. ⁹ pigranimis KTV: pigra nimis *plerique codd.*
tanto (= *tam parvo*) T *Rawl., Pet.*² : tantos GC*m*².
¹¹ decolor A*m*¹KPT : discolor A*m*² *Ashb.*

734

THE FABLES OF AVIANUS

XXXIV

THE ANT AND THE GRASSHOPPER

[The man that has allowed his youth to go by in idleness and has not taken anxious precautions against the ills of life—that man, foredone with years, will in the presence of burdensome old age often ask in vain, alas, for a neighbour's help.]

An ant reserved for the winter the fruits of toil snatched during sunny hours and stored them betimes in her tiny hole. But when earth assumed its white robe of hoar frost and fields lay hid beneath unyielding ice, then, quite idle and unfit bodily to face the rain-storms, she picked out the moistened grain in her own abode. A grasshopper in her varied hues, who before had cleft the fields with plaintive note, amid prayers and supplications begged the ant for food. For her part, she said, when the threshing-floor was bruising the ripened harvest, she had worked out the summer days in song. Then with a laugh the tiny ant thus addressed the grasshopper (for their wont is to prolong their life equally)[a]: " Since *my* subsistence has been secured by dint of hardest toil, I draw out long days of ease in the midst of the frost. But *you* now have your last days left for dancing, since your past life was spent in song."[b]

[a] *i.e.* continue their life from year to year, as neither dies in the winter.

[b] The ant's ironic gibe is that, as the grasshopper has been an inveterate singer, she can conclude her days in dancing with her song as an accompaniment.

XXXV

De Simiae Gemellis

Fama est quod geminum profundens simia partum
    dividat in varias pignora nata vices;
namque unum caro genetrix educit amore,
    alteriusque odiis exsaturata tumet.
coeperit ut fetam gravior terrere tumultus,
    dissimili natos condicione rapit:
dilectum manibus vel pectore gestat amico,
    contemptum dorso suscipiente levat.
sed cum lassatis nequeat consistere plantis,
    oppositum fugiens sponte remittit onus.
alter at hirsuto circumdans bracchia collo
    haeret et invita cum genetrice fugit.
mox quoque dilecti succedit in oscula fratris,
    servatus vetulis unicus heres avis.

sic multos neglecta iuvant, atque ordine verso
    spes humiles rursus in meliora refert.

XXXVI

De Vitulo et Bove

Pulcher et intacta vitulus cervice resultans
    scindentem adsidue viderat arva bovem.
" non pudet heus " inquit " longaevo vincula collo
    ferre nec haec positis otia nosse iugis ?
cum mihi subiectas pateat discursus in herbas
    et nemorum liceat rursus opaca sequi."

XXXV. [11] ad P : et *Pet.*[1] : ab *cett. codd.* : at *vulgo.*
[16] *fortasse* rursus spes humiles *Ellis.*
XXXVI. [4] haec positis *Ellis* : expositis *codd.*

THE FABLES OF AVIANUS

XXXV

THE MONKEY'S TWINS

The story goes that a monkey gave birth to twin offspring and assigned her children each to a different destiny. One the mother reared in fond affection, and she rankled with superabundant hatred for the other. When a perilous attack began to alarm the mother she hurried her young apes off, meting out unequal treatment. The favourite she carried in her paws or her tender bosom; the despised one she lifted up and carried on her back. But when she could not stand upright on her wearied feet, in mid-flight she gladly let go the one that burdened her in front. But the other, throwing his arms round his mother's hairy neck, clung to her and shared her escape against her will. Besides, he soon succeeded to the caresses his favoured brother had enjoyed, and survived to be sole heir to his ancient lineage.

Thus do many come to like what once they slighted; and hope, changing the order of things, carries the lowly back into happier fortune.

XXXVI

THE CALF AND THE OX

A fine calf, skipping to and fro and never yoked as yet, had seen an ox busily ploughing the fields. "You there," he said, "are you not ashamed to have your aged neck fastened, unable to throw off the yoke and know the leisure that is mine? For I am free to range at will over the low-lying pasture, and then again I can make for the shade of the

at senior, nullam verbis compulsus in iram,
    vertebat solitam vomere fessus humum,
donec deposito per prata liceret aratro
    molliter herboso procubuisse toro.   1·
mox vitulum sacris innexum respicit aris
    admotum cultro comminus ire popae.
" hanc tibi " testis ait " dedit indulgentia mortem,
    expertem nostri quae facit esse iugi.
proderit ergo graves quamvis perferre labores,   1·
    otia quam tenerum mox peritura pati."

est hominum sors ista, magis felicibus ut mors
    sit cita, cum miseris vita diurna negat.

XXXVII

De Cane et Leone

Pinguior exhausto canis occurrisse leoni
    fertur et insertis verba dedisse iocis.
" nonne vides duplici tendantur ut ilia tergo
    luxurietque toris nobile pectus? " ait.
" proximus humanis ducor post otia mensis,
    communem capiens largius ore cibum."

[11] sertis *Cannegieter*.
[13] testis CK *Reg.*: tristis *cett. codd.*
[18] miseris B *m. pr.*: miseros *cett. codd.* negat B b² *m. sec.*:
regat *cett. codd.*: necat *Ellis*.

---

[a] The epimythion 17–18 is perhaps spurious, as it partly
contradicts lines 15–16, which may be taken to point the moral
and which advocate endurance.
[b] *verba dare* has not necessarily in late Latin the classical
sense of gulling: *cf.* ix. 20, xxxviii. 6: contrast i. 14.

grove." But the old ox, not at all angered by the
words, went on wearily turning the soil as usual with
the share, till he was allowed to drop the plough and
to lie at his ease on a grassy bed in the meadows.
Soon afterwards he saw the calf brought by a leading-
string to the sacrificial altar and coming close to the
knife of the priest's attendant. As he witnessed
this he said, " Such is the death given you by the
forbearance that leaves you free from my yoke. So
then it will be better to endure toil however burden-
some than to experience when young an ease that is
soon to be lost."

This is the lot of mortals; death comes swift to
the happier ones, while the daily life of the unfortunate
refuses them death.[a]

XXXVII

THE DOG AND THE LION

A well-fed dog is said to have met an exhausted
lion and to have addressed [b] him with taunts in his
words: "Don't you see," he said, "how my flanks
dilate under my back's double ridge [c] and my fine
breast has handsome muscles? When resting-time
has come, I am brought close up to the tables where
men eat, my mouth getting in ample measure the
fare my master shares with me." "But what is that

[e] Heinsius explained *duplici tergo* as *lato tergo*, like Virgil's
duplex agitur per lumbos spina, G. III. 87 (of a horse), where
Servius interprets "aut revera duplex aut lata." The
depression along the back of a horse in good condition gives
the appearance of a double spine. Ellis suggests that *tergo*
is used of the ridge or projecting surface of the skin covering
the dog's flanks, which is called "double" from inequalities
produced by outstanding muscle or fat.

" sed quod crassa malum circumdat guttura ferrum ? "
  " ne custodita fas sit abire domo.
at tu magna diu moribundus lustra pererras,
  donec se silvis obvia praeda ferat.   10
perge igitur nostris tua subdere colla catenis,
  dum liceat faciles promeruisse dapes."
protinus ille gravem gemuit collectus in iram
  atque ferox animi nobile murmur agit.
" vade " ait " et meritis nodum cervicibus infer,   15
  compensentque tuam vincula dura famem ;
at mea cum vacuis libertas redditur antris,
  quamvis ieiunus quae libet arva peto.
has illis epulas potius laudare memento,
  qui libertatem postposuere gulae."   20

XXXVIII

DE PISCE ET PHYCIDE

Dulcibus e stagnis fluvio torrente coactus
  aequoreas praeceps piscis obibat aquas.
illic squamigerum despectans improbus agmen
  eximium sese nobilitate refert.
non tulit expulsum patrio sub gurgite phycis   5
  verbaque cum salibus asperiora dedit :
" vana laboratis aufer mendacia dictis,
  quaeque refutari te quoque teste queant.

XXXVII. [7-8] *hos versus post* 10 *collocavit Cannegieter, post*
12 *Schenkl et Baehrens, post* 14 *Barth.*
  [7] quo *Cannegieter* : quod *codd.*
  [13] gemitu *codd.* : gemuit *Baehrens.*
  [16] compescant BX *Pet.*[1] *Pet.*[2]
  XXXVIII. [5] phycis *Cannegieter* : phoecis CK : phocas
GLOT *Rawl. Pet.*[2]

villainous bit of iron round your brawny throat?"
"That's to prevent my leaving the house I have been
guarding. But you for a long time wander through
the wilds dying of hunger, until your victim meets
you in the jungle. Proceed, therefore, to bow your
neck to the chains I wear, till you can earn an easy-
won feast." At once the lion with a growl worked
himself into a violent rage and in haughty spirit
uttered a lordly roar. "Begone," he said, "set
bonds on your neck as it deserves, and may the
galling chains take the place of hunger in your case;
but when I am restored still free to my solitary den,
famished though I be, I make for any field I please.
Mind you commend such junketing more especially
to those who have sacrificed independence for
gluttony."

XXXVIII

The Fish and the Lamprey

Driven by the rush of a river out of its fresh pools,
a fish darted headlong to the waters of the sea.
There it arrogantly looked down on the ranks of
scaly fish and averred that its high birth gave it
distinction. A lamprey in its ancestral depths could
not endure the *émigré*, and spoke [a] to it sharply in
satiric vein. "Away with empty falsehoods from
your affected language! away with what can be
disproved even on your own evidence! For I will

---

[a] *Cf.* note on *verba dedisse*, xxxvii. 2.

---

[6] salibus *codd. fere omnes contra metrum*: sociis G: salsis
Lachmann: ? sannis *Ellis*: probris asperiora *vel* salibus liberiora
Withof.

nam quis eat potior populo spectante probabo,

    si pariter captos umida lina trahant.   1●

tunc me nobilior magno mercabitur emptor,

    te simul aere brevi debile vulgus emet."

XXXIX

De Milite Arma Cremante

Voverat attritus quondam per proelia miles

    omnia suppositis ignibus arma dare,

vel quae victori moriens sibi turba dedisset

    vel quicquid profugo posset ab hoste capi.

interea votis fors adfuit, et memor arma

    coeperat accenso singula ferre rogo.

tunc lituus rauco deflectens murmure culpam

    immeritum flammis se docet isse pyrae.

" nulla tuos " inquit " petierunt tela lacertos,

    viribus affirmes quae tamen acta meis ;   1●

sed tantum ventis et cantibus arma coegi,

    hoc quoque submisso (testor et astra) sono."

ille resultantem flammis crepitantibus addens

    " nunc te maior " ait " poena dolorque rapit ;

    9 erit *codd.* : eat *Baehrens.*

    XXXIX. **8** esse prius *codd.* : piis *Canneg.* : cibum *Withof* : in flammis se d. esse pyrae *Froehner* : isse pyrae *Ellis.*

    13 resultantem *codd.* : reluctantem *ed. vetus.*

    14 dolorque *plerique codd.* : colorque B : calorque *Ellis.*

prove to you who passes for better in the eyes of the people, should a dripping net catch and land us both at the same time. In that case a purchaser of high rank will pay a lot for me, while the feeble rabble will give but a brass farthing for you."

XXXIX

The Soldier who Burned the Weapons

Once upon a time a soldier worn out in the wars had vowed to light a fire and devote to it all his arms, both those yielded to him in his hour of victory by numbers of dying combatants and aught that could be taken from the foe in flight. Time passed and chance favoured his hopes; so, mindful of his vow, he kindled a pyre and began bringing his weapons to it one by one. At that moment a trumpet with a harsh blare, deprecating all guilt, declared that it went innocent to the flaming pyre. "Never," it said, "were your brawny arms struck by missiles which you could, by way of plea, assert were hurled by strength of mine. No, I only mustered the weapons of war with wind and note, and that only (the stars be my witness) in a sound subdued." The soldier added the trumpet to the crackling flames and made it bounce, saying, "Now a severer punishment[a] and pain hurries

---

[a] " A severer punishment " (Ellis says " an extra severity of punishment ") befalls the trumpet; for, whereas the weapons only suffer the burning, it suffers first the violence of being thrown against the weapons and is then destroyed by fire. This supports *resultantem* rather than *reluctantem*, which otherwise is a good suggestion.

nam licet ipse nihil possis temptare nec ausis,
  saevior hoc, alios quod facis esse malos."

XL

DE PARDO ET VULPE

Distinctus maculis et pulchro pectore pardus
  inter consimiles ibat in ora feras;
sed quia nulla graves variarent terga leones,
  protinus his miserum credidit esse genus.
cetera sordenti damnans animalia vultu
  solus in exemplum nobilitatis erat.
hunc arguta novo gaudentem vulpis amictu
  corripit et vanas approbat esse notas:
" vade " ait " et pictae nimium confide iuventae,
  dum mihi consilium pulchrius esse queat,
miremurque magis quos munera mentis adornant,
  quam qui corporeis enituere bonis."

XLI

DE IMBRE ET TESTA

Impulsus ventis et pressa nube coactus
  ruperat hibernis se gravis imber aquis;
cumque per effusas stagnaret turbine terras,
  expositum campis fictile pressit opus:
mobile namque lutum tepidus prius instruit aer.
  discat ut admoto rectius igne coqui.

XL. ² inira CK : in ira A *m. pr.* : mira P : inire GLT
Rawl., Reg. : in arva A *m. sec.* V *m. sec.* BX *Petrenses* : in ora
Ellis : abnuit ire *Lachmann.*

you off. For, though you cannot yourself attack at all or venture on anything, you are a more cruel foe in that you make others dangerous."

XL

THE LEOPARD AND THE FOX

A fine-breasted leopard in his dappled glory went to parade himself among the beasts which were his compeers. But because the surly lions had no varied hues upon their back, he straightway formed the belief that theirs was a sorry tribe. Condemning all the other animals as mean-looking, he took himself for the one pattern of noble breed. As he was rejoicing in the garb of youth, a wily vixen chid him and showed the uselessness of his markings. " Go," said she, "keep your excessive confidence in your gorgeous youthfulness, so long as I can surpass you in fine counsel, and so long as we can admire those adorned by gifts of intellect more than those who shine in bodily charms."

XLI

THE SHOWER AND THE JAR

Impelled by the winds, a heavy rain-storm had gathered with the pressure of cloud upon cloud and burst in wintry torrents. And as its whirling deluge made a lake over the widespread lands, it struck some potter's work set outside in the fields; for warm air shapes the plastic clay beforehand, to train it for being baked more perfectly when fire is applied.

tunc nimbus fragilis perquirit nomina testae.
  immemor illa sui " Amphora dicor " ait ;
" nunc me docta manus rapiente volumina gyro
  molliter obliquum iussit habere latus."   1(

" hactenus hac " inquit " liceat constare figura :
  nam te subiectam diluet imber aquis."
et simul accepto violentius amne fatiscens
  pronior in tenues victa cucurrit aquas.
infelix, quae magna sibi cognomina sumens   1[
  ausa pharetratis nubibus ista loqui !

haec poterunt miseros posthac exempla monere,
  subdita nobilibus ne sua fata gemant.

XLII

DE LUPO ET HAEDO

Forte lupum melior cursu deluserat haedus,
  proxima vicinis dum petit arva casis ;
inde fugam recto tendens in moenia cursu
  inter lanigeros adstitit ille greges.
impiger hunc raptor mediamque secutus in urbem   5
  temptat compositis sollicitare dolis :
" nonne vides " inquit, " cunctis ut victima templis
  immitem regemens morte cruentet humum ?
quod nisi securo valeas te reddere campo,
  ei mihi, vittata tu quoque fronte cades."   10

XLI. ⁹ nunc *codd.* : nam *edd.*
¹⁶ pharetratis *codd.* : foret tantis *Cab.*, *Baehrens* : foret
atris *Wopkens* : *fortasse* erat iratis *Ellis.*
¹⁸ ne B : ut *cett. codd.*

ᵃ *i.e.* conceitedly elated by its beauty as described in 9–10,
it forgets what a frail thing it is.

Then the rain-cloud asked the name of the brittle jar, which, forgetting itself,[a] said, " My name is Amphora. As you see me now, a craftsman's hand, by means of the wheel's swift revolutions, has ordained the gentle slope of my side." " Till now, but no more," said the other, " think yourself permitted to bear this shape, for rain is about to whelm you in its waters and wash you away." And thereupon, taking in the wild rush of the flood, and cracking open, the jar yielded and dashed headlong into the flowing waters. Ill-fated one, to take a proud name to itself and venture to speak thus to clouds which have their quivers in readiness!

This example will serve in future to warn the wretched not to lament their destiny when it is under the control of the great.

XLII

THE WOLF AND THE KID

It happened that a kid, while making for the fields which lay nearest to some neighbouring huts, had baffled a wolf by faster running. Then, directing his flight straight for the city walls, he came to a halt among flocks of wool-clad sheep. The beast of prey was unwearied and, pursuing the kid into the heart of the town, tried to lure him with studied wiles. " Do you not see," he said, " how in all the temples a victim amid repeated groans stains the pitiless ground with its life-blood?[b] But if you are not able to return to the safety of the meadow, ah me, you too will die with the sacrificial fillet round your brow."

[b] The fable, Ellis points out, belongs to a time when sacrifices in heathen temples might still take place: cf. the pagan atmosphere of XXIII and XXXVI (see also Introd.).

ille refert: "modo quam metuis, precor, exue curam
   et tecum viles, improbe, tolle minas;
nam sat erit sacrum divis fudisse cruorem
   quam rabido fauces exsaturare lupo."

sic quotiens duplici subeuntur tristia casu,   1
   expedit insignem promeruisse necem.

  XLII. [13] sat erit *plerique codd.* : satius *Withof.*

The kid replied, " Just drop, I pray you, the anxiety which is your dread, and take yourself off and your trumpery threats too, you rogue. I shall be content to pour out my blood in a sacrifice to the gods rather than gorge the throat of a ravenous wolf."

So every time we face disaster of twofold hazard, it is the noble death which it is expedient to achieve.

RUTILIUS NAMATIANUS

INTRODUCTION

TO RUTILIUS NAMATIANUS

THE last of the classical Latin poets, Claudius
Rutilius Namatianus, or (as is quite possibly the
correct order for his name) Rutilius Claudius Nama-
tianus, belonged to a Gallo-Roman family [a] and was
born late in the fourth century, most likely at
Toulouse. His father, almost certainly the Lachanius
of his poem, and more or less plausibly identified
with different official Claudii of the period, passed
through a distinguished public career and had been
honoured with a statue at Pisa, a visit to which is
described with filial pride.[b] Rutilius held high
appointments under the emperor Honorius, who
reigned A.D. 395–423. We must, however, beware
of being misled by distinctions spuriously thrust
upon him in the title of the Bologna edition; he
was not a *vir consularis*, though he was a *vir claris-
simus*; he had been neither a *tribunus militum* nor a
praefectus praetorii, but he had attained to the
influential positions of *magister officiorum* [c] and
praefectus urbis.[d] It can be shown that he held the
former office in A.D. 412 and that he immediately

[a] I. 20.　　　[b] I. 575–596.　　　[c] I. 563.
[d] I. 157–160 and 427.

753

preceded his friend Albinus [a] as prefect of the city for part of the year A.D. 414.

Educated on the lines of the ancient learning, Rutilius, as his poem indicates, was a man of literary knowledge and taste, an adherent of paganism, and influenced by Stoic philosophy. The times in which he lived had brought devastation again and again into Italy at the hands of northern barbarians. In A.D. 410, six years before he undertook the journey back to his native Gaul which makes the subject of his poem *De Reditu Suo*,[b] Rome had witnessed in a three days' sack the culmination of the third siege of the city by Alaric, King of the Visigoths.

That same year men had seen the burial of the Gothic chief under the diverted waters of the Busento; and in 412 Ataulf, the successor of Alaric, had withdrawn his Goths from Italy into Gaul, whence he had been forced across the Pyrenees into Spain to meet his death by assassination in 415. Soon afterwards, under their King Walia, the Visigoths concluded peace with Rome; but years of merciless ravage had left in Italy and Gaul scenes of depressing desolation which are reflected in our author's realistic allusions.[c] The misery of it all touched him closely as he was planning his route in 416 from the one devastated country to the other, and so he decided to coast northwards from the mouth of the Tiber rather than face the dangerous roads and broken bridges of Italy. The motive for his journey has been questioned: it is at least more likely that he

[a] I. 466–474.
[b] A slightly more satisfactory title than the alternative *Itinerarium*.
[c] I. 21, 39–42.

may have wished to inspect some property of his own in Gaul than that his paganism had somehow lost him favour in Rome.[a]

It was autumn when he started from the city, and in the extant portion of the poem we can read an entertaining elegiac journal for two months from September 22nd to November 21st, A.D. 416,[b] when his second book breaks off at the 68th line after the arrival at Luna. This was something more elaborate as a travel-poem than Horace's journey to Brundusium or Ovid's sketch of his voyage in the *Tristia* or Statius' send-off to his patron bound for Egypt.[c] We may guess that the composition of the poem followed not long after the time of the journey; but our knowledge of the author and of his fortunes stops short with the interruption of his work. Only half-a-dozen lines before the end, as we now have it, the author had contemplated the continuance of his narrative. Is the conclusion lost or was it never written?

A brief summary will enable us to follow him on his voyage so far as his poetic record runs. A long exordium (1–164) is largely a rhetorical eulogy on

[a] H. Schenkl, *Rh. Mus.* 66 (1911), pp. 393 *sqq.*, argues that Rutilius' attacks on Christian monks do not prove his pagan creed, and it is true that some Christians have censured monasticism severely. But this is not the whole case. Rutilius' tone elsewhere seems inconsistent with Christian belief. Labriolle quite reasonably distinguishes it from that of a professing Christian like Ausonius, *Rev. des études latines*, 6 (1928), pp. 30 *sqq.*

[b] Carcopino, *Rev. des études lat.*, 6, 180 *sqq.*, 1928, argues for 16th Oct. 417 as the date of the departure from Rome. Both Helm and Préchac agree in their editions.

[c] Hor. *Sat.* I. v (partly suggested by Lucilius' *Iter Siculum*); Ovid, *Trist.* I. x; Stat. *Silv.* III. ii.

the majestic greatness of Rome and her gift of unifying nations. After the start from the city (165) Rutilius was weather-bound for fifteen days at Ostia in the harbour of Claudius and Trajan. When his sailors had once found a fair wind, the coasting and mainly daylight voyage began, and, as related in Book I, lasted six days (or, according to Vessereau, seven). The first day (217–276) brings them to Centumcellae, where they spend the night. On the second day (277–312) they sail at dawn, pass off the mouth of the Munio and the pinewoods of Graviscae, sighting Cosa before putting into Portus Herculis at nightfall. On the third day (313–348), sailing still earlier, before sunrise, they coast along Monte Argentario, pass the island of Igilium (recently a refuge for fugitives from the Goths), touch, without staying, at the Umbro mouth, and are forced, when overtaken by night, to bivouac ashore. The fourth day (349–428) finds them compelled to take to oars in the morning: and after sighting Ilva (Elba), whose mines suggest to the poet the praises of iron, they land in a state of fatigue before midday at Faleria, where they chance upon an Osiris fête in progress. Their most unpleasant experiences with an extortionate landlord, a Jew, lead to an outburst against Judaism. Subsequent rowing brings them to Populonia, where they are rejoiced to get news from Rome. With the fifth day (429–510) we have the distant view of Corsica chronicled, and when Capraria rises in sight, the opportunity is seized for an onslaught on the monasticism of its inhabitants. The travellers later reach Volaterrana Vada. A visit is paid to the villa of a good friend, Albinus, and the processes of the neighbouring salt-pans are described. The welcome meeting with Victorinus, a friend from Toulouse, compensates for the delay caused by a gale. During the early part of the sixth day [a] (511–540) they find themselves off the dangerous rocks of Gorgon island, the home of a hermit whom Rutilius regards as one of a group of misguided fanatics, more bewitched, he thinks, than the victims of Circe's enchantments. They next arrive at the villa Triturrita, built on an artificial causeway near a harbour protected by a curious barrier of seaweed. Here, in spite of the inducement to proceed with the voyage in fair weather, an interruption is made, as Rutilius cannot resist the temptation to visit his friend Protadius in the neighbouring town: so Protadius' merits, Pisa itself and the statue erected there to his own father are in turn touched upon. This voluntary delay (541–614) is followed by a compulsory one (615–644); for on coming back to Triturrita, the travellers being storm-stayed have to occupy their time in a boar-hunt: and for the moment horn and song appear to be echoed in one of Rutilius' couplets.[b] A long stay is made in this district, Book I ending in a description of violent and continued storm.

Book II in its 68 lines narrates only the voyage from Portus Pisanus to Luna, but it also contains a description of Italy, a furious invective against the dead general Stilicho, and an account of the marble quarries in the Luna district.

[a] Vessereau makes this the seventh day, as he estimates that the distance from Populonia to Vada and the visit to Albinus would need more than a single day. The sixth day may therefore have been spent at the villa; but the poem does not clearly indicate this.   [b] 629–630.

His poem, in some ways the better for those digressions which make it more than a journal of travel, exhibits Rutilius as a man with an eye for the scenery of the Italian coast, interested in the affairs of the places touched at during his voyage northwards, and stirred by warm affection for friends [a] no less than by frankly expressed dislike for Jews, Christian monks and Stilicho. It is pleasant to note his joy at meeting friends and his regret at parting: it is an equally human trait that he is a good hater. His tender Stoic melancholy, coloured rather than seared by the memory of Rome's recent capture by the Goths, does not prevent him from cherishing an optimistic confidence in her recovery, even as in long-past history she had recovered after the Allia and Cannae. And so in his encomium upon the imperial city, sincere enough in feeling and yet in phrasing more rhetorical than poetic, Rutilius has uttered the swan-song of Rome.

Nor is it a song unworthy of the classical tradition. His Latin has a prevailing lucidity which befits his theme; and, despite the influence of Virgil and Ovid, his work, thanks to concentration upon his own experiences, which are narrated in a vivid and realistic style, bears a definitely individual mark. But it is rare for this individual note of his to show itself in mere linguistic usage such as *decessis* (if that be the true reading at I. 313) or the archaistic *propudiosa* (I. 388). As to metre, it is true that *amphitheatrum* is not a Virgilian ending for a hexameter, nor *sollicitudinibus* an Ovidian ending for a pentameter. [b] It is true also that Rutilius is too free

---

[a] See notes on the translation.
[b] There are some sixteen exceptions in Rutilius to the dissyllabic close of a pentameter.

in his employment of spondees. There is, further, little *enjambement* between hexameter and pentameter, so that his lines tend to be monotonously self-contained.[a] Yet, on the whole his versification must be called graceful,[b] and at times his elegiac couplets gain greatly in strength by a kind of Propertian force which Rutilius succeeds in conferring upon the pentameter.

EDITIONS

J. B. Pius. Editio princeps. Bologna, 1520.

Onuphrius Panvinius. In his *Reipublicae Romanae Commentarii*. Venice, 1558.

J. Castalio. Rome, 1582.

C. Barth. Frankfort, 1623.

Th. J. Almeloveen (c. not. variorum). Amsterdam, 1687.

P. Burman. *P. L. M.* II. pp. 1–184. Leyden, 1731.

C. T. Damm. Brandenburg, 1760.

J. C. Wernsdorf. *P. L. M.* V. i. pp. 1–202. Altenburg, 1788.

A. W. Zumpt. Berlin, 1840.

L. Mueller. Leipzig, 1870.

Itasius Lemniacus (A. v. Reumont). Berlin, 1872.

E. Baehrens. *P. L. M.* V. pp. 3–30. Leipzig, 1883.

---

[a] Usually hexameter and pentameter constitute a unity, as in I. 65–66, or the second line takes up and completes the first, as in I. 91–92, 331–332. Only occasionally does a sentence run into more than one distich, as in I. 403–408, 519–522.

[b] The elisions are 61 in 712 lines. There are no elisions of a long vowel before a short, nor of a monosyllable, nor at the caesura, nor in the second half of a pentameter.

INTRODUCTION TO

J. Vessereau (text, French prose transln. and essays). Paris, 1904.

C. H. Keene (Eng. verse transln. by G. F. Savage–Armstrong). London, 1907.

G. Heidrich (introd. and crit. appar.). Vienna, 1911.

V. Ussani. Florence, 1921.

R. Helm. Heidelberg, 1933.

J. Vessereau and F. Préchac (texte établi et traduit). Paris, 1933.

RELEVANT WORKS

E. Gibbon. *Decline and Fall of the Roman Empire* (esp. chaps. xxviii–xxxi for historical background).

T. Hodgkin. *Italy and her Invaders*, Vol. I. Oxford, 1880–1899.

Fr. Mueller. *De Rutilio Namatiano stoico*, progr. Soltquellae (= Saltwedel), 1882.

H. Schiller. *Geschichte der röm. Kaizerzeit*, II. Gotha, 1887.

P. Monceaux. *Les Africains : étude sur la littér. latine d'Afrique*. Paris, 1894.

C. Hosius. *Die Textgeschichte des Rutilius*, Rh. Mus. 51 (1896), pp. 197–210.

P. Rasi. *In Cl. Rut. Namatiani libros adnotationes metricae*. Turin, 1897.

S. Dill. *Roman Society in the last Century of the Wn. Empire*. London, 1905.

R. Pichon. *Les derniers écrivains profanes* (ch. v, " un grand fonctionnaire gallo-romain : le poète Rut. Nam."). Paris, 1906.

H. Schenkl. *Ein spätrömischer Dichter u. sein Glaubensbekenntnis*, Rh. Mus. 66 (1911), pp. 393–416.

P. de Labriolle. *Rut. Nam. et les moines* in *Rev. des
études latines*, VI. pp. 30–41. Paris, 1928.

J. Carcopino. *À propos du poème de Rut. Nam.* in
Rev. des études latines, VI. pp. 180–200. Paris,
1928.

M. L. W. Laistner. *Thought and Letters in Wn.
Europe*, A.D. 500–900 (opening chapter on
" Empire and its Invaders "). London, 1931.

E. S. Duckett. *Latin Writers of the Fifth Century*.
New York, 1931.

SIGLA

V = Codex Vindobonensis 277 (olim 387), qui, post
membranas vetustas Ovidii Halieutica et Grattii
Cynegetica continentes, foliis 84^a–93^b saeculi xvi
nostrum carmen habet.

[:$f\cdot$ = the symbol accompanying some of the marginal
corrections in the Vienna MS.: it has been
variously interpreted as *fortasse* (L. Mueller,
Baehrens), *fiat* (Hosius), or *fuit* (Purser).]

B = editio princeps, Bononiae anno 1520 emissa.

R = Codex Romanus : saec. xvi, Romae anno 1891
repertus.

On these three sources of the text, two MSS.
and the editio princeps, a few notes are desirable.
Baehrens in his edition of 1883 based his text upon
the Vienna manuscript (now denoted by V, the colla-
tion of which by Huemer was called c by Baehrens)
and upon Mau's collation of the editio princeps
published by Battista Pio at Bologna in 1520 (here
denoted by B but in Baehrens by b). Since
Baehrens' time a second manuscript, denoted by R,
has become available : it was discovered in the library

of the Duke of Sermoneta at Rome in 1891. V and R, both written in the sixteenth century, are indirectly and independently derived from an archetype found at Bobbio in 1494 or 1493. This archetype may be conjectured to have been written in Lombardic characters in the eighth or ninth century; but it has been lost since its removal from Bobbio in 1706. In 1495 Inghiramius, surnamed Phaedrus of Volaterra, afterwards librarian at the Vatican, made a copy of it at Bobbio and took it to Rome before 1506. About that time the poet Sannazaro had brought with him from France to Italy the newly-discovered *Halieutica* of Ovid and *Cynegetica* of Grattius and of Nemesianus; and in his enthusiasm for new works he either acquired or transcribed Phaedrus' copy of the manuscript. According to Baehrens and to Vessereau, V is Sannazaro's copy, though, according to Hosius, the descent of V is traceable back through Sannazaro and then through Phaedrus to the codex Bobiensis. The Vienna MS. is on paper, of the sixteenth century, bound up at the end of a volume immediately after Ovid's *Halieutica*, also on paper and preceded by seven older manuscripts on vellum of smaller dimensions than the paper MSS. Among these vellum MSS. certain lines of Eucheria and another copy of the *Halieutica*, with Sidonius Apollinaris and Grattius, have been identified with the actual poems which Sannazaro brought from France.

The editio princeps published by Battista Pio at Bologna in 1520 has a value for determining the text, as it represents Phaedrus' copy according to Hosius, and thus offers a testimony earlier than Sannazaro's copy and its derivative V.

RUTILIUS NAMATIANUS

R is dated by Vessereau a quarter of a century after V, *i.e.* in 1530, as he holds V to be Sannazaro's copy. Hosius, who collated R in *Rh. Mus.* (1896), vol. li, inferred that it was written within 30 or 40 years of the discovery of Rutilius' poem in 1493.[a] The corruptions shared by V and R prove their common descent, but R cannot have come from Phaedrus' copy (represented in the editio princeps B), because R sometimes preserves the true reading in contrast with V and B. On the other hand, a consensus of V and R virtually establishes a reading in the lost codex Bobiensis of the eighth century.

[a] The comparative value of V and R is hard to estimate. Keene points out that while R has the advantage in I. 178 *tenet*, 211 *curae*, 235 *largo*, 265 *lymphas*, 461 *algam*, 552 *utramque*, V has the superiority in I. 22 *miseranda*, 232 *Inui*, 317 *ternis*, 573 *Elide*, II. 62 *propositum*. R certainly has serious disfigurements due to one or other of its three hands. Recently L. Bartoli (*Athenaeum* ix. 3, 1931), writing on the two codices, has awarded the palm to the Vienna manuscript.

Bibliographical addendum (1982)

Rutilius, *De reditu* (with Italian translation and commentary), ed. E. Castrina, Florence 1967.

Rutilius, *De reditu*, ed. E. Doblhofer, Heidelberg: I (introduction, text, German translation, index verborum) 1972; II (commentary) 1977.

RUTILIUS NAMATIANUS

DE REDITU SUO

LIBER PRIMUS

VELOCEM potius reditum mirabere, lector,
  tam cito Romuleis posse carere bonis.
quid longum toto Romam venerantibus aevo?
  nil umquam longum est quod sine fine placet.
o quantum et quotiens possum numerare beatos
  nasci felici qui meruere solo!
qui Romanorum procerum generosa propago
  ingenitum cumulant urbis honore decus!
semina virtutum demissa et tradita caelo
  non potuere aliis dignius esse locis.   10
felices etiam qui proxima munera primis
  sortiti Latias obtinuere domos!
religiosa patet peregrinae Curia laudi,
  nec putat externos quos decet esse suos;
ordinis imperio collegarumque fruuntur   1
  et partem Genii quem venerantur habent:

---

⁵ quater *Heinsius, Mueller, Baehrens.*

ᵃ *Potius* supports the view that the opening of the poem
is lost.
  ᵇ The poet is to praise Rome at length (3–164). He claims
that nothing can be tedious in the eulogy of a city which
every age has held in honour—the *urbs aeterna* calls for
eternal veneration.

RUTILIUS NAMATIANUS

A VOYAGE HOME TO GAUL

BOOK I

RATHER [a] will you marvel, reader, that my quick
return journey (to Gaul) can so soon renounce the
blessings of the city of Romulus. What is too long
for men who spend all time in venerating Rome? [b]
Nothing is ever too long that never fails to
please. How greatly and how often can I count
those blest who have deserved birth in that happy
soil! Those highborn scions of Roman nobility
crown their honourable birth with the lustre of the
Capital! On no other land could the seeds of virtues
have been more worthily let fall by heaven's assign-
ment. Happy they too who, winning meeds next
to the first, have enjoyed Latin homes! [c] The
Senate-house, though fenced with awe, yet stands
open to foreign merit, nor deems those strangers
who are fittingly its own. They share the power
of their colleagues in the senatorial order, and possess
part of the sacred Genius [d] which they revere, even

---

[c] *i.e.* though not born in Rome, like those in 5–6.

[d] The *Genius* is the indwelling spirit of the Roman People,
shared by such provincials as were admitted into the senate.
Their union is compared with the heavenly council under
the presidency of the supreme god (Jupiter is not named).

quale per aetherios mundani verticis axes
  concilium summi credimus esse dei.

at mea dilectis fortuna revellitur oris,
  indigenamque suum Gallica rura vocant.   20
illa quidem longis nimium deformia bellis,
  sed quam grata minus, tam miseranda magis.
securos levius crimen contemnere cives :
  privatam repetunt publica damna fidem.
praesentes lacrimas tectis debemus avitis :   25
  prodest admonitus saepe dolore labor.
nec fas ulterius longas nescire ruinas
  quas mora suspensae multiplicavit opis :
iam tempus laceris post saeva incendia fundis
  vel pastorales aedificare casas.   30
ipsi quin etiam fontes si mittere vocem
  ipsaque si possent arbuta nostra loqui,
cessantem iustis poterant urgere querelis
  et desideriis addere vela meis.
iam iam laxatis carae complexibus urbis   35
  vincimur et serum vix toleramus iter.

electum pelagus, quoniam terrena viarum
  plana madent fluviis, cautibus alta rigent.
postquam Tuscus ager postquamque Aurelius agger,
  perpessus Geticas ense vel igne manus,   40
non silvas domibus, non flumina ponte coercet,
  incerto satius credere vela mari.

  17 aetherias . . . arces *Baehrens.*
  22 veneranda R : miseranda VB.
  34 verba *vir doctus apud Wernsdorf* : *accepit Baehrens.*
  37 vetabant *Baehrens.*

766

as from ethereal pole to pole of the celestial vault
we believe there abideth the council of the Deity
Supreme.

But 'tis my fortune that is plucked back from the
well-loved land; the fields of Gaul summon home
their native.[a] Disfigured they are by wars im-
measurably long, yet the less their charm, the more
they earn pity. 'Tis a lighter crime to neglect our
countrymen when at their ease: our common
losses call for each man's loyalty. Our presence
and our tears are what we owe to the ancestral
home: service which grief has prompted ofttimes
helps. 'Tis sin further to overlook the tedious tale
of disasters which the delay of halting aid has multi-
plied: now is the time after cruel fires on ravaged
farms to rebuild, if it be but shepherds' huts. Nay,
if only the very springs could utter words, if only our
very trees[b] could speak, they well might spur my
laggard pace with just complaints and give sails to my
yearning wishes. Now that the dear city slackens
her embrace, my homeland wins, and I can scarce
feel patient with a journey deferred so late.

I have chosen the sea, since roads by land, if on
the level, are flooded by rivers; if on higher ground,
are beset with rocks. Since Tuscany and since the
Aurelian highway,[c] after suffering the outrages of
Goths with fire or sword, can no longer control
forest with homestead or river with bridge, it is
better to entrust my sails to the wayward sea.

[a] Rutilius feels the call of his ravaged estates in Gaul: see
Introduction.

[b] *arbuta* is not used here in the restricted sense of *arbutus*.

[c] The Via Aurelia was the road by the coast of Etruria to
the Italian Riviera. *Cf.* sense of *agger* in *medio in aggere*,
Avianus, xvii. 15.

crebra relinquendis infigimus oscula portis:
  inviti superant limina sacra pedes.
oramus veniam lacrimis et laude litamus,   4
  in quantum fletus currere verba sinit:

" exaudi, regina tui pulcherrima mundi,
  inter sidereos Roma recepta polos,
exaudi, genetrix hominum genetrixque deorum,
  non procul a caelo per tua templa sumus: 50
te canimus semperque, sinent dum fata, canemus:
  sospes nemo potest immemor esse tui.
obruerint citius scelerata oblivia solem,
  quam tuus ex nostro corde recedat honos.
nam solis radiis aequalia munera tendis,   55
  qua circumfusus fluctuat Oceanus.
volvitur ipse tibi, qui continet omnia, Phoebus
  eque tuis ortos in tua condit equos.
te non flammigeris Libye tardavit harenis,
  non armata suo reppulit Ursa gelu: 60
quantum vitalis natura tetendit in axes,
  tantum virtuti pervia terra tuae.
fecisti patriam diversis gentibus unam:
  profuit iniustis te dominante capi.
dumque offers victis proprii consortia iuris,   6.
  urbem fecisti quod prius orbis erat.

" auctores generis Venerem Martemque fatemur,
  Aeneadum matrem Romulidumque patrem:

---

52 sospes VRB : hospes *Cuperus, Baehrens.*
58 ortus VB : ortas R : ortos *Castalio.*
64 iniustis VB : inustis R : invitis *Juretus, Damm, Mueller,*
Baehrens : invictis *Castalio* : infestis *Schrader.*

---

* Baehrens' alteration to *nutrix* is purely arbitrary, even
in the light of *altricem* in 146.

Repeated kisses I imprint on the gates I have to leave: unwillingly my feet cross the honoured threshold. In tears I beseech pardon (for my departure) and offer a sacrifice of praise, so far as weeping allows the words to run:

"Listen, O fairest queen of thy world, Rome, welcomed amid the starry skies, listen, thou mother [a] of men and mother of gods, thanks to thy temples we are not far from heaven: thee do we chant, and shall, while destiny allows, for ever chant. None can be safe if forgetful of thee. Sooner shall guilty oblivion whelm the sun than the honour due to thee quit my heart: for thy benefits extend as far as the sun's rays, where the circling Ocean-flood bounds the world. For thee the very Sun-God who holdeth all together [b] doth revolve: his steeds that rise in thy domains he puts in thy domains to rest. Thee Africa hath not stayed with scorching sands, nor hath the Bear, armed with its native cold, repulsed thee. As far as living nature hath stretched towards the poles, so far hath earth opened a path for thy valour. For nations far apart thou hast made a single fatherland; under thy dominion captivity hath meant profit even for those who knew not justice: [c] and by offering to the vanquished a share in thine own justice, thou hast made a city of what was erstwhile a world.

"As authors of our race we acknowledge Venus and Mars—mother of the sons of Aeneas, father of

[b] *Cf. Einsied. Ecl.* I. 29-31 and note *b*, p. 329 *supra*.
[c] *iniustis* has its point in relation to *iuris*, l. 65.

mitigat armatas victrix clementia vires,
   convenit in mores nomen utrumque tuos: 70
hinc tibi certandi bona parcendique voluptas:
   quos timuit superat, quos superavit amat.
inventrix oleae colitur vinique repertor
   et qui primus humo pressit aratra puer;
aras Paeoniam meruit medicina per artem,   75
   factus et Alcides nobilitate deus:
tu quoque, legiferis mundum complexa triumphis,
   foedere communi vivere cuncta facis.
te, dea, te celebrat Romanus ubique recessus
   pacificoque gerit libera colla iugo.   80
omnia perpetuo quae servant sidera motu,
   nullum viderunt pulchrius imperium.
quid simile Assyriis conectere contigit armis?
   Medi finitimos condomuere suos;
magni Parthorum reges Macetumque tyranni   85
   mutua per varias iura dedere vices.
nec tibi nascenti plures animaeque manusque,
   sed plus consilii iudiciique fuit.
iustis bellorum causis nec pace superba
   nobilis ad summas gloria venit opes.   90
quod regnas minus est quam quod regnare mereris:
   excedis factis grandia fata tuis.

[70] numen *Barth, Baehrens.*
[76] fretus VRB (*in marg.* factus · f · V): factus *multi editores:*
cretus *Canneg.*: fertur *Baehrens:* fretus it *Barth.*
[81] perpetuos . . . motus VRB: *corr. Baehrens.*
[84] condomuere *Mueller:* cum domuere VRB.

---

[a] *i.e.* of the two divinities Venus and Mars.
[b] The three alluded to are Athene (Minerva), Bacchus, and
Triptolemus.

the scions of Romulus: clemency in victory tempers
armed strength: both names [a] befit thy character:
hence thy noble pleasure in war and in mercy:
it vanquishes the dreaded foe and cherishes the
vanquished. The goddess who found the olive-
tree is worshipped, the deity too who discovered
wine, and the youth who first drove the ploughshare
in the soil; [b] the healing art through the skill of
the god Paeon [c] won altars: Hercules by his re-
nown was made divine: thou, too, who hast em-
braced the world in triumphs fraught with law,
dost make all things live under a common covenant.
Thee, O goddess, thee every nook of the Roman
dominion celebrates, beneath a peaceful yoke hold-
ing necks unenslaved. The stars, which watch all
things in their unceasing motion, never looked on a
fairer empire. What like unto thy power did it
fall to Assyrian arms to link in one? The Persians
only subdued neighbours of their own. The mighty
Parthian kings and Macedonian monarchs [d] im-
posed laws on each other through varying changes.
It was not that at thy birth thou hadst more souls
and hands: but more prudence and more judgement
were thine. By wars for justifiable cause and by
peace imposed without arrogance thy renowned
glory reached highest wealth. That thou reignest
is less than that thou deservest to reign: thy deeds
surpass thine exalted destiny. To review thy high

[c] *Paeǒniam:* the Greek adjective is παιώνιος. Rutilius
is not, however, unclassical here; for Ingram (*Hermathena*
ix. 407) illustrates the use of *Paeonius* in Virgil, Ovid, and
other poets: *cf.* Avianus vi. 7, *Paeonio magistro.*
[d] The Seleucid kings of Syria, who succeeded to part of the
empire won by Alexander of Macedon, and whose wars with
Parthia brought sometimes victory, sometimes defeat.

percensere labor densis decora alta tropaeis
  ut si quis stellas pernumerare velit;
confunduntque vagos delubra micantia visus: 9⸱
  ipsos crediderim sic habitare deos.
quid loquar aerio pendentes fornice rivos,
  qua vix imbriferas tolleret Iris aquas?
hos potius dicas crevisse in sidera montes;
  tale giganteum Graecia laudet opus.   10⸱
intercepta tuis conduntur flumina muris;
  consumunt totos celsa lavacra lacus.
nec minus et propriis celebrantur roscida venis
  totaque nativo moenia fonte sonant.
frigidus aestivas hinc temperat halitus auras,   10⸱
  innocuamque levat purior unda sitim.
nempe tibi subitus calidarum gurges aquarum
  rupit Tarpeias hoste premente vias.
si foret aeternus, casum fortasse putarem:
  auxilio fluxit, qui rediturus erat.   11⸱
quid loquar inclusas inter laquearia silvas,
  vernula qua vario carmine ludit avis?
vere tuo numquam mulceri desinit annus;
  deliciasque tuas victa tuetur hiemps.

---

⁹⁶ credideris hic *Burman*.   ¹⁰⁹ externus R.
¹¹¹ inter VRB : subter *Baehrens*.
¹¹² quae VR : qua *Castalio*. ludat VRB : ludit *Panv.* :
laudat *Baehrens*.

ᵃ The aqueducts of Rome, massive enough to be called
"Cyclopean" (*giganteum opus*, 100), like the masonry at
Tiryns or of the Lion Gateway at Mycenae. In the time of
Frontinus, who was *curator aquarum* A.D. 97–106, there were
nine aqueducts; later, this number was increased.
  ᵇ The hyperbole means that hardly any rainbow in the sky
could reach the same height as the span of the arches of the
aqueducts. Burman suggested that *quo* might be clearer
than *qua*.

honours amid crowded trophies were a task like endeavouring to reckon up the stars. The glittering temples dazzle the wandering eyes: I could well believe such are the dwelling-places of the very gods. What shall I say of streams suspended on airy arches,[a] where scarce the Rainbow-Goddess could raise her showery waters?[b] You might rather call them mountains grown up to the sky: such a structure Greece would praise, as giant-wrought. Rivers[c] diverted are lost sight of within thy walls: the lofty baths consume whole lakes.[d] No less are thy dewy meads filled also with their own rivulets, and all thy walls are a-babble with springs from the soil. Hence a breath of coolness tempers the summer air, and the crystal well relieves a harmless thirst. Nay, once a sudden torrent of waters seething hot broke forth, when thine enemy[e] trod the roads by the Capitol: had it lasted for ever, mayhap I had deemed this mere chance; but it was to save thee that it flowed; for it came only to vanish. Why speak of woods enclosed amid thy panelled palaces,[f] where native birds sport with varied song? In the spring that is thine never does the year fail in its mildness: baffled winter respects thy charms.

[c] *e.g.* water from the Anio supplied the aqueducts called *Anio Vetus* and *Anio Novus*.

[d] *celsa* refers to the imposing loftiness of the public baths; *lacus* to such lakes as Alsietinus, Sabatinus (Lago di Bracciano) and Sublacensis (near Subiaco), from which water was brought into Rome by aqueducts and stored in large cisterns.

[e] Legend had it that when Titus Tatius and his Sabines reached the gate of Janus under the Capitol, the god sent out boiling water from the earth and discomfited the enemy.

[f] The reference is to gardens enclosed within colonnades which had panelled ceilings.

" erige crinales lauros seniumque sacrati   11⟨
    verticis in virides, Roma, refinge comas.
aurea turrigero radient diademata cono,
    perpetuosque ignes aureus umbo vomat!
abscondat tristem deleta iniuria casum :
    contemptus solidet vulnera clausa dolor.   12⟨
adversis sollenne tuis sperare secunda :
    exemplo caeli ditia damna subis.
astrorum flammae renovant occasibus ortus ;
    lunam finiri cernis, ut incipiat.
victoris Brenni non distulit Allia poenam ;   12⟨
    Samnis servitio foedera saeva luit ;
post multas Pyrrhum clades superata fugasti ;
    flevit successus Hannibal ipse suos :
quae mergi nequeunt nisu maiore resurgunt
    exsiliuntque imis altius acta vadis ;   13⟨
utque novas vires fax inclinata resumit,
    clarior ex humili sorte superna petis.
porrige victuras Romana in saecula leges,
    solaque fatales non vereare colos,
quamvis sedecies denis et mille peractis   13⟨
    annus praeterea iam tibi nonus eat.
quae restant nullis obnoxia tempora metis,
    dum stabunt terrae, dum polus astra feret !
illud te reparat quod cetera regna resolvit :
    ordo renascendi est crescere posse malis.   14⟨

116 recinge VRB, *Vessereau* : refinge *Heinsius et fere omnes.*
137 maestis *Baehrens.*

---

a Cf. Lucan I. 185–190, where Roma, wearing a mural
crown, appears to Caesar at the Rubicon, *turrigero canos
effundens vertice crines.*
    b Four examples of recovery are cited : (1) the defeat of
Rome at the Allia in 390 B.C. was soon avenged by the death
of Brennus, the Gallic leader; (2) the subjection of the
Samnites compensated for the severe terms imposed by them

" Raise, O Rome, the triumphal laurels which wreathe thy locks, and refashion the hoary eld of thy hallowed head to tresses fresh and fair. Golden let the diadem flash on thy tower-crowned helmet[a]; let the golden buckler belch forth perpetual fires! Let forgetfulness of thy wrongs bury the sadness of misfortune; let pain disregarded close and heal thy wounds. Amidst failure it is thy way to hope for prosperity: after the pattern of the heavens losses undergone enrich thee. For flaming stars set only to renew their rising; thou seest the moon wane to wax afresh. The Allia did not hinder Brennus' penalty; the Samnite paid for a cruel treaty by slavery; after many disasters, though defeated, thou didst put Pyrrhus to flight; Hannibal himself was the mourner of his own successes.[b] Things which cannot be sunk rise again with greater energy, sped higher in their rebound from lowest depths; and, as the torch held downward regains fresh strength, so from lowly fortune thou dost soar more radiant aloft. Spread forth the laws that are to last throughout the ages of Rome: alone thou needst not dread the distaffs of the Fates, though with a thousand years and sixteen decades o'erpast, thou hast besides a ninth year in its course.[c] The span which doth remain is subject to no bounds, so long as earth shall stand firm and heaven uphold the stars! That same thing builds thee up which wrecks all other realms: the law of thy new birth is the power to thrive upon thine ills.

on the Romans at the Caudine Forks, 321 B.C.; (3) King Pyrrhus' successes in his invasion changed to disaster at Beneventum, 275 B.C.; (4) Hannibal's victories in the Second Punic War ended in defeat.

[c] The year 1169 of Rome gives the date A.D. 416.

" ergo age, sacrilegae tandem cadat hostia gentis:
    submittant trepidi perfida colla Getae.
ditia pacatae dent vectigalia terrae:
    impleat augustos barbara praeda sinus.
aeternum tibi Rhenus aret, tibi Nilus inundet,   145
    altricemque suam fertilis orbis alat.
quin et fecundas tibi conferat Africa messes,
    sole suo dives, sed magis imbre tuo.
interea et Latiis consurgant horrea sulcis,
    pinguiaque Hesperio nectare prela fluant.   150
ipse triumphali redimitus harundine Thybris
    Romuleis famulas usibus aptet aquas;
atque opulenta tibi placidis commercia ripis
    devehat hinc ruris, subvehat inde maris.

" pande, precor, gemino placatum Castore pontum; 155
    temperet aequoream dux Cytherea viam,
si non displicui, regerem cum iura Quirini,
    si colui sanctos consuluique patres;
nam quod nulla meum strinxerunt crimina ferrum,
    non sit praefecti gloria, sed populi.   160
sive datur patriis vitam componere terris,
    sive oculis umquam restituere meis,
fortunatus agam votoque beatior omni,
    semper digneris si meminisse mei."

---

    [a] For the ancient idea that the north wind brought to Africa rain-clouds gathered in Italy cf. Stat. *Theb.* VIII. 411; Lucan, III. 68-70; IX. 420-423.
    [b] The prayer is that traffic and trade may revive, now that Alaric has withdrawn.
    [c] The name of either of the twin Dioscuri may do duty for the other: cf. Hor. *Od.* III. xxix. 64, *geminusque Pollux*; in Catull. iv. 27 both are invoked, but only one named, *gemelle*

RUTILIUS NAMATIANUS

" Come, then, let an impious race fall in sacrifice at last: let the Goths in panic abase their for-sworn necks. Let lands reduced to peace pay rich tribute and barbarian booty fill thy majestic lap. Evermore let the Rhineland plough for thee, for thee the Nile o'erflow; and let a teeming world give nurture to its nurse. Yea, let Africa proffer to thee her fertile harvests, rich in her own sun, but richer for thy showers.*a* Meanwhile may granaries too arise to house the furrow-crops of Latium, and with the nectar of the West may sleek wine-presses flow. Let Tiber's self, garlanded with triumphal reed, apply his waters to serve the needs of Romulus' race, and 'twixt his wealthy peaceful banks bear for thee down-stream the wealthy cargoes of the fields and up-stream those of the sea.*b*

" Outstretch, I pray, the level main lulled to rest 'neath Castor and his twin brother; *c* be our Lady of Cythera the guide to smooth my watery path, if I found favour when I administered Quirinus' laws,*d* if to the venerable senators I showed respect and from them asked advice; for that ne'er a crime unsheathed my magisterial sword must be the people's, not the prefect's, boast.*e* Whether 'tis granted to lay my life to rest in ancestral soil or whether thou shalt one day be restored to my eyes, blest shall my life be, lucky beyond all aspiration, if thou deign always to remember me."

Castor et gemelle Castoris. There was a temple of Castor and Pollux at Ostia, and one of Venus on the island at the Tiber-mouth; hence the allusion to *Cytherea.*

d Rutilius had been *praefectus urbis* in A.D. 414; *cf.* I. 423–428; 467–468.

e The absence of capital punishment during Rutilius' prefecture was a credit to the Roman people.

his dictis iter arripimus : comitantur amici :   165
  dicere non possunt lumina sicca " vale."
iamque aliis Romam redeuntibus haeret eunti
  Rufius, Albini gloria viva patris ;
qui Volusi antiquo derivat stemmate nomen
  et reges Rutulos teste Marone refert.   170
huius facundae commissa palatia linguae :
  primaevus meruit principis ore loqui.
rexerat ante puer populos pro consule Poenos ;
  aequalis Tyriis terror amorque fuit.
sedula promisit summos instantia fasces :   175
  si fas est meritis fidere, consul erit.
invitum tristis tandem remeare coegi :
  corpore divisos mens tamen una tenet.

tum demum ad naves gradior, qua fronte bicorni
  dividuus Tiberis dexteriora secat.   180
laevus inaccessis fluvius vitatur harenis ;
  hospitis Aeneae gloria sola manet.

166 non possum sicca dicere luce vale *nonnulli editores.*
175 imitantia V : imitatio RB (*sic etiam in marg.* V, *sed expunctum*) : instantia *Mueller.*
178 ter et (*in marg.* tenet · f ·) V : tenet R.
180 secat V : petit R.

---

a Ceionius Rufius Volusianus belonged to an official family of ancient pedigree. He had been proconsul of Africa with his headquarters at Carthage (I. 173), and as a youthful imperial quaestor had performed the duty of reading before the senate communications from the Emperor (I. 171). Rutilius expresses his delight over the news of his friend's appointment to the city prefecture (I. 415–428).
b Rufius Albinus, prefect of the city in A.D. 390, should be distinguished from the Albinus of I. 466.

With these words we take the road: our friends attend. Eyes cannot tearless say " good-bye." And now while others wend their way back to Rome, Rufius,[a] the living glory of his father Albinus,[b] clings close to me on my way. He draws his name from the ancient pedigree of Volusus, citing Rutilian princes on the witness of Virgil.[c] To his power of eloquence was entrusted the imperial palace: in youth he was the fitting spokesman of the emperor. Still earlier, a mere stripling, he had governed as pro-consul the Carthaginian peoples and among the Tyrian folk inspired dread and love alike. His zealous energy gave promise of highest office: if it is permitted to trust desert, a consul he will be. In the end I sadly forced him to go back reluctant: yet, though in body severed, one mind keeps us linked.

Then at length I proceed to the ships,[d] where with twy-horned brow the branching Tiber cleaves his way to the right.[e] The channel on the left is avoided for its unapproachable sands: its one remaining boast is to have welcomed Aeneas.[f] And now the

---

[c] The family claimed descent from the Volusus addressed by Turnus, prince of the Rutuli, in *Aeneid* XI. 463.

[d] There were several boats (*cymbae* I. 219) used by Rutilius' company on their coasting voyage northwards: *cf.* I. 559, *puppibus ergo meis*.

[e] About eighteen miles from Rome and some miles from the sea the Tiber branches so as to form the Isola Sacra (*cf. Aeneid* VIII. 727, *Rhenusque bicornis*, referring to the two mouths of the Rhine: the " horn " idea is associated with the bull-like force of rivers in flood). At the mouth of the left branch was Ostia, the ancient port of Rome, which in time became blocked up with silt and sand. On the right branch harbour-works were undertaken by the Emperor Claudius and improved by Trajan.

[f] For Aeneas' landing see *Aeneid* VII. 29 *sqq.*

779

et iam nocturnis spatium laxaverat horis
    Phoebus Chelarum pallidiore polo.
cunctamur temptare salum portuque sedemus,   185
    nec piget oppositis otia ferre moris,
occidua infido dum saevit gurgite Plias
    dumque procellosi temporis ira calet.
respectare iuvat vicinam saepius urbem
    et montes visu deficiente sequi,   190
quaque duces oculi grata regione fruuntur,
    dum se, quod cupiunt, cernere posse putant.
nec locus ille mihi cognoscitur indice fumo,
    qui dominas arces et caput orbis habet
(quamquam signa levis fumi commendat Homerus,   195
    dilecto quotiens surgit in astra solo);
sed caeli plaga candidior tractusque serenus
    signat septenis culmina clara iugis.
illic perpetui soles atque ipse videtur
    quem sibi Roma facit purior esse dies.   200
saepius attonitae resonant Circensibus aures;
    nuntiat accensus plena theatra favor:
pulsato notae redduntur ab aethere voces,
    vel quia perveniunt vel quia fingit amor.

[188] cadit VRB : calet *Mueller* : cadet *Ussani*.
[191] feruntur *Baehrens*.

---

[a] The Scorpion is next to Libra among the signs of the Zodiac : the sun enters Libra at the autumnal Equinox. Poets use either *Chelae* (claws) or *Libra* (balance) in reference to this season.

sun in the paler sky of the Scorpion's Claws had lengthened the space of the night-watches.[a] We hesitate to make trial of the sea; we tarry in the haven, unreluctant to endure idleness amid the delays which bar our voyage, so long as the setting Pleiad storms upon the treacherous main, and the anger of the squally season is hot.[b] It is a joy to look back many a time at the city still near, and with scarce availing sight to trace its hills, and look where the guiding eyes[c] feast on that dear scene, fancying they can see what they desire to see. Nor is yonder place, which holds the imperial citadels and the world's capital, recognised by me in virtue of the smoke which marks it out (and yet 'tis the signs of light smoke which Homer[d] praises whensoever it rises starward from a well-loved land); nay rather a fairer tract of sky and a serene expanse marks the clear summits of the Seven Hills. There 'tis lasting sunshine: the very daylight which Rome makes for herself seems purer than all else. Time and again our spell-bound ears ring with the noise of the Circus games;[e] a blaze of cheers proclaims the crowded theatre: familiar shouts are sent back by the echoing air, whether it is that they really reach us or that affection fancies so.

[b] If *cadit*, 188, is kept in the sense of " subsides," it involves taking *dum* as " while " in 187 and as " until " in 188 (unless *cadit* can here mean " descends " or " swoops " upon the sea). *Calet* is accepted from L. Mueller.

[c] Cf. *oculique duces rem credere cogunt, Aetna* 189. He can just make out the hills of Rome, and part of the city he can see in imagination only, his eyes directing him to where it should be.

[d] Cf. *Odyss.* I. 57–59; X. 29–30.

[e] The *Ludi Romani* began in Rutilius' time on Sept. 21 and so fit into the autumnal setting of his voyage.

explorata fides pelagi ter quinque diebus,　　　　　205
　　dum melior lunae se daret aura novae.
tum discessurus studiis urbique remitto
　　Palladium, generis spemque decusque mei.
facundus iuvenis Gallorum nuper ab arvis
　　missus Romani discere iura Fori.　　　　　210
ille meae secum dulcissima vincula curae,
　　filius affectu, stirpe propinquus, habet:
cuius Aremoricas pater Exuperantius oras
　　nunc postliminium pacis amare docet;
leges restituit libertatemque reducit　　　　　215
　　et servos famulis non sinit esse suis.

solvimus Aurorae dubio, quo tempore primum
　　agnosci patitur redditus arva color.
progredimur parvis per litora proxima cymbis,
　　quorum perfugio crebra pateret humus.　　　220
aestivos penetrent oneraria carbasa fluctus:
　　tutior autumnus mobilitate fugae.
Alsia praelegitur tellus, Pyrgique recedunt—
　　nunc villae grandes, oppida parva prius.
iam Caeretanos demonstrat navita fines:　　　225
　　aevo deposuit nomen Agylla vetus.
stringimus ⟨hinc effractum⟩ et fluctu et tempore
　　　　Castrum:
　　index semiruti porta vetusta loci.

205 explorata VRB: expectata *Schrader*.
206 fideret VRB: se daret *Heinsius*: *alii alia* (*e.g.* sideret,
funderet).
211 cunę V: curę R.
227 *lacunam alii aliter suppleverunt*: hinc exesum *Barth*:
hinc effractum *Keene in not.*: expugnatum *Baehrens*.

---

^a Palladius, the last of Rutilius' circle to take leave of him
before his voyage, was a young relative of his who had come

Thrice five days we watched the trust to be placed in the sea, until a new moon's more favourable breeze should present itself. Then on the eve of going I send back to his studies and the city Palladius, the hope and honour of my race.[a] That eloquent youth had been sent of late from the lands of the Gauls to learn the laws of the Roman courts. My son in affection and kinsman by blood, he holds the fondest ties of my regard. Even now his father Exuperantius trains the Armoric sea-board to love the recovery of peace; he re-establishes the laws, brings freedom back and suffers not the inhabitants to be their servants' slaves.[b]

In the half-dawn we weigh anchor, at the hour of day when colour is first restored and lets the fields grow visible. In little boats we make way along the nearest shores, so that a beach might always lie open as refuge for them. Let cargo-ships 'neath canvas plough through the summer waves: safer is autumn if we have quickness to escape. The Alsian land is skirted, and Pyrgi fades into the distance[c]—to-day large country-houses, in earlier days small towns. Now the sailor points out the bounds of Caere: the ancient Agylla has lost its name through time.[d] Next we coast by Castrum, shattered both by wave and time: an age-worn gateway marks the half-ruined place. O'er it

from Gaul to study law in Rome. His father, Exuperantius, had restored order to the Armorican regions in Gaul, which had followed the example of revolt from the empire set by Britain in A.D. 407.

[b] The reference is most probably to a servile insurrection which Exuperantius checked.

[c] Alsium, now Palo, was an ancient Etrurian town. Pyrgi, now Santa Severa, was a seaport for Caere.

[d] Caere, now Cervetri, had Agylla as its Greek name.

praesidet, exigui formatus imagine saxi,   230
    qui pastorali cornua fronte gerit:
multa licet priscum nomen deleverit aetas,
    hoc Inui castrum fama fuisse putat,
seu Pan Tyrrhenis mutavit Maenala silvis
    sive sinus patrios incola Faunus init;
dum renovat largo mortalia semina fetu,   235
    fingitur in venerem pronior esse deus.

ad Centumcellas forti deflximus Austro:
    tranquilla puppes in statione sedent.
molibus aequoreum concluditur amphitheatrum,
    angustosque aditus insula facta tegit;   240
attollit geminas turres bifidoque meatu
    faucibus artatis pandit utrumque latus.
nec posuisse satis laxo navalia portu;
    ne vaga vel tutas ventilet aura rates,
interior medias sinus invitatus in aedes   245
    instabilem fixis aera nescit aquis;
qualis in Euboicis captiva natatibus unda
    sustinet alterno bracchia lenta sinu.

nosse iuvat tauri dictas de nomine thermas;
    nec mora difficilis milibus ire tribus.   250

229–230 *distichon post* 232 *posuit Damm.*
232 Inui VB : Iani R.
235 dumve novat *Baehrens.* longo V : largo RB. semina
VRB : saecula *Mueller.*
250 difficilis VRB : distantis (*sc.* thermas) *Baehrens.*

---

a Rutilius confuses Castrum Novum in Etruria with
Castrum Inui in Latium : *cf. Aen.* VI. 775. *Init* in 234 is
an attempt to explain the name Inuus, here identified with
the Greek Pan or the Latin Faunus.
    b For *dum* causal, assigning a reason, *cf.* Plaut. *Trin.* 1149–
50 *dum vereor sermonem interrumpere, solus sto*; and Cic. *Ad Att.*

stands guard, fashioned as a little statue in stone, the figure of one with horns upon his shepherd's brow: although long years have blotted out the earliest name, legend considers this was once " Castrum Inui," [a] whether it be that Pan exchanged Maenalus for Tuscan woods or that Faunus comes in to haunt his native dells: since [b] he reneweth the offspring of mankind with plenteous births, the god is represented over-prone to venery.

To Centumcellae [c] we changed our tack before a strong South wind: our ships find mooring in the calm roadstead. An amphitheatre of water is there enclosed by piers, and an artificial island shelters the narrow entrances; it rears twin towers and extends in both directions so as to leave a double approach with narrow channels. Nor was it enough to construct docks of wide harbourage; to keep the vagrant breeze from rocking the craft even when safe in port, an inner basin has been coaxed into the very midst of the buildings, and so, with its surface at rest, it knows naught of the wayward wind, like the water imprisoned in Cumae's baths [d] which buoys up the unhurried arms plied by the swimmer in alternate sweep.

We pay a pleasant visit to the hot springs named after a bull: [e] the distance of three miles seems no

---

I. xvi. 2 *qui (sc. Hortensius) dum veritus est . . . non vidit illud.* . . . Rutilius I. 443 may also be a parallel.

[c] Now Civita Vecchia. The port was constructed under Trajan: see the description in Plin. *Ep.* VI. xxxi. 15–17.

[d] Cumae, on the bay of Naples, was partly settled by Euboeans: *cf.* Virg. *Aen.* VI. 2: *Euboicis Cumarum allabitur oris.*

[e] Aquae or Thermae Taurianae, three miles N. of Civita Vecchia.

non illic gustu latices vitiantur amaro
  lymphave fumifico sulphure tincta calet:
purus odor mollisque sapor dubitare lavantem
  cogit qua melius parte petantur aquae.
credere si dignum famae, flagrantia taurus   255
  investigato fonte lavacra dedit,
ut solet excussis pugnam praeludere glaebis,
  stipite cum rigido cornua prona terit:
sive deus, faciem mentitus et ora iuvenci,
  noluit ardentis dona latere soli;   260
qualis Agenorei rapturus gaudia furti
  per freta virgineum sollicitavit onus.
ardua non solos deceant miracula Graios!
  auctorem pecudem fons Heliconis habet:
elicitas simili credamus origine lymphas,   265
  Musarum ⟨ut⟩ latices ungula fodit equi.
haec quoque Pieriis spiracula comparat antris
  carmine Messallae nobilitatus ager;
intrantemque capit discedentemque moratur
  postibus affixum dulce poema sacris.   270
hic est qui primo seriem de consule ducit,
  usque ad Publicolas si redeamus avos;

---

²⁵³ labantem VB, *corr. Simler*: molisque . . . labentem R.
²⁶¹ tecti *Baehrens.*
²⁶³ solos . . . Graios V : solum . . . Graiis R.
²⁶⁵ en medicas *Baehrens.* nymphas V *et pler. edd. vett.*:
lymphas *corr. Castalio et sic legitur in* R.
²⁶⁶ ut *addidit Damm.*

  ᵃ *i.e.* whether for drinking or bathing.
  ᵇ The bull that unearthed the hot wells may have been a
disguised god, just as, according to the myth, the bull that
carried off to Crete Europa, the daughter of the Phoenician
king Agenor, was really Jupiter.
  ᶜ The fountain Hippocrene on Mount Helicon in Boeotia,

troublesome delay. There the wells are not spoiled
by a brackish flavour, nor is the water coloured and
hot with fuming sulphur: the pure smell and delicate
taste make the bather hesitate for what purpose
the waters should better be used.[a] If the legend
deserves credit, it was a bull that first revealed
these hot baths by tracking out the source, when,
tossing aloft the sods, as is a bull's way to prelude
a fight, he grazed his downbent horns upon a hard
tree-stump: or else a god, counterfeiting an ox-like
shape and visage, would not permit the gift of the
warm soil to lurk unseen; like the god who, bent
on snatching stolen joys from his theft of Agenor's
daughter, bore across the seas the terror-stricken
maid.[b] Not Greeks alone must have the glory of
marvels which o'ertop belief! The fount of Helicon
has for its begetter an animal:[c] let us believe that
through like origin these waters were drawn forth,
as the steed's hoof dug out the Muses' well. The
land also, blazoned in Messalla's poetry,[d] has these
outlets to vie with the Pierian grots: and his sweet
lines, affixed to the hallowed portals, capture the
eye of him who enters, and makes him linger as he
leaves. This is the man who traces his descent
from the first consul, if we go back as far as his
ancestors the Publicolae: he too with his nod as

sacred to the Muses, was fabled to have been produced by a
stroke of the hoof of the winged horse Pegasus.

[d] Valerius Messalla, praetorian prefect in A.D. 396, is often
mentioned in the Code of Theodosius. He claimed descent
from Valerius Publicola, who became colleague to Junius
Brutus on the retirement of Tarquinius Collatinus; so that
"primo de consule," 271, is not literally accurate. Sym-
machus (VII. 81–92) addresses letters to him, and Sidonius
Apollinaris admired his intellectual qualities (*Carm*. 9, 302).

hic et praefecti nutu praetoria rexit.
  sed menti et linguae gloria maior inest.
hic docuit qualem poscat facundia sedem: 27*
  ut bonus esse velit, quisque disertus erit.

roscida puniceo fulsere crepuscula caelo:
  pandimus obliquo lintea flexa sinu.
paulisper litus fugimus Munione vadosum:
  suspecto trepidant ostia parva salo.   28*
inde Graviscarum fastigia rara videmus,
  quas premit aestivae saepe paludis odor;
sed nemorosa viret densis vicinia lucis,
  pineaque extremis fluctuat umbra fretis.
cernimus antiquas nullo custode ruinas   28*
  et desolatae moenia foeda Cosae.
ridiculam cladis pudet inter seria causam
  promere, sed risum dissimulare piget.
dicuntur cives quondam migrare coacti
  muribus infestos deseruisse Lares!   29*
credere maluerim Pygmaeae damna cohortis
  et coniuratos in sua bella grues.
haud procul hinc petitur signatus ab Hercule portus:
  vergentem sequitur mollior aura diem.

[277] fulsere VB : luxere R.

---

[a] Quintilian repeatedly insists on character as indispensable in an orator: I. *proem.* 9–10 (*qui esse nisi vir bonus non potest*); II. ii. (the whole section); II. xv. 1; XII. i. 1 (*is qui a M. Catone finitur, vir bonus dicendi peritus*): *cf.* Cic. *de Orat.* II. 85.

prefect held praetorian control. Yet greater glory dwells in his mind and tongue. He has shown what kind of dwelling-place eloquence demands: each man's power in oratory will depend on his desire to be good.[a]

The half-light of dewy morn gleamed from a purple sky; we spread our sails bent in curves slantwise; and for a time give a wide berth to the shore which the Munio[b] blocks with shoals: the narrow river-mouth heaves restlessly with treacherous surf. Thereafter we sight the scattered housetops of Graviscae,[c] plagued often with a marshy smell in summer-time; and yet the wooded neighbourhood is green with close-grown groves, and pine-tree shadows wave o'er the margin of the sea. Then we descry, all unguarded now, desolate Cosa's ancient ruins and unsightly walls.[d] 'Tis with a qualm that I adduce mid serious things the comic reason for its downfall; but I am loath to suppress a laugh. The story runs that once upon a time the townsfolk were forced to migrate and left their homes behind because rats infested them! I'd sooner believe in losses suffered by the Pygmies' infantry[e] and in cranes leagued solemnly to fight their wars. Not far from here we make the port which the name of Hercules distinguishes: a softer breeze follows

[b] Now the Mignone.
[c] Graviscae, the port of Tarquinii, being in the Maremma, had unhealthy air. Like its pine-groves, this small place has disappeared.
[d] Cosa is now Ansedonia: its harbour was the Portus Herculis, now Porto Ercole.
[e] The first mention of Milton's " small infantry warred on by cranes " is in Homer, *Iliad* III. 3-6.

inter castrorum vestigia sermo retexit   295
  Sardoam Lepido praecipitante fugam;
litore namque Cosae cognatos depulit hostes
  virtutem Catuli Roma secuta ducis.
ille tamen Lepidus peior civilibus armis
  qui gessit sociis impia bella tribus,   300
qui libertatem Mutinensi Marte receptam
  obruit auxiliis urbe pavente novis.
insidias paci moliri tertius ausus
  tristibus excepit congrua fata reis.
quartus, Caesareo dum vult irrepere regno,   305
  incesti poenam solvit adulterii.
nunc quoque—sed melius de nostris fama queretur:
  iudex posteritas semina dira notet.
nominibus certos credam decurrere mores?
  moribus an potius nomina certa dari?   310
quicquid id est, mirus Latiis annalibus ordo,
  quod Lepidum totiens reccidit ense malum.

necdum discussis pelago permittimur umbris:
  natus vicino vertice ventus adest.

---

³⁰² pavente V : gemente R : favente B.
³¹³ decessis VRB : discussis *Almeloveen* : detersis *Heinsius.*
permittitur VRB : permittimur *Castalio.*

---

^a Four Lepidi are here alluded to : (1) M. Aemilius Lepidus,
declared a public enemy by the Senate in 77 B.C., was after
his defeat at the Mulvian Bridge pursued by Catulus into
Etruria. He eventually fled from Portus Herculis to Sardinia.
(2) His son, M. Aemilius Lepidus, who had long wavered

declining day. Amid the traces of his camp our
conversation weaves again the tale of Lepidus in
headlong flight to Sardinia; [a] for 'twas from Cosa's
shore that Rome, following the lead of valiant
Catulus, drove off the foes of her own blood. Yet
was that Lepidus more a villain, who mid civil strife,
in a confederacy of three, waged impious warfare;
whose reinforcements—to the city's dread—crushed
the freedom recovered in battle at Mutina. A
third of the name ventured to contrive a plot against
the peace and met a fate that fits luckless de-
fendants. A fourth, aiming at a stealthy inroad on
imperial power, paid the penalty of foul adultery.
To-day also—but of the Lepidi of our day fame
will draw up a better indictment: let posterity be
the judge to brand the ill-omened stock. Am I to
believe that definite characters descend from names
or rather that definite names are given to characters?
However that be, it is a strange routine in the
chronicles of Latium that misfortune has so often
recurred through the sword of the Lepidi.[b]

The shades of night as yet are undispelled when
we entrust ourselves to the sea. Born of the neigh-
bouring hill-crest, a breeze befriends us. Mount

between Mark Antony and the Senate, joined forces with
Antony after the battle of Mutina in 44 B.C. The allusion in
l. 300 is to his membership of the triumvirate with Antony
and Octavian. (3) The triumvir's son plotted in 30 B.C.
to murder Octavian, but was arrested and sent to Octavian,
then in the East, where he was put to death. (4) M. Aemilius
Lepidus was the second husband of Drusilla, Caligula's sister.
He conspired against his imperial brother-in-law, and had
illicit relations with Agrippina and Livilla, two other sisters
of the emperor. He was executed in A.D. 39.

[b] *Lepidum:* genit. plur. rather than adjectivally with
malum.

tenditur in medias mons Argentarius undas   315
  ancipitique iugo caerula curva premit;
transversos colles bis ternis milibus artat;
  circuitu ponti ter duodena patet:
qualis per geminos fluctus Ephyreius Isthmos
  Ionias bimari litore findit aquas.   320
vix circumvehimur sparsae dispendia rupis,
  nec sinuosa gravi cura labore caret:
mutantur totiens vario spiramina flexu:
  quae modo profuerant vela repente nocent.
eminus Igilii silvosa cacumina miror,   325
  quam fraudare nefas laudis honore suae.
haec proprios nuper tutata est insula saltus,
  sive loci ingenio seu domini genio,
gurgite cum modico victricibus obstitit armis
  tamquam longinquo dissociata mari: 330
haec multos lacera suscepit ab urbe fugatos,
  hic fessis posito certa timore salus.
plurima terreno populaverat aequora bello
  contra naturam classe timendus eques:

ᵃ Monte Argentario, a rugged peninsular promontory over
20 miles in circuit, has two peaks (*ancipiti iugo*)—the southern
one above Porto Ercole, and the northern one above Porto S.
Stefano.
  ᵇ The promontory of Monte Argentario is likened to the
isthmus of Corinth (= *Ephyre*, frequently in the poets from
Homer onwards). In strict accuracy, the Ionian sea lies on
one side only of the isthmus, the Aegean being on the other
side.
  ᶜ Igilium, now Giglio, was, as an island, reasonably safe
from invasion by the Goths (l. 329), whether in A.D. 408

Argentarius juts out amidst the waves and with two-fold ridge *a* confines the blue waters of its bays, shortening the road across the hills to twice three miles, while its extent round by sea is three times twelve, even as the Corinthian isthmus betwixt twin floods cleaves the Ionian deep with shores which two seas wash.*b* We just succeed in doubling that long round of scattered crags, nor are the helmsman's anxious détours without heavy toil—so often puffs of wind change with each varying tack: the sails which helped a moment since are suddenly a drag. Far off I marvel at Igilium's *c* forest heights: 'twere sinful to cheat the island *d* of the homage which its fame deserves. Of late this isle defended its own glades, whether by natural position or by the emperor's supernatural powers,*e* when, though severed only by a moderate channel, it bade defiance to triumphant arms as if isolated by the far-dividing sea. It welcomed many refugees from mangled Rome: here might the weary drop their fear and find sure safety. A cavalry, which against nature's law spelt terror on shipboard, had harried many a sea with warfare suited to the land.*f* It is a miracle

when Alaric advanced to his first siege of Rome or in the following years. It offered refuge to fugitives from Rome when the city was sacked by Alaric in A.D. 410 (see l. 331).

d *quam*: *sc. insulam*, though its name Igilium is neuter.

e The alternatives (emphasized by a play on words) are that the island may have been protected either by the *ingenium* (= *natura*) *loci* or by the indwelling *Genius* of Honorius, which is viewed as a presiding *Fortuna* guarding the island against attack.

f The Gothic cavalry was reinforced by that of the Huns under Alaric's brother-in-law Ataulf. They sailed from island to island on marauding expeditions.

unum mira fides vario discrimine portum   335
    tam prope Romanis, tam procul esse Getis.
tangimus Umbronem ; non est ignobile flumen,
    quod tuto trepidas excipit ore rates :
tam facilis pronis semper patet alveus undis,
    in pontum quotiens saeva procella ruit.   340
hic ego tranquillae volui succedere ripae ;
    sed nautas avidos longius ire sequor.
sic festinantem ventusque diesque reliquit :
    nec proferre pedem nec revocare licet.
litorea noctis requiem metamur harena :   345
    dat vespertinos myrtea silva focos :
parvula subiectis facimus tentoria remis :
    transversus subito culmine contus erat.

lux aderat : tonsis progressi stare videmur,
    sed cursum prorae terra relicta probat.   350
occurrit Chalybum memorabilis Ilva metallis,
    qua nihil uberius Norica glaeba tulit ;
non Biturix largo potior strictura camino,
    nec quae Sardonico caespite massa fluit.
plus confert populis ferri fecunda creatrix   355
    quam Tartessiaci glarea fulva Tagi.

---

    [339] pronis *om.* R.
    [343] festinantem VRB : festinantes *Schrader, Baehrens.*
    [352] qua nihil . . . gleba V : qua mihi . . . terra R.

---

    [a] *i.e.* at the time of the sack of Rome and of the Gothic sea-raids.
    [b] *metari* is the regular verb for laying out a camp.
    [c] Lit. " mines of the Chalybes." The Χάλυβες of Pontus were renowned for their working of steel (χάλυψ).
    [d] Noricum, between the Danube and the Alps, corresponded to a great part of Styria and Carinthia and included the district round Salzburg. Its steel was famed : *cf.* Hor. *Od.* I. xvi. 9–10, *Noricus ensis.*

to believe that a single haven at crises different [a]
should be so near the Romans, and for the Goths so
far. We touch at Umbro's mouth: no inconsiderable
stream, it welcomes panic-stricken barques at a safe
entrance: such easy approach does the river-bed
with its descending current ever offer, as often as a
cruel tempest bursts upon the deep. Here I was
minded to land upon the peaceful shore; but, as
the mariners were greedy for further progress, I
e'en follow: so, speeding on, I find that with day-
light the breeze has failed: neither forward nor
backward can we make way. So on the sand of the
beach we mark out [b] our resting-place for the night:
a myrtle wood provides our evening fires. We raise
our little tents with oars as props: a pole set cross-
wise helped to form a hastily fashioned roof.

Day came: though pushing on with oars, we seem
to be at a standstill, and yet the receding land proves
the movement of the bow. Across our course lies
Elba, famous for its iron mines: [c] than it Norican [d]
soil has produced no richer yield; nor is the wrought
metal of the Bituriges preferable, though smelted
in great furnaces; [e] nor the molten mass which pours
from the Sardinian ore. [f] More good is done to
the world by teeming earth which gives birth to
iron than by the golden gravel washed down by the
Tagus in the distant West; [g] for deadly gold is the

[e] The Bituriges of Gallia Aquitanica have left their name
in Bourges. *Strictura*, wrought metal, implied smelting which
could be carried out where firewood was abundant. Ore from
Ilva (the modern Elba), which was short of fuel, had to be
taken to furnaces on the mainland.

[f] *caespes*, lit. the clod or lump containing ore: *cf. glaeba*,
352.

[g] From Tartessus in Spain *Tartessiacus* gets its meaning of
"Western."

materies vitiis aurum letale parandis :
   auri caecus amor ducit in omne nefas :
aurea legitimas expugnant munera taedas,
   virgineosque sinus aureus imber emit :   360
auro victa fides munitas decipit urbes :
   auri flagitiis ambitus ipse furit.
at contra ferro squalentia rura coluntur ;
   ferro vivendi prima reperta via est :
saecula semideum, ferrati nescia Martis,   365
   ferro crudeles sustinuere feras :
humanis manibus non sufficit usus inermis,
   si non sint aliae ferrea tela manus.
his mecum pigri solabar taedia venti,
   dum resonat variis vile celeuma modis.   370

lassatum cohibet vicina Faleria cursum,
   quamquam vix medium Phoebus haberet iter.
et tum forte hilares per compita rustica pagi
   mulcebant sacris pectora fessa iocis :
illo quippe die tandem revocatus Osiris   375
   excitat in fruges germina laeta novas.
egressi villam petimus lucoque vagamur :
   stagna placent septo deliciosa vado.

357 fatale *Burman* : ferale *Baehrens*.
371 laxatum *Castalio* : lassantem *Baehrens*.
373 fagi VRB : pagi *Castalio*.
377 lucoque vagamur V : lŭtoque vagamus (*contra metrum*)
P : petimusque luthoque vagamur B : ludoque vacamus
Werusdorf.

---

   a The allusion in l. 360 is to the myth of Danaë and in l. 361
to the bribery employed by Philip of Macedon to capture cities.
Cf. the attack on gold by Tiberianus, pp. 560–563 *supra*.

substance that makes vice: blind lust of gold leads
into every crime: golden gifts carry by storm the
troth of wedded brides: a golden shower can buy
the maid's embraces:[a] loyalty sapped by gold
betrays the well-walled town: by scandalous mis-
use of gold ambition itself pursues its wild career.
But not so iron: it is with iron that neglected fields
are tilled; by iron was the first way of living found.
Races of demigods, who knew not iron-harnessed
Mars, by iron faced the charge of savage beasts.
For human hands their unarmed use is not enough,
if iron weapons lent not other hands. Such thoughts
of mine beguiled the weariness of a laggard wind,
and all the time in varied notes the boatswain's
trumpery refrain rang out.

The neighbouring Faleria[b] checks our weary
course, though Phoebus scarce had reached his mid
career. That day it happened merry village-bands
along the country cross-roads soothed their jaded
hearts with festal observances; it was in truth the
day when, after long time restored, Osiris wakes
the happy seeds to yield fresh produce.[c] Landing,
we seek lodging,[d] and stroll within a wood; we like
the ponds which charm with their shallow enclosed

----

[b] It is now Falese, or Porto di Faliesi.

[c] The worship of Osiris, introduced from Egypt in republican
times, passed through vicissitudes of favour and disfavour,
but spread widely through the Roman Empire. A vegetation-
deity and patron of agriculture, Osiris was also a suffering hero
and became god of the dead. The priests of his sister-wife
Isis mourned his death or joyfully celebrated his periodic
resuscitation. Here he gives a fertilizing stimulus to
autumnal sowings.

[d] *Villam* here seems to mean an "inn": *cf. villicus* or
vilicus as "innkeeper," I. 623.

ludere lascivos intra vivaria pisces
    gurgitis inclusi laxior unda sinit.   380
sed male pensavit requiem stationis amoenae
    hospite conductor durior Antiphate!
namque loci querulus curam Iudaeus agebat,
    humanis animal dissociale cibis :
vexatos frutices, pulsatas imputat algas,   385
    damnaque libatae grandia clamat aquae.
reddimus obscaenae convicia debita genti
    quae genitale caput propudiosa metit :
radix stultitiae, cui frigida sabbata cordi,
    sed cor frigidius religione sua.   390
septima quaeque dies turpi damnata veterno,
    tamquam lassati mollis imago dei.
cetera mendacis deliramenta catastae
    nec puerum in somnis credere posse reor.
atque utinam numquam Iudaea subacta fuisset   395
    Pompeii bellis imperiisque Titi!
latius excisae pestis contagia serpunt,
    victoresque suos natio victa premit.

adversus surgit Boreas ; sed nos quoque remis
    surgere certamus, dum tegit astra dies.   400
proxima securum reserat Populonia litus,
    qua naturalem ducit in arva sinum.

[379] inter VRB : intra *Schrader.*
[382] dirior *Drakenborch* : crudior *Mueller.*
[394] pueros omnes VB : puer ōnes R : pueros parvos *vel* teneros *coniec. Baehrens* : pueros et anus *Keene in not.* : puerum in somnis *A. M. Duff.*
[395] Iudea capta R.
[396] imperioque B, *Baehrens.*

---

[a] The savage king of the Laestrygones devoured one of Ulysses' men and sank all his ships except that on which Ulysses sailed (*Odyss.* X. 114–132).

basin. The spacious waters of the imprisoned flood
permit the playful fish to sport inside these pre-
serves. But we were made to pay dear for the
repose of this delightful halting-place by a lessee
who was harsher than Antiphates as host![a] For a
crabbed Jew was in charge of the spot—a creature
that quarrels with sound human food.[b] He charges
in our bill for damaging his bushes and hitting the sea-
weed, and bawls about his enormous loss in water
we had sipped. We pay the abuse due to the filthy
race that infamously practises circumcision: a root
of silliness they are: chill Sabbaths are after their
own heart, yet their heart is chillier than their creed.
Each seventh day is condemned to ignoble sloth,
as 'twere an effeminate picture of a god fatigued.[c]
The other wild ravings from their lying bazaar
methinks not even a child in his sleep could believe.
And would that Judaea had never been subdued by
Pompey's wars and Titus' military power.[d] The
infection of this plague, though excised, still creeps
abroad the more: and 'tis their own conquerors
that a conquered race keeps down.[e]

Against us rises a North wind; but we too strive
with oars to rise, while daylight shrouds the stars.
Close at hand Populonia opens up her safe coast,
where she draws her natural bay well inland. No

[b] The taboo of the pig as unclean was unintelligible to
Romans, whose cuisine included fifty different ways of
serving swine's flesh.

[c] The reference is to the teaching of the Hebrew scriptures:
e.g. Genesis ii. 2–3; Exodus xx. 9–11, xxxiv. 21.

[d] The Maccabean monarchy fell after Pompey's three
months' siege of Jerusalem, 63 B.C. Titus captured Jerusalem
in A.D. 70.

[e] Cf. Hor. Epist. II. i. 156, Graecia capta ferum victorem
cepit.

non illic positas extollit in aethera moles
   lumine nocturno conspicienda Pharos;
sed speculam validae rupis sortita vetustas,   405
   qua fluctus domitos arduus urget apex,
castellum geminos hominum fundavit in usus,
   praesidium terris indiciumque fretis.
agnosci nequeunt aevi monumenta prioris:
   grandia consumpsit moenia tempus edax.   410
sola manent interceptis vestigia muris:
   ruderibus latis tecta sepulta iacent.
non indignemur mortalia corpora solvi:
   cernimus exemplis oppida posse mori.

laetior hic nostras crebrescit fama per aures: 415
   consilium Romam paene redire fuit.
hic praefecturam sacrae cognoscimus urbis
   delatam meritis, dulcis amice, tuis.
optarem verum complecti carmine nomen,
   sed quosdam refugit regula dura pedes.   420
cognomen versu † ⟨veniet⟩, carissime Rufi:
   illo te dudum pagina nostra canit.
festa dies pridemque meos dignata Penates
   poste coronato vota secunda colat:

---

[421] cogn. versu veneris VB: cognomen venens (*om.* versu
contra metrum) R: Veneri (*vocativus*) *Pith.*, *Burman*:
cognomen serva, Veneri *Barth, Schrader*: c. versus servet
Damm: c. versu dederis *Mueller*: c. versu capitur *Baehrens*:
c. versu veniet *Vessereau*: c. v. veneror *Helm*: c. v. vehĕris
Préchac.

---

[a] At Populonia, an ancient Etruscan town, there was an old
castle instead of a lighthouse like the famous one on the island
of Pharos off Alexandria.
   [b] Cf. in Sulpicius' letter of consolation to Cicero, *Ad Fam.*
IV. v., *nos homunculi indignamur, si quis nostrum interiit* . . .

Pharos,[a] conspicuous with nightly light, has piers built there which rise into the sky; but men long ago, finding a mighty cliff to serve as a look-out where the towering hill-crest overhangs the conquered waves, laid the foundations of a castle for twin services to man—a defence on land and signal-post for sea. The memorials of an earlier age cannot be recognised; devouring time has wasted its mighty battlements away. Traces only remain now that the walls are lost: under a wide stretch of rubble lie the buried homes. Let us not chafe that human frames dissolve: from precedents we discern that towns can die.[b]

Here a joyful piece of news spreads as we listen: it was almost my decision to go back to Rome. Here do we learn that the prefecture of the Sacred City has been bestowed upon your merits, beloved friend. I'd fain include your true name in my poem; but the strict law of metre avoids certain feet.[c] Your cognomen will come in a line,[d] dearest Rufius: by that name but recently my page has sung your praise.[e] Let a day of festivity, such as years ago honoured my own home with garlands on the door, now show respect to hopes fulfilled:[f] let green

---

[b] *quorum vita brevior esse debet, cum uno loco tot oppidum cadavera iacent?*

[c] Rufius' full name, Ceionius Rufius Vŏlŭsĭanus, is inadmissible in elegiacs.

[d] The vexed line, 421, whether *Veneri* is read as dative of *Venus* or as vocative of *Venerius*, offers no sure foundation for the addition of *Venerius* to the name of Rufius. Taking *Veneri* as vocative, some editors have thought Rutilius dedicated his poem to "Venerius" Rufius.

[e] *Supra*, lines 167–178.

[f] Rufius' elevation brings back to Rutilius' mind his own prefecture: *cf.* I. 157–160.

exornent virides communia gaudia rami: **425**
    provecta est animae portio magna meae.
sic mihi, sic potius, placeat geminata potestas:
    per quem malueram, rursus honore fruor.

currere curamus velis Aquilone reverso,
    cum primum roseo fulsit Eous equo.   430
incipit obscuros ostendere Corsica montes,
    nubiferumque caput concolor umbra levat:
sic dubitanda solet gracili vanescere cornu
    defessisque oculis luna reperta latet.
haec ponti brevitas auxit mendacia famae: 435
    armentale ferunt quippe natasse pecus,
tempore Cyrnaeas quo primum venit in oras
    forte secuta vagum femina Corsa bovem.

processu pelagi iam se Capraria tollit;
    squalet lucifugis insula plena viris.   440
ipsi se monachos Graio cognomine dicunt,
    quod soli nullo vivere teste volunt.
munera Fortunae metuunt, dum damna verentur:
    quisquam sponte miser, ne miser esse queat?
quaenam perversi rabies tam stulta cerebri,   445
    dum mala formides, nec bona posse pati?

---

    [a] *Cf.* I. 493, *nostrae pars maxima mentis*, and Hor. *Od.* I.
iii. 8, *animae dimidium meae.*

    [b] *dubitanda* = to be puzzled over, an object of uncertainty:
cf. Virg. *Aen.* VI. 454, *aut videt aut vidisse putat per nubila
lunam.*

    [c] Cyrnos (Κύρνος), or Corsica, lies about 55 miles off the
mainland. Itasius Lemniacus denies that it could be seen

boughs be the decoration for the joy we share: a great part of mine own life [a] has been advanced to high place. Thus, aye thus to me let this renewal of office bring pleasure: once again I enjoy dignity through the one for whom I wished it more.

When the North wind veered, we took pains to run with sails before the breeze, as soon as the Morning-star gleamed on his rosy steed. Corsica begins to show her dim mountains, and, matched in colour, the mass of shadow makes the cloud-capped crest look higher still: so 'tis the moon's way with slender horn to fade leaving us puzzled,[b] and e'en though found she yet lies hid for straining eyes. The short sea-passage here has given support to a lying legend; for folk say a herd of cattle swam across at the time when first it happened that a woman called Corsa in quest of a stray ox reached the shores of Cyrnos.[c]

As we advance at sea, Capraria now rears itself— an ill-kept isle full of men who shun the light. Their own name [d] for themselves is a Greek one, "mona-choi" (monks), because they wish to dwell alone with none to see. They fear Fortune's boons, as they dread her outrages: would anyone, to escape misery, live of his own choice in misery? What silly fanaticism of a distorted brain is it to be unable to endure even [e] blessings because of your terror of

from Populonia. The story ran that a herdswoman noticed an ox used to swim the sea and return fatter. This suggested that there was a fertile island not far away.

[d] *Cognomen* is the equivalent of *nomen* in several Virgilian passages: *Aen.* III. 163; VIII. 48. It is loosely used, *supra* I. 421.

[e] *Nec* has the force of *ne . . . quidem*, as in *nec puerum*, I. 394.

sive suas repetunt factorum ergastula poenas,
  tristia seu nigro viscera felle tument,
sic nimiae bilis morbum adsignavit Homerus
  Bellerophonteis sollicitudinibus :
nam iuveni offenso saevi post tela doloris
  dicitur humanum displicuisse genus.

in Volaterranum, vero Vada nomine, tractum
  ingressus dubii tramitis alta lego :
despectat prorae custos clavumque sequentem
  dirigit et puppim voce monente regit.
incertas gemina discriminat arbore fauces
  defixasque offert limes uterque sudes :
illis proceras mos est adnectere lauros
  conspicuas ramis et fruticante coma,
ut praebente algam densi symplegade limi
  servet inoffensas semita clara notas.
illic me rapidus consistere Corus adegit,
  qualis silvarum frangere lustra solet.
vix tuti domibus saevos toleravimus imbres :
  Albini patuit proxima villa mei.

[447] fatorum (*in marg.* factorum · f ·) V.
[456] derigit *Baehrens.*
[458] limus *Baehrens.*
[461] algam RB : viam V, *Baehrens* : ulvam *Kalinka,*
Préchac.
[463] rabidus *Mueller, Baehrens.*

---

[a] *Ergastula,* " prisons for slaves," prob. by metonymy here
for the inmates.

ills? Whether they are like prisoners [a] who demand the appropriate penalties for their deeds, or whether their melancholy hearts are swollen with black bile, it was even so that Homer assigned the ailment of excessive bile as cause of Bellerophon's troubled soul; [b] for it was after the wounds of a cruel sorrow that men say the stricken youth conceived his loathing for human kind.

Entering on the region of Volaterra, appropriately called "The Shallows," [c] I thread my way through the deep part of the treacherous channel. At the bow the look-out watches the water beneath and gives directions to the helm behind, guiding the stern with warning shouts. A boundary on each side marks the puzzling narrows by a pair of trees, and presents a line of piles hammered in there: to these it is the custom to fix tall laurels easy to see because of their branches and bushy foliage, so that, although the shifting bank [d] of thick mud shows its mass of sea-weed, a clear passage may keep the guiding-signs unstruck. There I was driven to make a halt by a tearing North-wester of the sort that is wont to shatter the depths of the woods. Scarce safe beneath a roof did we endure the pitiless rains: the neighbouring country-seat of my own Albinus was placed at my disposal. For my

[b] Homer in reality does not explain Bellerophon's misanthropy as due to black bile (μελαγχολία), though he describes him as "eating out his heart" (ὃν θυμὸν κατέδων Il. VI. 202). The true reason for his grief was the loss of his three children.

[c] The name is preserved in Torre di Vada.

[d] The shifting mud-bank is compared with the fabled Symplegades of the Euxine, the floating rocks which used to clash together and rebound.

namque meus, quem Roma meo subiunxit honori,
  per quem iura meae continuata togae.
non exspectatos pensavit laudibus annos;
  vitae flore puer, sed gravitate senex.
mutua germanos iunxit reverentia mores,
  et favor alternis crevit amicitiis.
praetulit ille meas, cum vincere posset, habenas;
  at decessoris maior amore fuit.

subiectas villae vacat adspectare salinas;
  namque hoc censetur nomine salsa palus,
qua mare terrenis declive canalibus intrat
  multifidosque lacus parvula fossa rigat.
ast ubi flagrantes admovit Sirius ignes,
  cum pallent herbae, cum sitit omnis ager,
tum cataractarum claustris excluditur aequor,
  ut fixos latices torrida duret humus.
concipiunt acrem nativa coagula Phoebum,
  et gravis aestivo crusta calore coit;
haud aliter quam cum glacie riget horridus Hister
  grandiaque adstricto flumine plaustra vehit.
rimetur solitus naturae expendere causas
  inque pari dispar fomite quaerat opus:
vincta fluenta gelu concepto sole liquescunt,
  et rursus liquidae sole gelantur aquae.

⁴⁷¹ amores *Baehrens.*
⁴⁸⁷ solitas natura VRB : solitus naturae *Castalio* : solitus
naturam *Baehrens.*
  ⁴⁸⁹ conspecto VRB *et vulgo* : concepto *Baehrens (cf. 483).*

  ᵃ Albinus succeeded Rutilius as Prefect of the city in
A.D. 414.
  ᵇ *i.e.* Albinus had been appointed to high office at a
singularly early age; but, if he fell short of the usual number
of years, he made up for this by his merits.

RUTILIUS NAMATIANUS

own he was whom Rome linked to me as successor
in office,[a] in whose person my civil jurisdiction
was continued. His merit outweighed years which
had not been waited for:[b] a lad in the bloom of
youth, he had the worth of age. Mutual respect
joined our kindred characters, and regard grew from
the friendship of one for the other. He preferred
that I should hold the reins of power, although he
might have surpassed me: yet his affection for his
predecessor has made him a greater man.

We find time to inspect the salt-pans lying near
the mansion: it is on this score that value is set
upon the salt marsh, where the sea-water, running
down through channels in the land, makes entry,
and a little trench floods the many-parted ponds.
But after the Dog-star has advanced his blazing fires,
when grass turns pale, when all the land is athirst,
then the sea is shut out by the barrier-sluices, so
that the parched ground may solidify the imprisoned
waters. The natural incrustations catch the pene-
trating sun, and in the summer heat the heavy crust
of salt cakes, just as when the wild Danube stiffens
with ice and carries huge wains upon its frost-
bound stream. Let him who is given to weigh
natural causes examine and investigate the different
effect worked in the same material:[c] frost-bound
streams melt on catching the sun, and on the other
hand liquid waters can be hardened[d] in the sun.

[c] *fomes* "touchwood" is here "matter," "material," or
"element"; and virtually "cause" in relation to *opus* =
"working," "effect." (*Cf.* note on *opus* in *Aetna*, 337, *supra*
p. 391.)

[d] *i.e.* by evaporation salt can be secured from brine.
Compare Lucretius' lines on the baking and the thawing action
of heat, VI. 962–969.

o, quam saepe malis generatur origo bonorum!
  tempestas dulcem fecit amara moram;
Victorinus enim, nostrae pars maxima mentis,
  congressu explevit mutua vota suo.
errantem Tuscis considere compulit agris   49
  et colere externos capta Tolosa Lares.
nec tantum duris nituit sapientia rebus:
  pectore non alio prosperiora tulit.
conscius Oceanus virtutum, conscia Thule
  et quaecumque ferox arva Britannus arat,   50
qua praefectorum vicibus frenata potestas
  perpetuum magni faenus amoris habet.
extremum pars illa quidem discedit in orbem,
  sed tamquam media rector in urbe fuit.
plus palmae est illos inter voluisse placere,   50
  inter quos minor est displicuisse pudor.
illustris nuper sacrae Comes additus aulae
  contempsit summos ruris amore gradus.
hunc ego complexus ventorum adversa fefelli,
  dum videor patriae iam mihi parte frui.   51

lutea protulerat sudos Aurora iugales:
  antemnas tendi litoris aura iubet.

---

493 laus (*vel* spes) *Baehrens.*   gentis *Burman.*
503 discessit VRB : discedit *Baehrens.*
504 medio . . . orbe VRB : media . . . urbe *Mueller,
Baehrens.*

---

a Like Shakespeare's " There is some soul of goodness in
things evil " (*King Henry V.* Act IV. Sc. i. l. 4).
b Victorinus, a Gaul like Rutilius (l. 510), had lost his home
in Toulouse owing to its capture by Ataulf, King of the

How oft the fount of blessings springs from ills![a]
The hateful weather produced an enjoyable delay;
for Victorinus,[b] more than half my soul, by meeting
me fulfilled our mutual hopes. The capture of
Tolosa had forced him, a wanderer in the lands of
Etruria, to settle there and dwell in a foreign home.
It was not only amid distress that his wisdom shone:
with heart unaltered he could face prosperity.
Well did the Ocean know his merits, well did the
Far North know them, and all the lands the untamed
Briton ploughs, where his self-restrained authority
as a Prefect's deputy[c] has earned him the lasting
interest paid by strong regard. That region is
parted from us far as earth's most distant bound,
but he was its ruler as it might have been in the heart
of Rome. A greater prize it is to have aimed at
popularity with those among whom it is less dis-
credit to be unpopular. Though attached of late
to our revered Court as Right Honourable Count,[d]
yet in his passion for country-life he disdained the
highest grades of advancement. Embracing him I
mocked the contrary winds, while I enjoyed already,
methought, a part of my own native land.

Saffron Aurora had brought forward her fair-
weather team: the breeze offshore tells us to haul

Visigoths, in A.D. 413 (l. 496). He had been *Vicarius* for the
Praetorian Prefect of Gaul and as such had exercised authority
in Britain. Though he held the distinction of *Comes Illustris*,
he preferred country-life in Etruria to attendance at court.

[c] Victorinus had been *Vicarius Britanniarum*: see preced-
ing note.

[d] The three classes of *Comites Illustres* were: (1) *in actu
positi*, holding office; (2) *vacantes*, on the list for appointment;
(3) *honorarii*, merely titular. Victorinus belonged to the
third class.

inconcussa vehit tranquillus aplustria flatus;
    mollia securo vela rudente tremunt.
adsurgit ponti medio circumflua Gorgon   51
    inter Pisanum Cyrnaicumque latus.
aversor scopulos, damni monumenta recentis;
    perditus hic vivo funere civis erat.
noster enim nuper iuvenis maioribus amplis,
    nec censu inferior coniugiove minor,   52
impulsus furiis homines terrasque reliquit
    et turpem latebram credulus exsul adit.
infelix putat illuvie caelestia pasci
    seque premit laesis saevior ipse deis.
num, rogo, deterior Circaeis secta venenis?   52
    tunc mutabantur corpora, nunc animi.

inde Triturritam petimus: sic villa vocatur,
    quae iacet expulsis insula paene fretis.
namque manu iunctis procedit in aequora saxis,
    quique domum posuit condidit ante solum.   53
contiguum stupui portum, quem fama frequentat
    Pisarum emporio divitiisque maris.
mira loci facies: pelago pulsantur aperto
    inque omnes ventos litora nuda patent;
non ullus tegitur per bracchia tuta recessus,   53
    Aeolias possit qui prohibere minas;

    518 conditus *Baehrens.*
    522 agit VRB : adit *Burman* : amat *Wernsdorf.*
    525 num VB : nuc (*sic*) R : non *Barth.*
    528 latet VRB : iacet *Heinsius* : patet *Burman* : latere *Keene* :
late *Mueller, Baehrens.*
    533 pulsatur VRB : pulsantur *Barth, Baehrens.*

---

    a This island, now Gorgona, lies about 22 miles S.W. of
Leghorn.   It was long occupied by monks.
    b Homer, *Odyss.* X. 135–405.

the sail-yards up. The gentle breath of the wind carries the stern-fittings on without vibration; softly flap the sails on rigging free from any strain. There rises in the midst of the sea the wave-girt Gorgon [a] with Pisa and Corsica on either side. I shun the cliffs, which are memorials of recent disaster; here a fellow-countryman met his doom in a living death. For lately one of our youths of high descent, with wealth to match, and marriage-alliance equal to his birth, was impelled by madness to forsake mankind and the world, and made his way, a superstitious exile, to a dishonourable hiding-place. Fancying, poor wretch, that the divine can be nurtured in unwashen filth, he was himself to his own body a crueller tyrant than the offended deities. Surely, I ask, this sect is not less powerful than the drugs of Circe? [b] In her days men's bodies were transformed, now 'tis their minds.

From there we make for Triturrita: [c] that is the name of a residence, a peninsula lying in the wash of baffled waves. For it juts out into the sea on stones which man's hand has put together, and he who built the house had first to make sure building ground. I was astonished at the haven close by, which by report is thronged with Pisa's merchandise and sea-borne wealth. The place has a marvellous appearance. Its shores are buffeted by the open sea and lie exposed to all the winds: here there are not sheltering piers to protect any inner harbour-basin capable of defying the threats of Aeolus.[d]

[c] The Villa Triturrita is conjecturally placed with the neighbouring Portus Pisanus (I. 531, II. 12) between Leghorn and the mouth of the Arno, but the coast has been greatly altered owing to alluvial deposits.

[d] Cf. Virg. Aen. I. 50-91, the Cavern of the Winds.

sed procera suo praetexitur alga profundo
  molliter offensae non nocitura rati,
et tamen insanas cedendo interligat undas
  nec sinit ex alto grande volumen agi.   54

tempora navigii clarus reparaverat Eurus;
  sed mihi Protadium visere cura fuit:
quem qui forte velit certis cognoscere signis,
  virtutis specimen corde videre putet:
nec magis efficiet similem pictura colore   54
  quam quae de meritis mixta figura venit.
adspicienda procul certo prudentia vultu,
  formaque iustitiae suspicienda micat.
sit fortasse minus, si laudet Gallia civem:
  testis Roma sui praesulis esse potest.   55
substituit patriis mediocres Umbria sedes:
  virtus fortunam fecit utramque parem.
mens invicta viri pro magnis parva tuetur,
  pro parvis animo magna fuere suo.
exiguus regum victores caespes habebat,   55
  et Cincinnatos iugera pauca dabant.
haec etiam nobis non inferiora feruntur
  vomere Serrani Fabriciique foco.

---

[539] caedendo V, *Baehrens*: cedendo B: credendo . . .
unda R.   interrigat VRB: interligat *Castalio*: internicat
Baehrens.
   [544] speciem VRB: specimen *Castalio*. vidente VRB:
vigente petat *Baehrens*: petat VB: putat R: videre putet
Heinsius.
   [552] utraque V: utrăque R.
   [555] rectores VRB: victores *Baehrens*.

---

   [a] Protadius corresponded with Symmachus, from whose
letters we learn that he came from Trèves (*cf.* 549–551). A

But, fringing its own deep-water domain, the tall
sea-weed is like to do no damage to a ship that
strikes it without shock; and yet in giving way it
entangles the furious waves and lets no huge roller
surge in from the deep.

A clear South-east wind had brought again the
moment for sailing; but I was eager to pay a visit
to Protadius: *a* whoever perchance may wish to
recognise him by sure signs should think in his
heart that he is looking upon a model of goodness:
no painting will ever give a truer portrait of him in
colour than will the image that comes from his
blended excellences. His prudence marked by
steady look is evident even to a distant eye; the
expression of fair-mindedness shines out, command-
ing respect. This tribute might perhaps be lessened
were it merely that Gaul was praising a fellow-
countryman; but Rome can bear witness to her
former prefect. Umbria *b* replaced his ancestral
home with but a humble abode: his virtue took
either lot as equal. The man's unvanquished mind
regards small things as great; for to his spirit great
things once had been but small. A petty farm used
to contain the conquerors of kings, and a few acres
yielded men like Cincinnatus.*c* Such contentment
in our view is deemed to fall not short of Serranus'
plough and Fabricius' hearth.*d*

learned official, he was the son of an eminent rhetorician
praised by Ausonius for his lectures in Constantinople, Rome
and Bordeaux.

b Either Protadius had some property in Umbria proper,
or " Umbria " here includes the part of Etruria round Pisa.

c For the story see Val. Max. IV. iv. 7.

d Rutilius here echoes Virg. *Aen.* VI. 844.

puppibus ergo meis fida in statione locatis
    ipse vehor Pisas qua solet ire pedes.   56
praebet equos, offert etiam carpenta tribunus,
    ex commilitio carus et ipse mihi,
officiis regerem cum regia tecta magister
    armigerasque pii principis excubias.
Alpheae veterem contemplor originis urbem,   56
    quam cingunt geminis Arnus et Ausur aquis;
conum pyramidis coeuntia flumina ducunt:
    intratur modico frons patefacta solo;
sed proprium retinet communi in gurgite nomen,
    et pontum solus scilicet Arnus adit.   57
ante diu quam Troiugenas fortuna Penates
    Laurentinorum regibus insereret,
Elide deductas suscepit Etruria Pisas,
    nominis indicio testificata genus.
hic oblata mihi sancti genitoris imago,   57
    Pisani proprio quam posuere foro.
laudibus amissi cogor lacrimare parentis:
    fluxerunt madidis gaudia maesta genis.
namque pater quondam Tyrrhenis praefuit arvis,
    fascibus et senis credita iura dedit.   58

559 fida VB : tuta R.
573 Elide VB : Aulide R.

---

  a The other route would have been by sea to the mouth of the Arno and then up the river.

  b The tribune had served in the *Scholares* or Imperial Guard, who were under the control of Rutilius when *Magister Officiorum* at the palace.

  c Pisa was reputed to have been founded from the Pisa in Elis, near the river Alpheus (*cf.* 573–574).

So then I moor my ships in the safe anchorage, and myself drive to Pisa by the road the wayfarer goes afoot.[a] I get horses and the offer of carriages too from a tribune personally endeared to me through former comradeship,[b] when as Master of Household Duties I was controller of the palace and of the pious emperor's armed guard. I scan the ancient city of Alphean origin,[c] which the Arno and the Ausur gird with their twin waters; at their junction the rivers form the cone of a pyramid: the opening front offers access on a narrow tongue of land; [d] but 'tis the Arno that retains its own name in the united stream, and in truth the Arno alone arrives at the sea. Long time ere fortune could enrol the house of Trojan birth among Laurentum's royal line,[e] Etruria welcomed Pisa as a colony from Elis, witnessing its origin by the evidence of its name. Here was shown to me the statue of my revered father,[f] erected by the Pisans in their market-place. The honour done to my lost parent made me weep: tears of a saddened joy wet my cheeks with their flow. For my father once was governor of the land of Tuscany and administered the jurisdiction assigned to the six fasces.[g] After he had passed

---

 [d] Those coming up-stream would face the apex of the triangle formed by the union of the two rivers, and by this tongue of land those going inland would enter on the opening "frons," the narrow strip gradually expanding into a broad front.

 [e] The claim implies that Pisa was founded before Aeneas arrived in Italy.

 [f] The name of Rutilius' father was Lachanius, I. 595.

 [g] The *arva* are identical with the *provincia* of I. 597. Six *fasces* were the insignia of the office of *Consularis Tusciae et Umbriae*. A consul in Rome had twelve *fasces*: cf. *Laus Pisonis*, 70 (*supra*, p. 300).

narrabat, memini, multos emensus honores
   Tuscorum regimen plus placuisse sibi ;
nam neque opum curam, quamvis sit magna, sacrarum
   nec ius quaesturae grata fuisse magis ;
ipsam, si fas est, postponere praefecturam   58
   pronior in Tuscos non dubitabat amor.
nec fallebatur, tam carus et ipse probatis :
   aeternas grates mutua cura canit ;
constantemque sibi pariter mitemque fuisse
   insinuant natis qui meminere senes.   59
ipsum me gradibus non degenerasse parentis
   gaudent, et duplici sedulitate fovent.
haec eadem, cum Flaminiae regionibus irem,
   splendoris patrii saepe reperta fides :
famam Lachanii veneratur numinis instar   59
   inter terrigenas Lydia tota suos.
grata bonis priscos retinet provincia mores
   dignaque rectores semper habere bonos,
qualis nunc Decius, Lucilli nobile pignus,
   per Coryti populos arva beata regit.   60
nec mirum, magni si redditus indole nati
   felix tam simili posteritate pater.

---

  [a] Rutilius' father had been Count of the Sacred Largesses,
Quaestor, and City Prefect.

  [b] The *praefectura* here is that of the City Prefect, not of
the Praetorian Prefect. Rutilius is apologetic (*si fas est*)
over the idea of preferring any dignity to the prefecture of
the august city of Rome.

  [c] *Canit* here implies laudatory lines on the base of the statue
rather than actual song.

  [d] The regions in mind were Umbrian and Tuscan districts
lying not far off the line of the great northern road from
Rome.

  [e] *Lydia* here means Etruria, which according to one ancient
account was settled from Lydia in Asia Minor.

through many offices,[a] he used to tell, I can recall, that his governorship of Tuscany had been more to his liking than any: for neither the management of the Sacred Largesses, important though it be, nor the authority of a quaestor had brought him more pleasure. His affection, inclining more towards the Tuscans, did not hesitate to give an inferior place, if piety lets it be said, even to his prefecture in Rome.[b] Nor was he mistaken, being an equal favourite with those whom he esteemed: their mutual regard inscribes in verse undying gratitude,[c] and old men who can remember him make known to their sons how firm of purpose he was and at the same time how kindly. They are glad that I myself have not fallen off from my parent's honours, and eagerly give me a warm welcome for his sake and for my own. Often as I traversed the lands near the Flaminian Way [d] I have found the same proof of my father's renown; the whole of Lydia [e] worships Lachanius' [f] fame like some divinity among the natives of her soil. A favourite with the good, this province keeps its old-world ways and deserves always to have good governors, like Decius, the noble offspring of Lucillus,[g] who among the peoples of Corytus [h] rules o'er these happy lands. Small wonder it is that the sire, reproduced in the character of his great son, feels blest in a descendant so like

[f] The fact that the name *Lachanius* does not occur elsewhere is not enough to justify Burman's substitution of *Laecanius*.

[g] Rutilius is our sole source of information about Decius, who was *Consularis Tusciae et Umbriae* in A.D. 416, and about his father, whose satiric powers are compared to those of Juvenal and Turnus.

[h] *Corytus* or *Corythus* (now Cortona) is here used for Etruria, as being one of its ancient towns.

huius vulnificis satira ludente Camenis
    nec Turnus potior nec Iuvenalis erit.
restituit veterem censoria lima pudorem;   605
    dumque malos carpit, praecipit esse bonos.
non olim sacri iustissimus arbiter auri
    circumsistentes reppulit Harpyias?—
Harpyias, quarum discerpitur unguibus orbis,
    quae pede glutineo quod tetigere trahunt,   610
quae luscum faciunt Argum, quae Lyncea caecum,
    inter custodes publica furta volant;
sed non Lucillum Briareia praeda fefellit,
    totque simul manibus restitit una manus.

iamque Triturritam Pisaea ex urbe reversus   615
    aptabam nitido pendula vela Noto,
cum subitis tectus nimbis insorduit aether;
    sparserunt radios nubila rupta vagos.
substitimus.   quis enim sub tempestate maligna
    insanituris audeat ire fretis?   620
otia vicinis terimus navalia silvis,
    sectandisque iuvat membra movere feris.
instrumenta parat venandi villicus hospes
    atque olidum doctas nosse cubile canes.
funditur insidiis et rara fraude plagarum   625
    terribilisque cadit fulmine dentis aper,

---

603 livente *Baehrens*.
612 custodes VRB (custodum ·f· *in marg.* V).   volant
VRB: vorant *Baehrens*.

---

a *Huius* applies to Lucillus, not to his son.   Turnus, though
a satirist, succeeded in surviving under Domitian (*vet. schol.*
on Juvenal I. 20; Martial XI. x, *contulit ad saturas ingentia
pectora Turnus*).   Juvenal belonged to the next generation.
Two lines of Turnus (one unintelligible) are given in Morel,
Fragm. Poet. Lat. p. 134.

himself. His satire, sportive in its mordant poetry, neither Turnus nor Juvenal [a] shall surpass. The censorious file has restored old-fashioned modesty: in attacking the bad, it teaches to be good. Did not that most upright dispenser of the Sacred Largess repel in his day the Harpies who gathered round it? [b] —Harpies, whose claws rend asunder the world, their sticky talons dragging off whatever they touch; creatures who make Argus one-eyed and Lynceus blind; [c] public thieves, [d] they flit among the guardians; but their hundred-handed pillaging did not escape Lucillus, whose single hand checkmated all their hands together.

And now returning from Pisa's city to Triturrita, I was setting the hanging sails to a clear Southern wind, when the sky turned foul under a sudden pall of rain-clouds; the cloven rack scattered its vagrant lightnings. We stopped; who 'neath a spiteful storm would dare to go on seas which threatened madness? The respite from our voyage we spend in the neighbouring forests, delighted to exercise our limbs in the pursuit of game. Our innkeeper supplies the implements for the chase, and hounds trained to discover a strongly scented lair. By means of an ambush and the snare of wide-meshed nets a boar, though terrifying in the flash of his tusks, is overthrown and falls—such a one as

---

[b] *i.e.* as *Comes Sacrarum Largitionum*, Lucillus balked the greedy " Harpies " in their designs upon public money.

[c] Their peculations are so smart that Argus of the hundred eyes would seem to have only one eye to watch them with, while the keen-eyed Lynceus would seem to be blind.

[d] *publica furta*, abstract for concrete, means the plundering Harpies: *custodes* means the *Comites Sacrarum Largitionum*.

quem Meleagrei vereantur adire lacerti,
    qui laxet nodos Amphitryoniadae.
tum responsuros persultat bucina colles,
    fitque reportando carmine praeda levis.   630

interea madidis non desinit Africus alis
    continuos picea nube negare dies.
iam matutinis Hyades occasibus udae:
    iam latet hiberno conditus imbre Lepus,
exiguum radiis sed magnis fluctibus astrum,   635
    quo madidam nullus navita linquit humum ;
namque procelloso subiungitur Oarioni
    aestiferumque Canem roscida praeda fugit.
vidimus excitis pontum flavescere harenis
    atque eructato vertice rura tegi ;   640
qualiter Oceanus mediis infunditur agris,
    destituenda vago cum premit arva salo,
sive alio refluus nostro colliditur orbe
    sive corusca suis sidera pascit aquis.

---

[630] reportando V : reportanda RB : reportanti *Castalio* :
reportantum *Heinsius, Baehrens.*
  [632] diem *Baehrens.*
  [643] alto *Baehrens.*

Meleager [a] of the strong shoulders might dread to approach, such a one as would slacken the joints of Hercules. Then mid the echoing hills leap the notes of the bugle-horn, and singing makes the booty light in carrying back.

Meanwhile the South-west wind on dripping wings fails not by means of pitch-black clouds to deny us day after day. 'Tis now the season [b] when the watery Hyades are at their morning setting, and now the Hare is buried and hidden by the winter's rain—a constellation of scanty beams but cause of mighty waves: no sailor puts out from the land which it has soaked; for it is closely linked to stormy Orion, and the dew-drenched prey flees from the heat-fraught Dog-star. We saw the sea yellowing with the disturbance of the sands and pastures covered with the scum it has belched forth, even as the Ocean pours into the midst of fields, when under errant brine it whelms the lands from which it must ebb; whether the truth be that back-flowing from another world [c] it dashes against this world of ours, or that with its own waters it feeds the twinkling stars.

[a] Meleager, son of Oeneus and Althaea (see II. 53), took part in the famous Calydonian boar-hunt.

[b] A wet and stormy period of the year coincides with the setting of the Hyades in morning twilight (late November) and with the setting of the Hare (early November). The Hare is near the left foot of Orion, and flees as a "dew-drenched prey" (638) before the burning Dog-star, Sirius.

[c] *Alio orbe* means the moon. Of the two theories here suggested regarding the cause of tides, the second refers to an ancient belief that sun and stars were fed on the waters of the ocean.

LIBER SECUNDUS

Nondum longus erat nec multa volumina passus,
    iure suo poterat longior esse liber :
taedia continuo timui incessura labori,
    sumere ne lector iuge paveret opus.
saepe cibis affert serus fastidia finis,   5
    gratior est modicis haustibus unda siti :
intervalla viae fessis praestare videtur
    qui notat inscriptus milia crebra lapis.
partimur trepidum per opuscula bina ruborem,
    quem satius fuerat sustinuisse semel.   10

tandem nimbosa maris obsidione solutis
    Pisano portu contigit alta sequi.
arridet placidum radiis crispantibus aequor.
    et sulcata levi murmurat unda sono.
incipiunt Appennini devexa videri,   15
    qua fremit aerio monte repulsa Thetis.

Italiam rerum dominam qui cingere visu
    et totam pariter cernere mente velit,
inveniet quernae similem procedere frondi,
    artatam laterum conveniente sinu.   20

[3] timuit cessura VR (censura *Mueller* : sessura *i.e.*
haesura *Baehrens in not.*) : timui incessura *Purser, Keene.*

---

[a] *i.e.* the parchment had not been rolled to a great extent
round its stick.
[b] One long book might prove too wearisome : hence the
author thinks it advisable to begin a second book. The tone
suggests that Book II either was actually or was intended
to be much longer than it now is.

RUTILIUS NAMATIANUS

BOOK II

My book had not yet grown too long nor under-
gone many windings of its scroll; [a] in its own right
it might have been longer: but I feared weariness
would come upon continuous toil—feared lest my
reader should shrink from handling an undivided
work.[b] Ofttimes the late-delayed end of a feast
brings distaste for viands: water in moderate
draughts is the more welcome to thirst: the stone
that by its lettering marks the many miles seems to
afford the tired wayfarer some breaks upon the road.
Between two booklets I divide my nervous modesty [c]
which it had been better to have faced once only.

Freed at last from the stormy blockade of the sea,
we had the fortune to make for the deep from Pisa's
harbour. Calm smiles the surface of the waters
as the sunbeams glitter: the furrowed wave whispers
with gentle plash. The Apennine slopes heave in
sight where Thetis [d] chafes at her repulse by a wind-
swept promontory.

He who would embrace in his view Italy, the queen
of the world, and form at once a mental picture of
the whole land, will find that she extends in shape
like an oak leaf,[e] contracted by the converging
indentation of her sides. In length the distance

[c] *i.e.* the blushing diffidence of a modest author is spread
over two books instead of one. He ought, he feels, to have
boldly met his qualms of modesty and concentrated on a
single book: he now has to meet them over again.

[d] Thetis, as a sea-goddess, is a metonymy for the sea.
Beyond Pisa spurs of the Apennines run out into a lofty
headland.

[e] *Cf.* Plin. *N.H.* III. 43, referring to Italy as *folio maxime
querno adsimilata.*

milia per longum deciens centena teruntur
  a Ligurum terris ad freta Sicaniae ;
in latum variis damnosa anfractibus intrat
  Tyrrheni rabies Hadriacique sali.
qua tamen est iuncti maris angustissima tellus,   25
  triginta et centum milia sola patet.
diversas medius mons obliquatur in undas,
  qua fert atque refert Phoebus uterque diem :
urget Dalmaticos eoo vertice fluctus
  caerulaque occiduis frangit Etrusca iugis.   30
si factum certa mundum ratione fatemur
  consiliumque dei machina tanta fuit,
excubiis Latiis praetexuit Appenninum
  claustraque montanis vix adeunda viis.
invidiam timuit Natura parumque putavit   35
  Arctois Alpes opposuisse minis,
sicut vallavit multis vitalia membris
  nec semel inclusit quae pretiosa tulit :
iam tum multiplici meruit munimine cingi
  sollicitosque habuit Roma futura deos.   40

quo magis est facinus diri Stilichonis acerbum,
  proditor arcani quod fuit imperii.

---

34 feris *Schrader* : suis *Baehrens* : viis VRB.
42 quod VRB : qui *vulgo*.

---

a A Roman mile was 143 yards less than an English mile,
so that 1000 Roman miles are approximately equal to 918
English miles. This estimate of Italy's length is virtually
that of Pliny, *loc. cit.* (1020 miles). But the length in a straight
line from the Simplon to Cape Lucca is about 700 miles.
Rutilius, as the phrase *milia teruntur* shows (*cf. terere viam*),
is calculating, like Pliny, by the roads usually travelled.
b In Calabria, which is, however, merely the "toe" of Italy,
the peninsula is only about 20 miles wide; but Rutilius follows

by road is one of a thousand miles [a] from the Ligurian territories to the Sicilian straits: on her breadth the destructive fury of the Tuscan and of the Adriatic main makes entry in varied winding curves; but where the land is narrowest between the neighbouring seas it stretches merely one hundred and thirty miles.[b] The central mountain-chain slopes towards the sundered billows where the rising and the setting Sungod brings and withdraws the day: its eastern peaks beset the Dalmatian waves, and its western spurs cleave the blue Tuscan waters. If we acknowledge that the world was made on a definite plan and if this great fabric was a god's design, then as a protective fringe for our Latin outposts he wove the Apennines, barriers scarce approachable by mountain paths. Nature feared men's jealousy (of Italy) and thought it scant defence to put the Alps in Northern invaders' way, just as she has fenced with many limbs our vital parts and placed more than one covering around the precious works she has produced. Even then the Rome that was to be deserved her encirclement of manifold bulwarks and had gods who thought anxiously for her.

Wherefore more bitter is the crime of cursed Stilicho [c] in that he was betrayer of the Empire's

Pliny's estimate of 136 miles from the Adriatic across country to Ostia (*N.H.* III. 44).

[c] For the career of Stilicho, ending with his disgrace and death in A.D. 408, see Gibbon's *Decline and Fall* and Hodgkin's *Italy and Her Invaders*. His victories over Alaric at Pollentia in 403 and over Radagaisus in 405 did not save him from charges of treasonable collusion with the barbarians. His ambition incurred relentless enmity. While the prose-writers Zosimus and Orosius take, like Rutilius, an unfavourable view of his character, Claudian is emphatic in his praises.

Romano generi dum nititur esse superstes,
  crudelis summis miscuit ima furor;
dumque timet quicquid se fecerat ipse timeri,   45
  immisit Latiae barbara tela neci:
visceribus nudis armatum condidit hostem,
  illatae † cladis liberiore dolo.
ipsa satellitibus pellitis Roma patebat
  et captiva prius quam caperetur erat.   50
nec tantum Geticis grassatus proditor armis:
  ante Sibyllinae fata cremavit opis.
odimus Althaeam consumpti funere torris;
  Nisaeum crinem flere putatur avis.
at Stilicho aeterni fatalia pignora regni   55
  et plenas voluit praecipitare colos.
omnia Tartarei cessent tormenta Neronis;
  consumat Stygias tristior umbra faces.
hic immortalem, mortalem perculit ille;
  hic mundi matrem perculit, ille suam.   60

---

⁴⁸ illato *Baehrens*: Iliacae cladis deteriore d. *J. S. Reid.*

  ᵃ By letting Alaric enter Italy (II. 46), Stilicho had revealed the "secret" that the barbarians could invade the empire with immunity.
  ᵇ The motive suggested for Stilicho's treachery is that he intended, by the ruin of the Roman race, to further his own interests: he counted on outliving the devastation of Italy.
  ᶜ The implication is that, though he had made himself feared through his influence with the Goths, he is now afraid of them.
  ᵈ The phrasing is difficult. If accepted, it seems to mean that it was safer for Stilicho to employ against Italy a secret pact with the Goths than a military invasion. But if the ablat. of comparison usually supplied with *liberiore* is dispensed with, the sense might be "with the over-bold fraud of ruin inflicted."
  Ovid and Claudian apply "pellitus" to the Goths.

secret.^a As he strove to live longer than the Roman race,^b his cruel frenzy turned the world upside down, and, while fearing that wherein he had made himself formidable,^c he let loose the arms of the barbarians to the death of Latium: he plunged an armed foe in the naked vitals of the land, his craft being freer from risk than that of openly inflicted disaster.^d Even Rome lay exposed to his skin-clad menials ^e— captive ere she could be captured. Nor was it only through Gothic arms that the traitor made his attack: ere this he burned the fateful books which brought the Sibyl's aid.^f We hate Althaea for the death which came of the brand she gave to the flames; ^g birds, so the fancy runs, weep for Nisus' lock.^h But it was Stilicho's will to hurl to ruin the eternal empire's fate-fraught pledges and distaffs still charged with destinies. Let every torment of Nero in Tartarus now halt; let an even more miserable ghost consume the Stygian torches.ⁱ Stilicho's victim was immortal, Nero's was mortal; the one destroyed the world's mother, the other his own.

^f Rutilius is the sole authority for the allegation that Stilicho burned the Sibylline books which the Romans consulted in times of crisis. Their destruction thus preceded the fall of Rome by only a few years.

^g Althaea caused the death of her son Meleager by burning the magical firebrand on which his life depended: *cf.* note on Pentadius I. (*De Fortuna*) 21–22, *supra* p. 545.

^h Scylla caused the death of her father Nisus by depriving him of the purple lock on which his life depended: see the *Ciris* in the *Appendix Vergiliana*: *cf. crinem Nisi*, Nemes. *Cyn.* 44.

ⁱ *i.e.* Stilicho should suffer under the torches of the Furies even more horrible punishment than that inflicted upon the matricide Nero in Tartarus.

sed deverticulo fuimus fortasse loquaces :
   carmine propositum iam repetamus iter.
advehimur celeri candentia moenia lapsu :
   nominis est auctor Sole corusca soror.
indigenis superat ridentia lilia saxis,   65
   et levi radiat picta nitore silex.
dives marmoribus tellus, quae luce coloris
   provocat intactas luxuriosa nives.

. . . . .

[62] propositum V : preposito R : proposito B.

RUTILIUS NAMATIANUS

But in this digression we have perhaps been garrulous: let us now resume in verse the voyage we had set ourselves. On swiftly gliding course we bear towards white glittering walls: the sister who draws her radiance from the Sun is the bestower of the city's name.[a] In the colour of its native rocks it surpasses smiling lilies, and the stone flashes bedecked in polished radiance. Rich in marble, it is a land which, revelling in its white light, challenges the virgin snows.

.   .   .   .   .

[a] With this allusion to the town of Luna and the brief glance at its marble quarries, the poem, as we have it, ends abruptly.

INDEX

OF PROPER NOUNS AND ADJECTIVES

The numbers refer to pages of the Latin text: adj. = adjective.

A

Acanthis, 276
Acarnan, 168
Achaemenius, 182
Achaia, 202
Achilles, 308, 414
Acidalius (*adj.*), 302
Acragas, 202
Acrisius (*adj.*), 578
Actius (= Apollo), 124
Adonis, 156, 470, 526
Adriacus (*adj.*), 490: *see also* "Hadriacus"
Aeacus, 364
Aeetes, 130
Aegon, 276
Aegyptus, 662
Aenaria, 398
Aeneadae, 768
Aeneas, 778
Aeneius (*adj.*), 312
Aeolius (*adj.*), 154, 810
Aeolus, 656
Aesopus, 680
Aetna, 358, 364, 366, 374, 376, 386, 388, 390, 394, 396, 400, 410, 416
Aetnaeus (*adj.*), 202, 362, 384, 400, 536
Aetolus (*adj.*), 168
Africa, 776
Africus (*sc.* ventus), 262, 820
Agamemnonius (*adj.*), 328
Agenoreus (*adj.*), 786
Agylla, 782
Alabandius (*adj.*), 154
Alanus, 446
Albinus, 778, 804: *see note b*, 778
Alcides, 126, 770
Alcippe, 238

Alcon, 268, 270, 464, 468, 470
Alexis, 250
Allia, 774
Aloides, 128
Alpes, 200, 824
Alphesiboeus, 234
Alpheus (*adj.*), 814
Alsius (*adj.*), 782.
Althaea, 826
Altinas (*adj.*), 162
Amaryllis, 246
Amor (personified), 128, 432, 524, 534, 538, 540, 512
Amphinomus, 418
Amphitryoniades, 820
Amphora (personified), 746
Amyclae, 160
Amyntas, 244, 250, 472, 482
Ancaeus, 156
Antiphates, 798
Aonius (*adj.*), 124, 308, 484
Ap(p)enninus (*sc.* mons), 514, 822, 824
Apollineus (*adj.*), 308, 634
Apollo, 244, 248, 250, 270, 278, 284, 328, 334, 428, 456, 462, 468, 470, 680, 716: *see also* "Actius," "Castalius," "Cynthius," "Phoebus," "Sol," "Titan"
Aquilo, 394, 802
Arabs, *plur.* Arabes, 488, 656, 662
Arar, 490
Arcadius (*adj.*), 160
Arctos, 492
Arctous (*adj.*), 824
Aremoricus, 782
Arethusa, 540
Argentarius (*sc.* mons), 792
Argo, 130
Argolicus, 360

INDEX

INDEX

Circe, 488
Circenses, 780
Cirrha *vel* Cyrrha, 202
Cirrhaeus (*adj.*), 652
Clementia (personified), 222
Clio, 434, 634
Cnosis *vel* Gnosis (= Ariadne), 544
Colchi, 360
Colchis (= Medea) 130, 414, 488, 540, 542
Comes, 808
Corsa, 802
Corsica, 802
Corus, 804 : *see* " Caurus "
Corycius (*adj.*), 132
Corydon, 218, 244, 248, 250, 278, 284
Corytus, 816
Cosa, 788, 790
Cresius (*adj.*), 252
Creta, 172
Crocale, 226, 230, 232
Cumae, 398
Cupido (= Cupid), 524, 526, 528, 532, 534, 536, 538 : *see also* " Amor "
—— (= Desire *sc. opum*), 650
Curae (personified), 650
Cureticus (*adj.*), 252
Curia, 222, 764
Cyaneus (*adj.*), 130
Cyclopes, 362
Cyclopius (*adj.*), 526
Cycnus, 488
Cylleneus (*adj.*), 654
Cynicus, 566
Cynthius (= Apollo), 326
Cynthos, 358
Cypris (= Venus), 432, 526, 530, 534, 536
Cyrnaeus (*adj.*), 802
Cyrnaicus (*adj.*), 810
Cyrrha *vel* Cirrha, 202
Cyrus, 182
Cythere (= Venus), 524, 538
Cytherea (= Venus), 536, 776

D

Daedalus, 544
Dalmaticus (*adj.*), 824
Danaë, 366, 560
Danaus, 486
Daphnis, 234
December, 232
Decius, 816
Delos, 358

Delphicus (*adj.*), 680
Dēō (= Demeter), 468
Dercylos, 160
Deucalioneus (*adj.*), 650
Diana, 150, 152, 160, 162, 198
Dianius (*adj.*), 176
Dictaeus (*adj.*), 252
Didon (= Dido), 540
Diogenes, 566
Diomedes, 128
Dione, 468, 558
Dirce, 486
Dis (= Pluto), 158, 342, 364, 376, 540, 560 : *see* " Pluton "
Ditis (= Dis), 418
Dodone, 358
Donace, 464, 466, 468, 470
Doricus (*adj.*), 560
Dorylas, 234
Drusus, 134
Dryades, 226, 466, 494
Dryas, 548

E

Echo, 462, 494, 548
Egestas (personified), 650
Eleus (*adj.*), 200
Elis, 814
Emathius (*adj.*), 124
Encelados, 364
Eous (*sc.* ventus), 546
—— (*adj.*), 124, 164
—— (= morning-star), 802
Ephyreïus (*adj.*), 792
Erato, 434, 634
Erigone, 412
Eriphyla, 578
Erymanthus, 126
Eryx, 468
Etruria, 814
Etruscus (*adj.*), 120, 446, 824 : *see also* " Tuscus," " Tyrrhenus "
Euboicus (*adj.*), 302, 784
Euhadne *vel* Evadne, 540
Europa *vel* Europe, 366
Eurotas, 412
Eurus, 228, 374, 388, 478, 546, 812
Eurydice, 542
Euterpe, 434, 634
Experientia (personified), 192
Exuperantius, 782

F

Fabricii, 812
Faleria, 796

INDEX

INDEX

INDEX

INDEX